The Beacon Best of 1999

Ntozake Shange, guest editor

The Beacon Best of 1999

creative writing

by women and men

of all colors

Beacon Press

Boston

Beacon Press
25 Beacon Street
Boston, Massachusetts 02108-2892
www.beacon.org

Beacon Press books
are published under the auspices of
the Unitarian Universalist Association of Congregations.

Printed in the United States of America
ISSN 1525-173X
ISBN 0-8070-6220-0
ISBN 0-8070-6221-9 (pbk.)

This book is printed on acid-free paper that meets the uncoated paper
ANSI/NISO specifications for permanence as revised in 1992.
Text design by Julia Sedykh Design
Composition by Wilsted & Taylor Publishing Services
05 04 03 02 01 00 8 7 6 5 4 3 2 1

contents

introduction

The impulse to depict is ancient. The bison, mammoths, reindeer, and rhinoceri painted along the fragile walls at Lascaux an Chauvet in France by early humans reveal what our forebears revered, what they saved from their lives to encounter again. *The Beacon Best of 1999*, this collection of poems, essays, and stories, is what I would like to remember as the year 2000 approaches, sketches of what we hold sacred and keep for those to come. The cave drawings, sometimes taking on the contours of the earth itself, rarely depict people, but the human spirit is clearly present. The selections included here rarely connote the mystery of animals, rock, and water, but they do assume the shapes of lives lived or shattered, myths sustained or battered, loneliness in its solemn beauty, and memory of the imagined. We leave written drawings of ourselves, literate *homo sapiens* who have encountered in one another the Self and the Other, the cherished and despised.

The Beacon Best of 1999 gives voice to the Other, those who have been marginalized, at times demonized publicly or privately ignored. For decades, "protest art" was rejected as histrionic, only to have the same principles/situations put forth as legitimate once the voice of the artist was brought over to the side of the dominant culture. For example, vilified during his lifetime, Jack Johnson's story was never told from his perspective, but instead evolved as the tale of "The Great White Hope." But in Kevin Young's poem included here, Johnson's voice is given free reign:

> *. . . pummeling*
> *any black cat who crosses*
>
> *their paths.*
> *Neck tie*
> *parties cutting*
>
> *another grin*
> *below any raised*
> *Negro chins—*
>
> *JOHNSON WINS*
> *WHITES LYNCH*
> *70 ARRESTED*
>
> *BALTIMORE*
> *OMAHA NEGRO*
> *KILLED—*
>
> *all because I kept*
> *their hope*
> *on the ropes. . . .*

In Touré's adventurous "The Sad Sweet Story of Sugar Lips Shinehot and the Portable Promised Land," a whole new language dances with the idiosyncratic rhythms of its characters and time:

> *Sugar Lips was top dog, even Charlie Parker was scared ah him cuz anytime Sugar Lips wrapped them thick, pillow-soft lips round a mouthpiece, he swung hard nuf to make rain, thunder, and lightnin' stop and pay attention.*

Here the thick and colloquial, the tragic and hyperbolically humorous join in a colored irreverence that startles while teaching.

In the decade of Desert Storm, the tragedy of Waco, and the seizing of Columbine High School, as public events/catastrophes have become personalized within ourselves, the short story, poem, or essay has become at once an act of retreat and an act of seeking, broadening. In the poem "Licking the Woman," Brandel France de Bravo takes on the epic and intimate calamity of AIDS, looking for answers to questions that have none:

> *I am the harried health*
> *consultant just landed*
> *in Ghana. The taxi driver*
> *thinks he knows*
> *where it came from,*
> *how it spreads.*
> The foreign man. He come
> and lick the woman,
> *he says, flicking*
> *his tongue in and out*
> *like a snake. I laugh*
> *and tip him two condoms.*

In pieces such as this we leave our own country and become the foreigner, the Unknown. Yet the Other is not always distanced by time or location. The Other can be right next door, the Unknown in our midst. Jewel Mogan's short story "El Lobo Solo" takes us into the melodious cacophony of the mission districts of east Los Angeles to a micro-ritual known as the *quinceañera* (which, when I hear the excitement in the young girl's voice, is something I wish I'd done for my daughter).

The cave drawings of ten thousand years ago are thought to have been reserved for ceremonial or spiritual rites, but now our spiritual moments are made significant by the everyday, the unselfconscious activities of living. For instance, Patrick Sylvain writes in his poem "Volcanic Song" of a single creative performance that transformed him:

I will ever bury the images
of his back arched like a bow,
holding his guitar like an arrow
with its six strings and echoing
the messages of his fingers
in a theater where waves of macoutes
could not touch his shore.

I have been transformed as well. It has been moving, inspiring, and sometimes humbling to read the selections for this, the first Beacon annual, to have the privilege of experiencing these artful glimpses of life at the end of the twentieth century. These stories, poems, and essays pay homage to what's become of us, to what we bring to the next millennium—the sweet rememberings of the imagined.

Ntozake Shange

Reginald Shepherd

A Boy Called Risk

Winter wind that wears the ghost of light
away, whiteout shutting down days
months at a time. The pigeon soul
combs sidewalks cauterized with ice

for crumbs, wings frayed, lice-riddled. He walks
through snow-blind January, February
blusters wrapped in a black wool coat.
The body walks through half a year

to heat-dazed streets and avenues: looks up
into a face smudged in a windowpane
where one has no color to call his own
and one calls all of them by name. He lies

in the abandoned boyhood all afternoon
while blinds stir in a box fan's
unconvincing breeze, rain rubs through
closed eyes. That was a summer left behind, a hustler

in a backward baseball cap leaning on a corner
streetlamp, smoking an unfiltered cigarette. The body
burns to charcoal, smoke curls through the chest
and brands the lungs. He'd like to breathe

that burnished skin, he's leaning
out too far again, just for a glimpse.

Greg Bottoms

1967

he himself grows in me we eat our defeats
we burst out laughing
when they say how little is needed
to be reconciled

—Zbigniew Herbert
"Remembering My Father"

Here is how I imagine it, how I might begin the book of my father, with a vision of his mother, under a mottled Virginia sky that promises rain, gray rolling over bruise-colored gray, faint streaks of yellow from the sun like a healing outer edge. The dilapidated house on a street of dilapidated houses, all built in the thirties, during the Depression, when, as the rest of the country suffered, southeast Virginia grew fat and strong around a shipbuilding industry and military bases—the fear of fascism in Europe. A single chicken pecks hungrily in the overgrown yard. It is 1967. The old house, like every house on this short side street, has long since forgotten what prosperity was like: wind whips through its seams; the roof sags like the spine of an old horse. And a woman, old beyond her years, sits under the cracked and splintered porch eaves, dressed in a dirty pink nightgown, a single pale sagging breast hanging lifelessly out of the material. She is drinking the heart out of a darkening fall afternoon. A group of young boys on bikes laugh in the vacant street, never taking their eyes from the pink, misshapen nipple. It sparkles like a coin to them. Occasionally these boys shoot BB guns at the woman from the woods. Because children are innocent and cruel. Because they haven't thought much about her—except to ponder her misshapen breasts. She swats the BBs as if they are mosquitoes, gets a swatter to hold in her lap while she drinks, puts calamine lotion over the welts that, oddly, don't itch. Go to hell, she would shout in this opening scene, taking a drink.

And then: My father pulls his '65 Mustang, the best thing he has ever owned, into his mother's pocked driveway. It is three years before he is my father and twenty-six years before his funeral, when a great-uncle I barely know, almost weeping, gives me this story, the one that could begin a book, if I only had the patience and the strength, the memory and the nerve; it was, as he told it, a broken story in need of great repair, but also an interesting one, one that will trail me around for a good while. It was a backward story, the way he told it, an anti-tragedy, one that began with death and ended with life—a wishful story at a time when wishing seemed silly. And in this story, as it was told to me and as I might reimagine it, my father stands in the overgrown yard, staring at the boys in the street, making eye contact with the leader, giving his meanest look. Which, I remember, was fairly tepid. The kids, like kids, ride off, shouting, Nice tits!

He is medium-built, my father, in 1967, with dark blue eyes and freckles. His hair is reddish brown and wavy, fashionably unkempt, and long, bushy sideburns reach past his earlobes. He's wearing velour. He likes Creedence Clearwater Revival and The Who. He is unconventionally handsome, I think, in the few pictures I still have of him. He looks at his mother, his eyes moving immediately to her sagging breast, white as a new golf ball. Jesus, he thinks, not as prayer but lament. His father, her husband, has recently died, at the age of fifty, of a heart attack, and his mother, who has been drinking like this for years, has now been drunk for several straight weeks. Soon she will wreck a new car bought with insurance money; later, before she is put in Eastern State Mental Hospital, she will catch the house on fire by letting a cigarette fall drunkenly from her wet lips.

My father and his father barely spoke. My father loved his father, though, in a quiet, obligatory way. They never hugged, generally kept their distance, but they would have fought for each other, broken pool cues over foes' heads for each other. He made the funeral arrangements, spent all his money on the service, and still, as of fall 1967, owes some.

*

Something about my father's father. When my father decided he would return to high school after dropping out for two years, the old man resented him. He made fun of high school, talked of the righteousness of simple hard work with your hands and your back. He had been a migrant farmer as a boy, had worked hard and long, then spent years as a laborer, going where the work was, until he quit all of that toward the end of his life for some ill-advised moneymaking ventures: a flop of a grocery store in a bad part of town, a pig farm that put them immediately into debt. On my father's graduation day in 1962, as students two years younger than he huddled with their families for pictures and then went off to celebrate, my father walked to a friend's house, where several high school dropouts sat around drinking beer and watching baseball on an old TV. He got drunk and never mentioned the ceremony, which was, after all, just a ceremony.

Now, in this story, the one the great-uncle told me, he walks up the drive toward the small house. His mother sees him but says nothing. He loves his mother, too, but the love feels like an obligation, sometimes a curse. It is an exhausting sort of love. He thinks, and will always think until his death, that love is often more work than it deserves. He has come out here several times this month, to find her sleeping in the woods, sleeping with the oven on, sleeping in a neighbor's front yard at night with a group of boys around her, laughing. He imagined the boys pissing on her and chased them. He imagined the urine dripping off her forehead, her eyelashes, as she smiled in a dead sleep. To the neighbors, the scene must have been both sad and comical: the neighborhood drunk slumped half-dead in the yard, her half-crazy son chasing them damn boys again. The western sky, he notices, is the color of the veins in her legs. Her circulation is poor. Her blood is thin with alcohol, but her heart pumps slowly. Mr. Purcell, a neighbor, a kind old pipe fitter for NASA, called about the stink: I reckon a coon or a big old black snake mighta got up under the house and died, he had said that morning—and, hell, Ron, I didn't want to call the city. Reckon y'all been through enough. The phone call had alarmed my father. He remembers the last complaint about the smell.

*

Sometimes my father dreams of his father, as I will dream of him, and in the dreams things are extreme, feelings become literal, become actions. Dreams are like the best books, I think sometimes: they tell you important things you may not want to hear; they challenge you; they make you uncomfortable, because every dream, no matter what it is about, is about you. Dreaming, like reading, is a selfish act. In dreams, my father pushes his head down a hole in the street; his father shoots his mother for wildly fucking another man; his father gargles soup at the rusty, linoleum-topped table—that's it, just leans his head back and audibly, almost musically, gargles soup; he finds himself along the Chesapeake Bay, walking the beach, searching for his father's eyes like fiddler crabs (this one after watching a special of ancient religions on his small TV) so he can put him back together—everything depends on the finding of his eyes, which, of course, are nowhere to be found.

He is here, again, for the stink.

Something else that should go into this book I'm not going to write. Once, not long before his death, my father's father drove his old car off the Hampton Roads Bridge Tunnel. The tunnel was new. You could look through records and see that he was the first person to get a car to go off that bridge. People scratched their heads over this; it pointed out a design flaw. Cars weren't supposed to just go sailing into the bay. A sailor from Norfolk—this is true—jumped off the bridge and saved him. It was in the paper. It was like something from a movie—if you focused on the heroism of the sailor rather than all the complicated stuff about the victim. The logical question is: Did he try to commit suicide? People said: Yes; he was a sad, angry man; life was unfair and he wore the unfairness on his sleeve. Once he was well (his injuries were miraculously minor), he said: Course not; I was drunker'n piss. But when I ask family members about him, they say he never drank.

But about that earlier scene. He tucks his mother's breast in and she pays no attention. It is oddly cold in his hand. Her face is gaunt, collapsing, eyes yellow as a healthy boy's urine. However, she remarks with lucidity about the weather as she stares out at the thick, wet distance, says how it will be too rough to fish later, as if it were possible for her to fish later without doing her own falling off of bridges. So he would sit down on the bench beside his mother, surely he would do this, put his head in his hands, sigh—a practiced gesture.

His mother and father were separated at the time of his father's death. She was in the hospital getting surgery on an ulcer (they performed surgery on them back then). My father got a call from the cops. They had found his father after he'd been dead for three days from a massive heart attack. My father had to go to the house, sign some papers, answer some questions, identify, verify. It was still hot then. You can imagine. The body was swollen, as if full of water. The skin was gray. Eyes were open. It was as if he'd drowned, a delayed reaction to driving off the bridge. Maybe he'd been dead for a long time, my father might have thought, and had just now decided to lie down in darkness and start stinking to let everyone know. His dog, Henry, a little terrier mutt, was lying still beside the body, ready to go out. The dog perked its ears up, wagged its tail when my father opened the door. My father ejected sickness and disbelief into his open hands, instinctively trying to avoid making a mess in his father's house.

Something about my father's mother. He had a pet rabbit as a boy, my father, a little white one named Bugs—no kidding—my mother told me this not long ago—and his mother told him to go get it. She was sober. He handed it to her with complete trust. He was maybe ten, eleven, not yet cynical, wary. He knew nothing of alcoholism, madness, suicide. All of that was later; still too early for a boy, but later. She broke the rabbit's neck with her bare hands. It screamed. Rabbits scream like babies when excited. When he cried and refused to eat Bugs, his father said, Fine, more for me. On this fall afternoon in 1967, he thinks of this when the smell hits him, even, oddly, before he thinks of his dead father's swollen, gray body. He can't believe she could sit here, no matter how drunk, in this smell.

She keeps drinking and talking of fishing, of blue skies, of the time they went, just the two of them, right after they were married, down to Florida, to the Gulf Coast. Blue water and huge fish. These words could be anything: baby talk, the grocery list, another fishing story. She is unraveling, tiptoeing toward psychotic break. She doesn't look at my father. She goes on: He (my father's father) caught one so big that they grilled it and fed everyone at the hotel. They were heroes for a day. They smoked cigars in the sun. They were wearing new clothes. They both had jobs back in Virginia. It was a beautiful day. They had coleslaw and French fries and big hunks of fish. Her nightgown opens again. She doesn't notice, or simply doesn't care, he can't tell. She tries to conjure other good days, furrows her brow at the chicken pecking in the yard. She drinks from a tall, chipped tea glass. My father walks into the house to get a flashlight so that he can get under the house and see what's dead. He takes a bandana from his pocket, one of those red paisley ones, and ties it around his face like Billy the Kid. He feels like a boy.

The smell of death sends him reeling, thinking of the rabbit, his father's swollen body. The luck of this house. His life. He had dreams, my father, of playing Major League baseball, of living far from all this. (Certainly any story would incorporate dreams.) He'd gone out west with the national championship all-star baseball team from Virginia, 1960, and the sky, just like they said, was enormous, limitless, not like in the South, where it was low and thick and wet all the time, even when it was sunny. He dreamed of being somebody, a name, and living out in the open. Growing up he felt sometimes like a speck on the sad, wet earth. The shouting and the drinking and the occasional tossing of dishes had closed in on him like walls. Instead of getting tough, he became overly sensitive, withdrawn, lacking confidence in everything from school to girls, everything but his ability to hit and field a ball. And then he ruined his knee, just kidding around with dropouts, playing basketball in a pair of slippery loafers. (Are dreams so fragile that they can be taken by a pair of slippery loafers?) It kept him out of Vietnam, sure, but it also kept him out of baseball; it kept him away from what he imagined was his only chance to live a life that was not obscene.

But he did find ways. He kept his head above water. I'd want that to be clear.

*

So he rifles through drawers, looking for the flashlight. We are back in the opening scene of the imaginary book I will never write. The smell is strong, maybe too strong to be under the house. He can't find the flashlight. After hurting his knee, after the doctors told him it would never be right again, he found himself depressed, finally realizing that he was stuck in his life as it was. He ran his father's grocery store after dropping out of school. It was when the store went under that he returned to school and graduated. Then he took care of his father's pig farm, something he bought before he died, thinking it would make money. It didn't. Soon he would work in a bank. Then, finally, by 1970, the year I was born, he'd take a job at the Newport News Shipyard, this when he'd conceded that he would never fulfill his dreams and that he needed to imagine new things to dream. But on this particular day he is unemployed.

It's not under the house. It's Henry, my father's father's dog. That's the twist, the big moment of imaginary Chapter Uno. Dead in the bedroom, on the bed. Dead for a while, a few days. Jesus, he thinks, not as prayer but lament, what is it with this? How do these things go unnoticed? The dog is . . . collapsing . . . dead for a good while, Christ, maybe a week. He thinks Henry may have starved, but then pushes the thought away. Heart attack. Old age. Easier. Neater. He picks Henry up and thinks of the rabbit, his father, and now his mother out on the porch and those boys who go in the woods to shoot BBs at her, who stand around her when she's drunk and dare each other. If he were not himself, he thinks, holding the stinking dog, and he were instead one of those boys, he'd probably do the same thing. He imagines shooting BBs at his mother, standing over in the yard in the dark while she sleeps, totally unconcerned, daring the boys.

Here is how bad my father's luck—and by extension my own luck, my family's luck—was: He eventually died, almost twenty-six years to the day from the dog incident, of malignant mesothelioma caused by asbestos fibers, which he got while working for more than two decades at the Newport News Shipyard. That may seem too lachrymose, too contrived, to even put in a book. When I think of this, his illness, I think of baseball, of his knee, of dead rabbits and dogs and fathers, of dreams and dead dreams and dreams of death as ordered and uncomfortable as a good book, of the fact that his father and mother wouldn't take one fucking afternoon to go stand in a crowd for what was perhaps a pointless ceremony while my father graduated from high school at almost twenty years old (only slightly younger than I was when I received a bachelor's degree, for which my father went out and spent more money than he should have on a camcorder to capture my pointless ceremony, which he made sure I knew was anything but pointless), which was one of the most difficult things he ever accomplished, which is why I'm writing a story without the words "grandmother" or "grandfather."

Something about me, the narrator, the non-book-writer of this story. In college, for a time, I read Eastern philosophy (I might have grown a goatee if my face would have cooperated). I read Hesse and Kerouac. All that unencumbered ranting. Those books were about me. I wanted to be that sad happy tragicomic narrator bleeding that jazzy blues-filled bebop prose, a dirty reefer-stoked Buddhist martyr who considered myself no more or less important than anyone or anything else. One can incorporate, attribute, luck to the karmic wheel, to samsara, the endless cycle of birth, suffering, death, rebirth. To yin and yang, to universal equanimity, to positive and negative wrestling for space, et cetera. One can have a clean mind and body and a stoic understanding of tragedy, if trained properly. But I failed in every way. I am about as capable of following religious dogma as a dead mutt (dead for a week, let's say) is of winning the Blue Ribbon in a dog show. I took drugs and drank and ate bad food; the closest I came to stoicism was floating around in a haze, narcotized, untroubled.

And after college, I moved to Richmond, a couple hours up the James River from where I was born. My father was dying. I tried not to think about it; it became all I thought about. I had four jobs that year and quit them all. I fancied myself some kind of poet. I was filled with what I thought of as the necessary angst and turmoil; I just lacked talent. I read all the time and remember, on at least a couple of occasions, being an angry, drunk, pompous asshole. I drank all the time. I was as frightened of my father's death as if it were my own. I rarely went home to see my father, to look into my own face; instead, calling him, having incredibly positive, superficial conversations while he had trouble breathing. Distance, I hoped, would alleviate the obligation of love. It didn't, like I knew it wouldn't, like he knew it wouldn't. I was a coward. On the morning of the day my father would die, my younger brother called. He was sixteen and stayed home with my father and is much braver than I will ever be. I envy him his courage. He was crying. For a year after this he suffered panic attacks. He was just a kid. It fucked him up. On the phone, he really couldn't even speak, but I knew. I was broke. I hadn't worked in weeks. I didn't have money for gas to get home. I took quarters out of a jar in my roommate's room. I left him a note that I would pay him back. I realize now that I never did. All the signs along the highway were blank and I floated unmoored through timeless space without touching the accelerator or the steering wheel or hearing the radio that was on full volume. Two hours later, when I reached my house, there was a sign that said OXYGEN IN USE: NO SMOKING. I was stuck. I didn't want to go in. I thought, for just a second, about leaving. Inside, my father was in bed. The cancer had spread to his liver; his poisoned blood was recycling itself and pumping through his body. He was wearing a diaper. He weighed maybe eighty pounds, having lost half of his body weight in less than a year, a third of that in the month since I'd seen him. I barely recognized him. He was fifty-one. He used to run every day. I was twenty-two. I've erased a lot of it. I remember lying in the bed with him, both of us looking at the rough, white ceiling, both of us still shy about showing affection. I don't remember what I said, but I talked to him for a long time, calm but also urgent, every few minutes looking over to see his gaunt profile. He was on morphine, but he seemed to be listening, his legs slowly writhing like things under water. Less than two hours after I'd returned home, he died. I'd swear he waited for me, that he insisted on doing me that favor. My mother, my younger brother, and I stayed in the room with him. Had it been my choice, at that moment, I might have washed him and kept him for three more days.

But about the dog and my father's mother. The old great-uncle from North Carolina, after the funeral, back at my house, the two of us drinking and eating. He finished the story. He wasn't a good storyteller. He backtracked, said, No, wait; said, And then. My father's mother had had a nervous breakdown. She went into a hospital that year and actually got better eventually, not great but better. She couldn't touch booze ever again. The couple of times she did were disastrous. And my father, said the great-uncle, that dark fall day in 1967, walked out the back door, the stinking dead dog in his arms, the bandana over his face, to avoid having his fragile mother see. And that was a part of it. The point. The message, the moral. He wanted me to understand the kindness in that gesture. She was still talking to the chicken in the overgrown yard. The boys were in the street, on their bikes, drinking sodas, eating candy. My father buried Henry in the woods out behind the house. That was it. End of story. The old great-uncle looked at me. We both swigged beer. We were drunk now and I figured I might stay this way for a good while. Do you see, his eyes said, your father was a genuinely good man; he didn't have to pretend; he didn't have to talk about it.

After the funeral and the reception (or whatever you would call the non-party after funerals), after everyone had left, and my family was asleep, I was still drinking under a single lamp in the otherwise dark house, thinking about the story, picturing my father in 1967, mulling it over, storing it up. I thought of the story and the old great-uncle from Carolina whom I could not remember ever meeting until today. The story connected to other stories, stretching back through time, springing forward through my life, my future, even far beyond me, until I was nothing but a character in someone's story, but in that way, like my father, perhaps immortal. I slept on the couch in a stiff black suit.

The next morning, I sat at the kitchen table talking to my mother, my brother. People would come by the house later, but for now we were alone—together in the kitchen, but feeling more alone than we ever had, as if just out the window was nothing but a vast, empty desert. I can't remember what was said. But I remember we laughed somehow; we were all exposed nerves, and the moderately funny became uproariously hilarious. We laughed so hard we cried; we slapped our knees and gasped for breath. There were still funny things in the world. That amazed me. I kept the old uncle's story to myself that morning, tried to push it way back inside my head, afraid of puncturing our bubble of good, hard laughter.

Nadine Kijner

Water

My sister kisses me on the lips and her mouth lingers on mine, holds, the familiar smell of her skin hidden beneath smoke and cheap cabernet. She keeps her lips on mine for the benefit of the drunks at the bar, then floats her head back and laughs. *Look, lesbians,* a man says, gaping, and laughter erupts from her throat, volcanic, watery. Her skin turns a violent red. I never know for certain what's so funny—I mean, I know what's funny, but not *so.*

"Please, another glass," she says and strokes my chin, her cigarette grilling red in front of my eyes. Her lips twitch to the left. She leans forward and snaps her fingers, but the bartender is on the other side of the open-air bar. There is a moon and there is a breeze. She reels on high heels, knocks a glass down the front of her black beaded dress. Wine splats my hand in ruby freckles.

My sister looks at me. Flickers of rage disturb her pale blue eyes. Her cold fingertips pull my face to hers, then push me away. A new cabernet shines on the bar. She takes the stem of the glass between her fingers and says, "Dah-ling, you rilly are too kind," and I step up and out to the wood-planked deck and lean over the rail. The Intercostal looks silver beneath the moon, rippling. Fish breath rises in quiet pops. My sister's laughter rifles inside.

My sister and I once shared a bedroom. We would sleep together in summers, sweating, our backs hot, damp, and in the first morning breath, I wouldn't know where she ended and where I began.

My sister is a neighboring country. She talks, and this angular black woman with sad eyes and a sensitive mouth watches and nods. My sister's arms lunge and swipe the air, her words lurching, careening from her lips. Wine stumbles out her glass. Fish leap up and I watch their dark shapes swither and dash.

My sister and I had a language between Spanish and English. We used these private words after our mother's death. We soaked together in long baths until we raisined, skin pressed to skin. There was a river in our back yard. In winter it froze. When it thawed, we splashed our feet in it, brown mud clouding up around our white toes.

I take my sister's hand. Her wrist is the width of a child's. I have to begin the leaving. I discovered this bar, El Encanto, a rustic hideaway for boaters and locals on the Intercostal. The tired-looking owner with the growing paunch always greets us with a kiss on each cheek and a free drink. I hold my sister's hand and she looks at me, light knife-flashing in her eyes. Her skin is no longer flushed. I feel the small bones of her dry hand move beneath my palm.

The slap on my cheek is cold, flat, and sharp. My feet step back, my eyes water. Men, slumped over the bar, chuckle. My heart begins to gallop, sweat rushes and breaks through my skin. My sister, her pale blue eyes drag across my face. She is with the fish that dart below the dark moving water. There was a language we spoke I no longer remember.

My sister's breath is rancid. There is dried red wine at the corners of her mouth. She strokes my cheek. The moon has moved, but the stars have not shifted. Our feet lift and scrape against the unyielding wood. Fish scissor beneath the water's surface, restless, hungry, silent.

My sister's hair smelled like cake. When she wasn't looking, I put the long ends into my mouth, my tongue curling the thin strands into the fine point of a paintbrush. There was a sweetness hidden in there. I drew on my hand, with my saliva coating my sister's spun tip of hair. I made small square houses, tiny wet windows that looked out at the world.

These houses disappeared between the blink of your lashes, evaporated, homes once there, gone, as if they'd never existed.

My sister would lock me in the bathroom and read me portions of *Catch 22*. You didn't laugh, You're not listening, she'd say. I knew not to answer. She reread entire passages, one hand clasping the doorknob, the book's worn spine held open in the other. She was twelve and I was ten. There was strength in her legs, her forearms, a slew of freckles on her forehead. My sister had eyes like this, bright, hungry, quick. They could hold you as if you were the only one. With no warning, they might drop you.

You knew anger sluiced through her. It could be there at the end of a sentence, startling you like a shadow slinking by an open door.

There was a river in our back yard. In winter, it froze. When it thawed, we splashed our feet in it, brown mud clouding up around our white toes. There was an incline of earth, rocks your hands could hang on to as you descended. But still, you slid. Dirt and pebbles crumbled away beneath your sneakers the harder you slipped, sploshing, the river rippling. If you were the one down below along the edge, watching the earth pinch up, scatter, the pebbles and dry clumps of mud dappling the water, you could get wet. Splashed.

Maybe you would tumble headfirst and something that got cut would need tending.

I spent hours trying to see myself in the river. Knees pressed against my chest, edgily balanced on the balls of my toes, the soles of my sneakers bent far beyond the rubber's wish, I looked at the river's skin. Show me who I am. Changeable waters, first green, then brown, then silver beneath the sun, seemingly placid, always moving slightly away. Always washing through your fingers, dribbling, beading up and plopping on the river's surface, single drops falling down like a mother's tears. Drawing the river into your hand, wet, gleaming, it always disappeared, just when you had absolute conviction, gone, just when you felt, yes, I can hold you.

You could see the reflection of the river in my mother's vanity table. But I don't remember much about my mother's vanity. Her bed was the land. Creased sheets, the surprise of sour sleeping breath coming from that face. I sunk against my mother's hip, my head fit in the empty space at the curve of her waist, and I remember sometimes her fingers pressing my head soft, yes, stay there, yes, encouraging me against her, yes. I made no noise about it. Bones, breath, skin, malady, all of it was my mother and it was my territory.

My mother had a face that made you need to look. She had these certain laughing eyes, the color of weather. When storms grabbed on, the laughter vanished. It was true the storms could frighten.

Catch 22. Listen. Laugh. Why are you not laughing? It was a clear radio voice that my sister used to read aloud, spiced with the ironic tone of a twelve-year-old. But I didn't want to listen to the book, there were things out the door that I wanted. *Hurry, come quick,* they urged, the river in my back yard, the lake of the bed where my mother swam in sleep. *Come to me.* My sister's endless voice, the book's repeated pages, her eyes watching, waiting for laughter, it was the stuffed heat in the bathroom with the door locked, the light blazing, pointing out the dullness of the faucet with its haphazard fingerprints, the neediness of the words, the insistence I laugh out loud with her, that made me suddenly kick out with violence.

In the end there was no exit but through laughter. You jumped out the window and into laughter's arms.

I crawled into my mother's bed when she lay there in the afternoon and put my hand on her thigh. She'd be folded inside herself, her gaze like a lost river. There was the sound of neighboring mothers shrieking out front doors, of brakes squealing, of people and their afternoons unfolding. The sun beat against the window, bounced off my mother's vanity mirror. I rejoiced in the blinding white heat, how it shifted by centimeters, alive, breathing. Shadows fell across the carpet, elongating. We were alone, incubated, stuck between the normal neighboring noises and the oncoming sadness, lying in the lake of the bed. All the sleep made my mother's thigh soft to my pressing fingers.

But it was the Nazis' swift and fierce occupation of my mother's mind which led me back down to the river. I couldn't see the things she saw, or hear the threats she protested. She might scream out, debate and bicker with nothing in English, her voice round, accented, high-pitched.

I don't know, her Spanish was saved for me, my sister, my father. For Spanish songs. Inside songs, her voice quivered, the lilt of it, the high holding notes made a smile form on her lips. She might sing to the maid. Ramona. My mother, I remember when she sang, how music curved out her mouth in a snaking stream, her eyes wet, bright. My voice longed to join in, and yes, seeing this, my eyes flash, my lips part, my mouth open, she said yes, sing, sing.

My mother threw open the window. Out went our heads. The never-ending song—*estas son las mananitas.* It seemed weeks flew by where we sang for days.

Most often, however, there was sadness, inexplicable, strangling, a sudden possession so complete it took small children with it. You could get lost in the thicket if you didn't escape to the river. She was loyal to its pull and call and forgot everything else, as if this plunging sadness were the waters that birthed her.

You pant, scurry, scramble, dashing, dashing, and oh, there it is, the river, its leaving constant. You notice how, yes, you do breathe deeper when you see its waters waving, how they swathe from light to dark with each ripple. You dip your hand in and feel the river thrum and stroke you, its watery fingers wrapped loose around your skin. Quieted now, you curl up by its side. Sturdy earth, how it holds you, how it holds your river in its warm brown hands. This is your world, right here, right beneath your digging fingers. You feel certain, your head resting against the land's stomach, that you could not be dropped. Things are held to last. No one has fallen through.

It was a matter of time for the inside to darken, all light smothered out. Your mother did not tell you this. It breathed out her pores like smoke. You banged on the walls but that pointlessness just sat there enclosed in a small sealed box. And how does one break open a box of smoke?

There was a waterfall in the river in our back yard. If you dared, you could walk out on the slick rocks. Green moss covered over with the constant current. One summer my father bought a boat. Later that winter, it too froze in the river.

My sister and I once had a language between Spanish and English.

Tell me what you saw, my sister always asks me years later without saying it. Perhaps everyone has become afraid of what I've seen and perhaps they are afraid that I will tell it.

My mother picked me up from school because I called her. She arrived in the green station wagon. The heater was on. I don't remember it being cold. I don't remember anything outside the car except the tops of the trees whisking by. I remember the two of us sitting, driving. My mother said to me, *Uste es buena.* I remember wondering like how was I good, but I didn't ask it. I took that *Uste es buena* and pushed it inside, let it burrow. I wanted to shout it out the green station wagon's window.

I was sick. I had a headache. My mother was out of bed, she was wearing striped jeans, her hair fell down brown along her back. My mother drove into the garage and parked the car. I really hadn't been sick, something urged me to call my mother, so I did and she got me. I walked out of Hillel Academy's red brick entryway and saw the green station wagon, breathing. And there she was, my mother.

I walk up to my room, flip on the light, get on my bed, and lie down. *Uste es buena*—I push the words around, make them rise. I have a headache, a heaviness that throbs. I fall asleep, a lead pipe to the head sleep. My sister is not in the bed beside me, later she will not ask me, Tell me what you saw. Years will go by and she will not put together the words she presses into my flesh. Her words become liquid, our silence thickens.

The river, the waters are agitated, they brash and brack.

My sister's hair once smelled like cake. My mother went to work in the garage. She was a sculptor who worked beside the green station wagon. Her table to mold, the clay, the kiln, all these things were in the garage. I fell asleep, a heavy mashed-in sleep. I had to do an oral report on Munich, tell the class important things about Munich, but something happened. I called my mother to pick me up instead. She brought me home in the green station wagon, our hands warm in the heat of the car. The garage door closed. I remember the way the heavy door thundered, the abrupt way light was shut out as if there were no mercy.

My sister and I had a language between Spanish and English. We used these private words after our mother's death. There was a language we spoke I no longer remember. We had sounds no one else could enter.

Rafael Campo

Darkest Purple

for Michael Canfield, d. 1995

Among the mourners gathered there were three
Young women, dressed in gold, black—aubergine?
Faint, high-pitched whistle from the bright CD

Inside its player (glimpse on a table in
The corner): song rang out to my surprise,
More soothing than my strongest medicine.

I sniffed the scentless ninety-nine cent rose
I'd bought conveniently across the street;
Like anyone whose grief is all he knows,

Ungrateful, dumbly mad, disconsolate,
I wept, and listened. Mike, I thought of you.
The woman dressed in gold stood up to greet

A late arrival; I noticed that the other two
Held hands as if in love, as if the black
And purple—ashes, Kaposi's—could make a new

Protective color. One whose name was lack
And joy, one whose meaning was not to break.

Frank X. Gaspar

The Lemons

Forget the sun and the dizzy moths.
Forget the pieces of mockingbird that the cats have left by the side gate.
Forget the hose running under the honeysuckle:
the lemons are offering us holiness again.
They are making us go down on our knees to smell them.
They are making us think of our old loves, to grieve over them.
They are singing every little song, they are conjuring every temptation.
They have been having sex with the oranges and tangerines, the yard.
is rife with their pollens, they are sweeter than they even know.
They speak together. They are amazing me with their navels and nipples.
How they flaunt themselves on the spider-veined limbs all pained
with thorn.
They are trying to make me lazy, to turn me against my simple work—
they do not want to be plucked from their own dreaming.
They are telling us again how they come each year, bringing secrets
from their other world, and how we are never able to decipher them.
How long now before we put up the aluminum ladder
and pull on the leather-palmed gloves? How long with the shape
and heft of lemon voluptuous in my hand? How long
with the summer in its steep track, and the low cars cruising
out on the avenues, and the drone of the small airplanes
like bees over the far houses?

Marcus Cafagña

Gloomy Sunday

for Hayden Carruth

If the instrument of your beloved's
suicide is within your reach, get rid of it.
—Traditional

This was the time of year, this gloomy Sunday in October
when I descended our basement steps
to the bottom and found my wife hanging
as if the lord mayor of hell
had lured her to the other side. Don't let me forget
that Lansing place and wonder who lives there now
and what they make of our cracked foundation.
Let it be clear, but small, through a lens,
my wife's cropped hair, the chairs
so torn with fabric stripped from arms.
How she promised she'd stay in this poor little world
and redeem the diamond ring.
But the ulcers in her colon
did not stop bleeding and the face-lift seared her scalp
to the stitches and the manic depression coiled
her throat like a necklace, burning pearl by pearl,
or was suddenly relinquished
to the velvet box of failed attempt. She could not avenge
her first husband's fist, the psychiatrists
on a ward in Fort Myers who dilated

her pupils and left her gown on
backward, the snapshot posed on prom night
with her father, the secret bristling between them.
Now the dolorous wind swings branches
sharp-edged and shadowed
with clouds. Now the radio wakes me from a bathroom floor
in Pittsburgh, the clamor on every station
a summons through evening's
wormy pomp—acid guitar, sarabande whirling
under electric globes, voice of an angel
blown to dust—as if from my wife's dying breath the germ
I've caught will self-inflict. Ridiculous thought
but I'm throwing my extension cords away. The one she used
was polarized, white,
a 15-footer
and it shook her down to a hard-shelled silence.

Pat Mora

Reluctant Death

We all know anger,
how suppressed it seeps,
contorts, and against our will
bursts forth in startling shapes.

When the noble god Brahma
suppressed his fury,
fire appeared from all his
apertures as a scarlet
woman, her garments, eyes,
palms, and the soft soles of her feet
red, red, red, red, red.
Brahma called the maiden Death.

Fond of us, she bravely
resisted his wish by
supreme asceticism.
For fifty thousand
million years, she stood
on one foot.

Brahma said, "Obey my command."
She stood on one foot
for another twenty thousand
million years. She lived with
the teeth and claws of wild
animals for yet another
ten million million years.
"Obey my command."

For twenty thousand years,
the unwilling maiden
ate nothing but air.
For eight thousand years,
she stood silent in water.
At the Kausiki River,
she lived only on wind and water,
and at the Ganges and Mount Meru
she stood alone, still
as a piece of wood
to avoid harming
any one of us.

On the summit of Himalaya,
she stood on one big toe
for yet another thousand
million years. "Obey
my command," the lord,
the Grandfather, said,
assuring her, his voice
feather soft. "Humans
will not blame you."
Her teardrops became
the diseases that whisper
to our gauzy flesh
that its time has come,
and she comes, a friend

she hopes, as a man to men,
as a woman to women,
gathers us into her red
palms and bathes us
with holy water from her eyes.

Jewel Mogan

El Lobo Solo

His only child had come of age. To his unbelievable good fortune she came to this dump where he was living to invite him to her *quinceañera*. His ex-wife must be busy with the preparations to let Vickie stay so long, telling him all about it, black eyes big as any unbroken colt.

And he had had to tell her that he could not be there. He goes back to jail tomorrow to finish serving his sentence. His parole has been revoked because he never met with his parole officer. The parole officer told the judge he was sorry, but Gonzales had a communication problem.

"Would you send me the pictures?"

"Yes, Papa, I'll send you all the pictures. You'll see me in my dress and Ramon in his tuxedo. Mama wanted Noe to be my escort, and we had a terrible fight, but I was going to have Ramon or nobody at all."

He smiled at this. He guessed that Noe was her mother's boyfriend.

It was too soon for her. His baby. She was not yet shaped to womanhood and motherhood. She was one round bundle from neck to knees, bouncing around on his couch with no control over her hands and feet. Like a bird still in its soft feathers, not at home in the nest, on the ground, or in the air. He tried to frame those eyes, the round laughing face, her long black hair, in the center of his dismal dirty picture window, but she constantly fluttered in and out of the frame.

Yet when he had smoked cigarette after cigarette and watched her child's fingers draw her long dress and flower coronet in the thick dust of his coffee table, draw her attendants, their satin dresses and their names, the white tuxedo Ramon would wear with a pink cummerbund (she wrote VICTORIA and RAMON in capital letters in the dust), he allowed her to become a woman in his mind, and he realized that by some inexplicable boon from on high, he and Ramon would be *familia*, too. She was honoring him, Tonio, as her father, and his brother Ramon as her uncle. Ramon she had always loved in spite of, perhaps because of, his reputation. No doubt about it, his little brother had gone bad. He had a hideout, a den, a territory of his own, wore the red and black of the territory, and made too many moves for Tonio to keep up with, though he was only eighteen. Tonio had no more use for Ramon than one snake for another in the nest. Each male in the Gonzales family struck out on his own as soon as he had hair between his legs. *Machismo* was all one could call upon. *Cojones.* Others might call upon the bottle. A woman. The land. The faith. The military life. *Phut.* He fired a fragment of tobacco from his lip. Workmanship? One's work? All of these had failed him. Or he them. Life had pulled up these anchors as a tornado uproots a tree. He narrowed his eyes against the smoke of his cigarette. It is all we have, our manhood. A possession no one can take away. It will not desert me unless I dishonor it. Only my death can take it away.

Why, then, did he feel so sad to see his daughter entering her womanhood? It's not the same for a woman. He was sad and anxious for Vickie. "Not yet. Not yet."

"Mama and Aunt Angela and Aunt Victoria are cooking already. To freeze. Beef and chicken enchiladas. Tamales and *menudo*."

His ex-wife's side of the family was putting on the *quinceañera.* "I wish I could be there. I would not come to the reception, but I would come to the church if I could." He plugged his cigarette firmly into the corner of his mouth as he took out his wallet from a back pocket of his jeans. He gave her all the money in it, thirty-two dollars.

"I'll send you pictures of everything. You'll see me in my dress, Papa. I tried it on yesterday. It came from Juarez. And the cake. I wish you could see how unbelievable! At the top of a pedestal it will be in three tiers, with staircases of icing coming down to two more cakes and little figures of *da-*

mas and *chambelánes* in long dresses and tuxedos coming down these staircases. Mama and Aunt Angela and Aunt Victoria have been planning for months and months. I will walk with Ramon through a big archway of flowers into the hall and then there will be a dance. Mama will present me my heels on a pillow for the first dance. Oh, Papa, thank you for the money." She suddenly seemed to remember the bills crumpled in her hand. "Watch for all this in the pictures. I'll send you all of them."

As they sat on the battered couch, her words danced with no pauses and no more meaning for him than golden motes on the late afternoon air in the picture window. But he kept his eyes narrowed to her to draw in only her image as the afternoon blued into evening. She had plenty to tell him, and he recorded her voice and image, not the individual words.

She wanted to cut his hair. He needed a haircut, so he let her. He was surprised at the sure way her small fingers ruffled the long wavy ends of his hair, snipped them quickly, and as quickly brushed them from his neck, later gathering the towel from his shoulders and shaking it out the front door. She liked to do things with hair, she said. She said he had beautiful hair.

When Ramon appeared at the door as she was sweeping up the last of the hair clippings, it surprised him, for Ramon did not come often.

"Tony—" he said to his brother in a husky voice, ignoring Vickie. "Tony!"

"Ramon!" said Vickie, as if she owned him. "You can take me home. I need to get home or Mama will send for me." She crossed the picture window to go toward him, stepping over her father's long legs under the table, Ramon making a step toward her, dark-faced except for the whites of his eyes in the gathering darkness, his hands up suddenly in some familiar, deadly familiar, way—a way, a warning Tonio read instantly, but not quickly enough. "Vickie!" He threw his body up to his daughter, too late. Through the picture window, bullets winged into her body, the couch, the front door, crashed at their feet, bore into the meat of Ramon's leg, although Tonio didn't remember this until he saw Ramon at the funeral home limping under his black pants, refusing to use any crutch except one of his lieutenants.

The police questioned him and Ramon closely. In the three days' extension he was allowed on his reporting date at the jail in order to attend his daughter's funeral, Tonio hunted his daughter's killer on his own, independent of Ramon and his homeboys. He hadn't many clues except some names Ramon had confided to the police—names of the ones he had argued with that afternoon in some dispute over their turf. The bullets were intended for Ramon. He told the police that the two who most likely would have been shooting at him, Tonio, were already in prison. He went sleepless the first night, searching the streets. The next night would also be sleepless, at Victoria's wake; the next day would be the funeral, and then jail. Time enough then to eat and sleep.

They laid her out at Vallejo Funeral Home. Vallejo allowed all the coffee, all the candles you wanted, and space for all the wailing a woman needed to raise to heaven, all the cigarettes all the cousins and uncles could smoke who would stay the night smoking. And Ramon and his young bloods would smoke themselves into a stupor and fall asleep, collapsed together on the soft couches in their white T-shirts, black baggies, and red and black bandana headbands that had never soaked up sweat in a cottonfield. The candles burned over them and the brightly burnished open casket corners. The rest of the metal container was surrounded and nearly buried in flowers. She was beautiful in death. She had been not beautiful in life but lively as a brown field lark, always singing or talking about today and tomorrow. He put his head down in his hands.

He had come to the funeral home after the Rosary and after the women were taken away so that he would not have to face his ex-wife, her boyfriend, and her family. Enough of that at the funeral tomorrow, when they all would sit together. His brother, Victoria's favorite uncle, must sit with them, too, in the knowledge that the bullet that killed her was intended for him. That thought did not seem to cause Ramon guilt now. Perhaps it never would. His brother was on fire now for vengeance. Tonio saw them, all the young males, in metal coffins in these T-shirts they were now wearing the ones with "In Living Memory of Victoria" and "R.I.P., Vickie" printed in German letters that were hard to read. Others showed Selena or Jesus hovering over a sleek low rider. These shirts had been made up overnight for Vickie's and Ramon's friends. It was the only way they knew to memorialize anyone. Statements. Blood oaths. Cries. Words in the wind.

Ramon told him the paper said that the city had "taken young Vickie

Gonzales to its heart." He had not read this article nor heard it quoted, for he talked to no one. The words would have meant nothing, anyway. A snake, he told Ramon, is long on action and short on words. He said he had never heard a snake say anything, except a rattler, and he speaks too late. Your homeboys' oaths of vengeance mean nothing. Of all things in the world, he had the least use for words, spoken, written, or thought: the words of the law and the Church. The writers of books, how can they say everything? Or anything? The Congress and the President; the doctor; the *curandera* with her crazy chants; a woman's words of love; the empty boasts of soldiers; drunken promises. Above all, Tonio's own words.

The many candles flickered over the body. Her healthy glimmering hair covered the head wound completely. How could her black hair ever die? It was vibrant to its very roots, where it curled around her ears, made little spiral side curls where sideburns would be on a boy. He had never met a *hispaña* who was not proud of her hair. Such a symbol for life. Hair between the legs the sign above all signs one watched for. No sign so eagerly awaited. When a girl had her first bleeding, she began planning her *quinceañera.* Now the moment Vickie became a woman was caught and wrapped in that cold white dress and its layers and layers of frozen satin flounces and gathers, as if she had fallen into a snowbank that would never thaw.

He was still at the funeral home, still awake, when the women of the family came back in the morning for the procession to church. He did not go near the mother. He did not get in the same car with her, the limousine. He could not speak to her. Death was a woman's language, as was birth. He felt the responsibility of both in his heart.

Ramon arrived separately at the church. Tonio watched from a car window as he limped through a gauntlet of young brown hands waiting to give him the handshake. Most of these male teens seemed younger than Ramon, but they all wore the "R.I.P., Vickie" T-shirts. Some had red-figured black bandanas hanging from a pocket under the T-shirt tails, long as skirts on their skinny bodies. "Girls," Tonio scornfully called them. Tonio saw a black boy in the same mourning T-shirt hold out his hand tentatively to Ramon. Ramon either did not see his hand or chose not to shake it. The black boy self-consciously pulled a hair off the shirt in front of him to cover his gesture. Some of the teen girls had twisted their bandanas into their hair. The red-and-black patterns blindly twisted through the black hair like snakes.

As they got out of the automobiles and stood on the church steps in the morning heat, the sun drew forth, like incense, the dark sweet musks from their black glistening hair. Heady scents of tropical flowers and heavy ripe fruit made Tonio dizzy. He had not thought to eat anything for two days. The boys smelled sweeter than the girls. They were not tough; they were pretty girls, with hairnets over slicked-down sheaths of hair, and sunglasses perched backward on their skulls shaved below the ears. Tonio felt like an *antigua*, an old one drained of life. He was thirty-two years old. The young people were excited over Vickie's death, which linked them in a new blood tie. The males walked between a crouch and a slouch. He saw this walk in prison all the time, but it was more of a crouch, as if somebody's about to jump you. In prison, you never turn your back on anybody.

He had not been in this church in decades, but he remembered Jesus laid out in a glass case along the side aisle. Who would not remember such a thing? The bloody Crucifixion over the altar had lost its power to startle even the most pious, but this gray-fleshed young body dead of its wounds in a glass case—this could still stop the heart. He recognized that life has no joys equal to the sorrows of death. No one loves *el muerte* like us. We are in love with it.

In the noisy thump of people going into the pews, he began to go hypnotic, as he always did in a church. A priest and a tottery deacon came out, and Tonio stood with the rest like a block of wood. The priest, an Irishman, said some soft things while he looked directly at the mother. Tonio could not understand his brogue but was glad that he did this. The deacon read the reading in a heavy Spanish accent. "I have told you all this so that you may find peace in me. In the world you will have trouble, but be brave: I have conquered the world." Then Tonio's mind went numb again until the loud, wrenching groan of the pews and kneelers told him it was the Elevation. At Communion, he rose with the others and shuffled to the altar. He crossed his arms on his breast, did not partake, passed the dead Christ on the way back, the Christ not looking in the least at peace, but suffering still in death, with a terrible look of pain on his face. Strange that they chose to make Him look that way.

The Mass was almost over. With a final thunderous groan the kneelers accepted their load as bodies pressed on them for the final blessing, the cries of the wood overwhelming for a moment the priest's soft clear Irish words. His daughter would have "everlasting youth in heaven," the priest said when the rumble subsided, raising his arm over her coffin, and Vickie was thereby declared never to be a woman and was gone forever. When they raise the arm over you, that's it.

But there was only more, and worse, to come. If, somehow, the burial could only come first, and then the funeral Mass ... The mother broke down on the steps when the coffin was again loaded into the hearse. She leaned heavily on her boyfriend, sobbed and moaned, and threw back her black head, screaming words in staccato stabs at the sky.

Behind the family cars, high monster pickups and low riders loaded with teens growled in anticipation, red-and-black bandanas tied to their aerials. As they waited a few minutes in line for the procession of cars to move on, the rap beat heated up from vehicle to vehicle, and cigarettes lit up. The DJ shouted, "Cypress Hill! Playing 'How I Could Just Kill a Man'!" The beat goes on, thought Tonio, and stepped out of the car to light his cigarette. Then they were moving again. Soon they smoothly rolled away from the church with the help of a police escort. They glided through the barrio of San Francisco, past a Mexican eatery, over the tracks, past a white dust-coated concrete-block factory and a flea market. Traffic genteelly halted in respect, if not for death, for the mounted men in blue on motorcycles.

Lifted heavenward on the overpass, they looked down on distant joints in the inner city: redneck lounges (the Bowlegs Bar), black hangouts, and brown cantinas (El Lobo Solo, where he used to hang out). The tinted glass of a tall, clean bank building reflected clouds and a steeple, making the clouds and the church seem inside the bank. Other sharp spires, the old jail and the new courthouse, the college buildings, every institution in the city was stacked up all the way to the white-hot horizon.

A large percentage of the traffic stopped to let them pass, even on the freeway. This was an old local custom from horse-and-buggy days. A dangerous gesture, thought Tonio. But something in him appreciated the dangerous gesture. Even an eighteen-wheeler halted on an access road. In the car with Tonio was a little boy he did not know. This boy's white T-shirt, "R.I.P., Vickie," hung to his knees, and his baggy shorts went down to his ankles. "El Droopy" was printed on the front of his shirt. The boy, barely frying size, said to Tonio, "I think I will be a truck driver. I want to be a truck driver." Tonio looked him over and nodded. "You can do it."

On the edge of town, past the city limits, more joints, and then one liquor store after another on the Strip, where you had to go to get your liquor. As the buildings shrank and scattered, there were Texas Giant Fireworks stands, all shuttered up. Some trash pickers in Day-Glo orange vests stood at attention momentarily in whirling dust as the funeral contingent passed in a steady pace, the procession doing what it had to do. They traveled a few miles through dry brown fields, ending at quiet, dusty San Francisco Cemetery, with DIOS DA Y DIOS QUITA on the adobe archway, where you could drive no further but had to walk through. Everybody got out here, parked, and walked through the arch. Even though the rest of the cemetery was not fenced, it seemed not right to go in any way but through the arch. Sheep, thought Tonio.

The hearse, deacon's car, and limousine, however, entered another, more modern entrance, and drove right up to the gravesite.

There were puffs of cotton on the dirt here and there, matched by a few small puffs of clouds in the milk-blue sky. A dust devil swirled, and the procession made its own small dust cloud.

The family was guided to chairs draped with horrible green plush on an island of too-green plush carpet like no grass Tonio had ever seen. The carpet bulged in spots over clumps of some dry weed that dominated the sandy cemetery. He saw his parents and his ex-wife's parents, seated at opposite ends. Numerous aunts, uncles, and cousins from her side were seated in two rows, forming a bulwark for his ex-wife, the chief mourner and center of all their woe, sheltering her from the twin truths of the flower-draped casket and the open excavation waiting for it. She leaned heavily but quietly on her boyfriend.

Tonio squeezed his old mother's shoulders, shook hands with his father, and sat just behind them. He and his father had neither met nor spoken for years. There had been no open break, for there had been nothing there to break. He had left home at fifteen.

There was another round of gang handshakes beyond the immediate circle. Some of the boys wore black rosaries around their necks. Their heavy pomades mingled with the fruity, flowery scents of their girlfriends and Vickie's girlfriends. Ramon was beginning to grow a mustache.

Aiee, me. He thought of a cigarette. He knew their minds. They considered that they became men on this day. A supremely significant day for them. But "In Living Memory" T-shirts would tomorrow be replaced by the macho ones. Already, one kid had "Bad to the Bone," and another a basketball slam dunk star mouthing "Callin' Da Shots," even as they stood in the stupor of death. Tonio snorted softly. He felt as impotent as he had ever felt in his life. He wondered what shots would that kid call if that red and black bandana hanging limply out of his pocket turned into a coral snake? He had once been bitten by a coral snake, out of Loredo, on a lonely, dusty road. Attracted by something shiny in a clump of dried careless weed, he had foolishly reached in. The snake struck his wrist and almost before it settled back into its coils, his injured arm had shot forward, itself like a wiry brown snake, to seize the devil. He caught the mean end with his other hand, behind its black little eyes, twisted the head with all his strength, then bit it off. He gnawed his own wound larger, sucked it, and spat a few times into the dust. He pulled that killer inside out, made a tourniquet of the skin, twisted it tightly around him like an arm bracelet. He made his way back into Loredo, near fainting with pain, until someone took him to the clinic.

The deacon stepped up under the corrugated plastic canopy and sprinkled holy water around from a small plastic bottle. They crossed themselves and brought a thumbnail to the lips. Someone among the young males cracked his knuckles in the silence. He, the deacon, realized his inadequacy to the moment. He spared them a lot of words, saying only something about their "fellowship with the saints," and that there would be no more "whipping." He led them in "El Padrenuestro" and the "Salve Maria." When he left the gravesite, frail as he was, it seemed their supports were cut out from under them, their mouths were unstopped. Tonio's ex-wife broke into wreching moans and cries that set the other women and babies to crying. All cried in overlapping cadences, in waves of loud, then slowly dying, cadences. Every woman's way of crying is as individual as her laugh. Calling her daughter's name, Vickie's mother's cry flew out of her like a demon, its uniqueness overpowering all the rest, as it should have.

The funeral director addressed the family and friends and invited them to pay their last respects and sprinkle sand from a pail provided by Vallejo. Tonio wondered why they provided sand, when all one had to do was to reach down for dirt, acres of it, dry, sifting through the fingers.

His ex-wife sobbed through it all, as the wet-faced teens came up to contribute something to the big spray of innocent-faced flowers on the casket—a sprinkle of dirt, or a small bouquet, a single rose, or a rolled bandana. Someone started up Spanish rap on a jambox, Kid Frost doing "La Raza." The ceremony was coming apart now. The girls with red-and-black bandanas bound into their hair left with Ramon and their boyfriends. Cars could be heard spinning gravel just outside the arch of the cemetery. Vickie had mentioned an arch that was to be at her *quinceañera*. An arch of flowers, was it? He couldn't remember. The cars and pickups spun out in clouds of dust and a heavy basso music beat.

He did not want to be left with his ex-wife and the old ones, so he hitched a ride with a stranger back to town. He had the man—who was a friend of the boyfriend, he learned—drop him near the bank. At the bank he closed his account of $175 and mailed a cashier's check, minus $20, to his ex-wife. At El Lobo Solo he had a drink, a cigarette, and a plate of fajitas, his first meal in days. He then walked a single block of the free world, to the jail, checked himself in, and fell on a bunk in the holding cell.

When he awoke, he had no idea what time it was. It didn't matter anyway, anymore, such a thing. He was back on prison time, which is different from outside time. It was dark. They had put someone in the cell with him, the last thing he wanted, but of course the thing to be expected.

"Sleeping one off, old man?" asked the other guy.

It was not worth answering. He groaned and rolled over to go back to sleep.

"Do you know what time it is?"

What a chicken. "No."

"It must be past eleven-thirty. They just put me in here at eleven and I can't sleep. I don't know. . . . I told my mother to get me a lawyer. I have to see my lawyer first thing in the morning. I told her to get me a good one—man, the last part of his name is—man. It starts with an S. Stul—Stultzman, that's it. He can get off me of this thing. Did you hear of him?"

"No."

"I don't want no court-appointed lawyer."

He would be held forty-eight to seventy-two hours in this cell with this fish until the jailer knew if the fish would be bonded out right away. If not, he'd be put away in another cell. He was stuck with this girl for at least forty-eight hours. There was no hope of a Latino kid bonding out.

"I never been in jail except one night for simple burglary. I got off on probation. They can't pin this on me. They got nothing. They got the weapon, but they can't say I was the one did it."

"Was there a buddy with you—a witness?"

"Yes."

"Then if you did it, they got you."

"No, man, me and my homeboy, we're in tight."

Tonio laughed.

"Man, I tell you I can beat this with Stuze—, Stultzman. I don't need to talk to you or anybody until I see my lawyer."

"Who wants to talk? I don't."

"See, it got a lot of publicity. That's what's bad. That's always bad."

Something flashed in the dark cell, as a priceless silver coin shines out of darkness. It first glittered in a corner of his mind, then drew his entire being to it. Tonio said, "I don't read the papers. I just came here yesterday from Laredo and got picked up for public intoxication, vagrancy. What charge you caught?"

"What?"

"What's up?"

"A gang thing. Somebody got killed."

"They gonna charge you with murder one?"

"Yes, why not? Murder one, *bobo*," said the other, with an elevated tone in his voice.

Tonio cracked his knuckles in the darkness. "It was a fight to protect your turf?"

"It started that way."

"You jump somebody?"

"No, they jumped us first. They beat me and my homeboy bad. We paid them back."

"Who got killed?"

"A girl caught the bullet. But she was one of them."

"Ah." Everything had turned red—walls, ceiling, floor. It was as if he was looking through the bursting blood vessels of his own eyes. He rocked his body slowly on the bunk, and as he rocked one way he slipped a hand under his buttock and then a hand under the other buttock as he rocked the other way. Now their conversation must remain casual, in the everyday way. Let my tongue speak in the everyday way. "And you paid them back good."

"Yes."

"You—what's your name?"

"They call me Primo."

"You—Primo—you yourself got blood revenge."

"Yes."

"You were the trigger man, eh, *compañero?*"

"*Sí*, I became a man that night, *compañero.* When I get out, no one will touch me."

Yes, you became a man. I let you claim it, because I could not kill a boy. But I can kill a man. "Do you have a shank?" he asked, flinging himself on his back and speaking to the air.

"What?"

"You got a knife?"

"No, I don't have no knife on me."

Tonio ran his fingers thoughtfully around the neat scissor line that Vickie had made, ruffling his hair up along that line. He continued to speak to the ceiling, helpfully, confidentially. "Tomorrow, you might think about making yourself a shank."

Tonio would never again question fate. What he had been born for had come about. To find the serpent trapped in this concrete block cell. It was the way a wolf might trap his prey in a box canyon. He could not believe it. Thank you, Señor. He said it again, man to man. Thank you, Señor. Here was his Jesus free of his glass case. Señor Jesus Látigo. Jesus with the whip hand, who gets the job done.

Desire flowed from all the pores of his skin. He desired to do it now, before the jailers perhaps discovered their error and separated them. But experience told him to wait. The shifts had changed. They were well into the graveyard shift. Whatever one shift did, the next took for granted. This principle had aided many an escape, many a riot. And they never learned! He felt as high as he had ever been with a woman. Here was his pretty girl waiting on the other bunk.

Nothing was happening in his brain now, which was good. Many things were going on inside his body—trembling, nausea, diarrhea, inspired not by fear, but by desire.

His cellmate cursed him stinking up their space. "Gaaa! You fucking drunk! This is a shithouse. Jailer! Jailer! Give me a break. Get me out of here. In the hall. Please! Just a few minutes' break to breathe. I need a cigarette! Come on!"

The night jailer roared for them to shut the hell up. "Goddam pepper guts!"

The cellblock at last became quiet. Tonio lay still on his bunk. His bowels had done their worst, and they too lay quiet. He did not dare to get up to drink water. He did not flex his fingers for fear they would crack.

It was hot. The man opposite him turned on his bunk, sighed impatiently, mumbled, flopped around, writhed, and twisted the sheets around his body. It would be a long wake, spent marking his rising and falling breath, his suspended breaths, followed by sharp snorting inhalations to make up for the breaks in his respiration. A long time later, perhaps an hour after the man began to breathe evenly and deeply, Tonio rose slowly. So, you are laid out at last.

To within two inches of the other man's throat, he willed his hands to stay leashed. Then they struck simultaneously, as he had planned for hours; for a lifetime he had rehearsed this moment. The thumbs cut off the wind, the victim made not a sound, but silently writhed. No viper ever was more silent. Neither did Tonio make a sound. The eyes were open wide. In the half-light he could see the whites bulging out with black dilated pupils. Larger even than Vickie's deep dark eyes had ever been. He felt he could have twisted the head from the muscular neck, such strength was in the grasp of his hands.

When the man was dead, perhaps too easily dead, Tonio spat on him and returned to his bunk. Done. Thanks be to God. Now I will sleep, dead to the world, dead as Christ in the tomb. He saw a pall covering a casket. In spite of the heat, he felt a chill. A cold moist slime, like a skin, seemed to draw up over his body. *Muerte chiquita*, he said to himself, surprised. A little nervous shiver. He pulled the sheet over himself and slept, cold as his companion.

The next morning at six A.M., the jailer brought their breakfast trays. Tonio pointed out to him that the other man was dead. The jailer didn't believe him. "Put a mirror to his mouth," said Tonio.

While they "investigated," he sat on his bunk and ate his cellmate's breakfast and his own. He ate until the food filled him to his very throat. He could swallow no more.

Janice Mirikitani

For a Daughter Who Leaves

More than gems in my comb box
shaped by the God of the Sea,
I prize you, my daughter . . .
—Lady Otomo of Sakanoue
Japan, eighth century
Translated by Geoffrey Bownas

A woman weaves
her daughter's
wedding slippers.
They will carry
her steps into a new life.
But the mother
weeps alone
into her jeweled sewing box.
She slips red thread around its spool,
the same she used
to make her daughter's first
silk jacket embroidered
with turtles
that would bring luck,
long life.
All the steps she took
on her unbound, quick feet
her mother remembers:
dancing on the stones
of the yard among yellow

butterflies and white breasted
sparrows.
    And she grew, legs strong,
body long, mind
independent.
Now she captures all eyes
with her hair combed smooth,
and her hips
gently swaying like bamboo.

Hanif Kureishi

Intimacy

It is the saddest night, for I am leaving and not coming back. Tomorrow morning, when the woman I have lived with for six years has gone to work on her bicycle, and our children have been taken to the park with their ball, I will pack some things into a suitcase, slip out of my house, and take the tube to Victor's place. There I will sleep on the floor in a tiny room next to the kitchen. Each morning I will heave the thin single mattress back into the airing cupboard and stuff the musty duvet into a box and replace the cushions on the sofa.

I will not be returning to this life. I cannot. Perhaps I should leave a note. "Dear Susan, I am not coming back. . . ." Perhaps it would be better to ring tomorrow afternoon. Or I could visit at the weekend. The details I haven't decided. I will not tell her this evening. I will put it off. Why? Because words make things happen. Once they are out, you cannot put them back. I am trembling, and have been all afternoon, all day.

This, then, could be our last evening as an innocent, complete family; my last night with a woman I know almost everything about and want no more of. Soon we will be like strangers. No, we can never be that. Hurting someone is an act of reluctant intimacy. We will be dangerous acquaintances with a history.

I perch on the edge of the bath and watch my sons, aged five and three. Their toys float on the surface, and they chatter. They are ebullient and fierce, and people say what happy and affectionate children they are. This morning, before I set out for the day, the elder boy, insisting on another kiss before I closed the door, said, "Daddy, I love everyone."

Tomorrow I will damage and scar them.

The younger boy was wearing chinos, a gray shirt, blue braces, and a policeman's helmet. As I toss the clothes in the washing basket, I am disturbed by a sound outside. I hold my breath.

Already!

She is pushing her bicycle into the hall. She is removing the shopping bags from the basket.

During the last few days, I have been trying to convince myself that leaving someone isn't the worst thing you can do to a person. It doesn't have to be a tragedy. If you never left anything or anyone, there would be no room for the new. Naturally, to move on is an act of infidelity—to others, to the past, to old notions of yourself. Perhaps every day should contain at least one essential infidelity. It would be an optimistic, hopeful act, guaranteeing belief in the future—a declaration that things can be not only different but better.

Eight years ago my friend Victor left his wife. Since then he has had only unsatisfactory loves, including the Chinese prostitute who played the piano naked and brought all her belongings to their assignations. If the phone rings he does a kind of panicky dance, wondering what new opprobrium may be on the way. Victor has always given women hope, if not satisfaction.

Susan is in the room now.

She says, "Why don't you ever shut the bathroom door?"

"What?"

"Why don't you?"

I can't think of a reason.

She kisses the children. When we really talk, it is about them—something they said or did.

She presents her cheek a few inches from my lips, so that to kiss her

I must lean forward. She smells of perfume and the street. She goes to change and returns in jeans and sweatshirt, with a glass of wine for each of us.

"Hallo. How are you?"

She looks at me hard in order to have me notice her. I feel my body contract. I smile. Does she notice anything different in my face today? Usually, before seeing her, I prepare two or three possible subjects, as if our conversations were examinations. Today I have been too feverish to rehearse. She accuses me of being silent. But silence, like darkness, can be an act of kindness; it, too, is a language.

The boys' bathwater drains away slowly—their toys impede the plughole. They won't move until the water is gone, and then they sit there making mustaches and hats with the remaining bubbles. Eventually, I lift the younger one out. Susan takes the other.

We wrap them in thick hooded towels. With damp hair and beads of water on their necks, the boys look like diminutive boxers after a fight. They argue about what pajamas they want to wear. The younger one will only wear a Batman T-shirt. They seem to have become self-conscious at an early age. They must have got it from us.

Susan gives the younger boy a bottle, which he holds up to his mouth two-handedly, like a trumpeter. I watch her caressing his hair, kissing his dimpled fingers, and rubbing his stomach. He giggles and squirms. What a quality of innocence people have when they don't expect to be harmed. Who could violate it without damaging himself?

We take the children downstairs, where they lie on cushions, nonchalantly sucking their pacifiers, watching "The Wizard of Oz" with their eyes half open. They look like a couple of swells smoking cigars in a field on a hot day. They demand ginger biscuits. I fetch them from the kitchen without Susan's noticing me. The boys extend their greedy fingers but don't look away from the TV. After a while, I pick up the crumbs and, having considered what to do with them, fling them into a corner.

Susan works in the kitchen, listening to the radio. Her own family life, like mine, has mostly been unpleasant. Now she goes to a lot of trouble to make good meals. Even if we're having a takeaway, she won't let us eat in a slew of newspapers and children's books. She puts out napkins and a bottle of wine, and lights candles, insisting we have a proper family meal, including nervy silences and severe arguments.

I sit on the floor near the boys and examine them, their feet, ears, eyes. This evening, when I am both here and not here—almost a ghost already—I want to be aware of everything; I want a mental picture that I can carry around and refer to when I am at Victor's place. It will be the first of the few things I must, tonight, choose to take with me.

The boys have fallen asleep. I carry them upstairs, one by one. They lie side by side under vivid duvets. I am about to kiss them when I notice their eyes are open. I dread a second wind.

"If you lie still I will read to you," I say.

They regard me suspiciously, but I find a book and make a place between them. They stretch out across me, occasionally kicking each other.

It is a cruel story, as most children's stories are, and it involves a woodcutter. But it also concerns a conventional family, from which the father has not fled. The boys know the story so well they can tell when I skip a bit or attempt to make something up. When they stop asking questions I put the book down, creep out of the room, and switch off the light, then return to find their faces in the covers and kiss them. Outside I listen for their breathing. If only I could stand here all night. Then I hear them whispering to one another and giggling.

Old wives; old story.

I always look at women—in shops, on the street, in the bus, at parties—and wonder what it might be like to be with one of them. I imagine that with each woman I could be a different person for a time. There would be no past. I could keep the world outside my skin, huddled up with a whispering woman who wanted me.

But now I am not sure that I can touch a woman as I used to—frivolously. After a certain age, sex is no longer casual. To lay your hand on another's body, or to put your mouth against another's—what a commitment that is! Your whole life is uncovered.

Maybe that is what happened with Nina. One day a girl walked past and I wanted her. I've examined the moment a score of times. She and I go over it repeatedly, in joy and puzzlement. I can remember how tall and slim she appeared; and then there was a jolt, a violent jolt, when we met. Something about her changed everything. She was from another world.

My young gay friend Ian liked to stand with me outside tube stations, where I would watch the flocks of girls in the summer and he would watch the boys. Looks would be exchanged between him and a stranger and off he would go, while I waited, having coffee somewhere. Sometimes he fucked five people in a day.

"I've never understood all the fuss you straights make about infidelity," he'd say. "It's only fucking."

Susan has already laid the table. I open the wine and pour it. The man in the off-license said it is an easy wine to drink. These days I find anything easy to drink.

Susan brings the food in and sets it down. I glance over the newspaper. As she eats, she turns on the TV, puts on her glasses, and leans forward to watch a soap opera.

"Oh, my God," she says, as something happens.

The noise presses into my head. I have begun to hate television.

After we clear up, Susan sits at the table, writing invitations for the boys' party. Then, making a shopping list for next week, she says, "What meals do you fancy?"

"I don't want to think about it now."

"What's your favorite ice cream flavor at the moment? Is it the nut crunch or the vanilla?"

"I don't know."

She says, "It's not like you to be unable to think of food."

"No."

I consider how well I know her. The way she puts her head to one side, and the grimace she makes when concentrating. She looks as she must have as an eleven-year-old taking an exam. No doubt she will have a similar look at seventy, her gestures unchanged, writing a letter to one of our sons.

I imagine her as a teen-ager, getting up early to study, and then preparing for school—making her sandwiches, leaving the house while her parents sleep. She got herself into Cambridge, where she insured that she knew the most luminous people. She is as deliberate in her friendships as she is in everything else.

She is effective and organized. Our fridges and freezers are full of soup, vegetables, wine, cheese, and ice cream; the flowers and bushes in the garden are labeled; the children's clothes are washed, ironed, and folded. Every day there are deliveries of newspapers, books, alcohol, food, and, often, of furniture. Our front path is a thoroughfare for the service industries.

There are also people who come to clean the house, tend the garden, and cut the trees, as well as nannies, babysitters, and au pairs, not to mention masseurs, decorators, acupuncturists, piano teachers, the occasional drug dealer, and people to organize all of the above. Chalked on a board are instructions for the week. Susan is always thinking of how to improve things. She will have strong, considered opinions on the latest films and music. In bed she reads cookbooks.

I am from the lower middle class and from the suburbs, where poverty and pretension go together, so I can see now how good the middle class has it—their separate, sealed world. They keep quiet about it, with reason. They feel guilty, too, but they insure that they have the best of everything.

It wasn't Susan's wit or beauty that attracted me. There was never great passion—perhaps that was the point. I liked her humdrum dexterity and ability to cope. She wasn't helpless before the world. I envy her capability, and wish I had half of it.

At the office Susan is too prudent to want power, but she is clear and articulate, and it is not difficult for her to make less confident people feel ineffectual. After all, she is cleverer than her colleagues, and has worked harder. Like many girls brought up to be good and well-behaved, she likes to please. Perhaps that is why young women are so suitable for the contemporary working world. They are welcome to it.

The range of her feeling is narrow; she would consider it shameful to give way to her moods. Therefore she keeps most of herself out of view. I would say this odd thing: because she has never been disillusioned or disappointed, her life has never appalled her. She has never lapsed into inner chaos.

"Sorry?" I say.

Susan is speaking—asking me to get my diary.

"Why?" I say.

"Why? Just do it, if you don't mind."

"Don't speak to me like that."

"I'm too tired for a negotiation. The children wake at six. I have to spend the day at work. What do you do in the afternoons? I expect you sleep then!"

I say, "You're not too tired to raise your voice."

"It's the only way I can get you to do anything."

"No, it's not."

"You exhaust me."

I could strike her. She would know then. I am about to say, "Susan, can't you see that, of all the nights we have spent together, this is the last one—the last one of all?"

My anger, usually contained, can be cruel and vengeful. But this should be satisfying: I don't want to discover tonight that Susan and I really are suited.

I murmur,"All right, all right, I'll do it."

"At last."

Sometimes I go along with what Susan wants, but in an absurd parodic way, hoping she will see how foolish I find her. But she doesn't see it, and, much to my annoyance, my cooperation pleases her.

I sit in front of her with my diary, flipping through the pages. After today the pages are blank.

She says how much she is looking forward to the weekend away that we have planned. We will stay at the country hotel we visited several years ago, when she was first pregnant. The weather was warm. I rowed her on a lake. We ate mussels and read the papers on the beach. It will be just us, without the children.

"The rest will do us good," she says. "I know things have been fraught."

"Do you think so?"

"You are gloomy and don't try. But... we can discuss things."

"What things?"

She says, "All this." Her hands flail. "I think we need to." She controls herself. "You used to be such an affectionate man." She reminds me that there are historic walks and castles in the vicinity of the country hotel. "And, please," she says, "will you remember to take your camera this time?"

"I'll try to."

"You don't want any photographs of me, do you?"

"Sometimes I do."

"No you don't. You never offer."

"No, I don't offer."

"That's horrible. You should have one on your desk, as I do, of you."

I say, "I'm not interested in photography. And you're not as vain as I am."

"That's true."

I pace up and down with my drink, agitatedly. She takes no notice.

Fear is something I recognize. My childhood still tastes of fear. Fear of parents, aunts, and uncles, of vicars, police, and teachers, and of being kicked, abused, and insulted by other children. The fear of getting into trouble, of being discovered, castigated, smacked, ignored, locked in, locked out. There is, too, the fear of your own anger, of retaliation and of annihilation, as well as the fear of who you might become. It isn't surprising that you become accustomed to doing what you are told while making a safe place inside yourself and living a secret life.

"By the way," she says, "Victor rang."

"Oh yes? Any message?"

"He wanted to know when you are coming." She looks at me.

"OK," I say. "Thank you."

After a bit she says, "Why don't you see more people? I mean proper people, not just Victor."

"I can't bear the distraction," I say. "My internal life is too busy."

"I can't imagine what you have to think about," she says. Then she laughs. "You didn't eat much. Your trousers are baggy. They're always falling down."

"Sorry."

"Sorry? Don't say sorry. You sound pathetic." She grunts. After a few moments she gets up.

"Put the dishes in the machine," she says. "Don't just leave them on the side for me to clear up."

"I'll put them in the machine when I'm ready."

"That means never." Then she says, "Are you coming upstairs?"

I look at her searchingly and with interest, wondering if she means sex—it must be more than a month since we've fucked—or whether she intends us to read. I like books, but I don't want to get undressed for one.

"In a while," I say.

"You are so restless."

"Am I?"

"It's your age."

"It must be that."

I find myself thinking of the last time I saw Asif. He doesn't often come into the city; the rush and uproar make his head whirl. But when he and I have an "old friends" lunch, I insist he meet me in the center of town. I take him to clamorous places where there will be fashionable young women in close-fitting items.

"What a picture gallery you have brought me to!" he says, rubbing his hands. "Is this how you spend your life?"

"Oh yes."

I indicate their attributes and inform him that they prefer mature men.

"Are you sure?" he says. "Have you tried them all?"

"I'm going to. Champagne?"

Our talk is of books and politics and of mutual university friends. At university he was the brightest of our year, and was considered something of a martyr for becoming a teacher. Soon after finals he and Najma married.

I get him to confess that he wonders what another body might feel like. But then he imagines his wife's putting out flowers as she waits for him. He says he sees her across the bed in her negligee, three children sleeping between them.

I recall him describing how much he enjoys sucking her cunt, grunting and slurping down there for hours, after all this time. They massage each other's feet with coconut oil. In the conservatory their chairs face each other. When they are not discussing their children or questions of the day, they read Christina Rossetti aloud.

A few months ago I asked him to tell Susan that I had been with him when I had been with Nina.

He was dismayed.

"But don't ask me to do that."

"What?"

"Lie for you," he said.

"Aren't we friends?" I said. "It's a sensible lie. Susan doubts me. It is making her unhappy."

He shook his head. "You are too used to having your own way. You are making her unhappy."

"I am interested in someone else," I said.

I told him little of my relationships with women; he imagined such fabulous liaisons that I didn't want to disillusion him. He said to me once, "You remind me of someone who reads only the first chapter of a book. You never discover what happens next."

"How old is she?" he asked.

There was a discernible look of repulsion on his face, as if he were trying to swallow sour milk.

"It's only sex, then."

"There is that," I said.

"But marriage is a battle, a terrible journey, a season in Hell, and a reason for living. You need to be equipped in all areas, not just the sexual."

"Yes," I said, dully. "I know."

Oh to be equipped in all areas.

Asif's favorite opera is *Don Giovanni*, and *Anna Karenina* and *Madame Bovary* are his favorite novels. Testaments of fire and betrayal. But people don't want you to have too much pleasure; you might start wanting it all the time. Desire is naughty. It mocks all human endeavor (and makes it worthwhile).

Once I tried out on Asif the idea of my leaving Susan.

"I can just about see why someone might leave their spouse," he said. "But I can't understand how someone could leave their children."

It is the men who must go. They are blamed for it, as I will be.

Comfortable chairs, old carpets, yards of books, many pictures, and piles of CDs: my study. I've always had a room like this. I take my weekend bag from the cupboard and open it. I stare into the bottom. What do you take when you're never coming back? I throw a book into the bag—something by Strindberg—and then replace the book on the shelf.

I stand here for ages. I am afraid of getting too comfortable in my own house, afraid that once I sit down I will lose my resolve. Above my desk is the shelf on which I keep my prizes and awards. Susan says it makes the place look like a dentist's waiting room.

An inventory, perhaps.

The desk—which my parents bought me when I was taking my A-levels—I lugged around from shared houses to council flats, until it ended up here, the first property I have owned. A significant decision, getting a mortgage. It was as if you would never be able to move again.

I'll leave the desk for the boys. And the books?

Fuck it, I will leave everything here. My sons, wandering in this forsaken room, will discover, perhaps by mistake, the treasures they need.

After school or college, in my bedroom, I used to pile up Father's classical records on the spindle of my record player, and the symphonies would clatter down, one by one, until supper. In those days it was rebellious for someone my age to like music that didn't sound better the louder it was played.

Then, surrounded by my father's books, I would reach up and pull down a few volumes. Father, like the other neighborhood men, spent most of his day in unsatisfying work. Time was precious, and he had me fear its waste.

I will regret forfeiting this room.

I know how necessary fathers are for boys. I would hang on to Dad's hand as he toured the bookshops, climbing ladders to pull down rotting tomes. "Let's go, let's go," I'd say.

The writers Dad preferred are still my favorites, mostly nineteenth-century Europeans, the Russians in particular. The characters—Goriot, Vronsky, Mme. Ranevskaya, Nana, Julien Sorel—feel part of me. It is Father's copies I will give to the boys. Father took me to see war films and cricket. Whenever I appeared in his room, his face would brighten. He loved kissing me. He, more than anyone, was the person I wanted to marry. I wanted to walk, talk, laugh, and dress like him. My sons are the same with me, repeating my phrases in their tiny voices, staring admiringly at me and fighting to sit beside me. But I am leaving them. What would Father think of that?

Six years dead, he would have been horrified by my skulking off. It would have been undignified. Susan used to go to him when we fought and he would take her side, phoning me and saying, "Don't be cruel, boy." He said she had everything I could want. He didn't approve of leaving. He believed in loyalty.

Father was a civil servant who later worked as a clerk at Scotland Yard, for the police. In the mornings, he wrote novels. He must have completed five or six. A couple of them were admired by publishers, but none of them got into print. They weren't very bad and they weren't very good. He never gave up; it was all he ever wanted to do. The book on his bedside table had a picture of a middle-aged writer sitting on a pile of books, a portable typewriter on his knees. It was *Call It Experience*, by Erskine Caldwell. Under the author's name it said, "Reveals the secrets of a great writer's private life and literary success." The writer did look experienced; he had been around. He was tough. That's what a writer was.

Failure strengthened Father's resolve. He was both brave and foolish. He wanted me to be a doctor, and I did consider it, but in the end he told me it was hopeless to take up something that wasn't going to please me. He was wise in that way. I was successful as a writer a couple of years after I left university. I could do it; I just could. Whether it was a knack or trick or talent, I didn't know. It puzzled both of us. Art is easy for those who can do it and impossible for those who can't.

What did Father's life show me? That life is a struggle, and that struggle gets you nowhere. That there is little pleasure in marriage; that it is like doing a job one hates. You can't leave and you can't enjoy it. Both he and Mother were frustrated, neither being able to find a way to get what they wanted. Nevertheless, they were loyal and faithful to each other. Disloyal and unfaithful to themselves. Or do I misunderstand?

Separation wouldn't have occurred to a lower-middle-class couple in the fifties. My parents remained in the same house all their lives. When we were older, money was short. Father refused to look for a better job and wouldn't move to a different part of the country. Nothing was allowed to happen until he "made it." Mother was forced to find employment. She was a school dinner lady; she worked in factories and offices; she worked in a shop.

The day I left home, my parents sat in separate armchairs, watching me carry out my records. What was there left for them to do?

But once I had gone my parents started going to art galleries, to the cinema, for walks, and on long holidays. They took a new interest in each other and couldn't get enough of life. Victor says that once the lights on a love have dimmed, you can never illuminate them again, any more than you can reheat a soufflé. But my parents went through the darkness and discovered a new intimacy.

I turn out the lights and find myself climbing the stairs to the bedroom. What am I doing? If this is my last night here, hadn't I better get packed and ready? I leave the light on in the hall. I step into our bedroom.

It's been weeks since we fucked. I've stopped approaching Susan in that way, to see if she desires me. I have waited for a flicker of interest. I am a dog under the table, hoping for a biscuit.

Without removing my clothes I lie down. Yellow light streaks the room from the street lamp opposite, a harsh, sickly color, reminding me of the smell of gas. I look at the ceiling where the roof has been leaking.

I am getting warm and dozy. The bed is comfortable. The house is silent; the children sheltered, healthy, and asleep.

Susan stirs.

I stroke her back. I am convinced she can feel my thoughts. If she wakes up, puts out her arms, and says she loves me, I will sink back into the pillow and never leave. But she has never done such a thing. Sensing my fingers on her, she moves away, pulling up the covers.

I rub myself through my jeans. I wish I had someone to do this. Not everything can be achieved alone. I won't do it here. Susan is offended by my solo efforts. She is of a disapproving generation of women. She thinks she's a feminist, but she's just bad-tempered.

Nina encouraged me to masturbate on her back, stomach, or feet while she slept. She liked me to do it before she rushed off, to have me on her on the tube.

I want Nina, but then I always want Nina when I have an erection. I raise myself quietly and tiptoe to the bathroom.

I push down my trousers and look for a suitable lubricant. The last time I did this, when Susan had some friends round for dinner, I used my children's shampoo, and felt as if a wasp had been pushed into my urethra. I find a greenish cream in the cupboard. It's anti-aging unguent. God knows how much Susan has spent on this pig fat. Catching me once using it as hand cream, she became incensed. Maybe if I apply this every day to my prick it'll become fourteen again.

I stick my penis in it.

What if I met Susan now, for the first time, at a party? I would look at her twice, but not three times. It is likely that I would want to talk to her. Fearing those she can't seduce, she can be overattentive to certain men, looking at them with what I call "the enraptured gaze," until they wonder why she wants to appeal to their vanity rather than their intelligence. I should have gone out with her for six months. Or maybe a one-night stand. But I wasn't ruthless enough, and I didn't know what I wanted.

I sort through the laundry basket and extract a pair of Susan's knickers, pulling them from her tights and laying them on the sink. Here we go. No; the gray knickers lack the *je ne sais quoi.* The white might do the trick.

I run through my library of stimulating scenes. Which one will I replay—the time in Berlin or the middle-aged Italian who wept? What about the girl who rode her bicycle knickerless? In the old days I had possible scenes—scenes that might actually occur—which I used as an aid, rather than this nostalgia. And then, by mistake, I glance into the mirror and see a gray-haired, grimacing, mad-eyed monkey with a fist in front of him (his other hand placed delicately on his side because his back hurts from lifting the children). I suddenly feel that I am more likely to weep than ejaculate.

I will think of Nina. Nina's face; then the way she turns over and offers her arse to me. That should do it.

Suddenly I hear a noise. Quickly I close my pants. The bathroom door is pushed open, as if by a ghost. I watch and listen.

From the darkness of the hall, a child's luminous pacifier bobs into the room, a tiny circle of green light. The boy's eyes are shut as he stands there in his Batman T-shirt, pajama bottoms, and furry slippers, three years old. Actually, he is asleep. He staggers suddenly, and automatically raises his arms as if he has scored a goal. My hands fit under his arms; I pull him up along my body, and smell and kiss his hair.

"What are you doing here, my beautiful boy?"

I carry him downstairs, lay him on the sofa, and pull off his bottoms and soggy nappy. The smell is unpleasantly sharp and familiar at the same time; it is him. He is willful and keeps trying to turn over, so I place one hand on the middle of his chest and push down while grasping his ankles with the other, as if I were about to hang him upside down from a hook. He thrashes and blinks as I wipe him. Then I shove and push to get the nappy in the right position. It is like trying to change the tire of a moving car. At last I replace his pajama bottoms.

"Have I been good enough to you, little boy?"

I didn't enjoy him as a baby, dreading the crying and whining, the refusal to get dressed, eat, or go to sleep. I was astonished how whole days would pass when there was no time for anything but him, not even in the evenings. Having considered several books on the upbringing of children, often with feces or vomit on my fingers, I once threw him backward into his cot, hitting his head. I put brandy in his milk. I booted him hard up the nappy before he was even walking.

Susan cut me out, keeping the babies and the competence to herself, her female friends, and her mother. It has been only in the past few months that I've made myself useful. And only recently that I have fallen in love with my son. Now the boy and I talk ceaselessly. Where does the light go at night, what do spiders eat, why do women have "bosoms," where do people go when they die, and why do they have eyebrows? Where will he get the answers when I'm not here?

I am leaving this woman alone with two young children. My presence, however baleful, has perhaps reassured her. Now she will work, buy their clothes, feed them, tend them when they are sick. I'm sure she will ask herself, if she hasn't already, what men are for. Do they serve any useful function? They impregnate women. Occasionally they send money. What else could fathers be? It wasn't a question Dad asked himself. Being a father wasn't a question then. He was there to impose himself, to guide, exert discipline, and enjoy his children. We had to appreciate who he was and see things as he did.

I pick up my son. Holding his head with one hand and supporting his back with the other—his eyes are closed and his mouth open—I carry him to bed. But as I am about to lay him down, I have a strange feeling. Sometimes you look into a mirror and can't always remember what age you are. Somehow you expect to see a twelve-year-old or an eighteen-year-old looking back at you. Now I feel as if I am looking at myself. He is me; I am him; both of us are part of one another but separate in the world. For now it is myself I am carrying in my arms.

I lay him down and cover him up.

I wonder when I will sleep beside him again. He has a vicious kick and a tendency, at unexpected moments, to vomit in my hair. But he can pat and stroke my face like a lover. His affectionate words and little voice are God's breath to me.

I creep down the stairs. I put my jacket on. I find my keys. I get to the door and open it. I step out of the house. It is dark and cold. The fresh wind sweeps through me. It invigorates me.

Go. You must go.

Steve Faulkner

Common Water

In early April, my son and I launched our canoe into a broad and gentle current. It was unseasonably warm. South winds were blowing, gusting up our river valley, shaking life into the winter-withered limbs of willows, cottonwoods, and oaks that fringe the Kansas River. Justin and I were keeping a long-delayed promise.

Dipping our paddles into the mud-brown river that flows through our city we could see, a half-mile downstream, the high concrete bridge that carried Highway 75 over the river, one of several bridges that connect north and south Topeka, Kansas. Its tall piers and swift curve of concrete speeds people over this easygoing, meandering river. For years we had hurried across that bridge and glanced down at the several currents wandering through the sandbars, and I had said to my children, "We've got to take a canoe down that river this spring when the banks are full." But working seven nights a week, carrying one, sometimes two day jobs, and taking classes in the afternoons had eroded my good intentions.

Like so many other parents these days, my wife and I constantly struggle to salvage hours with our children. Already our two oldest boys were away in college, and we had never taken that canoe trip. Years ago, when my wife didn't have to hold down a job, and I could get by on forty or fifty hours a week, I had taken those older boys rabbit hunting, squirrel hunting, fishing, or just exploring. But it's hard, very hard, to make a living now, and three jobs barely scrape us past the bill collectors. I had not hunted and fished with Justin, our third son. I remember looking over at him as we raced over the river on that concrete bridge. He was already growing tall, strong, and willful, and I was beginning to feel that gradual void that lengthens between teen-agers and parents, and deepens as a young adult follows his desires down paths he no longer feels obliged to share with Dad and Mom. Time was parting us. So I had repeated the old promise, this time determined to keep it.

The Otoe Indians called this sand-bedded, mud-banked river Topeka, "Good Potato River" in their language, but the early settlers called it Kansas, after another tribe that had long lived in the area, and gave the Otoe name to the city on its banks. So, oddly, Good Potato River is now the capital city, and Kansas is the river that flows through it. Farmers still grow potatoes along these banks, but the making of those good potatoes, along with wheat, milo, soybeans, and other crops, has polluted the waters with atrazine and other herbicides, insecticides, and fertilizers. According to a recent national report, the state of Kansas now has the most polluted rivers in the nation. This section of the Kansas River is among the worst in the state. The waters run chocolate brown in the spring, with the mud and silt of surrounding farmlands, while invisible chemicals soak into the banks and settle into layer after layer of sediment.

Still, it seems to me that a man and his son should take a boat to the waters near home, whether to sea or lake or river. We have more than an economic connection with such waters, for they convey the shapes and sounds and smells—the very personality—of a place. Such waters take up in sound and movement the land's own choreography, and we cannot feel the habit of our place or sense its unique rhythms until we follow its course. Here, along the Kansas, or Kaw River, as the locals call it, we have no rapids or crashing waves, just the slow idle of a wide current that moves quietly between oak-thatched hills and stubble fields, carrying, on a warm spring afternoon, that first scent of thawing soil.

We had made no plans for this journey. I had no idea how fast we could travel. I had only a rudimentary idea where the river went, where we would find ourselves by sundown, where we would disembark, and how we would then contact my wife to pick us up. One thing was certain: I absolutely had to be at work just after midnight or face the danger of losing my job. But we had ham sandwiches in a cooler, hats against the sun, jackets against the wind, a city map in my pocket, and the devil take the details.

Who, after all, can plot a single day's journey on the water, much less foresee a life that follows no riverbed? Or, for that matter, who would want to? Who would go adventuring, or plant crops, or even take up employment at a particular firm, much less marry and have children, if we could see the future? Enough today to have looked at a rough map and said, "Perhaps here by seven this evening, but if not, I'll find a way to call."

We stroked out into the current. Both of us were inexperienced canoeists, but I knew we would have to learn to read the ripples and swirls if we were to avoid the many sandbars. Scarcely fifty yards into our journey, our aluminum craft ground to a halt in midriver. We tried shoving off with our paddles, but the steady thrust of moving water pressed us into the sand. We stepped out into the cold water and shoved off. I had a momentary sense of being sucked down into swirling sand, but managed to clamber back into the canoe, recalling rumors of quicksand. Our feet would be wet the rest of the way. But in that first hour, nothing could dampen our enthusiasm for our little adventure. We stroked powerfully through the sparkling waters, pulling for speed as we ran with the current, the wind at our backs.

High up along the ridge to our right, and hard by Menninger's famous clinic, stands the residence of our state's governor. Cedar Crest has been the governor's mansion since 1962. Built after the fashion of the French-Norman mansions of the Loire Valley, its white towers and gables look far across the river valley and hills to the north and back at the city to the south, east, and west. The builders of this beautiful home were childless and patriotic. They offered the mansion and twenty acres of pasture and cedar trees to the state, but the governor at the time called the lovely home a white elephant and turned the offer down. Years later, another governor saw, as all politicians do, his predecessor's folly and moved in.

Far below, Justin and I were happy. We pulled strongly at our paddles, skimming beneath the highway bridge and threading our way along the deeper currents. In that first hour of adolescent energy and a father's awkward navigation, we struck sand four times. But gradually we learned to read the riffles that signaled shallow water and to steer wide of protruding sandbars.

We were paddling east. Far off to our left, tall concrete grain elevators stood against a blue sky; on our right, the distant dome of the capitol rose among office buildings. We passed an anchored barge that pumped a slurry of sand and water up a long black pipe and sprayed it onto a conical sand hill in a ready-mix concrete plant. Near the bank, a long-necked duck, perhaps a migrating merganser, dove beneath the waves and surfaced yards away. A few pigeons paced about a sandbar in midriver, their feathers ruffled by the gusting winds.

Ahead of us we saw a long line in the water where the current swirled over some obstruction. I had read about the concrete barrier the city built to divert water into the water plant's intake pumps in times of drought, but I hadn't realized it stretched so far across the river. I stood up in the canoe to get a good look at it. The spring flood roiled over the long ridge of concrete, dropping perhaps a foot on the other side; I decided to run right over it. We leaned into our paddles and charged straight for it, but the canoe crunched to a stop on the concrete. Immediately the current began to capsize us.

Justin and I jumped out onto the dam in about four inches of flowing water and shoved with all our might. Little by little we jerked and shoved the canoe over the concrete and into deep water just as a clever burst of wind ripped my new hat from my head and flipped it into the water. Conspiring with the wind, the river sucked the hat beneath the surface at the very moment my son reached for it. It popped up a few yards away. We paddled madly after it, and Justin swashed it out of the water with his paddle just as Old Man River tried to swallow it again. We shouted our success to a bemused fisherman and his boy on the far bank. With a wet hat upon my head and soaked socks on my feet, we paddled on.

To our left a huge grain elevator lay all along the horizon like some great skyscraper fallen on its side. To our right, above rocky dikes, a hill sheltered the Potwin district, old Victorian homes, elaborately painted, and still inhabited by the rich, though ruined rental housing is creeping up on all sides of this old bastion of wealthy Topeka.

I glanced at my watch. We had been on the water for about two hours. In the city I rely on regularity: five minutes to the grocery store, fifteen minutes to the cleaners. Detours are a necessary evil. I detest surprises: the car engine dies, a child is late getting out of school. I grow quickly angry when the machinery of life breaks down. But escape to the hills, or onto a river, and the mood changes. Time relaxes, and surprises please: high against a bright limestone embankment, a great horned owl sits blinking blindly into the sun, apparently enjoying the warmth.

We passed under the Union Pacific train bridge and then under the elaborate Topeka Avenue Bridge, with its detailed arches and columns of poured concrete grown old and grainy with time. Justin pointed out the place he had hunted old bottles with some friends on Sunday afternoons last winter. Both times he had gone bottle hunting, he had fallen through the ice up to his waist. But adventures are worthwhile, and I regretted not being with him those winter afternoons.

Time keeps running past us. Brief conversations between homework and television, a few words on the way to cross-country practice, judging another request to go out with friends—these are not enough to tie two minds, two wills together. I knew Justin to be a collector of bottles and shells and feathers, a boy who would point out an odd cloud formation or a scattering of wildflowers. But he could be stubborn, too, and contradictory. Between a man of middle age and a boy just now leaning toward manhood, tensions are inevitable. No matter that his mother and I provide him a place to throw off his shoes, wolf down his meals, and read his Louis L'Amour novels. No matter that we have helped pass on to him language and customs and standards—still, he will be a passionate, stubborn son, and I his impatient, demanding father.

The conflicts darken our relationship, as do my absences, which leave serious gaps, for I am always preoccupied with work and school, other children, other people, other necessary responsibilities. The watch is a tyrant; I am constantly asking its permission: Do I have time to listen to both sides of this argument between my son and his little sister? Can I spare five minutes for a math problem? Ten minutes for a stumbling story from my seven-year-old about the "house" she built of sticks at recess? Our busy, time-dictated schedules deprive us of one another.

Our paddles dipped simultaneously through the waters as we approached the Santa Fe Railroad Bridge. We were gradually learning to steer together, Justin anticipating the need to paddle on the other side of the canoe as wind, current, and my erratic steering veered us one way and then the other. It was hard to believe steamships had once maneuvered between here and Kansas City; we were having trouble with a single canoe.

The wind was slinging sand in our faces, but we caught sight of metal posts just breaching the surface ahead of us. Lined between concrete piers, from bank to bank, a line of ragged, rusty I-beams cut the current, spaced less than a foot apart. We shouted at each other above the wind and chose a spot where the river overflowed some broken beams. The current swept us a little left of our goal, and we heard the brutal scrape of an I-beam grooving the bottom of the canoe. I was glad for an aluminum canoe in a river staked with iron posts.

The river turned north, and we noticed that the wind had changed. To our left, we could see the sun declining in the west. A cool, brusque wind ran down across the current and made for choppy waters and difficult paddling. My long-unused muscles advised rest, but circumstances required redoubled work. A deep aching in my lower back argued we beach the canoe, but a father wants to keep up with his growing boy, and Justin showed no signs of tiring.

After our long, hard pull, we found the river turned sharply southeast, and we had the wind more or less to our backs again. I lay back in the stern and complained of an aching back. Justin laughed and kept churning the waters. But being older and more cunning, I mentioned food. His paddle came quickly out of the water, and he turned himself around. For almost a half hour, we drifted with the current, ate thick ham and cheese sandwiches my wife had prepared, and drank down bottles of apple juice.

We paddled on, my back still murmuring slanderous things against my age and strength. On the left bank, a farmer had parked his broken-down cars. Old, rusted hulks from the forties and fifties decayed among dry sunflower stalks above us; some had fallen halfway down the bank; pieces of fender and bumper protruded here and there from the weedy cliff. Justin was much interested in these, so I steered near. The rains and river were doing their work on these once-proud markers of material prosperity.

An hour later, the sun settled in toward the bank behind us; the day had already grown old. The river was running east, away from the sun. We should have been looking for a place to disembark and call my wife, but we had started late, and neither of us wanted to end this so soon, so we refused the little stream near Tecumseh, where we could have called home from a friend's house.

Beyond the stream, the river calmed into a long, wide pool. We stopped paddling for a time and turned to see the setting sun dye river and sky in crimson. Air and water seemed all one, of one color and translucence. The wind had died; a great stillness enveloped us. We rested together, drifting slowly backward through fiery waters, content simply to gaze as the red waters of the river slipped away into reddening skies, briefly obstructed by a dark silhouetted line of leafless trees on the far bank.

Night was upon us. A hundred lights glimmered from the city's old brick power plant on the right bank. Our paddles rose and fell. A high half-moon drifted through patches of cloud. On either bank, dark gatherings of old trees leaned together. We were well past the city now, and a chill had settled along the river. To our left we heard a tractor plowing a field; at times we could see its quivering headlight as the farmer stretched another day into darkness.

We talked about climbing the bank and asking him for the use of his home phone, but the bank was high, and the farmhouse lights seemed far away. We paddled on into a formidable silence, peering intently into the darkness to avoid the sand, but we could no longer judge the ripples and swirls, and several times found ourselves sliding suddenly through clawing branches of half-submerged trees or grinding against sand in shallow waters. Every so often, across the fields to the north, we would hear the muffled rhythms and the hoarse wailing of passing trains. Then all would grow silent again, but for the endless dipping of our paddles.

Some distance ahead we heard voices, harsh voices on the river. We wondered what fools would be out on the river so late. But it was only a few geese on a sandbar protesting our intrusion into their moonlit refuge. They took flight at our approach, passing over us like gray, querulous ghosts.

Two more hours, and we were cold and dog tired, still searching for the lights of some home or a lowering of the bank on either side that would allow us to bring the canoe to rest.

Off to the south, we saw distant lights, and I decided we must stop, even if we had to walk a mile to the farmhouse. A log protruded from the bank, and I steered us alongside. Justin grabbed for a broken limb and stepped carefully onto the floating trunk. He reached down and held the canoe steady while I stepped onto the log. But the bank was ten feet high and muddy. I pulled myself up, grasping roots and dead vines. Justin threw me the rope and I began pulling up the prow while he pushed the stern, but we could not muscle the eighteen-foot canoe up and over the vertical bank. We gave up, muddy and disgusted.

We pushed off and slipped back out into the steel-gray current. We were cold. I was getting worried. It was after nine o'clock, and I didn't relish knocking on farmhouse doors this late. Farmers and their dogs are wary of night-walking strangers.

Ahead of us the river ran under a black wooded hill. The place seemed familiar. We had once done some target shooting near here. I reminded Justin of this and said I thought the banks were lower ahead. He nodded and kept paddling; we were too weary for many words. We drifted past high cliffs where pale limestone outcroppings shone in the moonlight and hundreds of tree frogs croaked with their peculiar grating, clicking sound from the trees above us.

Spotting a low place in the bank, we coasted in and climbed out, flipped the canoe upside down, hoisted it on our shoulders, and carried it up and over a steep railroad embankment and onto a gravel road. We dropped the canoe in a weedy ditch and walked toward a well-lit, well-kept home with three cars in the driveway. Seven or eight little yapping dogs charged us as we crossed the road, but we were too tired to be dissuaded by such paltry opponents. Justin picked up a stick to keep the yappers at bay while I walked around a trimmed hedge and onto the brightly lit porch. The little fiends kept darting in and out, raising an almighty ruckus, but no one inside moved. I couldn't blame them, really. Who would open up to these two muddy creatures limping up out of the black waters? As I left the porch, the irritating beasts renewed their attack. Justin swung at them half-heartedly, and we walked away. I have never been fond of dogs of the small noise-making variety, and now I was having black thoughts about how right and just it was that Indians could kill and eat their dogs.

We shoved cold fingers into our pockets and shuffled off down the gray gravel road, trying to stomp life into our frozen feet. A half mile of walking brought us to another neat little brick home with a lighted barn in which two men were repairing a cello. When we called, they came to the door, a short white-haired man and a big, bearded fellow in bib overalls. They were friendly and curious, and allowed us to use the phone. I called my wife. A half hour later she picked us up as we were pacing up and down the gravel road to stay warm.

Five months after this, Justin and I, along with his two younger sisters and little brother, followed the setting sun into the highest range of hills near Topeka. The air was cool on this late September evening. We climbed through barbed wire, and then the younger children, suddenly released, charged away down the hill, laughing, leaping, and shouting. Far away, the blue-gray hills folded and faded into the evening mists. It seemed as if my children were running away into time itself.

Great bands of saffron, red, and gold swept the sky. I remarked to Justin, who still stood beside me, that it was the most beautiful sunset I could remember. He looked away toward the west for a time, then muttered something about another sunset more beautiful. I turned and looked at him. He shoved his hands into his pockets and said, "On the river."

Gish Jen

Who's Irish?

In China people say mixed children are supposed to be smart, and definitely my granddaughter Sophie is smart. But Sophie is wild, Sophie is not like my daughter, Natalie, or like me. I am work hard my whole life, and fierce besides. My husband always used to say he is afraid of me, and in our restaurant busboys and cooks all afraid of me, too. Even the gang members come for protection money, they try to talk to my husband. When I am there, they stay away. If they come by mistake, they pretend they are come to eat. They hide behind the menu, they order a lot of food. They talk about their mothers. Oh, my mother have some arthritis, need to take herbal medicine, they say. Oh, my mother getting old, her hair all white now.

I say, Your mother's hair used to be white, but since she dye it, it is black again. Why don't you go home once in a while and take a look? I tell them, Confucius says a filial son knows what color his mother's hair is.

My daughter is fierce, too, she is vice-president in the bank now. Her new house is big enough for everybody to have their own room, including me. But Sophie take after Natalie's husband's family, their name is Shea. Irish. I always thought Irish people are like the Chinese, work so hard on the railroad, but now I know why the Chinese beat the Irish. Of course, not all Irish are like the Shea family, of course not. My daughter says I should not say the Irish this, the Irish that.

How do you like it when people say the Chinese this, the Chinese that, she says.

You know, the British call the Irish heathen, just like they call the Chinese, she says.

You think the Opium War was bad, how would you like to live right next door to the British, she says.

And that is that. My daughter has a funny habit when she win an argument, she take a sip of something and look away, so the other person is not embarrassed. So I am not embarrassed. I do not call anybody anything, either. I just happen to mention about the Shea family, an interesting fact: four brothers in the family, and not one of them work. The mother, Bess, has a job before she got sick, she was executive secretary in a big company. She is handle everything for a big shot, you would be surprised how complicated her job is, not just type this, type that. Now she is a nice woman with a clean house. But her boys, every one of them is on welfare, or so-called severance pay, or so-called disability pay. Something. They say they cannot find any work, this is not the economy of the fifties, but I say, Even the black people doing better these days, some of them live so fancy, you'd be surprised. Why the Shea family have so much trouble? They are white people, they speak English. When I come to this country, I have no money and do not speak English. But my husband and I own our restaurant before he die. Free and clear, no mortgage. Of course, I understand I am just lucky, come from a country where the food is popular all over the world. I understand it is not the Shea family's fault they come from a country where everything is boiled. Still, I say.

She's right, we should broaden our horizons, says one brother, Jim, at Thanksgiving. Forget about the car business. Think about egg rolls.

Pad thai, says another brother, Mike. I'm going to make my fortune in pad thai. It's going to be the new pizza.

I say, You people too picky about what you sell. Selling egg rolls not good enough for you, but at least my husband and I can say, We made it. What can you say? Tell me. What can you say?

Everybody chew their tough turkey.

I especially cannot understand my daughter's husband, John, who has no job but cannot take care of Sophie, either. Because he is a man, he says, and that's the end of the sentence.

Plain boiled food, plain boiled thinking. Even his name is plain boiled: John. Maybe because I grew up with black bean sauce and hoisin sauce and garlic sauce, I always feel something is missing when my son-in-law talk.

But, OK: so my son-in-law can be man, I am baby sitter. Six hours a day, same as the old sitter, crazy Amy, who quit. This is not so easy, now that I am sixty-eight, Chinese age almost seventy. Still, I try. In China, daughter take care of mother. Here it is the other way around. Mother help daughter, mother ask, Anything else I can do? Otherwise daughter complain mother is not supportive. I tell my daughter, We do not have this word in Chinese, supportive. But my daughter too busy to listen, she has to go to meeting, she has to write memo while her husband go to the gym to be a man. My daughter says otherwise he will be depressed. Seems like all his life he has this trouble, depression.

No one wants to hire someone who is depressed, she says. It is important for him to keep his spirits up.

Beautiful wife, beautiful daughter, beautiful house, oven can clean itself automatically. No money left over, because only one income, but lucky enough, got the baby sitter for free. If John lived in China, he would be very happy. But he is not happy. Even at the gym things go wrong. One day he pull a muscle. Another day, weight room too crowded. Always something.

Until finally, hooray, he has a job. Then he feel pressure.

I need to concentrate, he says. I need to focus.

He is going to work for insurance company. Salesman job. A paycheck, he says, and at least he will wear clothes instead of gym shorts. My daughter buy him some special candy bars from the health-food store. They say THINK! on them, and are supposed to help John think.

John is a good-looking boy, you have to say that, especially now that he shave so you can see his face.

I am an old man in a young man's game, says John.

I will need a new suit, says John.

This time I am not going to shoot myself in the foot, says John.

Good, I say.

She means to be supportive, my daughter says. Don't start the send-her-back-to-China thing because we can't.

Sophie is three years old American age, but already I see her nice Chinese side swallowed up by her wild Shea side. She looks like mostly Chinese. Beautiful black hair, beautiful black eyes. Nose perfect size, not so flat looks like something fell down, not so large looks like some big deal got stuck in wrong face. Everything just right, only her skin is a brown surprise to John's family. So brown, they say. Even John says it. She never goes in the sun, still she is that color, he says. Brown. They say, Nothing the matter with brown, they are just surprised. So brown. Nattie is not that brown, they say. They say, It seems like Sophie should be a color in between Nattie and John. Seems funny, a girl named Sophie Shea be brown. But she is brown, maybe her name should be Sophie Brown. Nothing the matter with brown, they are just surprised.

The Shea family talk is like this sometimes, going around and around like a Christmas tree train.

Maybe John is not her father, I say one day, to stop the train. And sure enough, train wreck. None of the brothers ever say the word brown to me again.

Instead John's mother, Bess, says, I hope you are not offended.

She says, I did my best on those boys. But raising four boys with no father is no picnic.

You have a beautiful family, I say.

I'm getting old, she says.

You deserve a rest, I say. Too many boys make you old.

I never had a daughter, she says. You have a daughter.

I have a daughter, I say. The Chinese don't think a daughter is so great, but you're right. I have a daughter.

I never was against the marriage, you know, she says. I never thought John was marrying down. I always thought Nattie was just as good as white.

I was never against the marriage either, I say. I just wonder if they look at the whole problem.

Because of the whole problem. She sighs.

Exactly, I say.

Of course, you pointed out the problem, you are a mother, she says. And now we both have a granddaughter. A little brown granddaughter, she is so precious to me.

I laugh. A little brown granddaughter, I say. To tell you the truth, I don't know how she came out so brown.

We laugh some more. These days Bess need a walker to walk. She take so many pills she need two glasses of water to get them all down. Her favorite TV show is all about bloopers, and she love her bird feeder. All day long, she can watch that bird feeder, like a cat.

I can't wait for Sophie to grow up, Bess says. I could use some female company.

Too many boys, I say.

Boys are fine, she says. But they do surround you after a while.

You should take a break, come live with us, I say. Lots of girls at our house.

Be careful what you offer, says Bess, with a wink. Where I come from, people mean for you to move in when they say a thing like that.

Nothing the matter with Sophie's outside, that's the truth. It is inside that she is not like any Chinese girl I ever see. We go to the park, and this is what she does. She stand up in the stroller. She take off all her clothes and throw them in the fountain.

Sophie! I say. Stop!

But she just laugh like a crazy person. Before I take over as baby sitter, Sophie has that crazy-person sitter, Amy the guitar player. My daughter thought this Amy very creative—another word we do not talk about in China. In China we talk about whether we have difficulty or no difficulty. We talk about whether life is bitter or not bitter. In America, all day long, people talk about creative, never mind that I cannot even look at this Amy, with her shirt so short that her belly button showing. This Amy think Sophie should love her body. So when Sophie take off her diaper, Amy laugh. When Sophie run around naked, Amy says she wouldn't want to wear a diaper, either. When Sophie go *shu-shu* in her lap, Amy laugh and says there are no germs in pee. When Sophie take off her shoes, Amy says bare feet is best, even the pediatrician says so. That is why Sophie now walk around with no shoes like a beggar child. Also why Sophie love to take off her clothes.

Turn around! say the boys in the park. Let's see that ass!

Of course, Sophie does not understand. Sophie clap her hands, I am the only one to say, No! This is not a game.

It has nothing to do with John's family, my daughter says. Amy was too permissive, that's all.

But I think if Sophie was not wild inside she would not take off her shoes and diaper to begin with.

You never take off your clothes when you were little, I say. All my Chinese friends had babies, I never saw one of them act wild like that.

Look, my daughter says. I have a big presentation tomorrow.

John and my daughter agree Sophie is a problem, but they don't know what to do.

You spank her, she'll stop, I say another day.

But they say, Oh, no. In America, parents not supposed to spank the child.

It gives them low self-esteem, my daughter says. And that leads to problems later, as I happen to know.

My daughter never have big presentation the next day when the subject of spanking come up.

I don't want you to touch Sophie, she says. No spanking, period.

Don't tell me what to do, I say.

I'm not telling you what to do, says my daughter. But I am telling you how I feel.

I am not your servant, I say. I am supportive. Don't you dare talk to me like that.

My daughter has another funny habit when she loses an argument. She spread out all her fingers and look at them, as if she like to make sure they are still there.

My daughter is fierce like me, but she and John think it is better to explain to Sophie that clothes are a good idea. This is not so hard in the cold weather. In the warm weather, it is very hard.

Use your words, my daughter says. That's what we tell Sophie. How about you set a good example.

As if good example mean anything to Sophie. I am so fierce, the gang members who used to come to the restaurant all afraid of me, but Sophie is not afraid.

I say, Sophie, if you take off your clothes, no snack.

I say, Sophie, if you take off your clothes, no lunch.

I say, Sophie, if you take off your clothes, no park.

Pretty soon we are stay home all day, and by the end of six hours she still did not have one thing to eat. You never saw a child stubborn like that.

I'm hungry, she cry when my daughter come home.

What's the matter, doesn't your grandmother feed you? laugh my daughter.

No! Sophie says. She doesn't feed me anything!

My daughter laugh again. Here you go, she says.

She says to John, Sophie must be growing.

Growing like a weed, I say.

Still Sophie take off her clothes, until one day I spank her. Not too hard, but she cry and cry, and when I tell her if she doesn't put her clothes back on I'll spank her again, she put her clothes back on. Then I tell her she's a good girl, and give her some food to eat. The next day we go to the park, and, like a nice Chinese girl, she does not take off her clothes.

She stop taking off her clothes, I report. Finally!

How did you do it? my daughter ask.

After thirty-five years' experience with you, I guess I learn something, I say.

It must have been a phase, John says, and his voice is suddenly like an expert.

His voice is like an expert about everything these days, now that he carry a leather briefcase, and wear shiny shoes, and can go shopping for a new car. On the company, he says. The company will pay for it, but he will be able to drive it whenever he wants.

A free car, he says, how do you like that.

It's good to see you in the saddle again, my daughter says. Also she says, a little later, Some of your family patterns are scary.

At least I don't drink, he says. He says, And I'm not the only one with scary family patterns.

That's for sure, says my daughter.

*

Everyone is happy. Even I am happy, because there is more trouble with Sophie, but now I think I can help her Chinese side fight against her wild side. I teach her to eat food with a fork or spoon, she cannot just grab into the middle of a bowl of noodles. I teach her not to play with garbage cans. Sometimes I spank her, but not too often, and not too hard.

Still, there are problems. Sophie like to climb everything. If there is a railing, she is never next to it. Always she is on top of it. Also, Sophie like to hit the mommies of her friends. She learn this from her playground best friend, Sinbad, who is four. Sinbad wear army clothes every day and like to ambush his mommy. He is the one who dug a big hole under the play structure, a foxhole he call it, all by himself. Very hardworking. Now he wait in the foxhole with a shovel full of wet sand, and when his mommy come he throw it right at her.

Oh, it's all right, his mommy says. You can't get rid of war games, it's part of their imaginative play. All the boys go through it.

Also, he like to kick his mommy, and one day he tell Sophie to kick his mommy, too.

I wish this story is not true.

Kick her, kick her! Sinbad says.

Sophie kick her. A little kick, as if she just happened to be swinging her little leg and didn't realize that big mommy leg was in the way. Still I spank Sophie and make Sophie say she is sorry, and what does the mommy say?

Really, it's all right, she says. It didn't hurt.

After that Sophie learn she can attack mommies in the playground, and some will say, Stop, but others will say, Oh, she didn't mean it, especially if they realize Sophie will be punished.

This is how, one day, bigger trouble come. The bigger trouble start when Sophie hide in the foxhole with that shovel full of sand. She wait, and when I come look for her she throw it at me. All over my nice clean clothes.

Did you ever see a Chinese girl act this way?

Sophie! I say. Come out of there, say you're sorry.

But she does not come out. Instead, she laugh. Naaah, naah-na, naah-naah, she says.

I am not exaggerate: millions of children in China, not one act like this.

Sophie! I say. Now! Come out now!

But she know she is in big trouble. She know if she come out what will happen next. So she does not come out. I am sixty-eight, Chinese age almost seventy, how can I crawl under there to catch her? Impossible. So I yell, yell, yell, and what happen? Nothing. A Chinese mother would help, but American mothers, they look at you, they shake their head, they go home. And, of course, a Chinese child would give up, but not Sophie.

I hate you! she yell. I hate you, Meanie!

Meanie is my new name these days.

Long time this goes on, long long time. The foxhole is deep, you cannot see too much, you don't know where is the bottom. You cannot hear too much, either. If she does not yell you cannot even know she is still there or not. After a while, getting cold out, getting dark out, there is no one left in the playground, only us.

Sophie, I say. How did you become stubborn like this? I am go home without you now.

I try to use a stick, chase her out of there, and once or twice I hit her, but still she does not come out. So finally I leave. I go outside the gate.

Bye-bye! I say. I'm go home now.

But still she does not come out and does not come out. Now it is dinnertime, the sky is black. I think I should maybe go get help, but how can I leave a little girl by herself in the playground? A bad man could come. A rat could come. I go back in to see what is happen to Sophie. What if she has a shovel and is making a tunnel to escape?

Sophie! I say.

No answer.

Sophie!

I don't know if she is alive, I don't know if she is fall asleep down there. If she is crying I cannot hear her.

So I take the stick and poke.

Sophie! I say. I promise I no hit you. If you come out, I give you a lollipop.

No answer. By now I worried, worried. What to do, what to do, what to do? I poke some more, even harder, so that I am poking and poking when my daughter and John suddenly appear.

What are you doing? What is going on? says my daughter.

Put down that stick! says my daughter.

You are crazy! says my daughter.

John wiggle under the structure, into the foxhole, to rescue Sophie.

She fell asleep, says John the expert. She's OK. That is one big hole.

Now Sophie is crying and crying.

Sophie, my daughter says, hugging her. Are you OK, peanut? Are you OK?

She's just scared, says John.

Are you OK? I say, too. I don't know what happen, I say.

She's OK, says John. He is not like my daughter, full of questions. He is full of answers until we get home and can see by the lamplight.

Will you look at her? he yell then. What the hell happened?

Bruises all over her brown skin, and a swollen-up eye.

You are crazy! says my daughter. Look at what you did! You are crazy!

I try very hard, I say.

How could you use a stick? I told you to use your words!

She is hard to handle, I say.

She's three years old! You cannot use a stick! says my daughter.

She is not like any Chinese girl I ever saw, I say.

I brush some sand off my clothes. Sophie's clothes are dirty, too, but at least she has her clothes on.

Has she done this before? ask my daughter. Has she hit you before?

She hits me all the time, Sophie says, eating ice cream.

Your family, says John.

Believe me, says my daughter.

A daughter I have, a beautiful daughter, I took care of her when she could not hold her head up. I took care of her before she could argue with me, when she was a little girl with two pigtails, one of them always crooked. I took care of her when suddenly we have to escape from China, I took care of her when suddenly we live in a country with cars everywhere, if you are not careful your little girl get run over. When my husband die, I promise him I will keep the family together, even though it was just two of us, hardly a family at all.

But now my daughter take me around to look at apartments. After all, I can cook, I can clean, there's no reason I cannot live by myself, all I need is a telephone. Of course, she is sorry. Sometimes she cry, I am the one to say everything will be OK. She says she has no choice, she doesn't want to end up divorced. I say divorce is terrible, I don't know who invented this terrible idea. Instead of live with a telephone, though, surprise, I come to live with Bess. Imagine that. Bess make an offer and, sure enough, where she come from, people mean for you to move in when they say things like that. A crazy idea, go to live with someone else's family, but she like to have some female company, not like my daughter, who does not believe in company. These days when my daughter visit, she does not bring Sophie. Bess says we should give Nattie time, we will see Sophie again soon. But seems like my daughter have more presentation than ever before, every time she come she have to leave.

I have a family to support, she says, and her voice is heavy, as if soaking wet. I have a young daughter and a depressed husband and no one to turn to.

When she says no one to turn to, she mean me.

These days my beautiful daughter is so tired she can just sit there in a chair and fall asleep. John lost his job again, already, but still they rather hire a baby sitter than ask me to help, even though they can't afford it. Of course, the new baby sitter is much younger, can run around. I don't know if Sophie these days is wild or not wild. She call me Meanie, but she like to kiss me, too, sometimes. I remember that every time I see a child on TV. Sophie like to grab my hair, a fistful in each hand, and then kiss me smack on the nose. I never see any other child kiss that way.

The satellite TV has so many channels, more channels than I can count, including a Chinese channel from the mainland and a Chinese channel from Taiwan, but most the time I watch bloopers with Bess. Also I watch the bird feeder—so many, many kinds of birds come. The Shea sons hang around all the time, asking when will I go home, but Bess tell them, Get lost.

She's a permanent resident, says Bess. She's not going anywhere.

Then she wink at me, and switch the channel with the remote control.

Of course, I shouldn't say the Irish this, the Irish that, especially now I am become honorary Irish myself, according to Bess. Me! Who's Irish, I say, and she laugh. All the same, if I could mention one thing about some of the Irish, not all of them of course, I like to mention this: their talk just stick. I don't know how Bess Shea learn to use her words, but sometimes I hear what she says a long time later. *Permanent resident. Not going anywhere.* Over and over I hear it, the voice of Bess.

Ha Jin

A Young Girl's Lament

In the first lunar month of my seventh year
my earlobes were pierced for gold rings.
I was told a girl had to suffer twice—
having her ears pierced and her feet bound.
My binding began in the third month
after Mother asked an old man for a good day.
I wept and hid in a neighbor's house,
but Mother found me and dragged me home.
She shut our door, boiled water,
and took out scissors, binding cloths,
bowed shoes, a knife, needles and thread.
I begged her to postpone for another week,
but she said, "Today is a lucky day.
If bound now, your feet will never hurt."

She bathed my feet, put them on a stool,
sprinkled alum, and cut the nails.
Then she bent my toes toward the sole
and tied them with a cloth twelve
feet long and two inches wide—

first she did my right foot, then my left.
I was soaked in sweat and tears
but dared not make any noise,
biting a brush to suppress my screams.
She told me, "With lotus feet
you'll marry a nice man. You know
we aren't rich and you have an ordinary face,
so I'm giving you a second chance."

Done with the binding, she ordered me to walk.
When I did, I fell on the floor,
my feet, my feet no longer my own!

That night Mother wouldn't let me remove the shoes.
My feet felt on fire and I couldn't sleep.
The next day I got into a haystack
but was found and forced to walk.
From then on, beatings and curses
became a part of my life
because I'd loosen the wrappings in secret.

Four months later all my toes
were pressed against the soles except
my big toes, which were bound too,
the narrow cloths forcing them upward
into the shape of a new moon.
Whenever I ate fish or freshly killed meat
my feet would swell and pus would drip.
Mother scolded me for putting pressure
on the heels when I walked, declaring
my feet would never have a pretty shape.
She'd remove my binding and wipe the pus
saying only with the loss of flesh
could my feet grow slender and small.
If I pricked a sore by mistake
blood would trickle like a stream.

Every two weeks I changed to new shoes.
Each new pair was a fifth of an inch smaller
than the previous one. It took pressure
to get into the unyielding shoes.
I wanted to stay in bed, but Mother
always made me move around.
After changing a dozen pairs
my feet were reduced to three inches.

Then my younger sister began her binding.
When no one was around, we'd weep together.
In summer my feet smell of a chicken coop;
in winter they are icy cold for lack
of circulation. On each foot
the toes curl in like dead caterpillars.
Who would think they belong to a human being?
My toenails press the flesh
like scabs, and the folded soles
cannot be soothed when they ache
or scratched when they itch.
My shanks are thin, my feet humped,
ugly, rotten, clumsy, useless.
How I envy our maid who has natural feet!

Marilene Phipps

pink

The *I love New York* and silver heart
you see on my T-shirt, is not
what I like most about it. It's the pink.
I don't know how to read and I may
not be pretty, but I can tell what looks good
on me. With my black skin, bright pink is it.

Every day, going home from work,
I walk by Jésusla's stand at the corner
of Panaméricaine and Grégoire streets. Every day,
I think "God I want that shirt!" But one day
I have three dollars in my pocket. Some woman
is bargaining for *my* T-shirt. I snatch it from her,
push all the money I own in Jésusla's hand,
said I'd bring the remaining five later, walk away fast.

My husband has not found work for five years.
The minute he sees me, he grabs for the pink.
I grab back, run inside, lock myself in,

hide the shirt so he can never find it. He looked everywhere.
The children, he and I live in just one room.
You'd think it'd be hard to hide anything? Not for me.

Next morning I walk out of the house wearing it.
He stops me. Holds me by the tits. He is pissed.
"Where was it?!" "I'm not telling! Not telling! Not telling!"
In the evening, my daughter hid in the room
to find out where I was stashing the shirt. "I know

where you put it! I am going to tell my
Daddy! I saw you sewing it inside his pillow!
I am going to tell unless I can wear it too!"
"Not if you don't want me to tear the eyes
out of that ugly face of yours!" I meant it.
You've got to know what's yours in life. Set
some limits. If you leave your stuff
out in the open, it's family that will rob you first.

John Edgar Wideman

What Is a Brother?

Perhaps you've seen the famous image that decorated everything from medallions to Wedgwood plates in the eighteenth century: a black slave bound, kneeling, eyes fixed heavenward, who asks, "Am I not a man and a brother?" Lincoln freed the slaves, so the story goes, and all men are created equal and therefore deserve equal protection of the law, but a brother... brother's a different matter altogether, isn't it.

I mean, if we're brothers, who's the mama? Who's the daddy? Are we talking literal brothers here or some metaphysical tarbrush staining us all just because we all wiggle through the birth canal, born of woman, born to die?

Brother. Isn't that what black guys call one another, and isn't it reverse discrimination—a watered-down, conspiratorial echo of black power? Doesn't the phrase "brotherhood of man" suggest a primal division—God's separate creation of his creatures, multiple evolutionary bloodlines of white, black, red, and yellow—that it's our duty to keep pure? *Broederbond.* Aryan brotherhood. The lost and found Nation of Islam.

On the other hand, don't brothers bring chaos into the world? Didn't Cain murder Abel? Didn't Joseph's jealous brothers try to waste their younger sibling? What about Osiris and Set, Ahriman and Ahura Mazda, all those cosmic wombmates who went their separate ways established warring kingdoms of light and dark, good and evil, the mythic Manichaean polarities that plague mankind even to this very moment?

We love our younger brothers, don't we. Cute little buggers. We hate the sight of the tattling, tagalong nuisance, the late arrival who dares claim an equal share of our parents' attention. An older brother is our first taste of tyranny. The big guy who shields us from bullies. When we're really tight with somebody, we say, I love him like a brother. Big Brother spies on us. We grow unspeakably close to, unspeakably distant from, our brothers. We lose a brother, but he never goes away, his absence as tangible as the ghost pain of an amputated limb.

When we look at a brother, do we see ourselves—similar features and faults, our shared humanity, common destiny, brothers beneath the skin in spite of our differences? Or do we see what we aren't—the dark side, the bad seed, the evil twin?

Is *brother* mired in the language and politics of male domination? *Brother* a means of extending, naturalizing patriarchal power, identifying family, passing property along the male lines? Recalling the chronicles of bloody feuds, fierce implosions of clans when women bear illegitimate heirs?

Did the revolutionary slogan *Liberté, Egalité, Fraternité* leave someone out? Inevitably spawn a militant sisterhood still clamoring for a rightful share of the power its brothers usurped from the king?

If brothers weren't raised by their parents but sent away at birth to grow up in separate households with no knowledge of one another, would there be some twilight-zone vibe of recognition if they passed each other on the street as adult strangers? If your answer is no, then wouldn't you be within your rights if you responded to the kneeling slave by pointing out that maybe you are a man *and* a brother, since such categories are arbitrary, socially constructed? But so what. Why does that entitle you to any special consideration? If you say yes to the possibility of some transcendent, essential connector lodged in the souls of brothers, do you also believe that connection crosses race, gender, and class lines? Neither science nor religion has been consistently helpful to the kneeling slave.

The poor brother's still stuck on his knees, damned if he does, damned if he doesn't receive an answer. He should be asking a different question. Of course he's a man and a brother. Why should he put that call in anyone else's hands? His voice is the best, only, and final authority for membership in the human family. A better question might be, What kind of man or brother stoops to peddling human flesh?

Is it possible the enslaved man is lamenting not only the particular woes of his condition but also addressing, in his desperation, a universal dilemma that truly defines him as everyone's brother: the existential loneliness and fear that comes with the knowledge that we are born alone and die alone? Isn't that the daunting price of individual consciousness, the "I"? Eternal estrangement, the eternal threat of absolute extinction never more distant than the thickness of our skin. We know the inscrutable void that spit us out will one day just as abruptly gulp us down again. Isn't this knowledge the razor's edge we dance on all the days of our lives?

Brothers and sisters are a kind of hedge against oblivion. Although death remains a certainty, although time's always running out, a brother, a sister, diverts time's attention. Our attention. Multiplies our chances. Dilates time. Gives us more skin—thicker skin sometimes, thinner sometimes, more vulnerable—more time when we share joy, pain, terror, the bounties and threats out there. Share them with someone so much like us that the line dividing us blurs, becomes more like a permeable, Super Glue membrane.

If you're struggling to rise off your knees, shed your chains, wouldn't it be nice to find someone in this wide, surprising world who's been where you've been and understands what you're saying, who might be prepared to do unto you as he or she would have you do unto him or her if your circumstances were reversed? Someone behaving the way we dream a good brother would.

Kim Addonizio

Like That

Love me like a wrong turn on a bad road late at night, with no moon and
no town anywhere
and a large hungry animal moving heavily through the brush in the
ditch.
Love me with a blindfold over your eyes and the sound of rusty water
blurting from the faucet in the kitchen, runneling down through
the floorboards to hot cement. Do it without asking,
without wondering or thinking anything, while the machinery's
shut down and the watchman's slumped asleep before his small TV
showing the empty garage, the deserted hallways, while the thieves
slice through
the fence with steel clippers. Love me when you can't find
a decent restaurant open anywhere, when you're alone in a glaring
diner
with two nuns arguing in the back booth, when your eggs are greasy
and your hash browns underdone. Snick the buttons off the front of my
dress
and toss them one by one into the pond where carp lurk just beneath
the surface,
their cold fins waving. Love me on the hood of a truck no one's driven

in years, sunk to its fenders in weeds and dead sunflowers;
and in the lilies, your mouth on my white throat, while turtles drag
their bellies through slick mud, through the footprints of coots and
    ducks.
Do it when no one's looking, when the riots begin and the planes open
    up,
when the bus leaps the curb and the driver jams the brakes to the floor
    without resistance,
while someone hurls a plate against the wall and picks up another,
love me like a freezing shot of vodka, like dark rum, love me
when you're lonely, when we're both too tired to speak, when you don't
    believe
in anything, listen, there isn't anything, it doesn't matter; lie down
with me and close your eyes, the road curves here, I'm cranking up the
    radio
and we're going, we won't turn back as long as you love me,
as long as you keep on doing it exactly like that.

Brenda Miller

The Date

When I return naked to the stone porch,
there is no one to see me glistening.
—Linda Gregg

A man I like is coming for dinner tonight. This means I don't sleep very much, and I wake disoriented in the half light of dawn, wondering where I am. I look at my naked body stretched diagonally across the bed; I look at the untouched breasts, the white belly, and I wonder. I don't know if this man will ever touch me, but I wonder.

I get up and make coffee. While I wait for the water to boil, I study the pictures and poems and quotes held in place by magnets on my refrigerator. I haven't really looked at them in a long time, my gaze usually blank as I reach for the refrigerator door. But this morning I try to see these objects clearly, objectively, as if I were a stranger. I try to figure what this man will make of them, and so, by extension, what he will make of me.

He'll see pictures of my three nieces, my nephew, my godson. He'll see my six women friends hiking in a slot canyon of the San Rafael swell, straddling the narrow gap with their strong, muscular legs. He'll see the astrological forecast for Pisces and a Joseph Campbell quote that tells me if I'm to live like a hero, I must be ready at any moment, for "there is no other way." He'll see Rumi: "Let the Beauty we love be what we do. There are hundreds of ways to kneel and kiss the ground." He'll see me kayaking with my friend Kathy in the San Juan Islands; me sitting with my parents in the Oasis Cafe in Salt Lake City, the three of us straining to smile as the waitress snaps the photo; me standing on the grounds of Edna St. Vincent Millay's estate, my arms around my fellow artist-colonists, grinning as if I were genuinely happy.

Who is this person on my refrigerator door? I try to form these bits and pieces into a coherent image, a picture for me to navigate by as I move through my solitary morning routine of coffee, juice, cereal, a few moments of rumination before the stained-glass kitchen window. But I've seen these fragments so often, they've come to mean nothing to me; this collage exists only for others, a persona constructed for the few people who make it this far into my house—into my life. "Look," it says, "look how athletic, spiritual, creative, loved I am." And my impulse, though I stifle it, is to rearrange all these items, deleting some, adding others, to create a picture I think this man will like.

But how can I know? How can I keep from making a mistake? Besides, I tell myself, a mature woman would never perform such a silly and demeaning act. So I turn away from the fridge, leave things the way they are, drink my coffee, and gaze out the window. It's February, and the elm trees are bare, the grass brown between patches of snow. Tomorrow is Valentine's Day, a fact I've been avoiding. I think about the blue tulips I planted in the fall, still hunkered underground, and the thought of them down there in the darkness, their pale shoots nudging the hard-packed soil, makes me a little afraid.

I'm afraid because I'm thirty-eight years old, and I've been alone for almost three years now, have dated no one since leaving my last boyfriend, who is in California marrying someone else. Sometimes I like to be alone; I lie on my bed at odd hours of the day with a small lavender-filled pillow over my eyes, like the old woman I think I'm becoming. At times like these, the polish of light through the half-closed Venetian blinds seems a human thing, kind and forgiving, and my solitude a condition to be guarded, even if it means remaining unpartnered for life.

But other times I gaze into my bedroom and see no comforting light, smell no lavender. Instead, the empty room feels like a reproach—dark, unyielding. Unable to move beyond the threshold, I stand there paralyzed, panic gnawing beneath my skin. I try to breathe deeply, try to remember the smiling self on my refrigerator door, but that person seems all surface, a lie rehearsed so many times, it bears a faint semblance to truth, but not the core. I cry as if every love I've ever known has been false somehow, a trick. This loneliness seems more real, more true than any transient moment of happiness.

At these times I want only to be coupled, to be magnified in a world which too often renders me invisible. In my parents' house, an entire wall is devoted to formal family photographs, arranged in neat symmetry: my parents in the middle; my older brother, his wife, and their two children on one side; my younger brother, his wife, and their two children on the other. When I lived with my boyfriend Keith for five years, my parents insisted we have a portrait taken as well, and we did: me in a green T-shirt and multicolored beads, Keith in jeans and a denim shirt, the two of us standing with our arms entwined. So for a while my photo, and my life, fit neatly into the family constellation.

Then Keith and I split up, but the photograph remained on the wall another year, staring down at me when I came home to visit for Hanukah. I know my parents kept it up out of nostalgic fondness for Keith. "You have to take that down," I finally told them, and they nodded sadly. Now a portrait of myself, alone, hangs in its spot—a nice photograph, flattering, but still out of place amid the growing and changing families that surround it. Whenever I visit, my eight-year-old nephew asks me, "Why aren't you married?" and gazes at me with a mixture of wonder and alarm.

A man I like is coming to dinner, so I get out all my cookbooks and choose and discard recipes as if trying on dresses. I want something savory yet subtle, not too messy, and not too garlicky, just in case we kiss. I don't know if we will kiss, but just in case.

I don't know much about this man. He has two young daughters, an ex-wife, a hundred high school students to teach every day. He writes poetry. His hair is the same length as mine, curling just below the chin. I don't know how old he is, but I suspect he's younger than I am, so I need to be careful not to reveal too much too fast.

It will be our third date, this dinner. From what I've heard, the third date's either the charm or the poison. I have a friend who, in the last five years, has never gotten past the third date. She calls me at ten-thirty on a Friday night. "Third-date syndrome," she sighs. She describes the sheepish look on her date's face as he delivers the "let's just be friends" speech, which by now she has memorized: "You're great. I enjoy your company, but (a) I don't have a lot of time right now; (b) I'm not looking for a relationship; or (c) I'm going to be out of town a lot in the next couple of months." My friend tells me, "I just wish one of them would come right out and say, 'Look, I don't really like you. Let's just forget it.' It would be a relief, in a way."

I listen to her stories with a morbid fascination, as if she were a traveler returned from some foreign land to which I, thankfully, have been denied a visa. But then we hang up, and I turn back to my empty house: the bed, whose wide expanse looks accusatory; the pile of books, which has grown lopsided and dangerous. I stare at my fish, a fighting fish named Betty, who flares his gills at me and swims in vicious circles around his plastic hexagon, whipping his iridescent body back and forth. My friend Connie tells me this behavior indicates love, that my fish is expressing his masculinity so that I might want to mate with him. In my desperation, I take this as a compliment.

A man I like is coming to dinner, which means I need to do the laundry and wash the sheets, just in case. How long has it been since I washed the sheets? There's been no need to keep track. It's just me here, after all, and I'm always clean when I go to bed, fresh from the bath; nothing happens in that bed to soil it. When I lived with Keith, or Seth, or Francisco, I washed the sheets every week, but then I had someone in the laundromat to help me fold them when they were dry.

Today, as I dangle the dry sheets over the laundromat's metal table, I realize that I've never really dated before. I've always been transparent as a door made of rice paper: approach me and you can see inside; touch me and I open, light and careless. It's difficult to remember the beginnings of things. Was there always this dithering back and forth, this wondering, this not knowing? My first boyfriend and I took LSD and sat in a tree for five hours on our first date. We communicated telepathically, keeping our legs intertwined, sinewy as the branches of a madrone. We were eighteen years old.

Such a date, now that I'm thirty-eight, seems foolish, ridiculous. Now

I have to weigh everything: to call or not to call; whether to wait three days, or five, or six; whether to ask everyone who might know this man for information, then form a strategic plan. I shave my legs and underarms, make appointments for a haircut and a manicure, all of which will make no difference if nothing happens. I think about condoms and blush and wonder if he will buy any, wonder where they are in the store, how much they cost these days. I wonder about the weight of a man's hands on my shoulders, on my hair. Marilynne Robinson, in *Housekeeping*, writes that "need can blossom into all the compensations it requires. . . . To wish for a hand on one's hair is all but to feel it."

I want to believe her, so I wish for the hand. I close my eyes and try to picture this man's hands, to feel the soft underside of his wrist against my mouth. A man's wrists have always been the key to my lust; something rouses me in the power of a hand concentrated in that hinge. And yes, I feel it. Yes, my breath catches in my throat, as if he has stroked his thumb against the edge of my jaw. My body's been so long without desire that I've almost forgotten what it means to be a sexual being, what it's like to feel this quickening in my groin. It's all I need for now: this moment of desire unencumbered by the complications of fulfillment. Because craving only gives rise to more craving; desire feeds on itself and cannot be appeased. It is *my* desire, after all, *my* longing, more delicious than fulfillment, because over this longing I retain complete control. This arousal, breathless as it is, lets me know I'm alive. That's all I really wanted in the first place.

A *date.* The word still brings up visions of Solvang, California, and the date orchards on the outskirts of town, the sticky sweetness of the dark fruit. My family drove through the orchards on summer car trips, hot and irritable in the blue station wagon. But when we stopped at the stores with giant dates painted on their awnings, we grew excited, our misery forgotten. My mother doled out out the fruit to us from the front seat, her eyes already half-closed in pleasure. The dates—heavy, cloying, dark as dried blood—always made the roof of my mouth itch, but I ate them anyway, because they came in a white box like candy. I ate them because I was told they were precious, the food of the gods.

*

I lied. I changed everything on my refrigerator, my bulletin board, my mantelpiece; I put up a letter announcing a prize, took down my nephew's drawing because it ruined the aesthetics. I casually added a picture of myself on a good day, my long legs tan, my skin flawless as I pose in front of a blazing maple bush on Mill Creek. I try to suppress an unbidden fantasy: a photograph of me and this man and his two daughters filling the requisite place on my parents' wall. I know this is a dangerous and futile image, but it lodges stubbornly in my head.

I call my friend every half-hour or so with updates on my frame of mind, asking for reassurance that I am not a terrible person, asking questions as if she were a representative of the dating board: "On which date does one start holding hands? Kissing? If I ask him out again and he says yes, how do I know he's not just being polite?" If there were a guidebook, I would buy it; a class, I would take it.

Yesterday, I discussed this imminent dinner with my hairstylist, Tony, as he bobbed my hair. Tony and his boyfriend are essentially married, but he's had his share of dates, and he gave me both sides. "Well, on the one hand, you've *got* to play the game," he said, turning the blowdryer away from my hair, "but, on the other hand, you need to show some honesty, some of the real you. You don't want to scare him off. This is a good lesson for you: balance, balance, balance."

Tony is my guru. When I came to him the first time, I told him my hair was in transition: not long, not short, just annoying. "You can't think of it as a transition," said Tony, cupping my unwanted flip. "This is what your hair wants to be right now. There are no transitions. Right now, this is *it*."

Yesterday, Tony cradled my newly coiffed hair in his slender fingers, gazed at me somberly in the mirror. I smiled uncertainly, cocked my head. "Good?" he asked. "Good," I replied. Satisfied, he whisked bits of hair off my shoulders with a brush. "Don't worry," he said. "Play it cool." I nodded, gazing at myself in the mirror, which always makes my cheeks look a little too pudgy, my lips a little too pale. Whenever I look at my reflection too long, I become unrecognizable, my mouth slightly askew, a mouth I can't imagine kissing or being kissed. I paid Tony, then walked carefully out of the salon, my head level, a breeze cold against my bare neck. In the car, I did not resist the urge to tilt down the rearview mirror and look at myself again. I touched my new hair. I touched those lips, softly, with the very tips of my fingers.

A man I like is coming to dinner. In two hours. The chicken is marinating and the house is clean. If I take a shower and get dressed right now, I'll have an hour and a half to sit fidgeting in my living room chair, talking to myself and to the fish, whose water of course I've changed. "Make a good impression," I plead with Betty. "Mellow out." He swims back and forth, avoiding my eyes, butting his head against the plastic hexagon. I call my friend: Do I light candles? A fire in the fireplace? Use the cloth napkins? She says yes to the napkins, nix to everything else. I must walk the line between casual and formal, cool and aflame. Perfume? Yes. Eyeliner? No. I remake the bed, realizing only now how misshapen my down comforter is, all the feathers bunched at one end. The cover, yellow at the edges, lies forlornly against my pillows, and my pillowcases don't match. Skirt or pants? I ask my friend. Wine or beer? My friend, a saint, listens and finally says, "Why are you asking me? I never get past the third date!" I freeze. Suddenly, I want to get off the phone as quickly as possible, as if her bad luck might be contagious.

A man I like is coming to dinner. He's late. I sit on the edge of my bed, unwilling to stand near the front windows, where he might see me waiting. My stomach hurts and is not soothed by the smell of tandoori chicken overcooking in the oven. Like a cliché, my hands are sweating. I lie back on the bed, not caring at this point if I mess up my hair or wrinkle my green dress, chosen for its apparent lack of effort. Pale light sifts through the Venetian blinds at an angle just right for napping or making love. If I had to choose right now, I'd choose a nap, the kind that keeps me hovering on the edge of a consciousness so sweet it would seem ridiculous to ever resurface. My lavender eye pillow is within reach. My house is so small; how could it possibly accommodate a man, filling my kitchen, peering at my refrigerator door?

On my bedside table is the *Pillow Book* of Sei Shonagan, a tenth-century Japanese courtesan, a woman whose career consisted of waiting. In that expectant state, she observed everything around her in great de-tail, finding some of it to her liking and some not. I idly pick up the book, allow it to fall open, and read, "When a woman lives alone, her house should be extremely dilapidated, the mud wall should be falling to pieces, and if there is a pond, it should be overgrown with water plants. It is not essential that the garden be covered with sagebrush; but weeds should be growing through the sand in patches, for this gives the place a poignantly desolate look."

I close the book. I look around this apartment, this house where I live alone. My room feels clean, new, expectant. Right now, I want nothing more than to stay alone, to hold myself here in a state of controlled desire. But if this man doesn't show, I know my house will quickly settle into the dilapidation Sei Shonagan saw as fit for a single woman; the line between repose and chaos is thinner than I once thought. Despite all I've tried to learn in these years alone—about my worthiness as an independent woman; about the intrinsic value of the present moment; about defining myself by my own terms, not by someone else's—despite all this, I know that my well-being this moment depends on a man's hand knocking on my door.

The doorbell rings, startling me into a sitting position. I clear my throat, which suddenly seems ready to close altogether, to keep me mute and safe. I briefly consider leaving the door unanswered. I imagine my date waiting, looking through the kitchen window, then backing away, shaking his head, wondering. Perhaps he would think me crazy, or dead. Perhaps he would call the police, tell them there's a woman he's worried about, a woman who lives alone. Or, more likely, he would drive to a bar, have a beer, and forget about me. The thought of his absence momentarily pleases me, bathes me with relief. But of course I stand up and glance in the mirror, rake my hands through my hair to see it feather into place, then casually walk out to greet this man I like, this man who's coming to dinner.

Junot Díaz

The Sun, the Moon, the Stars

I'm not a bad guy. I know how that sounds—defensive, unscrupulous—but it's true. I'm like everybody else: weak, full of mistakes, but basically good. Magdalena disagrees. She considers me a typical Dominican man: a *sucio*, an asshole. See, many months ago, when Magda was still my girl, when I didn't have to be careful about almost everything, I cheated on her with this chick who had tons of eighties free-style hair. Didn't tell Magda about it, either. You know how it is. A smelly bone like that, better off buried in the back yard of your life. Magda only found out because home-girl wrote her a fucking *letter*. And the letter had *details*. Shit you wouldn't even tell your boys drunk.

The thing is, that particular bit of stupidity had been over for months. Me and Magda were on an upswing. We weren't as distant as we'd been the winter I was cheating. The freeze was over. She was coming over to my place, and instead of us hanging with my knucklehead boys—me smoking, her bored out of her skull—we were seeing movies. Driving out to different places to eat. Even caught a play at the Crossroads and I took her picture with some bigwig black playwrights, pictures where she's smiling so much you'd think her wide-ass mouth was going to unhinge. We were a couple again. Visiting each other's family on the weekends. Eating breakfast at diners hours before anybody else was up, rummaging through the New Brunswick library together, the one Carnegie built with his guilt money. A nice rhythm we had going. But then the Letter hits like a *Star Trek* grenade and detonates everything, past, present, future. Suddenly her folks want to kill me. It don't matter that I helped them with their taxes two years running or that I mow their lawn. Her father, who used to treat me like his *hijo*, calls me an asshole on the phone, sounds like he's strangling himself with the cord. "You no deserve I speak to you in Spanish," he says. I see one of Magda's girlfriends at the Woodbridge Mall—Claribel, the *ecuatoriana* with the biology degree and the *chinita* eyes—and she treats me like I ate somebody's kid.

You don't even want to hear how it went down with Magda. Like a five-train collision. She threw Cassandra's letter at me—it missed and landed under a Volvo—and then she sat down on the curb and started hyperventilating. "Oh, God," she wailed. "Oh, my God."

This is when my boys claim they would have pulled a Total Fucking Denial. Cassandra who? I was too sick to my stomach even to try. I sat down next to her, grabbed her flailing arms, and said some dumb shit like "You have to listen to me, Magda. Or you won't understand."

Let me tell you something about Magda. She's a Bergenline original: short, with big eyes and big hips and dark curly hair you could lose a hand in. Her father's a baker, her mother sells kids' clothes door to door. She's a forgiving soul. A Catholic. Dragged me into church every Sunday for Spanish Mass, and when one of her relatives is sick, especially the ones in Cuba, she writes letters to some nuns in Pennsylvania, asks the sisters to pray for her family. She's the nerd every librarian in town knows, a teacher whose students fall in love with her. Always cutting shit out for me from the newspapers, Dominican shit. I see her like, what, every week, and she still sends me corny little notes in the mail: "So you won't forget me." You couldn't think of anybody worse to screw than Magda.

I won't bore you with the details. The begging, the crawling over glass, the crying. Let's just say that after two weeks of this, of my driving out to her house, sending her letters, and calling her at all hours of the night, we put it back together. Didn't mean I ever ate with her family again or that her girlfriends were celebrating. Those *cabronas*, they were like, *No, jamás*, never. Even Magda wasn't too hot on the rapprochement at first, but I had the momentum of the past on my side. When she asked me "Why don't you leave me alone?" I told her the truth: "It's because I love you, *mami*." I know this sounds like a load of doo-doo, but it's true: Magda's my heart. I didn't want her to leave me; I wasn't about to start looking for a girlfriend because I'd fucked up one lousy time.

Don't think it was a cakewalk, because it wasn't. Magda's stubborn; back when we first started dating, she said she wouldn't sleep with me until we'd been together at least a month, and homegirl stuck to it, no matter how hard I tried to get into her knickknacks. She's sensitive, too. Takes to hurt the way water takes to paper. You can't imagine how many times she asked (especially after we finished fucking), "Were you ever going to tell me?" This and "Why?" were her favorite questions. My favorite answers were "Yes" and "It was a stupid mistake."

We even had some conversation about Cassandra—usually in the dark, when we couldn't see each other. Magda asked me if I'd loved Cassandra, and I told her no, I didn't. "Do you still think about her?" "Nope." "Did you like fucking her?" "To be honest, baby, it was lousy." And for a while after we got back together everything was as fine as it could be.

But what was strange was that instead of shit improving between us, things got worse and worse. My Magda was turning into another Magda. Who didn't want to sleep over as much or scratch my back when I asked her to. Amazing how you notice the little things. Like how she never used to ask me to call back when she was on the line with somebody else. I always had priority. Not anymore. So of course I blamed all that shit on her girls, who I knew for a fact were still feeding her a bad line about me.

She wasn't the only one with counsel. My boys were like, "Fuck her, don't sweat that bitch," but every time I tried, I couldn't pull it off. I was into Magda for real. I started working overtime on her, but nothing seemed to pan out. Every movie we went to, every night drive we took, every time she did sleep over seemed to confirm something negative about me. I felt like I was dying by degrees, but when I brought it up, she told me that I was being paranoid.

About a month later, she started making the sort of changes that would have alarmed a paranoid nigger. Cuts her hair, buys better makeup, rocks new clothes, goes out dancing on Friday nights with her friends. When I ask her if we can chill, I'm no longer sure it's a done deal. A lot of the time she Bartlebys me, says, "No, I'd rather not." I ask her what the hell she thinks this is and she says, "That's what I'm trying to figure out."

I know what she's doing. Making me aware of my precarious position in her life. Like I'm not aware.

Then it was June. Hot white clouds stranded in the sky, cars being washed down with hoses, music allowed outside. Everybody getting ready for summer, even us. We'd planned a trip to Santo Domingo early in the year, an anniversary present, and had to decide whether we were still going or not. It had been on the horizon a while, but I figured it was something that would resolve itself. When it didn't, I brought the tickets out and asked her, "How do you feel about it?"

"Like it's too much of a commitment."

"Could be worse. It's a vacation, for Christ's sake."

"I see it as pressure."

"Doesn't have to be pressure."

I don't know why I get stuck on it the way I do. Bringing it up every day, trying to get her to commit. Maybe I was getting tired of the situation we were in. Wanted to flex, wanted something to change. Or maybe I'd gotten this idea in my head that if she said, "Yes, we're going," then shit would be fine between us. If she said, "No, it's not for me," then at least I'd know that it was over.

Her girls, the sorest losers on the planet, advised her to take the trip and then never speak to me again. She, of course, told me this shit, because she couldn't stop herself from telling me everything she's thinking. "How do you feel about that suggestion?" I asked her.

She shrugged. "It's an idea."

Even my boys were like, "Nigger, sounds like you're wasting a whole lot of loot on some bullshit," but I really thought it would be good for us. Deep down, where my boys don't know me, I'm an optimist. I thought, Me and her on the Island. What couldn't this cure?

Let me confess: I love Santo Domingo. I love coming home to the guys in blazers trying to push little cups of Brugal into my hands. Love the plane landing, everybody clapping when the wheels kiss the runway. Love the fact that I'm the only nigger on board without a Cuban link or a flapjack of makeup on my face. Love the redhead woman on her way to meet the daughter she hasn't seen in eleven years. The gifts she holds on her lap, like the bones of a saint. "*M'ija* has *tetas* now," the woman whispers to her neighbor. "Last time I saw her, she could barely speak in sentences. Now she's a woman. *Imagínate.*" I love the bags my mother packs, shit for relatives and something for Magda, a gift. "You give this to her no matter what happens."

If this was another kind of story, I'd tell you about the sea. What it looks like after it's been forced into the sky through a blowhole. How when I'm driving in from the airport and see it like this, like shredded silver, I know I'm back for real. I'd tell you how many poor motherfuckers there are. More albinos, more cross-eyed niggers, more *tígueres* than you'll ever see. And the *mujeres—olvídate.* How you can't go five feet without running into one you wouldn't mind kicking it with. I'd tell you about the traffic: the entire history of late-twentieth-century automobiles swarming across every flat stretch of ground, a cosmology of battered cars, battered motorcycles, battered trucks, and battered buses, and an equal number of repair shops, run by any fool with a wrench. I'd tell you about the shanties and our no-running-water faucets and the sambos on the billboards and the fact that my family house comes equipped with an ever-reliable latrine. I'd tell you about my *abuelo* and his *campo* hands, how unhappy he is that I'm not sticking around, and I'd tell you about the street where I was born, Calle XXI, how it hasn't decided yet if it wants to be a slum or not and how it's been in this state of indecision for years.

But that would make it another kind of story, and I'm having enough trouble as it is with this one. You'll have to take my word for it. Santo Domingo is Santo Domingo. Let's pretend we all know what goes on there.

I must have been smoking dust, because I thought we were fine those first couple of days. Sure, staying locked up at my *abuelo*'s house bored Magda to tears; she even said so—"I'm bored, Yunior"—but I'd warned her about the obligatory Visit with Abuelo. I thought she wouldn't mind; she's normally mad cool with the *viejitos.* But she didn't say much to him. Just fidgeted in the heat and drank fifteen bottles of water. Point is we were out of the capital and on a *guagua* to the interior before the second day had even begun. The landscapes were superfly—even though there was a drought on and the whole *campo*, even the houses, was covered in that red dust. There I was. Pointing out all the shit that had changed since the year before. The new Pizza Huts and Dunkin' Donuts and the little plastic bags of water the *tigueritos* were selling. Even kicked the historicals. This is where Trujillo and his Marine pals slaughtered the *gavilleros*, here's where the Jefe used to take his girls, here's where Balaguer sold his soul to the Devil. And Magda seemed to be enjoying herself. Nodded her head. Talked back a little. What can I tell you? I thought we were on a positive vibe.

I guess when I look back there were signs. First off, Magda's not quiet. She's a talker, a fucking *boca*, and we used to have this thing where I would lift my hand and say, "Time out," and she would have to be quiet for at least two minutes, just so I could process some of the information she'd been spouting. She'd be embarrassed and chastened, but not so embarrassed and chastened that when I said, "O.K., time's up," she didn't launch right into it again.

Maybe it was my good mood. It was like the first time in weeks that I felt relaxed, that I wasn't acting like something was about to give at any moment. It bothered me that she insisted on reporting to her girls every night—like they were expecting me to kill her or something—but, fuck it, I still thought we were doing better than anytime before.

We were in this crazy budget hotel near the university. I was standing outside, staring out at the Septentrionales and the blacked-out city, when I heard her crying. I thought it was something serious, found the flashlight, and fanned the light over her heat-swollen face. "Are you O.K., *mami*?"

She shook her head. "I don't want to be here."

"What do you mean?"

"What don't you understand? I. Don't. Want. To. Be. Here."

This was not the Magda I knew. The Magda I knew was super courteous. Knocked on a door before she opened it.

I almost shouted, "What is your fucking problem!" But I didn't. I ended up hugging and babying her and asking her what was wrong. She cried for a long time and then after a silence started talking. By then the lights had flickered back on. Turned out she didn't want to travel around like a hobo. "I thought we'd be on a beach," she said.

"We're going to be on a beach. The day after tomorrow."

"Can't we go now?"

What could I do? She was in her underwear, waiting for me to say something. So what jumped out of my mouth? "Baby, we'll do whatever you want." I called the hotel in La Romana, asked if we could come early, and the next morning I put us on an express *guagua* to the capital and then a second one to La Romana. I didn't say a fucking word to her and she didn't say nothing to me. She seemed tired and watched the world outside like maybe she was expecting it to speak to her.

By the middle of Day 3 of our All-Quisqueya Redemption Tour we were in an air-conditioned bungalow watching HBO. Exactly where I want to be when I'm in Santo Domingo. In a fucking resort. Magda was reading a book by a Trappist, in a better mood, I guess, and I was sitting on the edge of the bed, fingering my useless map.

I was thinking, For this I deserve something nice. Something physical. Me and Magda were pretty damn casual about sex, but since the breakup shit has gotten weird. First of all, it ain't regular like before. I'm lucky to score some once a week. I have to nudge her, start things up, or we won't fuck at all. And she plays like she doesn't want it, and sometimes she doesn't and then I have to cool it, but other times she does want it and I have to touch her pussy, which is my way of initiating things, of saying, "So, how about we kick it, *mami*?" And she'll turn her head, which is her way of saying, "I'm too proud to acquiesce openly to your animal desires, but if you continue to put your finger in me I won't stop you."

Today we started no problem, but then halfway through she said, "Wait, we shouldn't."

I wanted to know why.

She closed her eyes like she was embarrassed at herself. "Forget about it," she said, moving her hips under me. "Just forget about it."

I don't even want to tell you where we're at. We're in Casa de Campo. The Resort That Shame Forgot. The average asshole would love this place. It's the largest, wealthiest resort on the Island, which means it's a goddam fortress, walled away from everybody else. *Guachimanes* and peacocks and ambitious topiaries everywhere. Advertises itself in the States as its own country, and it might as well be. Has its own airport, thirty-six holes of golf, beaches so white they ache to be trampled, and the only Island Dominicans you're guaranteed to see are either caked up or changing your sheets. Let's just say my *abuelo* has never been here, and neither has yours. This is where the Garcías and the Colóns come to relax after a long month of oppressing the masses, where the *tutumpotes* can trade tips with their colleagues from abroad. Chill here too long, and you'll be sure to have your ghetto pass revoked, no questions asked.

We wake up bright and early for the buffet, get served by cheerful women in Aunt Jemima costumes. I shit you not: these sisters even have to wear hankies on their heads. Magda is scratching out a couple of cards to her family. I want to talk about the day before, but when I bring it up she puts down her pen. Jams on her shades.

"I feel like you're pressuring me."

"How am I pressuring you?" I ask.

We get into one of those no-fun twenty-minute arguments, which the waiters keep interrupting by bringing over more orange juice and café, the two things this island has plenty of.

"I just want some space to myself every now and then. Every time I'm with you I have this sense that you want something from me."

"Time to yourself," I say. "What does that mean?"

"Like maybe once a day, you do one thing, I do another."

"Like when? Now?"

"It doesn't have to be now." She looks exasperated. "Why don't we just go down to the beach?"

As we walk over to the courtesy golf cart, I say, "I feel like you rejected my whole country, Magda."

"Don't be ridiculous." She drops one hand in my lap. "I just wanted to relax. What's wrong with that?"

The sun is blazing and the blue of the ocean is an overload on the brain. Casa de Campo has got beaches the way the rest of the island has got problems. These, though, have no merengue, no little kids, nobody trying to sell you *chicharrones*, and there's a massive melanin deficit in evidence. Every fifty feet there's at least one Eurofuck beached out on a towel like some scary pale monster that the sea's vomited up. They look like philosophy professors, like budget Foucaults, and too many of them are in the company of a dark-assed Dominican girl. I mean it, these girls can't be no more than sixteen, look *puro ingenio* to me. You can tell by their inability to communicate that these two didn't meet back in their Left Bank days.

Magda's rocking a dope Ochun-colored bikini that her girls helped her pick out so she could torture me, and I'm in these old ruined trunks that say "Sandy Hook Forever!" I'll admit it, with Magda half naked in public, I'm feeling vulnerable and uneasy. I put my hand on her knee. "I just wish you'd say you love me."

"Yunior, please."

"Can you say you like me a lot?"

"Can you leave me alone? You're such a pestilence."

I let the sun stake me out to the sand. It's disheartening, me and Magda together. We don't look like a couple. When she smiles, niggers ask her for her hand in marriage; when I smile, folks check their wallets. Magda's been a star the whole time we've been here. You know how it is when you're on the Island and your girl's an octoroon. Brothers go apeshit. On buses, the machos were like, "*Tu sí eres bella, muchacha.*" Every time I dip into the water for a swim, some Mediterranean Messenger of Love starts rapping to her. Of course, I'm not polite. "Why don't you beat it, *pancho*? We're on our honeymoon here." There's this one squid who's mad persistent, even sits down near us so he can impress her with the hair around his nipples, and instead of ignoring him she starts a conversation and it turns out he's Dominican, too, from Quisqueya Heights, an assistant D.A. who loves his people. "Better I'm their prosecutor," he says. "At least I understand them." I'm thinking he sounds like the sort of nigger who in the old days used to lead bwana to the rest of us. After three minutes of him, I can't take it no more, and say, "Magda, stop talking to that asshole."

The assistant D.A. startles. "I know you ain't talking to me," he says.

"Actually," I say, "I am."

"This is unbelievable." Magda gets to her feet and walks stiff-legged toward the water. She's got a half-moon of sand stuck to her butt. A total fucking heartbreak.

Homeboy's saying something else to me, but I'm not listening. I already know what she'll say when she sits back down: "Time for you to do your thing and me to do mine."

That night I loiter around the pool and the local bar, Club Cacique, Magda nowhere to be found. I meet a Dominicana from West New York. Fly, of course. *Trigueña*, with the most outrageous perm this side of Dyckman. Lucy is her name. She's hanging out with three of her teen-age girl cousins. When she removes her robe to dive into the pool, I see a spiderweb of scars across her stomach. Tells me in Spanish, "I have family in La Romana, but I refuse to stay with them. No way. My uncle won't let any of us out of the house after dark. So I'd rather go broke and stay here than be locked in the prison."

I meet these two rich older dudes drinking cognac at the bar. Introduce themselves as the Vice-President and Bárbaro, his bodyguard. I must have the footprint of fresh disaster on my face. They listen to my troubles like they're a couple of capos and I'm talking murder. They commiserate. It's a thousand degrees out and the mosquitoes hum like they're about to inherit the earth, but both these cats are wearing expensive suits, and Bárbaro is even sporting a purple ascot. Once a soldier tried to saw open his neck and now he covers the scar. "I'm a modest man," he says.

I go off to phone the room. No Magda. I check with reception. No messages. I return to the bar and smile.

The Vice-President is a young brother, in his late thirties, and pretty cool for a *chupabarrio*. He advises me to find another woman. Make her *bella* and *negra*. I think, Cassandra.

The Vice-President waves his hand, and shots of Barceló appear so fast you'd think it's science fiction.

"Jealousy is the best way to jumpstart a relationship," the Vice-President says. "I learned that when I was a student at Syracuse. Dance with another woman, dance merengue with her, and see if your *jeva's* not roused to action."

"You mean roused to violence."

"She hit you?"

"When I first told her. She smacked me right across the chops."

"*Pero, hermano,* why'd you tell her?" Bárbaro wants to know. "Why didn't you just deny it?"

"*Compadre,* she received a letter. It had evidence."

The Vice-President smiles fantastically and I can see why he's a vice-president. Later, when I get home, I'll tell my mother about this whole mess, and she'll tell me what this brother was the vice-president of.

"They only hit you," he says, "when they care."

"Amen," Bárbaro murmurs. "Amen."

All of Magda's friends say I cheated because I was Dominican, that all us Dominican men are dogs and can't be trusted. But it wasn't genetics; there were reasons. Causalities.

The truth is there ain't no relationship in the world that doesn't hit turbulence. Ours certainly did.

I was living in Brooklyn and she was with her folks in Jersey. We talked every day on the phone, and on weekends we saw each other. Usually I went in. We were real Jersey, too: malls, the parents, movies, a lot of TV. After a year of us together, this was where we were at. Our relationship wasn't the sun, the moon, and the stars, but it wasn't bullshit, either. Especially not on Saturday mornings, over at my apartment, when she made us coffee *campo* style, straining it through the sock thing. Told her parents the night before she was staying over at Claribel's; they must have known where she was, but they never said shit. I'd sleep late and she'd read, scratching my back in slow arcs, and when I was ready to get up I would start kissing her until she would say, "God, Yunior, you're making me wet."

I wasn't unhappy and wasn't actively pursuing ass like some niggers. Sure, I checked out other females, even danced with them when I went out, but I wasn't keeping numbers or nothing.

Still, it's not like seeing somebody once a week doesn't cool shit out, because it does. Nothing you'd really notice until some new chick arrives at your job with a big chest and a smart mouth and she's like on you almost immediately, touching your pectorals, moaning about some *moreno* she's dating who's always treating her like shit, saying, "Black guys don't understand Spanish girls."

Cassandra. She organized the football pool and did crossword puzzles while she talked on the phone, and had a thing for denim skirts. We got into a habit of going to lunch and having the same conversation. I advised her to drop the *moreno*, she advised me to find a girlfriend who could fuck. First week of knowing her, I made the mistake of telling her that sex with Magda had never been topnotch.

"God, I feel sorry for you." Cassandra laughed. "At least Rupert gives me some Grade A dick."

The first night we did it—and it was good, too; she wasn't false advertising—I felt so lousy that I couldn't sleep, even though she was one of those sisters whose body fits next to you perfect. I was like, She knows, so I called Magda right from the bed and asked her if she was O.K.

"You sound strange," she said.

I remember Cassandra pressing the hot cleft of her pussy against my leg and me saying, "I just miss you."

Another day, and the only thing Magda has said is "Give me the lotion." Tonight the resort is throwing a party. All guests are invited. Attire's formal, but I don't have the clothes or the energy to dress up. Magda, though, has both. She pulls on these supertight gold lamé pants and a matching halter that shows off her belly ring. Her hair is shiny and as dark as night and I can remember the first time I kissed those curls, asking her, "Where are the stars?" And she said, "They're a little lower, *papi*."

We both end up in front of the mirror. I'm in slacks and a wrinkled guayabera. She's applying her lipstick; I've always believed that the universe invented the color red solely for Latinas.

"We look good," she says.

It's true. My optimism is starting to come back. I'm thinking, This is the night for reconciliation. I put my arms around her, but she drops her bomb without blinking a fucking eye: tonight, she says, she needs space.

My arms drop.

"I knew you'd be pissed," she says.

"You're a real bitch, you know that."

"I didn't want to come here. You made me."

"If you didn't want to come, why didn't you have the fucking guts to say so?"

And on and on and on, until finally I just say, "Fuck this," and head out. I feel unmoored and don't have a clue of what comes next. This is the endgame, and instead of pulling out all the stops, instead of *pongándome más chivo que un chivo,* I'm feeling sorry for myself, *como un parigüayo sin suerte.* I'm thinking, I'm not a bad guy.

Club Cacique is jammed. I'm looking for Lucy. I find the Vice-President and Bárbaro instead. At the quiet end of the bar, they're drinking cognac and arguing about whether there are fifty-six Dominicans in the major leagues or fifty-seven. They clear out a space for me and clap me on the shoulder.

"This place is killing me," I say.

"How dramatic." The Vice-President reaches into his suit for his keys. He's wearing those Italian leather shoes that look like braided slippers. "Are you inclined to ride with us?"

"Sure," I say. "Why the fuck not?"

"I wish to show you the birthplace of our nation."

Before we leave I check out the crowd. Lucy has arrived. She's alone at the edge of the bar in a fly black dress. Smiles excitedly, lifts her arm, and I can see the dark stubbled spot in her armpit. She's got sweat patches over her outfit, and mosquito bites on her beautiful arms. I think, I should stay, but my legs carry me right out of the club.

We pile in a diplomat's black BMW. I'm in the back seat with Bárbaro; the Vice-President's up front, driving. We leave Casa de Campo behind and the frenzy of La Romana, and soon everything starts smelling of processed cane. The roads are dark—I'm talking no fucking lights—and in our beams the bugs swarm like a biblical plague. We're passing the cognac around. I'm with a vice-president, I figure what the fuck.

He's talking—about his time in upstate New York—but so is Bárbaro. The bodyguard's suit's rumpled and his hand shakes as he smokes his cigarettes. Some fucking bodyguard. He's telling me about his childhood in San Juan, near the border of Haiti. Liborio's country. "I wanted to be an engineer," he tells me. "I wanted to build schools and hospitals for the pueblo." I'm not really listening to him; I'm thinking about Magda, how I'll probably never taste her *chocha* again.

And then we're out of the car, stumbling up a slope, through bushes and *guineo* and bamboo, and the mosquitoes are chewing us up like we're the special of the day. Bárbaro's got a huge flashlight, a darkness obliterator. The Vice-President's cursing, trampling through the underbrush, saying, "It's around here somewhere. This is what I get for being in office so long." It's only then I notice that Bárbaro's holding a huge fucking machine gun and his hand ain't shaking no more. He isn't watching me or the Vice-President—he's listening. I'm not scared, but this is getting a little too freaky for me.

"What kind of gun is that?" I ask, by way of conversation.

"A P-90."

"What the fuck is that?"

"Something old made new."

Great, I'm thinking. A philosopher.

"It's here," the Vice-President says.

I creep over and see that he's standing over a hole in the ground. The earth is red. Bauxite. And the hole is blacker than any of us.

"This is the Cave of the Jagua," the Vice-President announces in a deep, respectful voice. "The birthplace of the Tainos."

I raise my eyebrow. "I thought they were South America."

"We're speaking mythically here."

Bárbaro points the light down the hole, but that doesn't improve anything.

"Would you like to see inside?" the Vice-President asks me.

I must have said yes, because Bárbaro gives me the flashlight, and the two of them grab me by my ankles and lower me into the hole. All my coins fly out of my pockets. *Bendiciones.* I don't see much, just some odd colors on the eroded walls. And the Vice-President's calling down, "Isn't it beautiful?"

This is the perfect place for insight, for a person to become somebody better. The Vice-President probably saw his future self hanging in this darkness, bulldozing the poor out of their shanties, and Bárbaro, too—buying a concrete house for his mother, showing her how to work the air conditioner—but me, all I can manage is a memory of the first time me and Magda talked. Back at Rutgers. We were waiting for an E bus together on George Street, and she was wearing purple. All sorts of purple.

And that's when I know it's over. As soon as you start thinking about the beginning, it's the end.

I cry, and when they pull me up, the Vice-President says, indignantly, "God, you don't have to be a pussy about it."

That must have been some serious Island voodoo: the ending I saw in the cave came true. The next day we went back to the United States. Five months later I got a letter from my ex-baby. I was dating someone new, but Magda's handwriting still blasted every molecule of air out of my lungs.

It turned out she was also going out with somebody else. A very nice guy she'd met. Dominican, like me.

But I'm getting ahead of myself. I need to finish by showing you what kind of fool I am.

When I returned to the bungalow that night, Magda was waiting up for me. Was packed; looked like she'd been bawling.

"I'm going home tomorrow," she said.

I sat down next to her. Took her hand. "This can work," I said. "All we have to do is try."

Ruth Prawer Jhabvala

A New Delhi Romance

Indu had married beneath her, but that was many years ago, and besides, she no longer lived with her husband. Everything else had changed too—her parents, who had so deplored her marriage, were long since gone, her brother and sisters had moved away, and the big house they had all lived in had been torn down and a block of flats built on its site. Indu herself still lived in the neighborhood, almost around the corner from the old house, in a complex of ramshackle hutments that had once been a barrack for policemen. She had lived here for twenty years and the rent was still the same, which was why she stayed on—who could have afforded anything else?—though it was far from her place of work. However, it did have the advantage of being near the university, so her son Arun, who was a student there, could easily come home if his classes were canceled due to a strike or the death of some important politician.

Arun, taking full advantage of the proximity of his home and his mother's day-long absence from it, didn't wait for classes to be canceled but cut them whenever he felt like it. Lately he had begun to bring his girlfriend Dipti there—though only after a struggle, not with Dipti, who was willing enough, but with himself. For one thing, he had to overcome his feelings of guilt toward his mother for doing this in her home; and then there was the shabbiness of that home—he was ashamed of it for himself and his mother, and angry with Dipti for maybe judging it in the same way he did. But Dipti was so happy to be there that she formed no negative judgments of it at all. On the contrary.

Yet Dipti herself lived in a very grand house and was brought to the college every day in a chauffeur-driven car. Her father was a politician, an important cabinet minister, and the family lived in luxury. They gave lavish parties at which everyone ate and drank too much; they brought back all the latest household gadgets from their trips abroad, even a washing machine, though they had their washerman living on the premises, along with their other servants. Dipti's mother was always going shopping, for saris and textiles and jewelry, and she bought fresh pastries and chicken patties, so that if Dipti brought her friends home, there was plenty to eat, as well as every kind of soft drink in the refrigerator. Long before he decided to bring Dipti to his own house, Arun had been visiting hers. He didn't eat the pastries—he didn't care for them—and made no attempt to ingratiate himself with her parents. But they liked him—approved of him, and of his mother. Dipti's mother was very gracious to her, not at all assuming the role of VIP's wife that she usually played to its full extent, as was her right. She brought Indu home, ostensibly consulting her on a question of interior decoration, and she even pretended to take her advice, though Indu's taste was not at all consonant with her own preference for rich ornamentation.

Indu accepted Dipti's mother's respect as her due and did not return it. But she liked Dipti—how could she not, for Dipti was everything a young girl should be: sweet and pretty and very much in love with Arun. It had not taken Indu long to discover that the two young people spent afternoons in her house. Dipti's floral perfume hung in the air hours after she had left, and once Indu found a white blossom on her pillow, which might have dropped out of the garland wound into a girl's hair. Indu's feelings as she picked it up were mixed: pride in a son's conquest, as well as a movement of jealous anger that made her indulge in a burst of outrage ("and on my bed!"). But as she sat on this bed, slowly rubbing the petal between her fingers so that it released its scent, memories of her own obliterated all thoughts of the young couple. She hardly needed the fragrance of the jasmine emanating from between her fingers to recall the secret nights on her parents' roof with Arun's father when the rest of the household was fast asleep. What more romantic than those nights drenched in moonlight and jasmine—or what more evanescent? The blossom in tatters between her fingers, she flung it away, her resentment now not against Arun and Dipti but against Arun's father, and also against her own stupid young self, who had tossed away all the advantages of her birth for the sake of those stolen nights.

Arun's father, Raju, had for years lived in Bombay, where he was involved in films. He had turned up throughout Arun's childhood, an unwanted guest who stayed too long, and far from contributing to the household or his son's support, borrowed money from Indu. Raju was good fun, especially for a young child—he sang, he played games, jokes, and magic tricks; but later Arun became as exasperated with him as his mother was. Dipti likewise expressed exasperation for *her* father: "Daddy works far too much! And all those people who come—does he have to see all of them!" But this was a pretense; she was proud of her father and the way crowds thronged to him. At certain hours of the day he sat enthroned on their veranda, an obese idol wrapped in a cloud of white muslin. Petitioners touched his feet in traditional gestures of respect; some brought garlands, some baskets of fruit or boxes of sweetmeats; poor people brought an egg or two, or milk from their cow. There were those who had traveled all night in crowded third-class railway carriages from his native state in order to present some petition to him; others came only to be in his presence, imbibing his aura of riches and power. He addressed them in a tangy native dialect, and his homilies were illustrated by examples drawn nostalgically from the simple life of thatched huts he had long left behind. He had a reputation for salty humor and liked the sound of appreciative laughter. That was one aspect of him—racy, earthy, a man of the people; at other times, with other guests, he was different. Big cars drew up outside his house; if there were too many of them, special police constables had to be called to supplement the guard on duty at his gate. Then he himself became obsequious—he hurried out to receive the visitors, his big bulk moving lightly and with grace. He led them inside and into his carpeted drawing room, where refreshments were served, not by servants but by his wife, her head covered as she offered silver beakers on a silver tray. Sometimes these visitors were led into a further room, where a white sheet had been spread on the carpet; here they all sat cross-legged in their loose native clothes, leaning against bolsters, some fat like himself, others scrawny from fasting and prayer. These powerful men weighed each other up like poker players, sometimes staying up all night while journalists waited outside; for the game that was being played involved millions not only of rupees but of lives. However, this was never a consideration in the minds of the players, who, like all true sportsmen, were sincerely dedicated to their game for its own sake.

■

One day Dipti and Arun's afternoon was disturbed by the arrival of Arun's father. He walked into the living room, which opened straight off the main compound around which all the barrack-like structures were grouped. "I'm here!" he called, like a most eagerly expected guest. In the bedroom, Dipti in a state of undress clapped her hand before her mouth and her wide eyes grew wider as she looked to Arun for rescue. As in all relations to his father, he was more exasperated than embarrassed. He got up and, winding a towel around his waist, went into the living room.

"Ah-ah-ah!" cried the father with delight at the sight of his son; and he hugged him tenderly, held him away for a moment to look at him, then hugged him again. Arun frowned all through this performance—he never liked to be embraced by his father and especially not now, for Raju was full of sweat and soot, as after a long train journey in an overcrowded carriage. But he pretended to have come by plane—"Indian Airlines is hopeless, hopeless! Two hours late and keeping us waiting without even a cup of tea! ... How are you? And your mother—I tried to call her in the office to tell her I was coming, but the connection between Delhi and Bombay—hopeless, hopeless! ... Did you get my telegram? No? That's funny. Why aren't you at college? Is it holidays? Good, we'll have a fine time, you and I, eh, what, ha? Pictures, coffee house, and so on."

Arun said, "I came home to study for my exam." He frowned more and added, "With a friend."

"Ah. A friend. Where is he? ... Understood!" cried Raju, his eyes dancing with pleasure and amusement as they roved over his son's handsome face and naked chest.

Arun went into the bedroom and, seeing Dipti fully dressed, told her, "You can come out. It's only my father. It's all right," he said in answer to her stricken look. When she still hung back, he took her hand and pulled her quite harshly through the curtain that separated the two rooms.

But Raju stilled her fears at once. Giving no sign that there was anything out of the way in a young girl appearing with his son out of the bedroom, he greeted her warmly and with obvious though highly respectful admiration for her beauty. He became the host of the occasion, largely gesturing everyone to sit. Apart from the couch, on which Arun slept at night, the furniture was scanty and makeshift; but Indu had made everything tasteful, with handloomed fabrics draped over oil cans and egg crates, and reproductions from art books hanging wherever new cracks appeared on the walls. Raju wanted to make a tea party of it, encouraging Arun to go for fritters and potato patties to the stall at the corner, even rummaging in his own pocket for money, but when he came up with nothing, the idea was dropped. He made up for it with his conversation, and while his son rolled his eyes up to the ceiling, Raju enjoyed his own skill as an entertainer and its effect on Dipti. She responded to him the way women, starting with Indu, had done all his life long—they didn't always believe what he said but liked his way of saying it. And he knew how to take the right tone with his audience. For instance, today, with Dipti, in telling her about the Bombay film industry, he did not stress its glamour but only its stupidity and vulgarity, adapting himself to what he guessed to be the opinion of someone like Dipti—a university student and, moreover, his scornful son's girlfriend.

"I *like* him," Dipti later insisted to Arun, and repeated it in spite of his "You don't know a thing." She did know some things—he had more or less told her the story of his parents' marriage—but she had not plumbed the depths of his feelings on the subject. And he had not described the scene on that night of Raju's arrival, when Indu got home from work. It was something that happened whenever Raju reappeared in the bosom of his family. When it came time to sleep, he carried his battered little suitcase into his wife's bedroom, on the assumption that this was his rightful place. Arun was already lying on the couch, which had been his bed ever since he had grown too old to share his mother's. He had turned off the light and shut his eyes, pretending to himself that he was too sleepy to listen to the altercation in the next room. He didn't have to; he knew exactly what course it would take. First they would keep their voices down—for his sake—but when Raju kept saying, "Sh-sh," Indu's rage rose till she was shouting, so that Raju too had to speak up to make his protests heard. That caused her to shout louder, till she was shrieking, and finally—Arun waited for it—Raju's little suitcase came flying out through the curtain, and he followed, groping around in the dark to retrieve its scattered contents while mildly clicking his tongue at his wife's unreasonable temper. Arun continued to pretend to be asleep, and with a sigh of patient resignation, Raju lay down on the floor mat. Arun then got up to offer him his place on the couch, and after some protests, Raju accepted. He was soon blissfully asleep, and Arun lay awake for hours, tossing and seething and aware of his mother doing the same in the next room.

Arun had grown up with such scenes, for his parents had been separated since he was two. Over the years, they had given him much occasion to ponder the relationship between men and women. Now he shared these thoughts with Dipti, though in a purely general way, careful not to give any insight into the particulars on which his theories were based. And that was the way she responded to him—also theoretically, with no reference to what she had observed between her own parents. For that marriage too, though enduring in the face of the world, had its own unmentioned, unmentionable areas on which no light was ever shed. Even in her own mind Dipti had veiled the scenes she had witnessed since her childhood—her father's outbursts when, for instance, a garment was not pressed well enough, or a stud was missing from his shirt. Then her mother would cower in a corner, with her arms shielding her head against the shoes he threw at her or the blows from his fist. Yet not half an hour later, when the defect in his toilet had been corrected and, starched and resplendent, he reclined among his guests, she was once more the modestly veiled hostess offering sherbet in silver vessels. It was only to Dipti that her mother sometimes whispered, in the dark and in secret, about the shame that it was the fate of wives to suffer: beatings and abuse, and also that other shame—she did not specify it further—that had to be undergone.

But Dipti knew, just as Arun did, that this was not how men and women should be together. They had formed their own idea on the subject, and it was the opposite of what they had observed between their parents. Their plan was to try out their theories on each other, and having already begun at the most basic, or essential, level in their afternoons together, they found that it was indeed a far cry from Raju's suitcase being flung out of Indu's bedroom, or that unspecified humiliation that Dipti's mother whispered to her about. Instead, they learned to grope their way around together in a completely new world that opened up for them, in infinite sweetness, at the touch of delicate fingers and the mingling of their pure breath.

"Yes, and if she gets pregnant?" Having found yet another blossom on her pillow, Indu could no longer refrain from confronting her son. He shrugged—his usual response to any of her questions he did not care to answer. But his father, who was still there and more and more on sufferance, interposed, "Ah, don't spoil it for him."

Indu seized the opportunity to turn on her husband. "Oh, yes—having ruined my life, now you send your son out to do the same to another innocent girl ... Not that *I* care what happens." She returned to Arun. "This time the shoe's on the other foot: it's not *you* who'll get pregnant and have to be married whether you want to or not."

If Raju had not been in such a precarious position in his wife's household—or if he had had the least bit of malice in him, which he did not—he could have pointed to himself as an unfortunate example of what Indu was talking about; for he, though still a student at the time, and from a very poor family, had been forced to marry Indu when she was found to be pregnant after their months of delight on her parents' roof.

This thought did arise in Indu, filling her with bitterness. "But, of course," she told her son, "you can always follow your father's fine example and never spend a single rupee on your child's support. Well, what else have you been doing your whole life long!" she said to Raju, as though he had dared utter a word of protest. "Sitting around in Bombay, running after film stars, while I'm working myself into a nervous breakdown to raise this child and give him a decent education fit for my father's grandson—oh, leave me alone, leave me alone!" she cried, though neither her husband nor her son had made a movement toward her. She ran into her bedroom—if there had been a door instead of only a curtain, she could have banged it—and flung herself face down on her bed.

Father and son remained together in silence. Raju would have liked to follow and comfort her but knew that his good intention would meet only with rejection. At last he said to Arun in a low voice, "Go. Go to her."

But Arun would not. It was not in his nature to dispense tender consolation to a woman in tears. He loved his mother fiercely and suffered because she did; but at this moment he also felt sorry for his father. Everything that Indu accused him of was true—Raju had got her pregnant and had never been able to provide for her and Arun, but had let them struggle along on their own. But this was because he couldn't provide even for himself, let alone a family, because he was—so his son thought with contempt and pity—just a poor devil. Raju would have liked to be generous, and if his pocket had not been chronically empty, he would have put his hand in it and pulled out bundles of bank notes to fling on his wife's table—"Here, take."

Dipti's feelings for her father were equally confused. Immensely proud of him for being what he was in the world, she could not forget what he was at home, behind closed doors, with her mother. At the same time, she blamed her mother for the way she submitted to his treatment, crouching under his fury like an animal unable to defend itself. Yet she was a proud woman, haughty and imperious with servants, with petitioners, with her husband's clerks; she passed among them like a queen, walking with slow majesty, as though her own massive weight and that of all her jewels and brocades were difficult to carry.

All this was before the scandal, which broke slowly, with a minor paragraph in one or two newspapers, and proceeded to mount, with headlines in all of them and photographs in the news magazines. At first Dipti's father brushed away the accusations against him; he joked with the visitors assembled around him on his veranda and made them laugh at the expense of journalists and other gossipmongers who had nothing to do in their offices except kill flies and make up lies about him. Then, when the stories persisted and questions began to be asked in Parliament, he grew angry and challenged his cowardly accusers—this too on his veranda amid his friends—to come out with one single fact against him.

And when they did—not with one but with many, how he had taken money from industrialists, businessmen, and foreign investors—he blustered and demanded proof. This was forthcoming; there were letters and diary entries as well as the huge unexplained wealth he had accumulated in movable and immovable properties. Denying everything, he demanded an inquiry, where he could, he said, easily prove himself as innocent as a newborn child. Cartoons of him in this latter role promptly appeared in the press. Although his resignation was demanded not only by the opposition but by his own party, he refused to submit it and hung on to his position, and to his official residence, until given the chance to clear himself before a committee to be appointed from the highest in the land.

During these difficult times, Dipti continued to attend her classes at the university, holding her head high. It was only when she was alone with Arun, during their afternoons in his mother's house, that she sometimes gave way to her feelings—and then only with silent tears, hiding her face against his chest. They never discussed the case and only referred to its essentials—as when she informed him that a committee of inquiry had been set up, or that her father had drafted his letter of resignation. Arun received the information without comment. Like Dipti herself, he had no desire to discuss the affair, and when other students did so within his hearing—and they spoke of it constantly, cynically, with jokes, everyone convinced of Dipti's father's guilt and gloating over it—he harshly reproved them. They nudged each other and grinned behind his back and called him "the son-in-law."

He also quarreled with his mother—his father was back in Bombay, where he claimed to have been hired as a scriptwriter for a major production—for Indu had strong opinions about the affair.

"What do you know about it?" he challenged her.

"I know what I read in the papers plus what I've seen with my own eyes. You're not trying to tell me," she went on, "that they were living on his salary? All that vulgar display—tcha, and everything in the lowest taste possible, of course, but what can you expect from people like that."

"People like what?"

She refused to be intimidated by his angry frown. "Uncultured, uneducated people. Peasants." She threw the word out with contempt.

"Oh, yes, only you're very grand and cultured."

"Yes, I am. And so are you." She tried to touch his face, glorying in his light complexion, his aristocratic features, but he jerked away and said, "And what about my father? Is he so very grand too?"

"Forget about your father. Think of your grandfather, who *he* was. God forgive me for what I did—dragged his name in the mud by marrying your father—all right, by getting pregnant from him, stupid, stupid girl that I was! . . . Arun, are you sure that you're doing everything—or she's doing everything—you know, so that she doesn't—?"

"Why, what are you afraid of?"

"That you'll ruin your life the way I ruined mine."

He wouldn't listen any more. He turned his back on her and went out of the house, through the compound, into the street, and walked for a long time through the lanes of the city, all the way to the old Mori Gate, where he sat outside a tea stall, smoking cigarettes, immersed in his thoughts.

A few evenings later he had to take the same walk again. It happened after his mother had come home from work and was cooking their dinner in the little attached shed that served as their kitchen. There was a commotion outside, and from the window he saw that the children of the compound, as well as one or two repressed little servant boys and the old sweeper woman employed by all the tenants, had come running to see the spectacle that was unfolding outside Indu's house. A long shiny car with satin curtains had drawn up; a chauffeur jumped out to open the back door, from which emerged Dipti's mother, in all the glory of an orange brocade sari with golden border and her full accoutrement of ornaments. Indu too had come to look but went quickly running in again to fix her hair, which was straggling over her forehead, damp with perspiration from her cooking. She was in the somewhat stained cotton sari she wore for housework, and with no time to change, she had to maintain her dignity with a display of the breeding and fine manners she had acquired in her father's house and at her convent school. The chauffeur carried in a basket of fruit and several boxes of pastries and other sweets, then returned to his car to chase away the children scratching at its bright blue enamel paint. Arun too had to chase them off when they peered in at the window of the living room to see what was going on. This was not anything that required Arun's presence, so he went out and repeated the walk to the tea stall outside Mori Gate, where he sat for a long time, not wanting to return and hear what Indu had to say about her visitor and the mission on which she had come.

But of course he had to hear all about it for days on end. Indu was indignant. "Yes, now they come running when they're in disgrace and think no one will take the girl off their hands. How old is she now?" Arun didn't answer, so she answered herself: "Old enough to have been married long ago, I'm sure, only now who'll have her?"

"Dipti wants to be a college lecturer."

"She may want, but her mother wants something different. . . . Who do they think we are?" She was incensed. "Who do they think they are?"

Arun did not tell Dipti about her mother's call or its purpose. Yet she may have suspected it—even saw signs of it on her afternoon visits. For days, the pastries that had been brought lay moldering in their golden boxes (Arun didn't like them, and his mother, who loved and could never afford them, was too proud to eat them). Dipti pretended not to see them. Secrets grew like a wall between her and Arun, making them often avoid each other's eyes. But as if to make up for the lack of words, their lovemaking became more passionate, and they clung to each other as if fearful of being torn apart. They also grew more careless, and when Indu came home from work, she sometimes found an undergarment forgotten on her bedroom floor.

Now she changed her tactics with her son. She sidled up to him with sighs; she took his hand in hers, and when he snatched it away, she smiled and said that, yes, he was too big now for her fondling. Smiling more, she recalled their past together, when he had been a little boy and had crept into her bed and kissed her and promised her that when he grew up, he was going to be a policeman and guard and take care of her forever. He squirmed at these memories—they were like little stab wounds in his soul—but she went right on, talking not of the past now but of the future she had always envisaged. No, he was not going to be a policeman, except perhaps a very high-ranking one who sat at a desk and controlled whole districts. A year from now, after he had graduated, he would take the entrance exam of the Indian Administrative Service, and he would pass with flying colors—ah, she knew it! Wasn't he his grandfather's grandson and with the same brains? He would rank among the country's ruling elite, rising from one eminent bureaucratic post to the next. As for marriage—everyone knew that once a boy had passed into that corps, all the best families would come running with their daughters and their dowries. Well, he was free to accept them or not, as he pleased, just as long as he kept himself unencumbered and at liberty to pursue all his advantages.

Arun broke away from her, for while she spoke she had drawn closer to him, winding a lock of his hair around her finger. "What is it?" he said through clenched teeth. "What are you trying to tell me?"

He knew it all too well, for it was his own thoughts she was expressing, digging up what he was trying to suppress and hide from himself.

Last year on her birthday Dipti had wheedled Arun to come to her house. "Yes, everyone knows you hate parties and all you do is sit there like a sick monkey—but you've *got to come!* Please? For me? Arun-ji?" He had sat at the side, watching the others dance, their friends from the college and some other friends she had from prominent political families like her own. Dipti herself was a terrific dancer and she had often tried to teach him, but he stubbornly refused to have anything to do with it. He frowned while he watched them, but secretly he enjoyed seeing her spin around on her slim feet, wriggling and waggling inside her tight silk kameez, her hair and long gauze veil flying behind her.

After her father's disgrace, she stopped having parties. In fact, it was Arun who asked her, a few days before her birthday, "Aren't you going to invite me?" She didn't answer for a while but turned away her face; then she said in a low voice, "Would you come?"

"What do you mean, would I come?" he answered her, doing his best to sound cross. "But of course if you don't want me—" Before he could finish, she had pressed her mouth against his, and he returned her kisses, pretending not to feel her tears on his cheek.

That evening he told his mother, "It's Dipti's birthday on Thursday."

"So?"

In the past, when he had gone to Dipti's birthday party, it was Indu who had bought the present for him to take. He relied on his mother's fine taste, and she always got a discount at the handicrafts emporium where she worked; besides, he had no money of his own.

"Don't tell me they're having a party," Indu said. "Surely they wouldn't, at such a time. And who would go to their house anyway."

"*I*'m going."

"You'll be the only guest then."

"Good. Get me a nice present to take; that's all I'm asking."

Later, while they were eating and she was serving him what she had cooked, she said, "I'll get her something very pretty, but give it to her at college. Don't go to their house," she pleaded, when he pretended not to understand.

He raised his eyes from his plate and looked at her. He had beautiful eyes, full of manly intelligence. She melted with tenderness for him, and pride, and also fear that he would not fulfill her hopes for him. "Oh, I feel sorry for her, poor girl," she said. "And I've always liked her, you know that. But people are very cruel—the world's very cruel, once you've lost your place in it." She stared into the distance for a moment, as though into her own past, before continuing, "If you go, her mother will get a wrong idea.... Why aren't you eating?" for he had pushed his plate away and got up.

"Just get me a present," he said and walked away from her.

She did bring a very beautiful gift for Dipti—even better than anything she had brought for her before—and Arun took it there. Although, as Indu had predicted, he was the only guest to celebrate Dipti's birthday, her mother had attempted to reproduce the atmosphere of previous occasions. The servants had been made to shine the silver and wash the chandeliers, and the pink birthday cake she had ordered was as huge as for the previous contingent of thirty guests. But she did not manage to dispel the fog of gloom that had settled over the house—not even when the twenty birthday candles were lit and flickered on their pastel stems over the lake of pink icing with its festive inscription in green. Dipti did her best to be cheerful and smiling, in gratitude to Arun for having come and also to her mother for her efforts. These never ceased; the mother bustled about and gave orders to the servants and, a fixed smile on her face, tried to get her husband and Arun to join her in singing "Happy

Birthday," and when they wouldn't, she sang it by herself. But most of her hard work was expended on Arun, for whom she couldn't smile enough. She had always been gracious to him, to demonstrate her acceptance of him as Dipti's friend, but now there was something desperate in her attitude, as if she were not bestowing but herself craving acceptance.

Dipti's father, too, had graciously patronized Arun in the past, sometimes singling him out among the crowd of admirers to address him with his pungently humorous remarks. Now Arun was their sole recipient, for there was no one else to hear them. And just as the mother had ordered the same size cake as for a large party, so the father, as voluminous as ever in his starched white muslin, spread out all his store of comment and conversation for Arun's sake alone. Supplying great gusts of laughter himself, he did not notice that Arun could only summon the faintest smile in response to his best jokes. And then, when he changed his topic and with it his mood, he needed no response other than his own mighty anger surging up in him. This was when he spoke of his case and of his enemies who had brought it against him; and from there he went on to announce what he would do to all of them, once he had cleared his good name and confounded all their schemes and dirty tricks. His voice rose; his face swelled out in a fearful way. Dipti implored, "Daddy!"' while his wife laid a hand on his arm to restrain him. "Leave off," she said. Then his anger burst like a boil: "Leave off! I'll show you how I'll leave off when I've crushed them under my feet and plucked out their eyeballs and torn out their tongues—rogues! Liars! I'll show them all. I'll teach them such a lesson—" His hands fumbled in the air as though to pluck down more threats—and then fumbled in a different way, like those of a drowning man attempting to save himself. His face swollen to a monstrous color, his words having changed to a gasp, he keeled over in the throne-like chair on which he was seated. His wife screamed; servants came running. Dipti and Arun tried to prevent him from falling out of the chair, holding his huge throbbing body in their arms. Bereft of his guidance, everyone was calling out confused orders; several hands plucked at him to undo the studs on his kurta. "I'm dying," he gasped. "They've killed me."

Dipti's father did not die, but he had suffered a stroke and was taken to hospital. There, he lay in a private room, monstrous and immobile, while his wife sat at his feet, moaning, "What will become of us?" The sight and sound of her drove him mad, but he could neither shout nor throw things at her, and she refused to be driven away. His eyes swiveled imploringly toward Dipti, who had taken over the duty of caring for him. Fully occupied with her father, she could no longer attend her classes, and once or twice Arun visited her in her father's hospital room. But he had always been impatient of anyone's sickness—whenever Indu felt unwell, she suppressed it in his presence as long as possible—and the sight of Dipti's father in his present state was intolerable to him. And in a different way what was almost worse was the mother groaning, "What will become of us?" and then looking with begging eyes at Arun, as though he alone held the answer to that question.

The final examination was drawing near, and Arun no longer had time to visit the hospital, or time for anything except his studies. His mother was delighted with the way he completely devoted himself to his work, and she did everything she could to encourage him. She fed him with his favorite foods, and in order to buy special delicacies for him, like ham or cheese, she gave up taking a rickshaw to work and went by the public transport—though secretly. She knew it would upset him to think of her in the reeking, overcrowded bus, being pushed and even pinched, for she was still attractive enough to draw such unwanted attention. It was her ambition—and his too, though he never spoke of it—that he should repeat the success of her father, who, in the same examination more than half a century earlier, had stood first in the whole university. The gold medal he had won then was one of her most precious possessions. These days she took it out frequently and gazed at it in its velvet-lined case, and also left it open on the table where she served Arun his meals. She was in an unusually good mood, and was completely free of the headaches and depression that so often plagued her.

Unfortunately, Arun's father, Raju, again turned up unexpectedly at this time, completely broke, for the film script he had set his hopes on had fallen through. But he was as cheerful as ever, and although he tried to be respectful of his son's studies, he could not refrain from expressing the thoughts tumbling around in his lively mind, or humming the tunes that came bubbling up there. He inquired after Dipti, and when he heard what had happened and how she had had to drop out of college, he shook his head in pity for her.

His thoughts reverted to her at odd moments. For instance, at night, while he was lying on the couch and Arun sat over his studies at the table, he suddenly said, "But she was a pretty girl. Really special. Intelligent but oomphy too."

Arun looked up, frowning. "What sort of word is that?"

"Oh, you know—like in 'She's oomphy—toomphy—just my moomphy,' " and he sang it, in case Arun didn't know this popular Hindi film song.

Indu thumped on the wall. "Are you disturbing Arun?"

"Oh, no. I'm helping him with his physics!" Raju called back. After a while, he spoke again. "How you must miss her—oh, oh, terrible! I know with Indu, when I had measles—can you imagine a youth of nineteen going down with measles—for three weeks I couldn't see her and I thought I would surely die with longing for her ... Yes, yes, all right!" he called when Indu thumped again. "I'm already asleep!"

After a few days of this, Arun complained to his mother, "He's driving me crazy." That night, when Raju already lay on the couch that was his allotted space, she called him into the bedroom. Raju raised his eyebrows at his son in pleased surprise. Arun too was surprised, and more so as the minutes passed and Raju was not sent out again. Arun found it difficult to return to his books. His attention was strained toward the other room; he heard their voices rising in argument till they shushed each other and continued their fight in whispers. Finally these too ceased, but by now Arun was completely incapable of concentrating on his work. What were they doing in there? He could not hear a sound. He walked up and down and cleared his throat to make them remember he was there; they continued silent, as though holding their breath for fear of disturbing him. He was no longer thinking of them but only of the room and its bed, on which they were together as he and Dipti had been together so many afternoons.

Dipti's father was in the news again when the results of the inquiry about him were made public. He had been found guilty on every count—taking money from interested parties, acquiring properties, accepting imported cars, and going on shopping trips to Hong Kong in return for favors received—and the report expressed itself in the strongest terms on his conduct. Although he was named as the prime culprit, several senior bureaucrats were drawn into the same web of accusations, as were other members of the cabinet. The whole government was brought under suspicion, and the opposition clamored for its resignation while frantic meetings were held at the highest level to save the situation. By then he had been discharged from the hospital and lay helpless and speechless on his bed at home, with his wife at his feet and Dipti ministering to his needs. No newspapers were allowed into his room, and when he made signs to ask for them, everyone pretended not to understand. All this time Arun had not seen or spoken to Dipti. He had tried to phone her once, from the college—he had no phone at home—but he knew she was in her father's room, with both parents present, so it was difficult for him to know what to say. And while he was groping for words, other students waiting behind him for the phone kept saying, "Come on, hurry up." After that he had not tried to contact her again.

When the report about her father came out, he had to listen to a lot of discussion about it but refused to participate, either at college or at home. When Indu said she had known it all along, that one look at the way they lived had told her it was all based on bribery and corruption, he cut her short with "You don't know what you're talking about."

"It's all here—in black and white."

"Oh, yes," he sneered. "You're just the type to believe everything that's written in some rag of a newspaper."

"*The Times of India*," she protested—but he was already out of the house and on one of his furious walks.

He had not yet returned when his parents were getting ready for bed. "He's thinking of the girl," Raju said to Indu in the bedroom, where he was still allowed to remain. "He feels for her—poor child; what is her future now? He loves her," he concluded in a musing, sentimental voice.

"He doesn't see her. Of course he doesn't! He's much too busy studying for his exam to waste his time on a girl."

Raju smiled. "Time spent on a girl is never wasted."

"That's your philosophy, but thank God it's not his."

"Yes, thank God," Raju echoed but continued smiling. His arms clasped behind his head, his eyes gazing at the ceiling, he began to recite, in a soft poetic voice: " 'My thoughts buzz like bees around the blossom of your heart—' "

"Sh-sh," she said, putting her hand over his mouth. "He's come home. Arun?"

She had to call twice more before Arun answered, "What do you want? Why do you have to keep disturbing me?"

"Are you studying?"

"Well, what do you think I'm doing?"

"He's studying," Indu said to Raju. She took her hand from his mouth. "Go on, but keep your voice down."

Raju continued, " 'My sting is transformed into desire to suck the essence of your beauty.' Do you like it?"

"Is it something you made up? I don't know why you can never think of anything except bees and flowers."

"Should I turn off the light?"

She assented, yawning to show how tired she was. "I must get to sleep. I have to be up early to go to work, unlike some people."

But once the light was off, it turned out she wasn't so tired after all, and although they tried to make no noise, they became so lively together that Arun in the next room had to cover his ears in an effort to muffle the sounds from the next room as well as those pounding in his head.

Next day Arun had an important pre-exam tutorial, but instead of attending, he went to see Dipti. He prepared himself to find her house as silent and gloomy as on her birthday, but instead it was in turmoil. They were moving out. Having lost his official position, the father also lost his official residence, and all its contents were being carried into cars and moving vans parked around the house. In supervising this operation, Dipti's mother had regained her former bustling, domineering personality. She was on the front lawn, fighting with a government clerk who had been sent to insure that no government property was removed. Whenever he challenged a piece of furniture being carried away, she told him that whatever was not theirs by private purchase had been earned by years of selfless public service, and, overruling his protests, she waved the coolies on with a lordly gesture.

Arun found her attitude to him completely changed. She greeted him haughtily, and when he tried to enter the house in search of Dipti, she barred his way. She told him that her daughter was busy, and, working herself up, went on indignantly, "My goodness, the girl has a sick father to look after, and here we are in the middle of a move to a big house of our own, not to mention other important family matters. You can't expect to walk in here whenever you please to take up our time."

Arun flushed angrily but was not to be put off. When she turned away to argue some more with the clerk, he strode past her into the house. He picked his way among sofa sets, chandeliers, and china services, through the courtyard full of packing cases and cooking pots, to the family rooms at the back of the house. All the doors here were wide open except one; he did not hesitate to turn its handle, and found himself in the father's room. The invalid had been placed in an armchair, with Dipti beside him, feeding him something out of a cup.

Her reception of him made Arun even more angry than her mother's had. "What a lovely surprise," she said in a bright, social voice. "And I was thinking of you only yesterday."

"I was thinking of *you*," he replied, but in a very different tone, his voice lowered and charged. "That's why I'm here."

"I was going to send you a note—to wish you good luck. For your finals. Aren't they next week? You must be so jittery, poor Arun."

"I have to talk to you."

"One more spoon, Daddy, for me." She put it in his mouth, but whatever was on it came dribbling out again.

"I must see you. Alone. Where can we go?" He didn't know if Dipti's father understood anything or not, and he didn't care. He thought only to leap over all the barriers between Dipti and himself—her huge helpless father, the house in upheaval, her mother, and, most of all, Dipti's manner toward him.

Her mother came in. She addressed Arun: "You must leave at once. You can see we're very busy." To Dipti she said, "The jeweler has come. I told him it's a bad day, but now he's here, we may as well look at what he's brought. There's not much time left."

"Not much time left for what?" Arun asked Dipti, ignoring her mother.

Dipti had her back to Arun, and instead of answering him, she scooped up the food from her father's chin back into his mouth.

Her mother told her, "Don't forget those people are sending a car for you in the afternoon. I said where is the need; we have plenty of cars of our own, but they insist. They like to do everything right—naturally, they can afford it. I'll call the jeweler in here; he can spread it out on the bed for us to see."

"It'll disturb Daddy."

But her mother went to the door to call for the jeweler. Quick as a flash, Arun drew near to Dipti and bent down to breathe into her ear. "Tomorrow. Four o'clock." She still had her back to him, and he laid one finger on the nape of her neck. It was the lightest touch, but he felt it pass through her like an electric current, charged with everything that had always been between them.

But it so happened that Raju stayed home the next day. Usually he accompanied his wife when she left in the morning and then remained in the center of town for the rest of the day, calling on friends, sitting with them in their favorite coffee houses, enjoying himself. But that day he had a cold, and, as always when he was sick, he looked at Indu with piteous eyes that said, "What has happened to me?" Before leaving for the office, she rubbed his chest with camphor and tied a woolen scarf around his neck. She left tea ready brewed for him on the stove, and two little pots of food she had prepared. He stayed in bed, mostly asleep; but as the day wore on, he became more cheerful, and by afternoon he had almost forgotten about his cold.

Arun arrived just before four, and as soon as he entered, he heard his father singing a lyric to himself, in that swooning way he had when deeply moved by a line of verse. "What are you doing here?" Arun said, in shock.

Raju stopped singing and pointed to the scarf Indu had tied around his neck. He coughed a little.

"Oh, my God," Arun said in such despair that Raju assured him in a weak voice, "It's just a cold, maybe a little fever." He felt his own forehead. "Ninety-nine. Perhaps a hundred."

There was a soft knock on the living room door, and Arun ran to admit Dipti. "Who is it, Arun? Has someone come?" Raju called from the bedroom. Dipti's eyes grew round in distress, and with the same distress Arun said, "My father has a cold."

Raju came shuffling out of the bedroom, and when he saw Dipti, he held his hands to cover the crumpled lungi in which he had slept all night and day. "Oh, oh!" he cried in apology. "I thought you were Indu come home early from the office. She was very anxious about me when she left."

But he quickly recovered and began to compliment Dipti on her appearance. She was dressed in pale torquoise silk, with little spangles sewn on in the shape of flowers; she also wore a pair of long gold earrings set with precious stones. "Are they rubies?" asked Raju. "All set around a lovely pearl. They say that older women should wear pearls, here, around their throat"—he touched the woolen scarf—"but I love to see them on a young girl."

"You could go back to bed," Arun suggested.

"And leave you alone here with this pearl?" A flush like dawn had tinted Dipti's face and neck. "Anyway, I feel much better. Completely cured by the sight of beauty, which is the best medicine in the world for a poor susceptible person like myself. I don't have a heart," he informed Dipti. "I have a frail shivering bird in here, drenched by the rains and storms of passion."

Arun exclaimed impatiently, but when he saw Dipti, still freshly flushed, smile at Raju's extravagance, irritation with his father turned to anger against Dipti. "You should ask her some more about those earrings," he said. "Ask her if they're her wedding jewelry—" Her flush now a deepest rose, Dipti's hands flew to her ears. "What was he doing there yesterday with you and your mother?" he challenged her more harshly. "What had he come to sell?"

"Whatever they are," Raju said, "she's come here wearing them for you. I wish I could say it were for me, but even I'm not such a conceited optimist. But I'm really feeling much better, and I think I might just lie and rest here a little bit on this couch. I won't disturb you at all—I'll shut my eyes, and I shall probably be fast asleep in a minute. But if you're afraid of waking me, you could go in the other room and keep very quiet in there."

He did exactly what he said—stretched himself on the couch and shut his eyes so that they would think of him as fast asleep. But they had no time to think of anything. Before they had even got into the next room, Arun was already tugging at her beautiful clothes, and she was helping him. It was many weeks since they had last been together, and they were desperate. Their youth, their lust, and their love overflowed in them, so that their lovemaking was like that of young gods. It is not in the nature of young gods to curtail their activities, and they forgot about keeping quiet and not disturbing Raju.

He *was* disturbed, but in a way he liked tremendously. He lay on the couch, partly listening to what was going on next door but mostly in his own thoughts. These made him happy—for the young people in the bedroom, of course, and for *all* young people, and these included himself. Raju was nearly forty; He did not have an easy life. He told no one about the many shifts he had to resort to in Bombay to keep himself going in between assignments, which often fell through or were never paid for. Nevertheless, he had not changed from the time he had been a student in Delhi and used to creep up to the roof of Indu's parents' house. She often had to put her hand over his mouth to keep him from waking everyone up, for in his supreme happiness he could not refrain from singing out loud. He knew all the popular hits as well as more refined Urdu lyrics, and they all exactly expressed what he felt about her and the stars above them and the white moonlight and scent of jasmine drenching the air around them.

But now the sounds from the next room changed. Raju propped himself up on his elbow. "I'll tear them off!" his son was saying. He was back on the subject of the earrings. The girl screamed, and Raju sprang up, ready to intervene. He knew there was something in his son that was not in himself—a bitter anger, perhaps transmitted to him by his mother during the years she had struggled to make a living for both of them. But somehow the girl pacified him, or it may have been his own feeling for her that made him hold his hand. She pleaded, "What else could I do? Arun, what could I do? With all that was happening, and Daddy's illness."

"You wanted it yourself. Because they're rich. Ah, don't touch me."

"Yes, they're rich. They can help Daddy."

"Who are they, anyway?"

She hesitated for a moment before replying, "They're Daddy's friends." He had to insist several times for a more definite answer before she came out with the name. Then Arun said, "Great. Wonderful." And Raju too on the other side of the wall was shocked, for the name she had mentioned was that of a tremendously wealthy family, notorious for their smuggling and other underworld activities and involved in several political scandals, including that of Dipti's father.

Dipti said with a touch of defiance. "They helped us when there was no one else." But her voice trembled in a way that made Raju's heart tremble, but not Arun's; he continued to speak harshly. "And you're madly in love with the boy . . . Why don't you answer!"

"I've met him twice. Arun, don't! I'll take them off. Here." She unhooked the earrings before he could tug at them again. He flung them across the room. One of them rolled under the partitioning curtain into the next room. Raju looked at it lying there but did not pick it up.

Arun said, "It's like selling yourself. It *is* selling yourself."

Again she spoke defiantly. "As long as it helps my parents in their trouble."

"Yes, and what about being a college lecturer? That was just talk. All you want is to be rich and buy jewelry and eat those horrible cream cakes."

After a while she said, in a very quiet voice, "That's not what I want."

"Then what? Don't try to fool me. I know you as no one else knows you. As no one else ever will know you. You can never forget me. Never. Never."

"No. I shall never forget you." Then she broke out, "But what can I do, Arun! You tell me; what else can I do!"

And on the other side of the curtain, Raju's heart was fit to burst, and it was all he could do not to cry out to Arun, "Tell her!" He was almost tempted to show him. Ah, with what abandon Raju himself would have acted in his son's place; how he would have flung himself at the girl's feet and cried, "I'm here! Marry me! I'm yours forever!"

But Arun was saying something different. "I'll haunt you like a ghost. You'll keep reading about me in the newspapers, because I'm going to be very famous. If necessary, I'll go into politics to clean up our country from all these corrupt politicians and smugglers who are sucking it dry. You'll see. You'll see what I'll do."

"I have to go. Let me get dressed."

"Not yet. Five minutes. Ten."

Then there was no more talking and almost complete silence in the bedroom, so when Indu came home, she didn't know anyone was in there and said to Raju, "Why aren't you in bed?"

He laid a finger on his lips and glanced toward the other room. She followed his eyes and gasped when she saw the earring that had rolled from under the curtain. "Sh-sh-sh," said Raju.

"He's got that girl in there," Indu whispered fiercely.

"You needn't worry."

"What do you mean, not worry? His finals are next week."

"Oh, he'll do very well. He's your son, and your father's grandson."

And for the hundredth time in their life she said, "Thank God anyway that he hasn't taken after you. Let go of me. Let go." For he had seized her in his arms and pressed his lips against hers. She thought at first it was to silence her but relaxed as his kiss became more pressing and more passionate, as if he wanted to make it up to her for his shortcomings, and then, giving himself over completely, to make it up to all women for the shortcomings of all men.

Yusef Komunyakaa

Venus of Willendorf

She's big as a man's fist,
Big as a black-pepper shaker
Filled with gris-gris dust,
Like two fat gladiolus bulbs

Grown into a burst of twilight.
Lumpy & fertile, earthy
& egg-shaped, she's pregnant
With all the bloomy hosannas

Of love-hunger. Beautiful
In a way that forces us to look
At the ground, this squat
Venus in her braided helmet

Is carved from a hunk of limestone
Shaped into a blues singer.
In her big smallness
She makes us kneel.

Marjorie Sandor

Orphan of Love

It was early in the morning, early spring in Indiana, bitterly cold. Imagine elm trees, a smooth gray sidewalk without cracks—exactly the kind of small town neighborhood my father used to fantasize about when he was a kid in Chicago. He'd picture his parents dead, perished in a big slum disaster, fire, or flood, and himself standing on a street corner just like this: all alone with his little suitcase, free to select his new family purely by the look of their house. My father, Abe Gershon, was twenty-eight years old when he stood on the Shapiros' porch in the spring of 1941, a medical resident on his first house call, but it came to him again, the brief, secret indulgence of childhood: *I hereby choose this family.* His belly tightened as if he hadn't eaten for days. He tugged at his pants so they'd hang right, so the lady of the house wouldn't immediately see that he had a bum leg. (*Stricken, not bum,* his mother always said. *Hold your head up high.*) Then, just as he raised his hand to knock, the door opened and before him stood a housewife neatly aproned and delicately built, the opposite of his own mother. That's how he knew the future had arrived.

My father's last stories often began with a little coincidence like this, a moment in which the world rose up to meet his secret wish. He lay in his hospital bed, the corners of his mouth whitened and sticky as he took a sip of water. "Just let me tell you this," he'd say. "Here's something your mother doesn't know." After he was dead she didn't deny his stories, but she didn't say they were true, either. "From what I can gather," she said bitterly, "his family had a different policy about the truth."

But what if she had loved this about him when they first began? She'd have been hungry for any kind of drama after a childhood in that nice town, that neat house, with a father who couldn't end a story and a mother who refused to begin. This young doctor, on the other hand, gave his stories the bright colors, the simple lines of a Sunday school book: the baby in the bulrushes rescued by a princess; the boy left in a pit for dead, only to become king of his enemies. He must have told her almost nothing true, and the one time she insisted on seeing a picture of his parents, he had nothing to say about them. I've seen this photograph: did my father choose it because it gave nothing away? There is his father, slender and slope-shouldered, and his mother huge beside him, both their faces austere and unreadable like those of circus performers resting between shows. Maybe my mother felt a first little question rising then, though it would have been nothing she could put into words, easy enough to brush away.

But this is supposed to be my father's version, my father who on his deathbed wanted to tell me a love story. He began it there on the porch, the hero at the first enchanted door, taking a deep breath and holding out his hand to a handsome matriarch. My mother later insisted it was nothing so grand. Her father, a diabetic, had walked into a wall in the dark one night and stubbed his big toe—the danger of infection was high.

"Dr. Gershon, from the hospital," said my father briskly. "How's the patient feeling this morning?"

He must have made a complicated first impression, this young doctor, with his slenderness, his shabby overcoat, the square small mustache like a felt patch under his nose. Slightly fraudulent, but attractively so, in Grandmother Eva's memory. The slump to the shoulders hinted at the truth: a deep and driving loneliness, a fragility at the core that drew women. She saw it, but it worked on her anyway. She leaned toward him, lifting his name tag in two fingers.

"Jewish," she said. "Where are your people?"

"Dead," said the doctor. "Everybody dead but me."

It was a stroke of genius. "*Mein Gott*, what a world," she said, her face swept pale. Then she regained herself. "Please come in, Doctor, don't stand in the cold. Only be a little quiet going up the stairs—our Clara's a light sleeper."

What Eva said about her daughter wasn't true either, and she later claimed never to know why she said it. "I stand accused," she'd tell me, shrugging. But it matters as much as my father's orphan lie, because my mother's sleeping was the dangerous thing about her. Once she went under, none of us could wake her; she went down into dreams like a spelunker, roped herself down and took the rope too, and only came up when she was good and ready. On their honeymoon my father saw this for himself, a little truth that had been kept from him in courtship, the way other families keep secret some inherited defect or story of dishonor. Their first morning together, he awoke in the gray light to see that his wife had pulled her pillow down over her ears and was holding it there, hard. Later she assured him it was against the roaring of the falls, but by then he already suspected the truth, that she wasn't in love with him and maybe couldn't love anyone really. He'd watched her sleep, a reasonable bridegroom thing to do, had seen her come up and out of her dreams as if she'd been on the longest train ride of her life and he was a servant sent to meet her at the station. Her face was pale blue in the morning light, a haughtiness in it he hadn't seen before. What if she wasn't the warm-hearted girl she seemed in daylight? A crazy idea, but it wouldn't go away—the possibility of cruelty. This isn't something he told me, but what if it had stayed with him, making him feel secretly justified years later when he stepped into his own dangerous dream of love?

My mother was a dreamer, too. She remembered the morning of that first house call and how my father's footstep—the way he came down heavily on his good leg—entered her life first through dream. "I've forgotten half my life," she'd say. "Why do I remember that?" In the dream she was performing, but the music on the piano had just revealed itself to be an unknown and maniacal piece, and just offstage somebody else was playing a waltz, so she was forced into a mad duet, a hectic parody of the Bach two-part invention she was preparing in real life for her upcoming college recital. Dragging herself awake, she still heard the off-beat heavily in her head. She was amazed later when she saw who had made that sound in real life, how small and slender he was, with a comedian's sad eyebrows, and so thin she could circle his wrist with her fingers.

But not yet. By this time sunlight had reached her bed, a deceptively warm yellow light that didn't want to let her go. She listened, feeling exactly the way she did in dreams, or when playing certain piano pieces she knew by heart: in a resting state, but keenly alert to the nuances of some other language or logic. She couldn't shake the dreamer's feeling of being guided along a necessary path, even as she came awake and recalled that a doctor was expected this morning. She smiled a little to think of the pretty sight she'd make in her nightgown, but surely something bigger, some buried desire for drama, sent her toward the bedroom door, wanting a crisis, wanting consequence. She couldn't know this, at nineteen. She only knew that her hair was beautifully unkempt and that when she stepped into the hallway, sunlight would stream out with her.

So she appeared, a girl in a white nightgown and a flood of light, at the very moment the doctor gained the top of the stairs. She looked him dead in the eye, not at all demure, not even human, but pure commandment: *Go ahead and fall in love with me.*

Then part of her woke up to the flat facts of him—facts she was about to spend months denying to herself. He was a skinny young man with a limp and a sad face. His eyes were beautifully blue, but dog-desperate, out for whatever he could get. And there was that awful mustache. In frank dismay she put her hand to her mouth and rushed back into her bedroom.

For Abe Gershon, it didn't matter. A beautiful girl from a good family had at last appeared in his life. She was gone, vanished, but for a second he still saw the wide white fan of her nightgown curving in the light, a vision meant only for him. Then nothing but a pure empty hallway, bereft of her.

The thrill of rising action, of medical crisis and the tough decision—this is what mattered in my father's telling, for even as he unwrapped the thin bandage around Jake Shapiro's big toe, he knew that the foot could not be saved and that the amputation itself might kill the patient. But underneath all this, did he also realize that the moment he hospitalized my grandfather he would lose access to the mysterious, essential thing he'd begun to crave? He must have felt suddenly that he couldn't live without this family, this girl. He needed their world: the hall hat tree, the bannisters, the dark and heavy European furniture, the piano with the music so seriously opened. All of it was like a painting of the life he'd always felt he was meant for but kept from. His heart tightened painfully when he imagined Eva and the girl Clara eating supper alone after the funeral, and he caught himself again. The strength of this desire made him restless and embarrassed.

The next morning when he woke in his own dark, cramped apartment, he vowed that on this new day he would be completely professional. They must never know that suspense was devouring him, that already he'd imagined Clara paying him a little visit in his apartment and being overwhelmed with pity and admiration, perhaps letting him kiss her and touch her hair. He went so far as to arrange his few knickknacks and bachelor dishes to make his loneliness look provisional, the necessary monastic phase in the ambitious life. He deliberately bathed in cold water, fought the urge to light the little gas heater, even denied himself the pleasure of a coffee and a roll at the bakery, knowing that the denial would translate into a look of hunger and sadness that might arouse Mrs. Shapiro's sympathies, reminding her just barely of her own lost history. He knew instinctively that the mother must be won before the daughter.

When he arrived at the Shapiros' that morning, waiting for him on the kitchen table was a cup of coffee, placed just so, with a sugar bun, a boiled egg, and a little note from Eva: "Eat. You're too thin."

So from the moment he stepped over their threshold he was two people: the calm professional and the secret hunter, watching and waiting for opportunity. The house itself became a landscape to be learned, inch by inch: Eva's downstairs, with its square yellow kitchen, the quiet front parlor, and dining room; and Jake's sickroom upstairs, with its stark white simplicity and the enormous purple beech pressing itself against the windows, the flattened, childlike form of Mr. Shapiro in the bed like a stage prop in this unfolding drama. Abe felt almost pure in this room, as if he really had no other motive than to save this man's life; yet the silver instruments in his own medical case shone with a faint air of judgment. He distracted himself by imagining the one place not given him to see: Clara's bedroom at the end of the hall. It was a mystery to be savored, his image of it elaborately Victorian, lacy, virginal. He actually averted his gaze to delay the pleasure whenever he walked past her door on his way to the lavatory. It was too late when she finally let him see it, after they were engaged. She showed it to him casually, almost roughly, with no ceremony whatever, and he was overtaken by a brief, crushing disappointment. It was no Victorian dream but an ordinary girl's room of the time: cheap magazine posters of Clark Gable and Cary Grant, textbooks and homework scattered on a plain desk, a white chenille bedspread identical to his own.

My mother, this Clara, never repeated her sunlit sleepwalker act, but she couldn't shake the dreamer's hypnotic feeling of moving steadily, blindly forward. Years later, she couldn't describe it any other way; it refused to come clear. It had been as if some story under the story wanted to rise up. She only knew that in the three days that the young doctor had come to her house, the downstairs rooms had begun to take on a malevolent, alien personality, particularly the front parlor, where her piano stood. In a stifling silence, the furniture leered at her: the stiff velvet davenport, the heavy mahogany sideboard with its scrolled legs, and the antique monk's chair. On the sideboard sat a mortar and pestle of blood-red glass, with which Clara now felt a faint thrill of complicity.

But the piano, of all things, had turned against her. The yellow Schirmer volume of Bach's two-and three-part inventions—the sublimely balanced piece of counterpoint her teacher had chosen, with Eva's blessing, for the recital—had gone as mad as in her dream. Why couldn't anybody else see the way the dark notes crowded together in a violent caprice, never letting a person breathe?

Maybe Eva wouldn't have been surprised to hear this, if Clara had tried to talk to her. But Eva wasn't really that kind of mother; as the daughter of immigrants, she'd been raised to believe in the virtue of silence. It was supposed to make a child strong. So I imagine she herself was left in the dark, feeling as if someone had moved a favorite vase a little to the left. She'd have known only that something had altered in her domestic composition, that there was suddenly no place for her in the new symmetry of the sickroom. And she was forced, on top of everything else, to submit to Clara's sudden imitation of the ideal daughter. Did Eva sense some parody aimed at herself? Clara was at last getting up on time, dressing modestly in a white blouse and dark navy skirt, pulling her hair up and back in schoolgirl barrettes to stand across from the young doctor, so priestlike in his tunic, tenderly bathing Jake's foot. Why did the scene irritate Eva so? Even the young doctor seemed to be getting bigger and straighter shouldered, as if the house itself were imbuing him with new powers. He was, by now, briskly in charge. When he arrived at the front door he immediately stepped in, bowed politely if hurriedly, and moved right past Eva, even past the sugar bun and coffee. "Oh, I can find my way, thank you."

Eva was right, of course—right and wrong. Clara intended no parody. I know this much about her, and about being nineteen: it is enough work to quiet the dark shameful thrumming in your body, the velvet on your skin, the fingertips alive with sensation as your father lies there, possibly dying. He doesn't seem real, exactly—more like a test of your powers of concentration. The white sheet, the coverlet, his sticky lips as he opens them: *Oh, what will he say?* There is, with fathers, always the sense that they are about to tell you the one thing you need to know—a deep family secret, a hint for your future conduct in life—or maybe just lay a hand tenderly on your head, as if in blessing. Some things don't change: how pale and small a father can be when he is dying, how he gets impossibly smaller each day, his dark eyes in their deep lavender folds rarely opening. Every once in a while he opens them and gives you a look of deep surprise, as if you are the one keeping secrets. It takes him a whole minute sometimes to know you. "Daddy," you whisper, as you did when you were small. "What happened next?" But he shakes his head. "I wish I could remember," he says, with the plaintive, withholding smile of all his unfinished stories.

The only time Jake roused to his old self was during the house calls—of this, Abe was proud. At morning and evening, a manly, companionable air entered the room. The patient lifted his head slightly, tried again to smile. "I should've looked where I was going, eh, Doc?" he murmured each time, and Abe patted his arm and laughed. Meanwhile, Clara couldn't look at the doctor without feeling a terrible excitement, mixed with gratitude for his kindness, for his comfortable authority with her father. Where had he come from? What had he lived through to be this strong? She must have wanted that life, whatever it was, and didn't dare look at him for fear she'd give herself away. She looked at anything else: the debriding instruments, the doctor's hands as he examined and cleansed the toenail and the entire foot, clipped the nail with a single decisive stroke. She was ready to fetch basins of warm water, to fumble in his medical bag for the gauze and a tiny scalpel. She felt as if she were in training for a new life, a real, deliciously raw and gritty one. That evening, as she sat in the bedside chair watching him unwrap her father's bandage, she pictured a little scene in which he asked her to please follow him into the small upstairs lavatory. There the young *lame* doctor would hurriedly push up her convent-blue skirt, back her up against the lavatory wall, reach swiftly and professionally around her back to undo her brassiere. Her heart was pounding; she looked at her father to steady herself.

"Damn it," said the doctor.

A fetid odor filled the room, as if a whole basket of fruit had rotted at once. She choked, and the next instant Abe Gershon's handkerchief was in her hand, the clean, slightly peppery smell of it saving her.

"I thought we could beat it," he said. "I really did."

Clara wasn't listening. She was looking at the dark yellow and violet stain on her father's big toe, the faint red streaks that seem to have arrived on the pale skin all at once, between the hours of the doctor's visit. How was it possible? Should she have been watching? She thought of the lavatory scene and flushed hot; wildly, she wondered if she'd brought on the infection herself by her sordid desires. Absurd, of course—she wouldn't confess this fear to anyone, certainly not to me—but surely it lay beneath the surface, weaving itself through the tangled lines of her desire for ravishment and escape.

The doctor seemed so sensitive to everything she felt. "Come downstairs with me, into your mother's kitchen," he said. "You need a break, and I can give you a little job, to help out. Has your mother got oranges?"

A few minutes later she held in her hand one of Eva's last winter oranges, and Dr. Gershon stood behind her, his own hand cupping hers as she squeezed the orange's skin into a little mound and plunged a hypodermic in. A strand of sunlight came through the window, lighting the orange and their four hands in a stark, vivid light: hers so pale, his darker, with the dark smooth hairs of his wrists emerging from the long white sleeves of his tunic. It took forever, this moment, long enough for her to fall in love with his hands—small but slightly square, a shape that suggested capability, authority, like those of the royal figures on cards, firmly gripping a scepter. Briskly, professionally, he let go of her. "Practice makes perfect, just like with your piano." His offhandedness was breathtaking; she ached to hear it again, to be destroyed by it.

But the doctor was worrying about his own next obstacle: how to get back upstairs with dignity. The house was terribly quiet, as if to test him. The ankle of his bum leg would of course click loudly all the way up the stairs, back to the sickroom and her father.

It did, but this was Abe Gershon's strange luck. Clara fell in love with that, too.

After the incident of the orange, Eva largely vanished from their stories, upstaged by a slant of pale sunlight, a piece of fruit. Jake Shapiro was admitted to the hospital, his case turned over to the surgeon, and the house seemed empty without his constant quiet presence. Eva stayed at the hospital herself most of the day, trapped in doorways, waiting rooms, straight chairs. For the first time, she was a receding figure in her daughter's life, and in those two days Clara experienced waves of euphoria, the sudden, wild conviction that freedom was possible. She opened her bedroom window at bedtime so that she could hear, in the dark, the minor notes of fast spring rain, and be awakened by first light, by mad birds, to watch the green emerging in the giant purple beech that leaned against the side of the house.

The doctor came to their house once more, briefly, to answer questions about the surgery and to offer what hope he could. But he was strangely formal and distant, and Clara felt a panic rising, the kind she remembered from childhood after guests departed, when the house fell into a deep, muffled, smoky silence that felt somehow permanent, and she had sobbed unconsolably. Now, with the strange irrational certainty of nineteen, she felt that if the doctor left her house, he would never come back, and she'd be trapped with her mother in that silence for life. So while he talked to Eva that evening, Clara wandered to the piano and tried a melancholy Chopin. She wanted to lure him to her like a siren, drive him into a hopeless passion, then reward him just a little. She sensed that the moment was crucial, that he had lost an important weapon: he could no longer deflate her power with a bit of instruction, a gentle sickroom admonishment. At the time she believed that in matters of love he was an infant, that she could destroy him.

He had, however, one weapon left. As she walked him to the kitchen door at the end of the visit, he said, "I can't ask you out while I'm on your father's case," and looked at her steadily for the first time.

"I know," she said, looking right back.

It is almost beautiful to me, and brave, the way neither of them would admit anything. They stood at the edge of Eva's domain, Clara on the top of the back steps, curving her foot seductively over the chipped concrete, with Abe just below her. It was as if a spell had been broken, or a new one cast, and I want to keep them there, at the exquisite edge, and tell them to be careful what they wish for. But it's too late, of course. Clara couldn't take her eyes off the doctor's hands, imagining for them a slightly alarming efficiency as she fell into fantasy: how he might remove her underclothes right there, his hands icy and swift on her tender skin. And what if her mother caught them, was wounded unto death by the sight of their violent passion?

But Eva left them alone, quite deliberately. This makes sense: he was, after all, going to make a good living as a doctor. She judged him to be a gentle, well-meaning young man, and Clara, left to her own devices, could easily do worse. So Clara was left on her own, without props or high drama, as the doctor raised his damp palms to her face and kissed her. It was an ordinary kiss, slightly hurried and a little too moist, and this, along with the lack of audience, irritated my mother. She was seized by restlessness, a bitter disappointment rising up.

The kiss was over. She lifted herself on her toes, narrowed her eyes, and smiled at him. "If I were you," she said, "I'd get rid of the mustache. It makes you look like Hitler."

My mother instantly regretted those words, and she always would. She felt it for life, a single corrupt little cell too far down to reach, suspended in the quiet depths of what she, too, had wanted to be a love story. How is it that something so small has a way of growing? At first there would have been just a slight souring that each of them felt, secretly, as they went about their lives. They saw each other only in the hospital corridors now, but they both felt it, the sudden tilt of romance into some other struggle, potent and unnameable. Abe felt shelved, somehow, and it was out of this that he played the aloof, distant professional until she was forced to lean, conciliatory, his way. Clara stopped him in the corridor outside her father's ward.

"I didn't mean it the way it sounded," she said.

"Never mind," he replied.

"How poor are you?"

He nearly (but not quite) smiled her own father's familiar, withholding look. "You don't really want to know."

"Oh, but I do," she said breathlessly. "I do."

She dressed carefully for her visit, in the blouse and convent-dark skirt she'd worn in the sickroom, and told Eva she was just going to run up to the college to check out the big piano. All the way to the doctor's apartment, she wasn't thinking of the doctor but of the exhilaration of the lie, the brief, almost violent sensation of freedom. Then she was at his door, and he was opening it, and she could see inside. The apartment was not quite as squalid as she'd imagined, and this vaguely disappointed her. But Abe, in his own way, had made preparations for this moment. He'd lit all his lamps and set out a teapot and two cups, and at last the details of the solitary life began to pull on her as they always did: the notion of a person choosing things for himself was beyond her experience. What she didn't know, of course, was that he was putting on a little show of his own, laying out a cozy bachelor scene: a select few pots and utensils neatly arranged to suggest self-sufficiency and hardihood, when in fact he took all his meals at the hospital. The nuns there felt a tremendous tenderness for him, as if he were the true invalid and their patients all imposters. It didn't matter, however; the possibility of ravishment was rising in Clara again, gorgeously blooming in her like a light, extending outward to the thin, ambitious young doctor bent helplessly over his teapot. Why else would she have moved toward him then, like the sleepwalking girl of that first morning, dreaming for herself the image of a girl from a life freer than her own? Such a girl would not hesitate to express herself. She came up behind him and put her hands lightly on his shoulders. That was all she had to do, and she knew it. He turned with the single swift gesture of her fantasies and put his hands on her waist. "You," he said.

"You yourself," she said with a teasing smile, and they leaned toward each other in the first natural movement they'd ever made together, leaning, leaning, their two stories in harmony at last—when there was a knock on the door.

The cold that ran through my father's body cannot be imagined.

"Can you hide?" he asked. "In that closet there?" He opened the door and shoved books and shoes aside; in his haste he bumped up against the hanging clothes so that everything, the whole meager display of shirts and trousers, cascaded down over his head.

At the time, my mother couldn't believe it. She tried to laugh as she got into the closet, but in their bitter middle years, when the silence of her childhood slipped into mine, it was the only story she'd tell about their courtship.

"It wasn't real life," she'd say, shrugging. "It was vaudeville."

The visitor, of course, was his dead mother—all two hundred pounds of her pressed into a blue-sprigged shirtdress and tiny pumps. Years later he'd struggle to sit up in bed to tell me this, his eyes briefly bright with anger, and I could see that she was the real story of his life, the one he couldn't get rid of. She showed up at his door because she had to, because she was the one person in the world who mortified him, and because of something my mother didn't yet know (and Eva only faintly suspected): her son was a terrible worry, somehow vulnerable, always tottering on the edge of incompetence. He had a look, which Eva had noticed from the start, a brave fraudulence that was keeping him from sinking into despair, a despair that would wait for him as long as he lived, looking for a way in.

His mother shifted uncomfortably at the door. She was not yet the size she'd be when she was my grandmother, but to my father she must have been big enough. The look on her face was eager, confident, as if she'd just stepped out of the kitchen and one of her card games to check up on him, to see if he needed a drink of water, or any little thing. What was it about this mother, of all possible mothers? She had a terrible, pure physicality about her, like a big rock in the road you can't get around. He told me how, when he was small, she used to hoist him up the easiest way, around the waist. His shirt rode up to his chest, and her big arm scraped roughly across his goose-fleshed belly. She carried him thus, log fashion, around the apartment. It made him shiver to think of it.

She'd already deposited her suitcase in the hotel downtown, she said, looking all around the room. She'd never dream of imposing. But surely he had time for a bite of lunch between patients. She winked broadly, lewdly, this uncanny mother. She'd noticed a nice restaurant by the train station—schnitzel, on a cardboard sign in the window, like a miracle. They wouldn't have to go out. Surprise! She had it right there in a box—and she held out the box with a magician's flourish, a box with a dark spreading stain along its rim.

"Actually, I'm expecting company, people from the hospital," he said. "Can I come to you at your hotel in an hour?"

She eyed him up and down.

"Mama—" he said. "Please don't say anything."

"I wouldn't dream of it," she said, winking again. "I'll be at the hotel when you're done."

Her coarseness astonished him, the way she slammed into the blunt ugly side of any life he might hope to have. He shut the front door and opened the closet to let Clara out. Not knowing what to expect, he braced himself for the end. But luckily there were tears in his eyes—genuine enough—as he slipped his arm around her waist. The tears must have moved her, for she shuddered against him. She sobbed once and buried her head on his shoulder like a daughter.

"You lied," she said, "about your *family*."

"Wouldn't you, with a mother like that?" he said.

What would have happened if his mother hadn't shown up—if, in fact, she had really been dead? Would there have been a luxurious slow rightness, a deepening of feeling? Could they have made love, and what sort of lovers would they have been? As it is, I imagine both of them to have been secretly relieved. My mother told me how she was raised by Eva to live in terror of "the sex act," and my father had never been with a virgin. The moment could have been disastrous if rushed.

Still, he had to do something. "I can't afford a ring right now," he told her, trembling. "But my intentions are honorable."

He must have seemed so deliciously unschooled. She raised her face to his. "Sh-sh," she said. "It's OK," She smiled, still faintly touched by his quaint, bookish phrase.

Not for years would they discuss it, my mother and father, but I think at the time she saw the lie as a mark in his favor. After all, she'd wished her own mother dead more than once, and he'd taken an incredible risk; it was oddly touching. A little worrisome, of course, but she could chalk it up to his struggle to rise in the world, the odds against him in every way: poverty, the leg ruined by polio, his slightly pathetic Jewish face. So she let it go, that hint of uncertainty that wouldn't quite show itself.

How is it that life conspires to make us rush past the moment that might illuminate our actions, that little spindly root already reaching up and out to make the future? Whatever the answer, it was at this precise moment that the crisis my father had anticipated began. The surgery was over, and Jake Shapiro was running a high fever. He was in shock, in and out of consciousness. In his brief awakenings, he had only one thing to say: "Make sure Clara plays the concert. She has to play." Then he opened his eyes only for Abe, who refused to leave Jake's side. Twice Eva put her hand on Abe's arm and let it rest there as if he were her own beloved son.

Meanwhile, Abe was avoiding his own mother, who was supposed to be dead but hovered at the margin of his new life, threatening to break out. He needn't have worried. She was nobody's fool; she must have sensed that he was on the verge of some conquest, and that it would be dangerous to get in his way. Maybe she was proud of his ruthless drive, even the insult to her. Because it was only that, a certain ruthlessness, that would stave off bad luck for her boy. She was a card player, after all; she understood the necessity of keeping things close to the chest. But two can play at this game, as she was fond of saying. So she refused to tell him when she was planning to leave town.

Clara's recital was the only pure thing in all this, and Abe was grateful for it, a focus away from his mother and from the patient's ghostly shape under a sheet, the stump of his right leg raised in a harness above his little white bed, his face blanched, his hands clammy and restless on the coverlet. When Abe offered to chaperone Clara to and from the college concert hall so that Eva could stay at Jake's side *in case there is any change*, Eva pressed her lips together. Did she feel a faint suspicion, an urge to refuse the doctor's offer? But Jake had opened his eyes. "Can you bring her here first? I want to see her in her dress before I die."

"Don't talk like that," said Eva. "Let them take a picture."

But Jake's eyes were wide open in a terrible lucidity she couldn't ignore.

So it was that the next night my father found himself escorting a young woman in black silk through the hospital corridors. Her hair was swept up and back in a chignon, her eyes bright green against icy skin, a late winter beauty in April. The nuns and other doctors winked slyly at him, and he was buoyed up by pride, by the feeling that she had transformed him, too.

Eva backed away from the bed as Clara approached, giving her a look of real fear, as if her daughter wasn't quite human but there on some dark errand.

"Why can't I see anything?" cried Jake. "Is she here?"

As Clara stepped closer, a nurse pulled the curtain around the bed, so she and Abe and Jake were caught inside, and Eva, in the confusion of the moment, was left out. My father felt it again: his strange sense of fortune, the coincidence only he could see.

"Mr. Shapiro," he whispered. "Your daughter is here. Can you open your eyes?"

In my father's telling, this was the climax, the moment he'd been waiting for his whole life, when the feeble king gives away his whole kingdom, his prized daughter, to the young hero from beyond the borders of the known province. That's how he would have finished the story, I'm sure, but he didn't finish. He had to close his eyes and rest.

"Dad," I said, but he only lifted his hand from the coverlet as if to put me off.

That's how this became my mother's story, took on my mother's ending. It had to, because as she stood there in her beautiful dress, her own father couldn't open his eyes. At last he managed to clear his throat, weakly professorial. "You'll marry that man," he said flatly. His eyes remained closed. A minute passed. It would have looked like sleep to anyone who didn't know better.

"Is he still with us?" she whispered.

The doctor expertly took up the dead man's wrist. "Yes," he said. "Sleeping."

Abe and Clara didn't dare look at each other, but they both knew the future had been settled. The dead have so much power; why do we give it to them? I imagine Abe looking wildly away from the girl to the hospital curtain, a pale wavery blue like a false sky closing in. She was so lovely, everything he'd always wanted. So why was he all heaviness and immobility? If Clara had just looked at him then, she might have seen his real helplessness, and that would have been a seed of truth between them. But she was stunned herself. It seemed like a judgment, the way her father kept his silence till the last moment and then decided her fate without looking at her. Still, the doctor said he was only sleeping; maybe she would wake him up and ask him again. So why was that old sensation of panic rising again? It felt a little different this time, a wider dark with no horizon. She told herself it was just the concert ahead of her, a bad case of stage fright. But I know what it was. It was the future: a clock ticking slowly in a handsome formal living room, a wife staring at a gold carpet and waiting for some murky truth to come clear at last.

The moment refuses to pass. I can't stop looking at my parents, wishing for them a different beginning. They seem so alone, with only their separate secrets for company, secrets that will grow the way a child does, with blood coursing along beneath the skin, carrying its invisible history of fantastic desire and ordinary betrayal. It's bound to be this way. God, how I want to change their stories before they become my own. I want to step inside that false sky and bring my parents' hands together just for a moment. I see them so clearly, trapped in there with a dead man, with a lie that I know must have seemed necessary at the time.

Susan Rosalsky

Closer

When I come to inspect the place, Stan the super does a stiff-armed Vanna White and I take a look at the prize. The toilet is in the kitchen; the tub, with a wooden plank over it, doubles as a love seat. Someone's left-over couch is bumped against the sink.

"It's one room," I say.

"That's the beauty part," says Stan. He has a mustache that hangs over his upper lip like his lip has something to hide. "It's like a loft, but your rent is way lower. Look at the closet space. It's practically another apartment. I could rent it out and get twice my money, but I'm too nice."

I like the sound of Stan's voice; it reminds me of Joseph's, the way he sounded after cigarettes and Heineken, scratchy and full at the same time. I say I'll think about it, hoping he'll say more, though I know I want it.

"You don't want to think too much. I got someone who's interested. It'll be gone by this evening." Stan scratches his armpit, and I hear his stomach. He says he wants to finish lunch, and that's when I say yes. In this apartment you can see everything from anywhere. No doors, except the closet. I feel close to being happy, though I have been closer. Like when I was in Boston and Joseph was still alive.

*

Here's a funny story. I come to New York to get my life together after the accident, but the first night I'm here I get up at four, thinking I'm still on Massachusetts Avenue. I can't get back to sleep, so I go out to buy the early paper. When I get to the street, things are not what they should be—the vertical skyline, the colors of the cop cars: this isn't Boston. And that's when everything comes back to me again.

The thing I do now is keep a lot of lists. Not just to cut back on forgetfulness but to save on the work of remembering. I have a morning list and an evening list; it's all there in front of me. I brush my teeth at the same time every day, and give myself thirty-two minutes to dress. This way I catch the right train.

It helps that in my new apartment nothing is out of reach. I want a banana? There it is on the counter; I can get it with my left hand. I want my heels? That's them under the sink; I grab with my right. Everything I need is within the distance of my sight. With the exception of the stuff in the closet. So the other day I call Stan to ask if he can remove the door.

"Now, 3B, why would you want to be doing that?" Stan calls everyone by their apartment number.

"It would make things more accessible. Like it would help me organize. See, I'm trying very hard to turn over a new leaf."

"A new leaf," he says. "Tell me this, 3B. Why are you people always trying to turn over new leaves? Why do you always come to my building?"

"I guess that's no?" I say.

"You guess that's no. That's a good one. Now I've heard it all."

I close my eyes, though I'm already in the dark, and imagine I'm talking to someone else. I want to hear his voice again, but he hangs up.

So I do the job myself. Take the door off its hinges, slide it under my bed, and now I'm thinking about the kitchen cabinets, where I keep my socks and dishes. You don't realize what you don't see until you see it.

How's this for happy. Once we were in a part of Roxbury we'd never been in before and walked into a little liquor store action. We saw a man pull a gun; we saw that man turn to look at us, the dumb white kids whose luck was running out.

And guess what happened?

Nothing.

We just walked away.

It was close, but we were so okay.

Laura Wexler

Waiting for Amelia

It is late in the afternoon, and no more visitors will ring the bell today. Through the parlor window I see Louise moving through the house, putting the brochures and guest book away. She gets out a throw pillow and her sewing, turns on the TV for the evening news. Then she moves the map from the parlor couch so that she can sit down and put her feet up. The map is for visitors; Louise doesn't need it to know that the red line tracing twenty-two thousand miles from Florida to New Guinea ends suddenly near a speck labeled Howland Island.

I am standing outside this rambling clapboard house high on a hill in Atchison, Kansas, the house where Amelia Earhart was born in 1897. A hundred years have passed since that July day when Amy Otis Earhart gave birth to her first girl in the master bedroom. Now tourists come to visit, and we are greeted at the door by a slight woman with a faint limp. Her name is Louise Foudray, and she is the one who lives here now; she is the caretaker and lives in an apartment on the second floor behind a door marked PRIVATE.

Earlier I—along with three other visitors—followed Louise on a tour through the house. She pointed, described, and spun tales. Here is the fireplace where Amelia and Muriel—Millie and Pidge—sat listening to their father's bedtime stories. There is the bannister Amelia used to slide down, learning at an early age about the pull of gravity on a body.

But Amelia's presence in the house is shadowy; there are only a few traces left of her childhood years spent here, and even these were arranged by Louise's hands. The stack of Amelia Earhart suitcases should go in the southwest bedroom. The photograph of Amelia—yes, the one with her plane, the Electra—should go in the front parlor. A wicker baby carriage—bought at a local antique shop—for Amelia's room, so things don't look so bare. A pair of stuffed bears wearing aviator goggles by the bed, yes.

When Louise stopped the tour in front of a wall of framed newspaper clippings, I scanned the headlines—EARHART PLANE DOWN . . . AMELIA LOST IN PACIFIC . . . LADY LINDY LOST. . . . Louise said then, "I think she's still living. I've felt all along that she survived."

Louise is more than a caretaker. Her presence is felt everywhere in the house, and with every word she utters, the difference between past and present, aviatrix and admirer, Amelia and Louise, blurs.

So Louise rearranges the furniture in Amelia's room, banking on the day an elderly lady—still tall and slender—will return to her childhood home. Maybe Louise believes this woman has already returned—a sly unnamed tourist—dropping two dollars in the jar, like any of us. Maybe Louise is on the couch now, sifting visitors' faces through her mind, wondering if Amelia's was among them.

I watch Louise for a moment more. Then I knock on the window and wave. She looks up and waves back. And I step off the porch and walk down the brick path to my car.

Once when I moved away from a place, I left a letter taped to the inside floor of my closet. *My name is Laura and I am a girl and I lived here once*, it said. These days I am caught up in the letters Amelia left behind. There are the childhood scribbles, written by the girl who cavorted around staid Atchison in the first pair of bloomers anyone had lain eyes on. There is Amelia writing her father, away on a trip, asking for footballs for Christmas. *We need them specially*, she wrote. Years later she would write her father a "popping off" letter, to be opened if she perished during her first Atlantic flight. *Dearest Dad: Hooray for the last grand adventure! I wish I had won, but it was worth while anyway. You know that I have no faith we'll meet anywhere again, but I wish we might.* These are words of hope and hopelessness. *I have no faith . . . but I wish . . .*

There is a famous letter from Amelia to her husband, George Putnam, on their wedding morning in 1931: *Dear GP . . . In our life together I shall not hold you to any medieval code of faithfulness to me, nor shall I consider myself bound to you similarly. . . . I must exact a cruel promise, and that is that you will let me go in a year if we find no happiness together.*

Then, there is the letter she wrote to her mother on the eve of her last flight: *Very confidentially I may hop off in a few days. So you don't know nothin'. While I am gone you will probably need a cool dress or two. . . . Herewith some doe.* Sometimes when I read these letters, full of nicknames, garbled words, wild punctuation, I forget she's not one of my college friends but Amelia Earhart—the one who stretched her flights longer and longer until flying the world seemed only logical. I forget she was a woman in the 1930s and not the 1990s. In her letters she seems so near, as near as when Louise tells her stories.

"There was a medical student who got hired as the caretaker for an elderly woman's estate in Virginia. The elderly woman had lots of animals and lots of land," Louise had told me earlier that afternoon. I'd stayed after the other tourists left, and we sat talking in high-backed chairs in the front parlor.

"After so much time had gone by, the elderly woman would write notes to this medical student, saying, *Gone flying. Be back later.* He got curious and asked her questions. But she would never tell him anything about her life before World War II. She just refused."

During the tour Louise had said, "I feel I know Amelia well enough to answer people's questions in the way she would have." Her story voice reflected that sureness.

"Well, one day he took one of those notes to a handwriting expert. They compared it with a letter of Amelia's. And the handwriting matched," Louise said, putting her hands in her lap.

I knew, and still I asked: *Was it Amelia?*

Louise shrugged. "The lady moved away, and the young man lost touch. . . ."

Then Louise started to tell me another story and stopped. "Some of this is still secret," she said.

These stories—they always begin as they should. There is a sighting, a happening too real to be coincidence, a glimmer of hope that unearths an old memory.

Faye Gillis Wells—a pilot who is now eighty-eight and has never broken any flight records—remembers Amelia at the first meeting of the Ninety-Nines in 1929, at Curtis Field on Long Island. "A voice, sure and steady, came from the back of the room, from a lady wearing a cloche hat and a suit and gloves. We were arguing over what to call our new group of lady pilots. This gal said we should count up how many of us were there and make that our name. Of course it was Amelia. We elected her first president of the Ninety-Nines."

Each summer, the Ninety-Nines return to Atchison to pay homage to Amelia. The sixty-seven-year-old organization of women pilots now has seven thousand members around the world. They hired Louise to be the caretaker and tour guide for the Amelia Earhart Birthplace. It was a dream job; years before, Louise would pass Amelia's house on walks with her children, always saying, "I'm going to live there someday."

There is a story about Albert Bresnik, Amelia's personal photographer. On the day Amelia went down, a man came into Bresnik's Hollywood studio. The man pointed at a photograph of Amelia and said, "The lightforce in the picture is gone. . . . " On January 5, 1939, when Amelia was declared legally dead, Bresnik sealed his negatives in wax. His wife says he didn't know what to do—he loved Amelia. Fifty years later he unsealed the negatives.

Now I have one of his photographs on my wall. In it there are creases on Amelia's pant legs—she'd been sitting awhile before coming out to pose in front of the Electra. A few crow's feet mark the skin surrounding her eyes, and the veins on her hands are raised, like the hands of any woman a few weeks shy of her fortieth birthday. A colored scarf is tied just below her chin. This is Amelia Earhart in 1937, the year she flew away and never returned.

There are as many stories as there are people to create them. One theory has Amelia captured by the Japanese and forced to make radio broadcasts as Tokyo Rose. This is part of a larger belief that Amelia wasn't just a pilot, but a spy taken by the Japanese and used as a bargaining chip with the United States in the tense days before World War II. The theory holds that when the bargaining failed, Amelia and her navigator, Fred Noonan, were executed and thrown in a ditch.

There are reports from Pacific islanders who say that a white woman and man were once in their island's prison. The white woman was pale, they say, and looked very much like a man. She gave someone a white-gold ring with a white stone, but that is long lost. There are bones and bits of wing and a pair of lady's shoes on an island called Nikumaroro, and this gives some enough hope to keep returning there.

Then there is the official conclusion: while circling the world, Amelia Earhart and Fred Noonan ran out of gas two hundred miles from Howland Island and fell to the ocean. According to government reports, Amelia Earhart spoke her last words at 8:45 A.M. on July 2, 1937. Her voice came in spurts over the radio. "We are running north and south," the radio man heard through the static.

Notice the straight plunge of the official conclusion. It has nothing of the stories' hope. Though the stories begin in certainty and trail off, most of them never end—the teller doesn't want Amelia to end, and so she doesn't. In fact, in the stories there is little thought of gravity at all, of the unavoidable tug that everything—even Amelia—feels toward earth. For some, Amelia hangs forever in the sky, and though they'll tell you differently, they always walk about with their heads cocked slightly upward.

That is why I believed Louise when she said she feels something. "I think I know what happened to her, but I don't have any proof," she told me.

Louise feels something. And I wait to feel something, too. I try to believe Amelia still lives. Then I try to believe she was executed on Saipan. I try to refute the government story. Then I try to believe it. I try to feel an instinct or a connection. I wait for my gut to send me a signal. But I can't come up with any answer but *Gone.*

*

On my way out of Atchison, I drive out to the Amelia Earhart Memorial Airport. Two men sit in a car by the runway there. They are World War II veterans—old pilots—who have come to listen to tapes of old radio shows, drink from a bottle, and watch the planes lift off and touch down. There's a man named Skip at the airport with a little yellow plane. We get to talking, and he says he'll take me up if I want.

From the air, I look down and think about how most things aren't made to be seen from above. Nothing looks very remarkable from up here, and that is the beauty of it. The church looks no more grand than the clean lines of a planted field.

It's very windy, and sometimes the wind shakes us a little, and I remember that I am moving through the air in something as improbable as a tiny yellow plane. Skip is steering us toward a certain hill in Atchison, the place where crop artist Stan Herd is creating his own story of Amelia, her portrait.

"See her dimple," I say to Skip. He nods and takes us a little closer. There is the trailing scarf, the leather jacket, the curly lock of hair—all cut from prairie grass.

It is strange to look down on Amelia—me in flight, she on the ground.

Then Skip offers to let me at the controls. His voice comes over my headphones in short bursts. "It's easy. Just keep the plane level," he says.

I shake my head no. I just want to watch.

I would like to know why Louise believes that Amelia lives. But she couldn't say it any differently than the trucker who knocked on the front door of the house that morning. He'd driven in from Ohio to buy books about Amelia for his wife—a woman, he said, who is unconventional, like Amelia. His wife wanted to drive the big trucks, so she quit a good job and took off for adventure.

I asked the man why Amelia was his wife's hero.

"I don't know," he said at first, shaking his head. But then he did know. "It's a love," he said.

Still, I have more questions. I would like to know if Amelia realized, standing at the window in her Atchison home, staring out at the Missouri River, that she would one day be a legend. Did she—that girl holding back the curtains with her hand—know that things as unsteady, as fragile as words would keep her alive?

I make up the answers, and sometimes they say yes. And they are always my own.

Terese Svoboda

Leadership

You strike me as a leader, says his father.

The boy turns his face—because the rest of him is being suited—toward his father raising the buttered toast. What kind of leader?

He's teasing, sighs the mother, who pats the boy down, extracting the dollar he got for switching line leader with a bigger boy, a much bigger boy, moving it from a pocket into an envelope. You *could* be a leader, she says and puts that bigger boy's name on the outside of the envelope and puts it into her pocket.

Both the boy and father hear how she puts the *could*, but the boy does not care, other than that is his dollar she has sealed up and tucked on her person, at least as far as he's concerned, and he is not going to show her any of those other dollars or any more that he gets if this is it, if this is how it is. Leading is not what he wants anyway. You get shoved from behind if you lead, you have to know which door. And if you talk, you have to go to the back of the line but the rest of them talk, yes they do.

A robin has set down in the too short grass and its hind end twitches like it tickles. The grass is too short like the truth she's putting out, that he cut himself on twice, it is so sharp, that short.

Eat your breakfast, she says to him who is so solemn with his empty pocket, sure she will look in another. He cranes his neck out toward the window.

A rocket has landed beside the robin. It is the size of a small dog and it appears to have legs that it is stretching like it has been doing a long trip. It's a what? he asks. On the grass. You have to see it.

Hush, she says. I see.

What are we going to do about it? she says. You—have a look.

His father drops his toast and his napkin upends on his knee as he too stands. Then the two males look at each other, one knowing the value of saying nothing, the other the value of looking away, of seeing nothing. You have to be careful, the father says, and the word *careful* rises in a bubble, getting bigger and bigger until the father could walk inside it like some future vehicle, like the answer vehicle to the one that is so improbably running beside the harried robin.

I saw somewhere that tomatoes are being grafted onto some important part of a chicken, you know, something small that doesn't count as a chicken, he says.

The mother and the son do not turn toward him, do not *hmmmmm*. The mother feels for the knob on the radio, for the comfort of emergency broadcast.

The boy has a gun. It's in a place his mother hasn't felt. So what if it's a toy. What it is is another bribe from the bigger boy, a real fake gun. He unlatches the door.

Get back in here, she says.

He walks into the prickly grass, holding the gun above his bellybutton and out. The rocketship stops running all over the yard and comes over and sort of sniffs his pants. The boy wants to say Good Boy but he doesn't, he fires away because he has this real fake thing in his hands.

The father comes up behind him. Furthest away the mother halts. They look up. The sky is going all slatey like in a painting people say is important. In the second they take to glance up, the rocketship retracts its legs and tail and plays dead.

Whether the weather, that sudden cover of sun, is part of the rocketship's strategy is not sure, but if the spiritual is at the bottom of what you believe and you believe the spiritual is not of this earth, then of course the rocketship could control the physical. It's now all foggy or that's what the mother swears later while she points at the rocketship on the shelf in her son's room for the cameras. But just then, the three of them in a line near this rocketship deployed yet finally quiet, they don't say much at all. Martha, the father murmurs as he has never murmured before, not even at night, Martha, hold my hand.

The boy wouldn't have answered to anything if anyone had asked. He throws himself to his knees and touches the rocketship because he knows what it wants: Take me to your leader. He is obeying, he is scooping it up in his arms, opening and closing all the little portholes. The bigger boy will let him in line now.

Sweetheart, says his mother. Give me that now.

Suzanne Kamata

Driving

Yvonne Hamada saw the cement mixer turn onto the narrow bridge, saw that it was coming straight at them, picking up speed as it rolled. She knew that Ryu's sedan was no match for that monster on wheels. There was hardly enough room for one car, let alone two; these roads had been built for cracker box-size economy cars, not the all-terrain vehicles and American-size dump trucks of '90s Japan.

Ryu let up on the accelerator ever so slightly.

Next to him, Yvonne closed her eyes, shrank back against the passenger seat—"the death seat," her brother had always called it. "This is it," she whispered. "I hope someone knows enough English to notify my parents in the States."

But then the car swayed as the truck whooshed past—within inches, no doubt—and Yvonne opened her eyes. They were safe. There were no other cars ahead of them. To her left, she could see jet skiers speeding over the river. On the opposite shore, boys cast their lines, as they did on any other Sunday afternoon.

Out of the corner of her eye, she could see Ryu's dark head leaning sideways as he fiddled with the radio dial in search of baseball. The car swerved toward the guardrail. This, just after they'd narrowly escaped death by two-ton truck.

"Ryu? Honey?" she said, her voice high and tight. "Do you mind, like, looking at where you're going?"

He looked at her instead, frowned, and then turned back to the road. "If you don't like my driving, you can drive."

Yvonne did not want to drive and she decided that she wouldn't make another sound. She saw the traffic signal a few meters ahead turn yellow, and she figured that Ryu would race through the red light as usual. She decided that for once she would hold her tongue, but then the car slowed and came to a stop. Yvonne smiled at her reformed husband.

He glanced at her, saw the grin, then began fussing with the radio again and didn't notice when the light changed.

Yvonne immediately forgot her vow of silence. "Sweetie? It's green. You can go now."

Ryu gripped the steering wheel once again. "*Ao*," he said, a smile playing at the corners of his mouth.

"It's not blue. Green. Just look at that light. How can you call that color blue?"

Ryu shrugged as they crossed the intersection. They'd had this exchange many times before. It was so familiar as to be comfortable to Yvonne. She settled back in her seat, finally content to enjoy the ride.

For ten years, Yvonne had cruised around in a banana-yellow hatchback, but since coming to Japan to teach English in the countryside of Shikoku, she didn't drive at all. Well, there had been that one time. Before she'd met Ryu, a Japanese suitor had rented a little red convertible as a surprise. Yvonne remembered the salty wind whipping her hair, the sight of the waves breaking on the shore, and then her date's absolute terror when she took a turn down the wrong side of the road. She was scared, too, when she nearly sideswiped a stop sign, having misjudged the distance between the side of the car and the edge of the road. Since then, Yvonne usually relied on public transportation or her mountain bike. Sometimes she allowed Ryu to drive her, though these days she preferred to stay in their recently mortgaged home, where she knew that she was safe and in no danger of breaking the law.

In Japan, driver's ed wasn't a school subject as it was in the States. Would-be drivers enrolled in private driving schools, where a series of lessons cost as much as a year at Yvonne's university. Not only was it expensive, but also inconvenient, as students had to sign up for lessons on a first-come first-serve basis, with everyone vying for the same time slots.

There were actually a lot of adults in Japan who didn't know how to drive. Her mother-in-law, Mrs. Hamada, for instance. She tooled around on a bright blue 50cc scooter. It was enough to get her to the hospital, where she worked as a cook, or to the store for groceries. For journeys to more distant places, her husband would drive. "You don't need a license," he told her. "I'll take you wherever you want to go."

Lying awake in bed one night, Ryu said, "I think my mother is going to divorce my father."

"What?" Divorce was a Western obsession. Here, women made do. They did *gaman*; they persevered.

"She said that she can't talk to my father anymore. He just drinks and plays Go."

Yvonne thought that maybe being married to an American made him see divorce as an option. She was always trying to explain her complicated family relations—half-cousins, stepfathers, adoptees, etc.

"If my mother leaves my father, can she live with us?" Ryu propped himself on his elbows so that he could look down at her moon-bathed face. "You two get along well. I think it would work out, don't you?"

Yvonne's limbs froze. She mumbled unintelligibly, trying to quell the sudden panic. Why not say yes? It would never happen, she thought. Mrs. Hamada would never ask for a divorce.

"Yvonne?"

"Sure, whatever," she said.

Ryu leaned down and kissed her, then fell back against the pillow. Seemingly content, he rolled over and began to snore softly almost immediately.

Yvonne tossed and turned until dawn. Before they'd married, Yvonne had paid close attention to how Ryu treated his mother. She'd always believed that men who were kind and considerate to the women who'd raised them would be the same way toward their wives. At family dinners, Ryu took his mother's side in arguments with his father. When the meal had ended, Ryu helped clear away the dishes, just as he did now at home. And he always spoke of his mother with words like "strong," "patient," and "brave."

When Ryu had asked her to marry him, Yvonne had made sure that they wouldn't be living with his parents. It wouldn't be good for their relationship, her friends and relatives had warned. Her grandmother had blamed her own divorce on an overbearing German live-in mother-in-law.

Early on in their relationship, Ryu and Yvonne had talked about living abroad—maybe in a third country that would be foreign to both of them. They had first been drawn together by mutual cultural curiosity—Yvonne's interest in traditional Japanese arts and Ryu's love of American freedom, frankness, and Major League baseball—and by a passion for travel.

Sometimes, as they lay together in bed just before sleep, they talked about the places they would visit. Yvonne was hungry for that initial burst of wonder she'd felt on first arriving in Japan. The novelty had long since worn off, and she was in need of a new fix. Ryu's job, however, kept him busy most of the year. The economy was failing, and he couldn't risk taking a vacation for a while. So far, most of the trips they'd planned were just wishes.

Yvonne remembered the first time Ryu's parents came to check out their new house—before they'd even decided to buy it.

They had discovered the place by chance—a two-story dwelling less than a kilometer away from the cramped apartment they'd been renting. After two years of breathing down each other's necks, they were ready for wide rooms filled with sunlight, a yard big enough for barbecues. Friends thought that they were being greedy—just the two of them moving into a house previously inhabited by a family of six—but Yvonne's American soul needed solitude.

The only problem with the house was the driveway, which was steep, narrow, and bordered by a cement wall. Ryu's father had parked on the street, not bothering with the challenge.

"So this is where you want to live," Ryu's father said as he wandered the empty rooms. "There's only one tatami room. No *tokonoma*." His own house was Japanese-style—weathered wood with a rock garden out front.

Mrs. Hamada trailed behind, a smile hiding her disappointment. "I was hoping we'd all live together," she nearly whimpered. "We added on last year . . ."

Yvonne knew about the twelve-mat room that had been adjoined to their house. She'd thought at the time that it was for Ryu's sister, who stayed there in the later stages of her two pregnancies. Now, she realized that in spite of their son's international marriage and his Western-style outspokenness, they still had hopes that he'd turn out traditional.

"We'll be nearby," Yvonne said. "It's only a fifteen-minute drive." She meant to remind them—Ryu, his parents, everyone—that her own family was thousands of miles away. That in agreeing to buy this house, rooting herself so near Ryu's birthplace, she was making concessions of her own. The dream of a life in Bali or Paris or Sydney was becoming dimmer and dimmer.

Mr. Hamada agreed to lend the couple money for a down payment on the house. They would take out a bank loan for the rest. Yvonne began fantasizing about leather sofas and oak tables, Georgia O'Keeffe prints for the walls, the tulips and irises she'd plant in the garden.

The next day she was in the kitchen working on a new concoction—a Thai dish involving lots of chilis. She had a CD playing, the music cranked up loud, and she danced while she chopped lemon grass.

She didn't hear the front door open.

"Konnichiwa!"

Yvonne jumped, nearly slicing her finger. She turned to find Ryu's mother right behind her. She was smiling broadly, flashing her gold teeth. She held a cloth bundle in one hand, then lofted it in the air to show what she'd brought.

Yvonne rushed over to the CD player to turn down the volume. Her scalp prickled with irritation. Why hadn't Mrs. Hamada called first? Why hadn't she locked the door?

In the now quiet room, she shoved a cookbook aside and motioned for her mother-in-law to sit. "I'll make you some tea," she said, setting a kettle of water to boil.

"No, no, that's not necessary."

"Please. I'd like a cup myself."

"I don't want to trouble you."

"It's no trouble."

Yvonne turned away and made a *tengu* face. Sometimes she got fed up with the verbal dance. She knew that if she didn't offer tea, her mother-in-law would think her rude. And she knew that Ryu's mother was a master at beating around the bush, exceptionally skilled at indirect response. She would have to invite her to stay for dinner, too.

As she poured hot water over tea leaves, she remembered Ryu's words of the night before. What if he was right? What if she really would rather live with her son than her husband? Hadn't she raised him to adore her? Hadn't she poured all of her efforts into making sure that he would never leave her?

She cast a glance at her abandoned culinary project. If Ryu's mother moved in with them, they'd have to forget about trying exotic new dishes. Ryu's parents lived on a strict diet of fish, rice, and miso soup. She'd once found the remains of a casserole she'd sent over in the trash of her in-laws' kitchen.

She'd have to give up her reading time to drink tea with her mother-in-law. They'd never be able to go on the trips that she and Ryu had talked about. Could she imagine Mrs. Hamada on a bus in Mumbai? No way.

And they would be forced to speak in Japanese all the time. This house, this former haven, would be an extension of the foreign world beyond its walls. Yvonne needed one place—just one—where she didn't have to worry about committing cultural blunders, where she could be wholly herself.

She brought the teapot and teacups on a tray to the table where her mother-in-law sat waiting. Normally, she wouldn't have bothered with the lacquer tray, but with a guest present, decorum was required. The two of them sat together sipping the hot tea. The room was silent except for the sound of Ryu's mother's slurping.

A month later, Mr. Hamada bade his wife goodbye as she hopped on her scooter for work. He read the newspaper, poured himself a second cup of tea, and got dressed. Sunshine was blessing all of the flowers and plants and tiny trees in his garden. He felt the warm rays on his taut-skinned face when he stepped outside. He bent to run his hands lightly over the leaves of a peppermint plant, then sniffed his fingers. Scent of gum. Then he began tugging at the weeds that had sprung up, tossing them into a pile at the center of the yard.

He went into the shed, took the trimming shears from their hook, and began snipping at twigs, giving the bushes form. He worked with total concentration. When the pain shot through his arm and chest, he dropped the shears and grabbed at his heart. That evening his wife found him staring at a bush with a look of surprise.

At least that's how Yvonne imagined it all. Heart attack. *Shinzo mahi.* It sounded like a Hawaiian fish, something you could order from a menu: "I'll have the shinzo mahi and a glass of white wine."

Throughout the wake, inappropriate thoughts kept popping into her brain. She wasn't sure what she was feeling. Sadness, sure, but underneath, panic was waiting to grab her by the throat. Mrs. Hamada was now alone. There was no need to even consider divorce.

The day of the funeral, Ryu brushed by Yvonne as if she were a stranger. He hovered at his mother's elbow, urging her to sit, to rest, to drink something. To Yvonne: "The priest is coming soon. Prepare the tray."

All the relatives were watching her. Would she sit with her legs sprawled open? Would she laugh and flap her arms around like a duck? Would she be like those Americans they'd seen on TV? Yvonne bowed to each aunt, uncle, cousin, neighbor who came to the door. She ushered them to the room where Mr. Hamada's body lay in a pine box. She brought them tea on a tray, set the cup down on the tatami near them with two hands.

In the kitchen, she hunched over the too-low sink and washed the teacups. Cousin Kanako joined her. "So will you live here from now on?"

Yvonne looked into the cousin's face. She was fortyish, earnest-looking. Kind. "I can't," she whispered. "In America . . ."

"But this is Japan. You can't just leave her alone in this big house. She'll have nothing to look forward to." Kanako leaned in closer. "I live with my mother-in-law. It's not so bad. We do embroidery together."

Yvonne shuddered, but Kanako didn't seem to notice. She should have been thinking about Mr. Hamada—reminiscing, perhaps, about the freshwater pearl necklace he had once brought her from Kyoto. Or the time he had tried to teach her how to play Go—the arrangement of black and white discs on the playing board. Or the time the four of them—Mr. and Mrs. Hamada, Ryu and Yvonne, had gone to a karaoke box and sung *enka* together. Instead, Yvonne could only think about herself. She could feel her future closing down on her like the lid of a box. It was getting harder and harder to breathe.

"Yvonne, the priest is here now." An aunt appeared to give directions. "Bring him the tray."

Later in the day, when most of the mourners had gone home, and it was just Ryu, Yvonne, and Mrs. Hamada in the kitchen, the older woman turned to her daughter-in-law and said, "Everyone said that you are a good bride. Not many young women know how to serve tea."

And then she saw the rest of her life as a succession of teacups. She'd fill them, place them before guests, and wash them, and this would go on and on and on. Every time one of Mrs. Hamada's friends or neighbors came to visit, she would be forced into this role.

"It's better to establish yourself as a bad daughter-in-law," her Japanese friend Maya had once told her. Now she understood.

"Mother," Ryu said. He sounded tired yet gentle. "We want you to live with us."

Yvonne could not move. Her head was becoming light.

"No, no, no. I can't leave this house. Your father and I lived here together for many years."

"He's dead now. It's time to move on."

Yvonne was stunned. Mr. Hamada's ashes had not yet cooled, and his son was already smothering the memory of him. He was already thinking of a new life where Yvonne would sit at the table in silence while the two of them rattled away in their language.

"Then we will move in here," Ryu said. "We can't leave you by yourself."

"I will be fine." Mrs. Hamada tried to smile, but her lips trembled. Yvonne could see the tears pooling in the corners of her eyes. "Your father wanted you to be happy in your new house. Please. Don't think of me."

That night, Yvonne slept in Ryu's childhood room. Ryu and his mother slept on futons in the room downstairs with Mr. Hamada's bones.

They burned candles and incense. Yvonne didn't understand any of the chants.

"You will have to learn to drive in Japan," Ryu said a few days later. "My mother has no license, and if there is some emergency, then you will have to help her."

"What about you?"

"I have to work long hours. I may be too busy."

Yvonne knew that all over Japan daughters-in-law were taking care of their husbands' mothers—bathing them, preparing soft meals, doling out pills, and spooning medicines into toothless mouths. The husbands were working, were drinking after hours with their co-workers in an effort to forget the heavy burdens of family and mortgage. Three generations under one roof, many hungry bellies—all this was on the husbands' shoulders. She tried to convince herself that her duty was to take care of Mrs. Hamada, but her only impulse was to run away to her new house and lock the door.

During the forty-nine days of mourning, she helped in the kitchen each week. She prepared the tray of tea and beancakes for the priest, set out slippers in a neat row in the entryway for visitors, chopped vegetables for the mourners' soup.

The fifth week, she found some carrots in the bottom of her mother-in-law's refrigerator. They'd be a good addition to the miso soup, she thought, a nice counterpart to seaweed and onions. She scrambled around in a drawer, dug up a scraper, and began peeling the carrots in long, curling strips. The aunts and cousins bustled around her.

"Yvonne-chan, what are you doing?" It was Kanako, there at her elbow. Her face too close to Yvonne's.

"Chopping carrots. For the soup."

"For the soup? Oh, no. There can be nothing red in the soup. Red's a color for celebration."

Yvonne stared at her for a moment. "Carrots are orange," she said.

"Almost red. *Dame, dame.*"

The other women glanced over and nodded their agreement. Yvonne sighed. She would never understand this family or this country. She picked up a chunk of carrot, popped it into her mouth, and crunched as carefully as she could. There was no way that the others could not have heard the sound, but they ignored it.

When, at last, Mr. Hamada's soul had been chanted into paradise, Yvonne waited for their lives to settle down. But things were far from normal.

"I have a duty," Ryu said. "I must take care of my mother. I will stay at her house three or four nights a week."

Yvonne thought that quiet and solitude would be a blessed thing. "If you must," she said. "But I will stay here."

Ryu nodded. He had given up trying to persuade her otherwise. Or maybe he was trying to wear her down, force her to see the ridiculousness of the situation. If they lived together, she wouldn't have to learn how to drive down the left side of the road, along with the maniacal motorists. She would be able to sleep next to Ryu every night. But she wouldn't budge. There was no welcome in her heart.

On Monday morning, Yvonne sat on the edge of the bed while Ryu packed. He took four pairs of balled-up socks out of the drawer and stuffed them into his duffel bag. He tossed four pairs of clean boxer shorts and his blue-striped pajamas in with the socks. She watched as he unhooked dress shirts on hangers from the closet pole. Usually, he asked her which tie went best with which shirt, but this time he chose silently.

Yvonne remained seated on the bed until he had departed. The house was quiet except for the sound of her breathing.

She went to work as usual, and bought a piece of chocolate cake at the bakery on her way home to eat for dinner. Why not? She deserved special treatment after seven weekends of slaving in her mother-in-law's kitchen. Back home, she lit a taper (Ryu hated eating by candlelight; said he couldn't see the food), put on her CD of *Madame Butterfly*, and arranged the wedge of cake on a china plate.

The icing was artfully arranged, but each forkful was airy and light—not the rich gooey concoction she'd hoped for. She ate slowly, scraped her plate clean of crumbs, but in the end she wasn't quite satisfied.

There was only a plate and a fork to wash instead of the usual sinkful of dishes. There were no inside-out socks to be picked up from the floor, no rumpled newspapers to be stacked, no empty beer cans. Yvonne had all evening to do as she pleased.

After a long soak in the tub (she'd added lavender-scented salts), she sprawled across the bed with a pile of fashion magazines. She flipped through a few pages of cosmetics ads, an interview with a rising young actress she'd never heard of, then glanced at the phone on the nightstand. It did not ring. He would not call tonight.

Ryu returned on Friday evening. As soon as she heard his car pull up next to the house, Yvonne rushed to the entryway to meet him. He pushed open the door and leaned in to kiss her. Yvonne reached for his bag.

"Mackerel," he said, sniffing the air. "We had that for dinner last night."

Yvonne bit the inside of her lips. She lugged his duffel bag to the laundry room, but when she unzipped it, she found that all of the clothes had been freshly laundered.

"So how is your mother?" she asked when they were seated at the table.

"Sad," Ryu said. "She wants to know why you don't visit."

Yvonne's jaw tightened. "She has her precious son," she wanted to say. "What does she need me for?"

From then on the week was divided—Mrs. Hamada's days and Yvonne's days. She knew that Japanese men, transferred by their employers to distant cities, often lived separately from their families, returning to their wives and children only on the weekends. In Japan, Yvonne and Ryu's new routine wasn't strange at all.

On Fridays, Ryu told Yvonne about taking his mother to the beauty salon, to the grocery store, to the art museum for a special exhibit of Picasso paintings.

"It's good that she's getting out and about," Yvonne said. She had stayed in the house reading books and staring out the window. Wondering if this semi-separation would go on forever.

"Yes," Ryu said. "She's smiling a bit more. She even laughed once."

"Great. Your being there must do wonders for her."

A few weeks later he started taking her to *ikebana* lessons. Mrs. Hamada also signed up for yoga and English conversation.

"She wants to be able to talk to you in English," Ryu said. "She's trying hard."

And then, most surprising of all, Ryu arrived home one Friday evening and announced, "My mother is going to driving school."

Driving school? At her age? She'd be embarrassed. She wouldn't last among all of those shrieking high school girls with orange-streaked hair, the boys with their pompadours and forced gruffness. Was this another ploy? Was Yvonne expected to realize that things had gone beyond all reasonable expectations, to relent, to consent to living together and driving Mrs. Hamada wherever she wanted to go?

"Tell her to do her best," Yvonne said coolly. "I'll be rooting for her."

She wondered if he was making everything up or if grief had touched him in a way that she hadn't imagined. She decided to give Mrs. Hamada a call. Just to see what was going on.

"*Moshi moshi.*" Mrs. Hamada's voice had the requisite phone cheer, but that didn't mean anything.

"What's this about driving school?" Yvonne asked, after enduring the niceties about health and weather.

"Oh-ho-ho. *Hazukashii!* I'm so old. They call me granny at the school!"

"So you really are learning to drive? A car?"

"I'm trying. Maybe someday I'll be able to drive to your house."

Yvonne grimaced. "That would be great," she said. "We could speak in English."

"Oh-ho-ho!"

Finally, around the time when buds began to appear on the branches of cherry trees, Ryu came home on Friday night and stayed until Tuesday. On Wednesday evening, he was still at home. Yvonne had made beef stew, and he'd eaten two bowls of it. Now, he was bathed, in his striped pajamas, and sitting in front of the TV with a can of beer.

Yvonne was afraid to ask when he was going back to his mother's house, but she had to know.

"How is your mother?" she asked. At first, Yvonne thought that Ryu hadn't heard. His eyes were fixed on news footage of a war in some distant country. The sound of gun shots blasted through the room.

"Ryu?"

"My mother is fine," he said, at last. "She's decided to go on a tour to

Malaysia next month with her friends." He chuckled. "She wants to go all over the world."

Mrs. Hamada? Yvonne felt something like envy rising in her gorge. Mr. Hamada's death had set her free. She was a fool to think that her mother-in-law needed her and Ryu to take care of her. Her world had suddenly burst open—a gallery of adventures waiting to be had.

Ryu's eyes were once again on the television screen. Relief workers were carrying injured Africans on stretchers while bombs exploded in the distance. After a few seconds, the carnage gave way to a shot of a suited announcer behind a desk, then a commercial featuring a muscle-bound actor exclaiming over sausages in a pan. Ryu reached for the remote control and flipped to a documentary—rare birds nesting on the Galapagos Islands, a strange and beautiful place.

Yvonne had thought that the new house would be a sanctuary, but it had become a fortress. She had imprisoned herself. She turned to Ryu, a sudden wildness in her eyes. "Give me your keys," she said.

"My keys?" He raised his eyebrows, but reached into his pocket and fished them out. Pitched them to her.

It was dark outside, the sky spangled with stars. The full moon shone upon Yvonne. She stood still for a moment, feeling the night breeze ruffle her hair, and then moved toward the car. It sat in the driveway, big and patient, like a promise. The moon's reflection bounced off the hood. Yvonne went around to the driver's side, unlocked the door, and eased in behind the dashboard. Just sitting there, with her fingers fitted into the ridges of the steering wheel, made her heart pound. She could hear the blood rushing through her head. She remained seated until the beat had slowed, then took a deep breath and went back into the house.

"What were you doing?" Ryu asked when she tossed back the keys.

"Nothing," she said. But next time, she would start the engine.

Neil Davidson

Goodbye, Johnnie Walker

Until recently, I hadn't gone to bed sober in twenty-five years. I was a drunk when I first met my wife of twenty-three years, and I have been one ever since. I have been a pretty good drunk, as drunks go, without the usual DWIs, abusive behavior, or too dear a price paid for being too honest after my seventh or tenth drink. I am a flirt when drunk but have never been unfaithful.

I worked hard while I drank, and once wrote three novels and hundreds of nonfiction articles in four years. I believe my work was more lyrical with the help of alcohol. The problem was that my love affair with the bottle finally began to threaten my continued existence on this shaky earth.

In the past year, I started drinking in the shower each morning. I was drunk by nine, drunk at noon, drunk at three, drunk at seven, and drunk at ten o'clock. I had pretty much stopped eating, although I still made dinner for my wife, our dogs, and myself, and pretended to enjoy a fine meal in a fine little house on a pretty street in a nice little town. Eventually, my body started eating itself to stay alive. Ketosis is the medical term.

Why my drinking got so out of control after so many years of my being a functioning and productive alcoholic remains a mystery to me.

I just know that I had become (and still am) one sick son of a bitch just a step away from the grave because I suffer from the disease of alcoholism. I drank too much. It is as simple, and as difficult, as that.

I love drinking, and am having a hard time accepting that being sober is somehow a superior state of being. It's also hard to accept that I have to expend even more energy to stay clean than I did when the first thing I thought about in the morning was whether I had enough Scotch for the following night. Never having had hangovers, I don't feel any better when I wake up now than I did when I drank, and I literally have to remind myself that I didn't drink yesterday.

I do not, however, miss all those questions for which I seldom found answers: Did I black out last night? Are apologies due? Is my wife pissed? How did I get home, and where the hell is the car? Who did I call, and did I insult them? What happened to all the money I had in my wallet? How much did I put on the card? Think now, Davidson. These are questions most drunks have had to ask themselves at one time or another. After a while, I just stopped asking them.

I want to run away and drink. If I die, I die. No excuses or regrets. I want to run away and drink, but I won't. I will try to make it in this new world I don't know. I will try those silly meetings that many drunks believe are chaired by God. I am scared now. I am afraid of success and failure in equal measure. But I will try.

If I didn't begin drinking early and keep drinking, I got the sweats so bad that my entire head became soaked with perspiration. My heart hurt so much, I was afraid a heart attack was imminent. My hands shook so much, I couldn't drink a glass of water, not that I was so inclined. But of course there was an antidote to my pain—a panacea so profoundly satisfying that virtually everything else became unimportant or nonexistent. One drink of good Scotch, and everything stopped. Well, almost everything. I still had quiet cries and a sadness that I just couldn't drown anymore. During my pre-admission interview with a counselor from Betty Ford, I asked her what I should do about needing a jolt in the morning. She said, "Take a drink and don't try to detox yourself, or you might not make it here." So I took a drink. It was now officially my medicine. My psychiatrist had once said that I was one of the most self-medicated persons he had ever met. At last, I understood precisely what he meant: I was the doctor with a fool for a patient.

I find most books that deal with drinking and rehab somewhat smug and self-congratulatory. I am neither confident enough nor sufficiently proud of getting through a day sober to take that attitude. Truth be told, I am confident only that I will have another drink at some point in my life. Maybe today.

I was surprised and more than a little delighted to find that at least some of the bars in the Philadelphia International Airport were open at six-thirty in the morning. Of course, I was prepared if they weren't. I had purchased twelve miniature bottles of Johnnie Walker Red for the trip.

I was on the way to the Betty Ford Center: sun and palm trees and drunken, pill-popping celebrities. Jesus, maybe I could get a free golf lesson. I was ready.

I remember having a few doubles in Philly before I took off, perhaps another five or so aboard the plane, five or six more in Denver, a few more after we took off again, and then, upon my arrival at Palm Springs at about twelve-thirty in the afternoon (California time), another seven or eight. These last drinks I downed after telling—in my most apologetic tone—the very nice gentleman from the center, who was there to pick me up and deliver me to my new life, that I needed to have a couple more belts before leaving. This very nice alcoholic stood with me at the bar in the Palm Springs airport, a tender hand on my shoulder, while I put away one after the other.

After that, I don't remember much. They told me later that I had my last five or six mini-bottles in the nurses' office. Once word got out that some guy was drinking over in "meds," my soon-to-be fellow patients came over as a group and carried me back to the dorm, singing, "Show him the way to the next whiskey bar. No, don't ask why." Several of them inquired as to whether I had any more booze and tried to impress upon me that sharing was a noble and selfless act. I didn't have anything left, I am happy to report. The damage I could have caused!

I am also told that, before going to bed that night, I asked the woman in charge of searching my bags for anything that might contain alcohol (including shaving cream) if she would tuck me in, and would it be possible to get a good-night kiss? She smiled and said no, then left with my razor. I was on suicide watch.

The next couple of days are fuzzy. I know that they were giving me some sort of drugs, but not enough, and that I was falling down a lot and hurting myself in the process, then crying when they told me I needed a wheelchair and round-the-clock nursing. A short time later, the maggots and leeches showed up. I kept telling my pretty nurse to find me some Raid. Then I told her to forget it, because my sweet black Lab puppy was somehow between my legs (even though I was damn sure Betty Ford had said no pets and that my dog was really three thousand miles away with my wife), and Raid would be toxic to her. I kept opening her mouth and pulling out maggots, but more kept coming from inside her. They were in my eyes and mouth, too, but I didn't care. I needed to help my innocent baby first.

In the beginning I was cranky and critical of what I perceived to be rather stupid and pointless rules at the center, such as no saying hello to anyone—especially women—from the other dorms; no newspapers, except from Saturday at five until Sunday night; no caffeine; no unauthorized books; no telephones, faxes, or televisions; no hats or sunglasses indoors; no walking alone after dark; no smoking in the boys' room or on our private verandas; and no removing the rubber mattress covering from your bed, no matter how much you suffered from the hot, then cold, sweats.

The fact that most of these rules came to make some kind of twisted sense as I progressed through the program was a revelation to me. The counselors talked often about the need to surrender, and, although the word *surrender* is not in my vocabulary—I have always been suspicious of anything even remotely smacking of authority—I did experience some sort of giving-in to many requirements I either hadn't agreed with or hadn't understood at the beginning.

The Betty Ford Center is located in Rancho Mirage, California (a small town with more than a hundred golf courses), on a beautiful campus covering some ten acres. It consists of four dormitories—two for men and two for women—housing twenty patients each, an overpriced bookstore that sells only approved drug- and alcohol-related books, a cafeteria, a swimming pool, a nursing station, an auditorium, and assorted office spaces. Although legally it is a hospital, it feels, at best, like a hotel; at worst, like a minimum-security prison.

In spite of its reputation as an expensive retreat (twelve thousand bucks up front, which our insurance company refused to help with) for rich elites and pretty people who just need to get straight for a while (there is an element of that), Betty Ford offers a program of tough love, a caring and talented staff with the patience of Job, and a rigid schedule designed to educate patients about substance abuse. Former first lady Betty Ford is on the board of the center and a frequent visitor (she lives nearby). Though not inclined to make small talk with patients, she will, with studied ease, stand up in front of a bunch of drunks and addicts and say, "Hi, I'm Betty Ford, and I'm an alcoholic and drug addict." And she will go on to tell her story of too much Valium and booze, usually mixed.

A normal day at Betty Ford begins with a six A.M. wake-up call. You shower, make your bed, visit meds, then do your daily chores. (Each person is given weekly job assignments that get easier as you make your way through the program. I started out cleaning the laundry room and ended up as clothing monitor, which consisted of telling people not to wear their hats or shades indoors.) After breakfast, there's a short meditation reading from two books of dated platitudes and wishes for drunks. The rest of the morning is taken up by a "meditation talk," a thirty-minute lecture on anything from anger management to the medical consequences of alcohol abuse (no lecture lasts longer than thirty minutes, since it is the contention at Betty Ford that the brains of alcoholics and addicts can absorb information for only that long), a peer review of the lecture, and then an hour of group therapy.

After lunch there is a "first step" session, in which a patient admits to his addiction and says how sorry he is for messing up. A first step can be boring, dramatic, touching, informative, or funny. For example: "I forgot my wife was with me and left the bar with another woman. I remembered my wife in the morning, though, but she wasn't there when I went back to pick her up. I guess she left when the place closed." After first step comes a mandatory recreation period (I never did get to it), then perhaps grief counseling or a smoking-cessation program. Before dinner you're expected to work on your assignment, such as writing in your diary (which goes to your counselor every day), or some other expressive activity. Then there's another visit to meds, and dinner.

After dinner (the food is quite good) you attend another lecture, another peer review of said lecture, and then an Alcoholics Anonymous meeting or a Narcotics Anonymous meeting for an hour. From nine P.M. until bed, you're expected to read alcohol-related materials or AA's "Big Book," but more often than not it's a chance for a snack, a smoke, or a stroll over to the women's dorms.

They dispense a minimum of drugs at Betty Ford and don't seem at all concerned when new arrivals show up at the dorm office complaining of thousands of insects in their beds. One young man, not yet familiar with just how tough the Betty Ford program can be, boasted that by putting half an Alka Seltzer tablet in his mouth and shaking uncontrollably, he could get the staff to give him morphine. He said he had done it successfully at other hospitals. Hearing of this, a counselor said, "You know what we would do? We'd throw the little shit out on the lawn and tell him he had an NA meeting in ten minutes and not to be late." I know from my own experience that the counselor was not exaggerating. The philosophy seems to be that a little suffering goes a long way toward helping you remember what it was that brought you there in the first place.

As I sobered up, I became very concerned about whether I would be able to write without my source of inspiration and comfort. The fact that I had become moderately successful in my chosen craft only while drunk did not escape me. The glib pronouncements of many people, both in and out of the program, that I would only be a better writer sober ("Just imagine how many new emotions you'll have!") was less than reassuring, since most of them couldn't write a simple declarative sentence if their lives depended on it.

I did worry, after reading over the few letters I wrote to people while at Betty Ford, that I was losing the ability to express myself on paper, not to mention finding it exceedingly difficult to write legibly, due to my uncontrollable shakes. A couple of weeks later, sans the tremors and with a more clear mind, I wrote the following for our last assignment before being released, a goodbye letter to whatever put us there, read aloud to the group:

Goodbye, Johnnie Walker

Unlike so many of my peers, I have not based my goodbye to you on the assumption that you are male or female, best friend or hated lover. In all the years of our dubious friendship, never once, even in my most drunken state, did you ever manage to pour yourself into my twelve-ounce glass, containing five half-moon ice cubes, and jump into my waiting hands. You are a fine bottle of whiskey—not a bad thing to be, by any means—but nothing more and nothing less.

It is late Friday night, and here I am having an illicit smoke in the bathroom at the Betty Ford Center and thinking about you. I am wondering if I will be able to find the words to tell you that, as much as I have enjoyed our reckless but enduring friendship, it's time for us to say goodbye. Alas, I will miss you terribly, but there comes a time when it is not only necessary, but best, to go our separate ways.

You have been a good and loyal friend. When my soul hurt, you were there to numb me. When my heart was broken, you helped me forget. When my dear old man died on Easter Sunday, I said, Goodbye, Daddy, with you in hand. But in the end, I was just another barfly, last guy down on the left. The last guy still there after my drinking friends had babies, changed jobs, bought new homes, or found other places that had five-buck all-you-can-eat lunches. I was left in a place I didn't like anymore, but I stayed anyway.

Then I saw your power: your ability to put me in the hospital, legs shot, liver wounded, cold sweats, a wheelchair. I saw maggots and leeches on my body, in my mouth. Even before, you made me sneaky, which, by nature, I am not. You made me think of Hemingway and putting a gun in my mouth, too. But then the dog barked and I took her for a walk. Maybe tomorrow. Maybe next week. But maybe, always maybe, when you are there.

I live in a small house at the end of a quiet cul-de-sac in the pretty town of Ardmore, Pennsylvania. It is a prosperous and safe place. I hap-

pily share my life with my wife of more than twenty years. She is beautiful and caring, but, best of all, she loves me. We have a fine dog—a black Lab named Samantha—who was born on the Fourth of July in 1995. I rake leaves in the fall, shovel snow in the winter, plant flowers in the spring, and take care of my little garden in the summer; last year—due to noisy storms and assorted quiet animals—it yielded exactly one fat green pepper, after an expenditure of $487.

I am an author—a profoundly satisfying calling—and work in a complete and attractive office on the second floor of our home. I am indeed a lucky man. And yet, with your help, I am killing myself, and I don't know why. So we are over, you and I. I take this action with a deep and abiding respect for both your power and your charm. I will miss you.

Since I began writing this, I have slipped three times. "Slipped" is the term AA uses to describe a relapse. The Betty Ford people say you "fucked up." I am neither proud nor ashamed that I did indeed fuck up. Nothing will give me back my yesterdays or allow me to relive them, so I won't try. I will just go on and hope that someday, somehow, I will finally win (if staying sober really is winning).

The first time I slipped, it was out of some strange curiosity about what a drink would do to me now and how it would taste. I decided to have a vodka and tonic. The biggest mistake I made (besides just having the drink) was to pour myself a drink of the same proportions—in the same fourteen-ounce glass, no lemon (it takes space away from the booze), just three small ice cubes—I'd used when I was a certifiable drunk. My preferred ratio was about 80 percent vodka to 20 percent tonic. So here I was, enjoying what I thought would be one little drink, and all of a sudden I was toasted, baked, fried.

Of course, once a drunk gets toasted, baked, and fried, all thoughts of moderation go out the window, and the only thought left is whether I *really* need three ice cubes in the second drink. I did, after a time, call the Betty Ford people to say that I had fucked up. I was crying and disappointed in myself and needed to hear some encouraging words. They were very nice and understanding and said that most of their lambs stray at some point, and that drinking is part of the recovery process, so I shouldn't be too hard on myself—but a little bit hard was OK.

They also suggested that I go to an AA meeting as soon as possible. Drunk but not disorderly, I went to a meeting that night and ended up being asked to leave and not come back if I'd had anything to drink. I was embarrassed and humiliated. The incident was a new one to everyone I told about it, especially to the Betty Ford people, who pointed out that membership to AA is open to all who have a desire to stop drinking. That's it. There are no other requirements to be a member of that august organization. Basically, I'd been tossed out of a club that will accept anybody.

Since then I've given up on AA and decided to make do with my trusty if expensive psychiatrist, my supportive and caring wife, our two dogs (who seem to have a great deal to say about everything that happens around here), my counselors from Betty Ford, and my fellow drunks and addicts and co-conspirators from the program.

I came to truly love and depend on the assorted wackos I lived with in the dorm at Betty Ford. There was a usually profane, even vulgar sense of shared pain, caring, and camaraderie among us. We banded together against the ignorance and antagonism many people showed toward our disease. One night on "Sixty Minutes," the resident curmudgeon and commentator, Andy Rooney, was discussing the Baltimore Ravens' chosen name. He pointed out that Edgar Allan Poe, whose poem "The Raven" had inspired the name, ended up dying in Baltimore on a barroom floor, penniless (certainly a crime in Rooney's neat white world of the Hamptons) and nothing more than a common *drunk*. He spit out the word *drunk* with a venom all too familiar to us alcoholics. So when we, the sick, have the chance to be together in a place where our flaws are not only accepted but embraced, it's a meaningful and transforming experience.

The first day or two that I was in the wheelchair, I decided—quite admirably, I thought—that I could do everything without help. But the damn doors were just too heavy, and the chair kept tipping, and I kept falling and was always late for meals because I wouldn't accept a helping hand. Finally, after a particularly nasty fall, I got up the courage to ask someone to help me back into the chair. It was then that I finally understood why Betty Ford urges people to ask for help: we all need it and can't make it without it.

After I was released from Betty Ford, my psychiatrist said that I'd been "engaged" there, and now needed sustained and continuing engagement if I was going to make it as a former drinker in a drinking world. So I have tried several private counselors who are supposedly experts in dealing with people like me—that is, drunks. The one I've settled on is a gray-haired woman, an M.D., smart and hard—and expensive. She told me the insurance companies "fucked her over" too much in the past, so she doesn't deal with them anymore. Another 120 bucks a week that we don't have, and for what? To try to keep me alive, I guess. She tells me I'm worth it, but for that much money she'll probably tell anybody anything. Nonetheless, I will see her again. My shrink said engagement, engagement, engagement. That's what I need. So I will try engagement.

I want to try heroin. I want to try prescription drugs. I want to get high again on my favorite Scotch. I want to lose myself. But right this minute, this second really, I am sober and I like it.

Brandel France de Bravo

Licking the Woman

1

I am the harried health
consultant just landed
in Ghana. The taxi driver
thinks he knows
where it came from,
how it spreads.
The foreign man. He come
and lick the woman,
he says, flicking
his tongue in and out
like a snake. I laugh
and tip him two condoms.

2

Juanita spoke Spanish,
lived in the apartment
next door, had the desk
next to mine at Booker T
elementary. In third

grade she taught me
the meanings of *saber.*
¿Cómo sabe?
How does it taste?
¿Cómo sabe?
How does she know?
Later that day
in Black History month,
during George Washington
Carver and his peanuts,
she brought her nose
to my forearm—the blond
hairs lay down beneath
her breath—and licked.
By the time Miss Baker
threw us out,
she was savoring
my apple-round shoulder.
Banished to the hallway,
we sat on the floor,
side by side, in silence.
I hugged my knees: my arm
smelled like plantains.

3

The man in Damascus
put whiskey in my beer
and his tongue between
my pinkie and ring finger,
ring and middle, middle
and index, index and thumb. . . .
I was in a divan-lined
living room, other people
present, so I thought,
what's the harm.

I'll let him
for a little. Avoiding
his eyes, I fixed mine
on the black velvet
Mecca above his head.
A couple of minutes
went by before I
jerked away, slapped him
with my wet palm.
They held him back
long enough for me
to leave. I would have
anyway. He already knew
too much.

Brian Hocevar

The Drowned Man's Notes

The final breath is where despair begins. For a lifetime, I took breath for granted; I let the diaphragm expand thoughtlessly, automatically; I drank up the air and, in that way, took the world inside me. Perhaps that is the problem. Perhaps we are only meant to know so much of the outside. I would have you know the easy brutality with which water intrudes on the lungs, the ease with which it presses the life out of you to make room for more water. You have, perhaps, sat beside rivers, lakes, or oceans with a lover or, later, maybe a child, and you may have spoken of infinities and forevers, as water is apt to make us do. We imagine some beauty in inundation. We think we want to be full of something else. But let no talk of the liquid womb deceive you: the body does not want to go into water.

First I went under, found some dank comfort in the mud of the riverbed, but now this ridiculous raft wants to float, and so I float. Face down, I do not need eyes anymore; the flesh is nothing but a hopeless, tangled mess of nerves. Along my back, moonlight stabs icy pinpricks through the sodden fabric of a shirt; it is night. In treetops along the river's edge, two crows call back and forth to each other: *He is dead? He is dead. He has drowned? He has drowned.* Lazy wakes lap against rocks along the bank, but the river will not climb ashore, so the living can sleep peacefully tonight. They pull covers over shoulders, they huddle together for warmth, and they leave this night to the dead and the drowned.

Rivers have names, but why bother? Somewhere to the east, mountains freeze over, then thaw, and that begins it. The melt-off makes its way west in creeks and streams, then finds the low passage and floods it. That's where I am. I hope for big water in the west: a lake, perhaps an ocean. Something vast into which I can disperse.

I expect no grace tonight. My prayers are all used up; there will be no murky hands to pull me back down into the quiet at the bottom, no angels with probing fingers and black wings to carry me to heaven, or something like it. Fully inflated now, there will be no more mindless sinking for me. Perhaps I will learn something in this dark, inky night, this weightless floating. One does not prepare oneself for these excursions on water.

A clearing comes up along the right bank. A shed, a tire swing, some bright plastic toys: a back yard. Tied to an old, gnarled sycamore, a black Labrador wakes from a dim, doggy slumber, and paces to the end of his chain. Nostrils flare as he catches the scent of something big and meaty and dead out on the water. He growls, moans, then lets out a sharp, hungry bark. No use in it. The feast floats by, untouchable, and now he won't be able to sleep for the pangs in his stomach. I have disturbed the little lamb.

Don't imagine there isn't some satisfaction in this.

The first glow of dawn illuminates a patch of buildings to the west. As the sun comes up, I drift closer, until the air is abuzz with the sound of traffic and industry, and I am drifting along a highway that pulses with early morning traffic. I'm sure they can see me from the road, and that someone will want to get his name in the papers for spotting the floater. Here I am, a little treasure for party conversation. If I had tears, this might be where they would flow, but I would still sell myself like a hawker pushing stuffed animals at a carnival. Make yourself famous, pedestrian, motorist: spot the floater.

Below me, a school of bream flash by, falter, then circle back around me. At my ankles, a ringed mouth puckers, sucking at the bony nub. Now they find my stomach, my neck, and they swarm me, sucking at the dead mass of my flesh. The first to venture to my face puckers on my lips, testing me cautiously.

How goes it, dead man?

Fuck off, fish. I've a float to conduct here. Leave me to it.

He laughs, presses his mouth to my neck, puckers.

No, you aren't so soft yet, but you've been gathering algae, old boy.

I cannot pull away, cannot flinch. I float.

My colleagues out there will make filets of you and yours. Don't forget that, fish.

Your colleagues? Don't fool yourself, dead man. You have no colleagues. Those are humans out there; you're just a barge of filth. What consequence in a drowned man?

To my starboard side, leaves chitter in a mild breeze. To my port, wind across an open field. I am out of the shadow of the buildings and the highway. I am still in the river.

The bream brushes against my swollen lids, his touch as light as a lover's.

Soften up, dead man. I may eat your eyes yet.

Choke on them.

The school, having fed, flashes away as quickly as they arrived, leaving a trail of bubbles in their wake. Do I hear laughter as they disappear? Have they seen the end of my float miles in advance? I can almost feel their mouths working at my hollow sockets.

A casket. With silk trimmings, even faux silk, even black velvet. Let the living cheer themselves with the sight of something worse off than they. Anything, just no more water.

■

But, of course, I drift. The press and surge of current thrums my eardrums with the dull insistence of a pulse. Even drowning has its rhythm, apparently, and I fall in for a while, let the beating river play me like a dumb lump of cork. Arms out, eyes peeled in milky stare, I drift.

Is time waiting for my right moment, perhaps? Did gravity cut me short of fate somehow, and will I have to wait that out? If that is the case, just imagine the chatter of a cemetery. What an insidious bore that must be, really, all the babbling dead waiting on a trumpet, a rallying cry. Saint Peter must have some disgruntled customers on his hands.

A dim shuffle breaks the silence somewhere ahead of me, an aural picture comes into slow focus. Along the water line, feet shuffle in tall grass and leaves, and a little girl's voice sings softly, secretly, *Ring around the rosy, pocketful of posy,* each syllable weighed, as though she is considering something: a chubby fistful of flowers, perhaps? A sodden mass approaching on the water, perhaps? Now close enough to feel her whole presence—the slow, controlled breathing, the strong pulse, the sweat of serious endeavor—I can venture a guess about this little girl. Eight years old. Hair: chestnut. Aquamarine eyes (light: not the heavy aqua of a river). Face amply fleshed, though her brow is drawn in tight, thoughtful lines; she is not the work of a frivolous God. A shifting rustle suggests that she has taken a seat, and now I can see her hands—dirty, reddened by stinging nettle—roving in tall grass, searching for posies.

And were I to raise my head, purse my blackened, swollen lips, what posy could I offer her? *Go now, while you still have the chance. Go back to your mother; confront her; demand to know what was so important about her and that man that they had to dabble in creation; demand to know how she thought she could get away with expelling you toward this; demand re-entry.* What would she make of this wreckage, this drowned man? Hands pressed to ears, eyes clamped tight, would she find the breath to scream? Or would I have taught her about silence? No, I have no desire to school this girl, not even if it were to mean the end of my drift, not even if I must float until I am a clump of mulch.

Her voice reaches a peak and then begins to fade; I am moving past her. Quietly, I hope. Without fanfare. Behind me, the girl carries on with her song, *Ashes, ashes,* her voice receding, each syllable as important as the next. Her hands, as I have imagined them, continue picking and plucking; they rove in the tall grass, fingers working on wildflowers, gathering posies that could be intended for a father, a boy, a man who—given different circumstances and simple breath—could be me.

My hands—the fraying, saturated clods—bob lazily, moving forward. I have to follow them.

Why do I have to follow them?

My unwinding begins on the sly; no one consults me on the matter. A day's float behind me, another about to begin, the sun comes up behind dense clouds in time for a school of perch to discover me and stop to feed. One of them, in gluttonous fervor, tears away a loose patch of flesh at my neck and, gulping that bit, works the ragged lesion with infantile conviction.

Now that I am unraveling, I wonder, How much will they have to eat before they begin to draw me out of this husk? Ten pounds? Twenty? Will one lucky fish sap this chatterbox in a single, convulsive gulp? Will its flat, vacant eyes roll as the shadow of me descends like a plague of locusts? Or will I go in refined segments, possibly small enough that I will not have this "I" to labor under anymore? I could end in a hungry thrashing of fins, a dumb, underwater stirring.

On the surface, a hiss and a splash, and something approaches from the starboard. Long and powerful, it coils slowly, tongue playing at the water as though testing the surface, moving toward me as a slither, a sliding, every inch announcing *serpent.* Brushing my arm, the moccasin's scales play lightly on dead flesh. Apparently satisfied with the full nature of my stillness, it slides up the hump of my back, my neck, ruffling my hair as it perches and nests.

A perch sucks carelessly at my lips and face; I can barely manage a whisper:

Moccasin . . .

The serpent's tongue flicks an earlobe.

Sh-sh. Have some decency, drowned man. Be silent.

Strike me. Strike me.

Don't waste my time. You are so much flotsam.

The moccasin coils itself in agitation. Beyond the rustle of the serpent, a new sound rises from somewhere up ahead: a watery rumble. The current picks up by the barest degree; I am drifting toward rapids.

Had I breath, I would scream now.

Kill me. End this.

Kill you? You are already dead.

The serpent moves out on a shoulder, pushes itself out onto the water, leaving me pleading, calling after it.

Just an ounce of venom . . .

Drowned man, you cannot drift forever.

The moccasin glides away, its wake describing half-circles that break apart against each other. I want to call after the moccasin, but he slithers onto the shore and disappears in the underbrush. As the rising current pushes me faster toward the rapids, the perch break away and disperse. Alone now, rushing in a suddenly terrifying current, I don't know whether to be angry or not. He could have at least tried.

Now the rumbling is on top of me, the current is turning me over, and I plunge into the rapids.

In my spinning, I consider the dead hulk on the water. Were I, for instance, the captain of this raft, I'd have some executive decisions to make. Jaw hanging slack in the quintessential expression of *Homo sapiens* breakthrough, I might grunt, *These are rapids.* That much established, I might make other discoveries. Portside, thick clusters of oak and willow crowd up to the water, but a long, gradual slope along the starboard shore would be easily accessible. The *Homo sapiens* navigator is a difficult buffoon to fathom, impossible to predict in terms of decision-making. I might raise a paddle above my head, shake it angrily at the sky. Rocking to and fro in the tantrum of mortal protest, I might capsize my raft and spill out into the water. Perhaps some sense of loyalty would urge me to salvage the vessel in the grand tradition of that *Homo sapiens* captain who goes down with his ship.

By the same token, I would want to get out of the rapids, and thus I might simply forget the raft and swim for it.

Or if I were a little girl picking posies by the river? Or if I were a dumb motorist, navigating early morning traffic? Or if I were a wife whose husband did not come back from his excursion on the river? The mind reels at the possibilities. The mind reels and turns, doubles back on itself. It putters on the verge of its deep ability to imagine. It reels, and it leaps forward.

And the drowned man lurches on, following the crescendo of the white water. He plunges headlong, turns in a violent squall, and, for a moment, the body is entirely submerged. Then it reappears, bobbing pathetically to the surface.

One might wince at the mindless buoyancy of the body resurfacing. Really. It's a terrible sight to behold.

Having seen the body bobbing in the river, one might have a thought or two on the pathology of drowning, perhaps even the nature of death.

It's obvious, really. When we die, angels come to carry our souls straight to heaven. Death is the merest exhalation.

Or, rather, we are in fact so much meat, and consciousness hinges on breath and pulse. When the meat dies, the consciousness simply ceases. Not even a breath, not even worth mentioning.

Or perhaps death happens in slow cycles, a continual molting, a changing of seasons. Consider the little girl by the river. One day, she may return to that spot a woman, her days of posy-picking long gone. Will her full-grown arms remember the sting of the nettle that hid in the tall grass? Will her fingers recall the rough stalk of the Queen Anne's lace, the pulpy flesh of the foxglove? She might walk slowly, gathering up these snippets as though she were collecting snapshots of dead relatives. She might kneel at the river's edge, dip a finger into the water, stare at her reflection.

Then again, this talk of death may be mere chatter, as meaningless as the buzz of gnats around a dead man's head.

Let's say I made it home after all. Let's say I'm in an easy chair—padded arms, footrest, yes—next to my bedroom window. Let's say I am reading a book, and I have just broken off in the middle of a sentence because I spotted something floating down the river out back.

■

The drowned man's hectic turning slows, stops, and he drifts steadily again. Equilibrium regained, his arms find their original position: shoulders hunched, hands up too high for crucifixion, too low for surrender. The back—still, undisturbed by breath—drifts slowly, cutting only a tiny wake, and his submerged, saturated head does not stir for the gnats that once again swarm his hair, nor for the clouds that break and dissipate on the horizon, nor for the dim chattering of voices in the trees downriver.

On the bank ahead, two fishermen tramp through a coppice, their boots sucking heavily in mud. They speak in the quiet tones of men who believe their voices stir the dumb silence of the riverbed; they are hoping for better fishing downriver. The shorter of the two takes the lead. Pushing his way through the branches and undergrowth, he laughs at some comment from his partner, turns his head to reply, and is cut short as if by a blow. Eyes widening, mouth falling open, he raises a hand and points out to the river.

The corpse takes no notice. Face down, eyes milky-blind, he floats. He does not hear the grunts of the fishermen as they push through the underbrush and splash out toward him; he does not feel the heavy hand that falls on his back, finds purchase; he does not feel himself being towed to shore. His water-logged arms drag in the current, but he does not twitch, does not stir. At the center of all this activity, the drowned man is beyond the jarring pull of the fishermen. He is dead weight.

Having dragged the carcass ashore and laid it in the mud, the fishermen back away, rinse their hands in the river. Their voices quiet now, they speak just loudly enough for the other to hear. Neither is certain what he should do with the dead man, but it is only so far to their vehicle, just a short hike, and they agree that were the tables turned, they wouldn't want to be left on the bank for any stray dog to pick at, so they fashion a makeshift stretcher from their ponchos, roll the dead man onto it, and bear him up.

Side by side, they trudge away from the river, up a sloping path into the woods, carrying the sagging form of the drowned man between them. The burden has silenced them, driven them down into parts of themselves that neither could ever fathom in the other, and that an outsider could only guess at. Perhaps they are thinking of how they will return to their respective homes, how they will have to explain what took them so long. They may still be revulsed by the mortifying feel of the drowned man's skin; they may be thinking of how they will have to shower before they touch children or wives. Perhaps they will toss sleeplessly tonight. Perhaps they will press themselves against their wives, as though grounding themselves deep in the act of breathing, pulsing.

Now the fishermen pick up their pace, hurrying to the top of the hill, as though they are quite ready to be rid of the drowned man, as though they have fully imagined their course beyond him.

Larissa Szporluk

Deer Crossing the Sea

Many things were like sleep,
wholly in the power of the forest,
the deep middle, deep shiver, deep shade,
from which many things ran, unawake,
in search of new mountains to graze,
covered in flowers, *my love, I am sick,*
or covered in snow, pink with algae,
in search of impossible light
made of water, whose sapphire waves
swathed their heads, *you were only a dream,*
as they swam out to meet it, kicking their hooves,
no longer breathing, because no one
or nothing can quit once the body gets wind
of an eden—the promise of nectar
haunts them forever, the shore pecked out
of their eyes, and there, in its stead,
something greater to catch,
a scent that would paralyze God.

Jane Brox

The Wilderness North of the Merrimack

I

As the Merrimack River gathers its water and its snowmelt, it descends through the worn slopes of New Hampshire's White Mountains past granite outcrops and hemlock, cone-heavy white pine, birch, maple, beech, through the cities of Concord, Manchester, Nashua, and into Massachusetts, where it bends eastward at the city of Lowell, and then, for the last thirty lateral miles of its journey to the Gulf of Maine, traverses the low rolling hills of a coastal plain. The bend in the river lies to the west of the town of Dracut, which is set among the hills on the northern bank, just past the inner crook where the Merrimack turns toward the sea.

On the early maps of New England—*being the first that ever was here; cut and done by the best Pattern that could be had, which being in some places defective it made the other less exact: yet doth it sufficiently shew the Scituation of the Country, and conveniently well the distance of Places*—the Merrimack appears as a central spine rising out of ship-laden waters, rising then branching off beyond the northern lakes and into the wine hills. The bend in the river is hardly discernible, and this town doesn't yet exist. You can clearly see how the first colonial settlements in the lower valley had spread out south and west of the river, the broad waters of which had been a barrier to the settlement of the north bank. The Pawtucket Indians, early inhabitants of this place, called it Augumtoocooke—the wilderness north of the Merrimack—a name it was known by until its seventeenth-century mapping, when surveyor Jonathan Danforth's plats divided twenty-two thousand acres into reserved lands and official grants for a handful of families and their descendants. The southern boundary was marked entirely by a calm stretch of the river. The first faint paths of settlement led to and from the ferry crossings.

Drawcutt, Draycott, Draycote, Dracut, Massachusetts. At 42°41′ latitude, 71°19′ longitude. Straight lines drawn across fishing places and hunting grounds. Boundaries marked by white oaks and brooks, by granite blocks and heaps of stones. Their plowing and planting and clearing, the modest homes they hoped would be permanent, the plat itself, marked the passing of an earlier world, though by the time Danforth drew his map, the Pawtucket Indians were already a remnant tribe. Explorers and fur traders had, years earlier, made their way up the river, bringing European disease with them. Between 1614 and 1617, more than three quarters of the Pawtuckets died of a sickness, still guessed at, that killed within three days of its first symptoms: *The living were in no wise able to bury the dead . . . hundreds without burial or shelter were devoured as carrion by beasts and birds of prey, and their bones were bleached by the sun.* They who'd trod paths along ridges and across the valleys, who'd found the shallow places to ford streams and the safest route to the sea, made trails that were narrow—*unmapped, unmarked except in the atlas of memory*—and worn so deep by years of use—two feet in places—that some are said still to be visible in parts of southern New England.

Brown ink washed out on parchment, black lines on bond. All the maps and all the dissolutions of time that render them inaccurate—scouring rains, disease, invasions, wars, and floods. Since the Danforth plats, the wilderness north of the Merrimack has been mapped and mapped again with topographic surveys, road maps, charts of the watershed and the milkshed, soil maps that follow the geological logic of the ice ages and have no center, assessors' maps squaring off the place to account for the ownership of every inch, zoning maps dividing the plots for purpose and use. Each illustrates a small part of the story and none begins to tell the whole, which, like the late April sun in a glass of clear water, can't ever be known by boundaries.

II

After syntax is gone, and the liturgy, the maxims, the songs—even after no one can read anything of the old alphabet, and the old names of things that remain are recognizable only to the few—ragged bits of story still come down from the old country and are told in a new tongue: dry, sturdy, thin as the last weeds to be covered by a January snow. Sometimes those stories feel like tests when they're told. *Don't you remember.... Haven't you heard*... how she was smuggled into this country under her mother's skirts... how they had to get him out after he'd killed that man in a fistfight... how they wanted to send her back because of the weeping in her eye?

I imagine the stories my Lebanese grandparents carried with them had been at first as bulky as a peddler's pack stocked with lace and thread and stockings. My grandmother, not yet eighteen, traveled with her goods along the roads surrounding Olean, New York. As she exchanged lace and thread and her own handiwork for pennies, she glimpsed, through each open farmhouse door, another life in the making—the rush of warmth from stove heat, the smell of hard soap, of johnnycake and drying apples. And with each open door, her pack lightened, and the stories shifted their place in her memory.

After Olean, the family moved to Lawrence, Massachusetts, known at the end of the nineteenth century as Immigrant City, the worsted and woolen capital of the world. For miles, red-brick textile mills lined the banks of the canals and the Merrimack River, and they contained so many looms and spindles that workers came to the city from Canada and all the countries of Europe and the Middle East to tend them. Within the central district you could hear forty-five—some say fifty or sixty—different languages and dialects spoken by dyers, cutters, spinners, and weavers, by men who fixed the looms and rigged the warps, and women who felt along the yardage for slubs. Their children hauled coils of sliver-spun wool and breathed in air that was white with cloth dust. Always cloth dust, falling constant as high mountain flurries.

The Italians settled near the commercial district; the Portuguese and Jewish neighborhoods were a little farther north and west. The Franco-

Belgians found a place by the Merrimack above the dam, the Poles along the thin, sinewy Spicket River, which wound through the north side of the city and eventually joined the Merrimack. The Syrians, as they were then known, settled several thousand strong on the slight-rise blocks above the commercial district and the river—several thousand who'd walked through night dust storms and across mountain passes and had sailed from Marseilles or Naples across the winter-gray Atlantic to pass, bewildered, through ports of entry so as to keep shop, and sell wares, and take up unskilled jobs in the mills, where they were among the lowest paid of all the workers. However far the journey, they continued to sing their Mass in Arabic, and their corner stores sold thyme, sesame paste, rose water, and the dried cherry kernels we call *mahleb*, which flavor our Easter sweets.

For my grandparents, the life they'd glimpsed in the offing wasn't there among the familiar language or aroma of spices in the neighboring shops. "God knows how they ever got the money together," my father once said, for twenty acres of tillage on the south side and an early-nineteenth-century farmhouse and fifteen acres on the north side of a dirt road—sometimes known as the Black North Road—in the town of Dracut, five miles west of Lawrence's tenement district and halfway to the city of Lowell.

A hundred years before they'd arrived in this country, a man named Moses Bailey had raised the first rough buildings on that property: a shed and a cottage he used as his shoe shop and living quarters, which in time became the central link in the long, curved spine of what we think of as a New England farm. Bailey's son extended the cluster of buildings eastward by raising a two-bay carriage house and a white clapboard cow barn, topped with a windmill. Westward he added an ell for a summer kitchen, and southward from that ell he built a two-story-and-garret home. It is a dream of the solid and ordinary, the gable roof with its plain sloping sides, the serene rows of windows—two lights over two—without ornament, the two chimneys breaching the roof beam. The eight fireplaces insured that even if the corners and attic remained cold enough to keep the summer harvest, there'd be a spot of warmth in every room.

If you were to slip off the leather latch of a farmer's diary from those years and turn the pages past the calendar, past the measure of length, the measure of surface, the measure of solidity, past the apothecary's weight and the diamond weight, the dry measures, the tests for death and the cure for cinders in the eye, you could read the concentrated words of those winter days: *Wednesday, January 4: Finished hauling in ice. Thursday, January 5: Got the sawdust back into the ice house. Tuesday, January 31: 6 below. Pump froze up. February 9: Zero. Sawing wood in the woodhouse. Cold windy day . . . Samuel Knight died this noon. Jim went down to his sister's . . . Mr. Knight's funeral . . . Tough New England storm. Snow flying. Hard wind blow. Sawing wood and churning.*

By the time my grandparents bought the farm early in this century, the chain of buildings Moses Bailey had started a hundred years before was as long and rambling as it would ever be. In a 1901 photograph I can count six different roof heights, the most prominent being that of the broad-peaked house. By then its separate doors led to separate worlds. The daily one faced the work yard and the outbuildings, the place where they made their repairs in spring, where they rigged up the bay mares and loaded the milk wagon. The front door—dressed with an overhang—was the one place that allowed for shade, the one place to shelter a formal visitor. It faced the road to the cities.

With the land and house came much of the life of those who'd gone before, their tools and cattle, their hens and chickens, and whatever they could coax out of wash and drift from the age of glaciers. My grandfather plowed the richest soils for the garden and the crop of hay; the indifferent, he used for pasture; the worst, let go to woods. The orchard spread across a droughty slope. Over time they came to judge for themselves the particular soils of the country—the sweet or sour, early or late. As they cleared stones and harvested potatoes and recorded their monthly payments to the bank, they would have been too intent on their work to notice that the last local map of agriculture was being drawn.

As I was going through my father's papers in the days after his death I came across what must have been that last map—the 1924 soil survey of Middlesex County. A booklet details the particular, elaborate name and best use of every soil to be found here, and the accompanying map lifts every inch of earth from its dun color and assigns it a rich, saturated one. The colors swirl and eddy—they remind me of Italian marbled paper—with fine distinctions and varying promises: the yellows of Hollis and the oranges of Sudbury loams, the pink of the Gloucester gravelly phase. The pale blue of Hinckley gravelly sandy loam: . . . *derived largely from coarse glacial drift . . . drainage, which is almost entirely internal, is usually excessive to the extent that crops suffer in dry seasons. . . . Crop yields are generally low. Hay cuts from one-half to three-fourths ton to the acre, depending on the season. . . . This land can be utilized for pasture, but it is not well suited to grass.* Merrimac gravelly sandy loam: *Nearly all the vegetables grown for market in this county are found on this soil, but asparagus is the only one grown on a large acreage. A few farmers make a specialty of chickens. Hay yields range from 1 to 1½ tons to the acre on the best-farmed land. . . . The soil is easy to cultivate. It is plowed 8 or 9 inches deep and can be brought into good tilth without difficulty. . . .* Coloma sandy loam, gravelly phase: . . . *differs from the typical soil in having a larger proportion of stones and gravel on the surface and throughout the soil. . . . It can be utilized for pasture land, but it furnishes only indifferent grazing. The rougher areas should be left in forest or should be reforested to white pine.*

The soft hills to our south are marked as drifts of Hinckley loamy sand—*a small acreage is in pasture, a still smaller area is in mowing*—and Gloucester stony loams. The soil of the river bank beyond those hills isn't deposited in pockets like most other county soils but has washed and settled in narrow bands along both sides of the watercourse—thin stretches, influenced by the drenchings and drainings of mountain water: . . . *brown mellow fine sandy loam . . . not inundated with every overflow but covered by the spring freshets. . . . The land is easily plowed and cultivated, coming readily into good tilth. . . . The overflow in spring is depended on in measure to keep up fertility.* This map is the only local one I've seen where the Merrimack's presence is so slight—really, it's almost lost amid the colors of over forty soil types, just a faint blue bend cutting through the reds and greens and oranges in its eastward turn to the sea, as if to suggest we were once a people defined by something other than the river and the red brick cities that line the drops along its lower course.

Any map is bounded by scope and hand and eye, by the particulars of the world it describes. I don't think the soils of Middlesex County will ever again be so painstakingly described and drawn. Contemporary soil maps consist of data imposed on aerial photographs. Colorless, perfunctory, stiff with information alone, the new maps chart moist bulk density and the shrink-swell potential of soils with exactitude, but the grain of the old language, with its good tilth and its indifferent pasture, is gone, just as *hames* and *traces* and *milk pungs* are gone from our conversations.

Our farm is no longer a self-regarding world. The barn and the silo have been lost to wind and rain, and with them the long protective curve of buildings around the east yard that shielded daily life. The house stands more prominent than the remaining farm buildings, and more solitary. A side porch makes it less plain; the maples shading the lawn, less blazed upon by the summer sun. And the crocus, then iris, then roses, until the rust chrysanthemums bloom in mid-October.

Moses Bailey's original cottage survives to this day in its place between the house and the carriage house, and we continue to use it as a storage room and toolshed. Its clean white clapboard exterior blends in with the line of remaining buildings. Walk inside, though, and you feel the length of its days. Its windows are blocked from full sun by two cedars so that, even at noontime, it's a pool of cool shadows. The boards of the interior walls are rough-sawn, not once sanded or painted in all their years. The smell of must. On the rafters a hundred nails have been sunk as a hundred hooks for lanterns, oilcans, chains. Look how everything is becoming the same color. The bins full of bolts and screws, the anvil and ax, the hammers, spades, and hoes, even the white pine floor and the hardwood rafters, the paper on crates and the notices pinned to the walls—all the same brown as acorns and fallen oaks.

If the interior of the farmhouse—its fireplaces blocked off, old papers piled in the bread ovens, half the clocks stopped—also feels like twilight, to think of it only as it is now is to miss much of the story, which continues to waken and glimmer in the eyes of those who lived there, in the eyes of one of my uncles remembering seventy years back to the May evenings he read to his mother as she darned socks and knitted sweaters. She'd want to hear the stories he was learning at college—Shakespeare was her favorite—so over and over again he read her *The Merchant of Venice.* By the late acts the sun had faded back from the dining room table and was retreating from the orchard, his dutiful voice was growing tired. Her knitting needles clicked: *The quality of mercy is not strain'd, it droppeth as the gentle rain from heaven upon the place beneath; it is twice bless'd. . . .*

The story never stopped on the last page. Days, months later he'd hear her tell a clear, clean version to his sisters as they made bread or pies or stuffed grape leaves. A version indiscernible in tenor from the stories she'd sometimes tell that she'd heard back in the dry hills of her own childhood. She'd begin: *There was an Italian* . . . and when she wanted to pause for emphasis or to keep up the suspense, she spent an extra moment pushing the silky dough away with the palm of her hand, then drawing it toward her again.

III

> *As we glided over the broad bosom of the Merrimack, between Chelmsford and Dracut, at noon, here a quarter of a mile wide, the rattling of our oars was echoed over the water to those villages, and their slight sound to us. Their harbors lay as smooth and fairylike as the Lido, or Syracuse, or Rhodes, in our imagination, while, like some strange roving craft, we flitted past what seemed the dwellings of noble home-staying men, seemingly as conspicuous as if on an eminence, or floating upon a tide which came up to those villagers' breasts. At a third of a mile over the water we heard distinctly some children repeating their catechism in a cottage near the shore, while in the broad shallows between, a herd of cows stood lashing their sides, and waging war with the flies.*
>
> —Henry David Thoreau,
> *A Week on the Concord and Merrimack Rivers*

The Dracut of slight sounds and home-staying people that Thoreau imagined as he sailed past on the cusp of the industrial revolution—a spare farming community separated from the world by a quiet stretch of river, a waylaid place between two mill cities, a promise glimpsed in the offing—has slipped into history, as have all the towns it's been since the first lands were granted to a handful of families and their descendants. Their records and maps, showing lands bought and sold over the nearly four hundred years of settlement, are stained with thumbprints and oils, and the corners are feathered from countless exchanges and handlings. Read closely the earnest markings of those documents and you read a world of boundaries marked by stakes and stones, by the trees and the fences that then stood: *The lot of tillage land on the southerly side of said Black North Road and bounded: Beginning on the south side of the said road at the corner of the wall by the old grave yard; thence southerly by said grave yard and by a wall to the road leading from the Methodist Church to the Whittier Brothers; thence by said road... thence westerly by said last named land by a fence to the corner in the wall by said Richardson... to the point of beginning. Said lot contains fifteen acres, more or less.*

To believe that Dracut is still a small place apart—to believe in the word *town* in its root sense as a world protected and enclosed—is as perilous as believing that the old maps suffice, with their hand-drawn lines describing assessments made with lengths of measured chain, with one eye squinting, tracing stone walls, defining borders by neighbors, knowing in some places that the map would be defective and make the whole that much less exact.

The Merrimack no longer divides us from the world or brings us the world, which comes in now by the road and leaves by the road, and distance everywhere is cut through by time. We are a town surrounded by two interstates. We are a reasonable commute to Boston. What had once been prime farmland, the best going for somewhere around eighty dollars an acre in the early decades of the century, is worth multiples of tens of thousands, and the map we live by now is the zoning map of the town, with its broad, direct lines designating solid areas of residential, business, and industrial lands. The shaded or hatched or dotted overlays, which obscure all delineations of ownership, old usages, soil types, elevations, the milkshed, the watershed, and the grid of roads, describe a world where old terms have slipped their meanings. In early documents sometimes the landlocked woods of the town—old pastures let go to pines, the pines now standing a hundred years—are notated as *vacant land.* Such a term has no place on the zoning map, just as *more or less* hardly fits our requirements for an exactitude greater than paces and strides and weighted observations can measure. Nor can *tillage* exist alongside the current concept of highest and best use, where, for final worth, the assessors reimagine fields and orchards and woods as house-lot parcels of one acre, no less.

Such efforts as we've made in these years—on the current map all the land surrounding our farm is zoned for industrial use—will take a long time to go to woods again. Hardly a mile away from the farm is an abandoned Esso plant that had been built—if I read the soil map right—on Gloucester sandy loam: ... *the weathered surface of a comparatively thin glacial-drift.... In cleared areas the soil, to a depth of 6 or 8 inches, is brown, mellow sandy loam ... one of the important soils, as it represents the best farming land in the region ... hay, the most important crop, yields from one-half to 1½ tons to the acre, depending on the season and seeding conditions....*

The rusting tanks of the old plant have been hauled away, but the flat-roofed brick and concrete buildings remain. Moss is creeping up the concrete walls, and mildew stains spread like shadows. A weedy, paved-over lot is scattered with rubbish. It remains a kind of no man's land, warning the world off with its chainlink fence topped with coiled barbed wire. Signs reading FOR SALE and NO TRESPASSING have been up for years, and the place is passed over by developers for old woods every time. I imagine, in spite of assertions that the land is not contaminated, investors are afraid of the future liabilities of building on such land, of what might be uncovered, afraid the work of cleaning the soils may be like cleaning up the river—long and laborious, and even so, not enough. It's easier to break new ground as long as there is new ground. Even the poorest soils keep a time different from human years, the way they build up out of the work of lichens wearing away the glacial rocks, the work of earthworms and sun, of voles and bacteria.

For as long as I can remember there's been a utility corridor along the eastern edge of the farm. I've never known where the high-tension wires link up, only that to our north they disappear into rising hills, and to our south they span the river and continue across the undulating plain toward Boston. This coming year Portland Natural Gas plans to put a 650-mile underground line through the corridor that will bring vast undersea gas reserves from off Sable Island, Nova Scotia, to New England. They'll cut an eighty-foot swath across part of the Maritimes, Maine, and New Hampshire, cut through the southeast corner of our property, and then link up with a national pipeline grid that begins in Texas and works north. Now that six of eight nuclear power plants that once produced electricity for the Northeast have shut down, everyone connected with the project easily says, *You know natural gas is the fuel of the future.* The Canadian reserves will last a hundred years.

Farther north in Maine, where the plan veers off the corridor and the proposed gas line crosses farmland and woods, some of the landowners have protested: *How can something be good for Richmond if it's not good for a group of people who have lived there for years?... If they ruin the land they'll ruin something we love.... I am fighting because I don't want to die in bitterness....*

Because the gas line here goes over a small portion of land already utilized by power lines, it will not encroach on us the way it will encroach on those in Maine. Yet I keep thinking of those protesters in Maine, though I don't know what to think myself, as the land agent from Portland Gas and I walk the utility corridor at the edge of the farm, finding our way through the brush by following a path made by deer and deepened by dirt bikes. He is a quiet, even man, with all his attention on the job in front of him. Nothing about him specifically makes me uneasy. But with my father's death has also come the unfamiliar responsibility of making decisions and negotiating with outside encroachments on the land, so even though I don't know what to think, my every word is guarded. Guarded maybe because one of my father's cautions to me was *Play your cards close to your vest.* And a little because really I'd just like to refuse every encroachment, now that development upon development has been coming in so quickly around us—trucking firms, concrete manufacturing, more trucking—and it just seems like too much too fast, and this, too, is part of all that.

"We all think, perhaps too much, of the piece of land where we were born and of the blood our ancestors gave us," said Jorge Luis Borges after the Falkland Islands War. "In ancient times the Stoics coined a word which, I think, we are still unworthy of; I am referring to the word *cosmopolitanism.* I believe we should be citizens of the world." I'm always arrested by Borges's words when I read them, and however much attachment I feel to this place, I also imagine I agree with him. What place, a citizen's duty? What place, the heart's affections? Where does the greater good lie? In a regional decision? In a local want? What choice, I wonder—to stand with the Mainers or simply let this one pass—would a citizen of the world make here and now?

The land agent and I talk about the lumber that they may need to cut, and the restoration of the woods, the price they'll pay for their easement. Orange flags mark the route of the future gas line, and we walk from flag to flag through the marsh across the brook to higher ground. The vegetation that has grown up along the corridor is not like any I see elsewhere here. The electric company keeps the woods back for the sake of the lines, but the land isn't tended or cultivated. Clumps of sun-loving sweetfern —its head-clearing scent rising when you walk on it—run scattershot through the highest dry ground. There's a stand of hazelnuts with their tiny nutmeats encased in elaborate husks. Sweetfern and hazelnuts both will be uprooted when they cut the trench for the gas line; they plan to replant the swath with grass. "They like to plant grass," the land agent tells me. "They know there's a leak when the grass dies."

We come up the crest of the hill just at the old mail road that runs through the woods. We stop and stand on the two discernible tracks where wagons once traveled across this hill toward the river. In the woods on either side of the corridor, trees have encroached on the old road, and branches lean over the last of it, which has narrowed to a footpath. Only underneath these power lines and on the stretch where our tractors still use the road can you make out the tracks defined over the years by wagons and oxcarts. The road had been on maps hundreds of years back, fifty years back, but on recent maps is no longer marked. "This is where our property ends," I tell the agent.

"I have you down as owning the other side of the road too."

"This is where our land ends," I say. "I'm sure of it." I remember my father in the lamplit circle of his desk showing me this boundary, telling me about the lumber they hauled out of the near woods after the hurricane of '38. In his last year, when I knew he was dying, when I knew many of the responsibilities he carried would fall to me, we hardly ever dared bring up the practical things. Our own deeds are old and inexact, and we probably should have had the land resurveyed before he died. But the most we managed was that sometimes he'd unroll one of the maps he kept stored in the ceramic crock in the corner of his office, and he'd show me the boundaries of our property, and fall into a story about how he came to own it: *I bought it because we needed wood for the winter. We'd go through fifteen cords. A French Canadian used to come out from Lawrence—carried his own ax—to do some of the logging. I paid him a dollar a day.*

When I think about all that went unsaid while he sat there remembering, I know that part of me didn't want to disturb his stories; it was easier—for us both—to abide their wanderings than to think about the future. If we'd had better maps or had spent more time going over what we had, would I be any more prepared for what I've had to face? Always the future is its own bewilderment, and has its own rewards and sorrows. Not long at all since my father died, and already I sometimes feel he wouldn't fit back into this world, that we've arranged our lives beyond him.

"I'm certain this is the property line," I repeat to the agent. "We've never owned that land." He begins flipping through the papers on his clipboard—back past the aerial maps of the property where I can count the trees in the orchard, can see the pattern of waterways through the woods and the clear edge of every field; back past the earlier hand-drawn maps with the stone walls painstakingly set down in a precise hand. He looks exasperated. He'll have to search through the old deeds to find the absent owner of the adjacent land. He begins to flip through more papers. As I wait, I look north up the long corridor where the power lines chase the retreat of the glacier and cut across every sea-flowing thing.

After a few minutes he says, "I'll have to get back to you." Then we begin our walk back down from flag to flag to the road below.

"You'll put all the stone walls back?"

"They have to restore everything."

A fine November rain is falling, and the dampness makes everything clear as rain falls into the last color of the season, bringing up the red at the branch tips on the birches, and the patchy green of the grass in the warmer places. I see black alder lining the low land along the brook, its silver-black bark shining, its red berries brighter than anything else on the land. Winterberries, they're called, because they stay on the branches until spring.

Late every year my father would take his truck down the back field and come home with a dozen cut branches for my mother, a little color at

Christmas to arrange in vases and pitchers. He called them foxberries—I don't know for sure why; I've never heard anyone else call them that, but it seems right. Foxberries. By the end of winter they're bird-pecked and shriveled, nowhere near as brilliantly red as they are in this November rain, but the light is softer and longer then, and what color remains is still apparent in the smoky March days.

Surveyors' chains and steel tapes sag over distances. They expand in the heat and sun, so you have to wait for a cool cloudy day for the best readings, and have to adjust readings done in full day to compensate for the inaccuracies. You need to keep an even stride over a rough road. The fog comes in, and you can't see benchmarks or the other members of the surveying team. You go back over the same ground to check and re-measure the work. It is an old trade, and I imagine its earthbound sounds—the tools clinking and creaking—will grow ever smaller and more distant, quieter and quieter with each successive map made, until they are nearly silent—hardly louder than key clicks.

What will determine our map of the future—the twenty-four satellites orbiting the earth that constitute the Global Positioning System? Each satellite emits precisely timed radio signals. An observer at any point on the earth's surface receiving signals from at least four of the satellites can figure the precise horizontal and vertical coordinates of any point on earth. The waves from the satellites can be read in snow and rain and fog. You can correct errors that have stood for centuries. You can map featureless lands. The only inaccuracy is a slight corruption the government figures for civilian use—the denial of accuracy—that will confound attempts to exactly locate sensitive military areas. The map you can compute from satellite readings can be freed from the eye and the subjectivities of the eye, the hand and the limits of the hand. A spatial database has no scale and no limits on the density of information. You can add the element of time and can capture the three-dimensional. Some farmers already use the system in conjunction with grid soil samples to determine the precise nutrient needs of every square inch of their fields. They use it to figure potential yield. Precision farming, farming by the inch. *Once you see a yield map, you never quite look at that field in the same way again.*

Surely one of those satellites is above us now, tumbling through soundless space, while the land agent and I make our way down the path beneath the power lines. As we approach the road, the sound of traffic swallows the hum of the wires. The light rain has stopped. Toward the west the clouds have lifted, and the branches and grasses and foxberries are shining in a brief moment of sun. I can't yet see a single star, just that incalculable deep blue of near twilight, vast and peaceful.

Denise Levertov

A New Flower

Most of the sunflower's bright petals
had fallen, so I stripped the few
poised to go, and found myself
with a new flower: the center,
that round cushion of dark-roast
coffee brown, tipped with uncountable
minute florets of gold, more noticeable
now that the clear, shiny yellow was gone,
and around it a ring of green, the petals
from behind the petals, there all the time,
each having the form of sacred flame
or Bo-tree leaf, a playful, jubilant form
(taken for granted in Paisley patterns)
and the light coming through them, so that
where, in double or triple rank, like a bevy
of Renaissance angels, they overlapped,
there was shadow, a darker shade
of the same spring green—a new flower
on this fall day, revealed within
the autumn of its own brief bloom.

Jamaica Kincaid

Garden of Envy

I know gardeners well (or at least I think I do, for I am a gardener, too, but I experience gardening as an act of utter futility). I know their fickleness, I know their weakness for wanting in their own gardens the thing they have never seen before, or never possessed before, or saw in a garden (their friends'), something which they do not have and would like to have (though what they really like and envy—and especially that, envy—is the entire garden they are seeing, but as a disguise they focus on just one thing: the Mexican poppies, the giant butter burr, the extremely plump blooms of white, purple, black, pink, green, or the hellebores emerging from the cold, damp, and brown earth).

I would not be surprised if every gardener I asked had something definite that they liked or envied. Gardeners always have something they like intensely and in particular, right at the moment you engage them in the reality of the borders they cultivate, the space in the garden they occupy; at any moment, they like in particular this, or they like in particular that, nothing in front of them (that is, in the borders they cultivate, the space in the garden they occupy) is repulsive and fills them with hatred, or this thing would not be in front of them. They only love, and they only love in the moment; when the moment has passed, they love the memory of the moment, they love the memory of that particular plant or that particular bloom, but the plant of the bloom itself they have moved on from, they have left it behind for something else, something new, especially something from far away, and from so far away, a place where they will never live (occupy, cultivate; the Himalayas, just for example).

Of all the benefits that come from having endured childhood (for it is something to which we must submit, no matter how beautiful we find it, no matter how enjoyable it has been), certainly among them will be the garden and the desire to be involved with gardening. A gardener's grandmother will have grown such and such a rose, and the smell of that rose at dusk (for flowers always seem to be most fragrant at the end of the day, as if that, smelling, was the last thing to do before going to sleep), when the gardener was a child and walking in the grandmother's footsteps as she went about her business in her garden—the memory of that smell of the rose combined with the memory of that smell of the grandmother's skirt will forever inform and influence the life of the gardener, inside or outside the garden itself. And so in a conversation with such a person (a gardener), a sentence, a thought that goes something like this—"You know when I was such and such an age, I went to the market for a reason that is no longer of any particular interest to me, but it was there I saw for the first time something that I have never and can never forget"—floats out into the clear air, and the person from whom these words or this thought emanates is standing in front of you all bare and trembly, full of feeling, full of memory. Memory is a gardener's real palette; memory as it summons up the past, memory as it shapes the present, memory as it dictates the future.

I have never been able to grow *Meconopsis benticifolia* with success (it sits there, a green rosette of leaves looking at me, with no bloom. I look back at it myself, without a pleasing countenance), but the picture of it that I have in my mind, a picture made up of memory (I saw it some time ago), a picture made up of "to come" (the future, which is the opposite of remembering), is so intense that whatever happens between me and this plant will never satisfy the picture I have of it (the past remembered, the past to come). I first saw it (*Meconopsis benticifolia*) in Wayne Winterrowd's garden (a garden he shares with that other garden eminence Joe Eck), and I shall never see this plant (in flower or not, in the wild or cultivated) again without thinking of him (of them, really—he and Joe

Eck) and saying to myself, It shall never look quite like this (the way I saw it in their garden), for in their garden it was itself and beyond comparison (whatever that should amount to right now, whatever that might ultimately turn out to be), and I will always want it to look that way, growing comfortably in the mountains of Vermont, so far away from the place to which it is endemic, so far away from the place in which it was natural, unnoticed, and so going about its own peculiar ways of perpetuating itself (perennial, biannual, monocarpic or not).

I first came to the garden with practicality in mind, a real beginning that would lead to a real end: where to get this, how to grow that. Where to get this was always nearby, a nursery was never too far away; how to grow that led me to acquire volume upon volume, books all with the same advice (likes shade, does not tolerate lime, needs staking), but in the end I came to know how to grow the things I like to grow through looking—at other people's gardens. I imagine they acquired knowledge of such things in much the same way—looking and looking at somebody else's garden.

But we who covet our neighbor's garden must finally return to our own with all its ups and downs, its disappointments, its rewards. We come to it with a blindness, plus a jumble of feelings that mere language (as far as I can see) seems inadequate to express, to define an attachment that is so ordinary: a plant, loved especially for something endemic to it (it cannot help its situation: it loves the wet, it loves the dry, it reminds the person seeing it of a wave or a waterfall or some event that contains so personal an experience such as, when my mother would not allow me to do something I particularly wanted to do, and in my misery I noticed that the frangipani tree was in bloom).

I shall never have the garden I have in my mind, but that for me is the joy of it; certain things can never be realized and so all the more reason to attempt them. A garden, no matter how good it is, must never completely satisfy. The world as we know it, after all, began in a very good garden, a completely satisfying garden—Paradise—but after a while the owner and the occupants wanted more.

Dorothy Allison

This Is Our World

The first painting I ever saw up close was at a Baptist church when I was seven years old. It was a few weeks before my mama was to be baptized. From it, I took the notion that art should surprise and astonish and make you think something you had not thought until you saw it. The painting, a mural of Jesus at the Jordan River, was on the wall behind the baptismal font. The font itself was a remarkable creation—a swimming pool with one glass side set into the wall above and behind the pulpit so that ordinarily you could not tell the font was there, seeing only the painting of Jesus. When the tank was flooded with water, little lights along the bottom came on, and anyone who went down the steps seemed to be walking past Jesus himself and descending into the Jordan River. Watching baptisms in that tank was like watching movies at the drive-in, my cousins had told me. From the moment the deacon walked us around the church, I knew what my cousin meant. I could not take my eyes off the painting or the glass-fronted tank. It looked every moment as if Jesus were about to come alive, as if he were about to step onto the water of the river. I think the way I stared at the painting made the deacon nervous.

The deacon boasted to my mama that there was nothing like that baptismal font in the whole state of South Carolina. It had been designed, he told her, by a nephew of the minister—a boy who had gone on to build a shopping center out in New Mexico. My mama was not sure that someone who built shopping centers was the kind of person who should have been designing baptismal fonts, and she was even more uncertain about the steep steps by Jesus' left hip. She asked the man to let her practice going up and down, but he warned her it would be different once the water poured in.

"It's quite safe, though," he told her. "The water will hold you up. You won't fall."

I kept my attention on the painting of Jesus. He was much larger than I was, a little bit more than life-size, but the thick layer of shellac applied to protect the image acted like a magnifying glass, making him seem larger still. It was Jesus himself that fascinated me, though. He was all rouged and pale and pouty as Elvis Presley. This was not my idea of the son of God, but I liked it. I liked it a lot.

"Jesus looks like a girl," I told my mama.

She looked up at the painted face. A little blush appeared on her cheekbones, and she looked as if she would have smiled if the deacon were not frowning so determinedly. "It's just the eyelashes," she said. The deacon nodded. They climbed back up the stairs. I stepped over close to Jesus and put my hand on the painted robe. The painting was sweaty and cool, slightly oily under my fingers.

"I liked that Jesus," I told my mama as we walked out of the church. "I wish we had something like that." To her credit, Mama did not laugh.

"If you want a picture of Jesus," she said, "we'll get you one. They have them in nice frames at Sears." I sighed. That was not what I had in mind. What I wanted was a life-size, sweaty painting, one in which Jesus looked as hopeful as a young girl—something otherworldly and peculiar, but kind of wonderful at the same time. After that, every time we went to church I asked to go up to see the painting, but the baptismal font was locked tight when not in use.

The Sunday Mama was to be baptized, I watched the minister step down into that pool past the Son of God. The preacher's gown was tailored with little weights carefully sewn into the hem to keep it from rising up in the water. The water pushed up at the fabric while the weights tugged it down. Once the minister was all the way down into the tank, the robe floated up a bit so that it seemed to have a shirred ruffle all along the bottom. That was almost enough to pull my eyes away from the face of Jesus, but not quite. With the lights on in the bottom of the tank, the eyes of the painting seemed to move and shine. I tried to point it out to my sisters, but they were uninterested. All they wanted to see was Mama.

Mama was to be baptized last, after three little boys, and their gowns had not had any weights attached. The white robes floated up around their necks so that their skinny boy bodies and white cotton underwear were perfectly visible to the congregation. The water that came up above the hips of the minister lapped their shoulders, and the shortest of the boys seemed panicky at the prospect of gulping water, no matter how holy. He paddled furiously to keep above the water's surface. The water started to rock violently at his struggles, sweeping the other boys off their feet. All of them pumped their knees to stay upright, and the minister, realizing how the scene must appear to the congregation below, speeded up the baptismal process, praying over and dunking the boys at high speed.

Around me the congregation shifted in their seats. My little sister slid forward off the pew, and I quickly grabbed her around the waist and barely stopped myself from laughing out loud. A titter from the back of the church indicated that other people were having the same difficulty keeping from laughing. Other people shifted irritably and glared at the noisemakers. It was clear that no matter the provocation, we were to pretend nothing funny was happening. The minister frowned more fiercely and prayed louder. My mama's friend Louise, sitting at our left, whispered a soft "Look at that," and we all looked up in awe. One of the hastily blessed boys had dog-paddled over to the glass and was staring out at us, eyes wide and his hands pressed flat to the glass. He looked as if he hoped someone would rescue him. It was too much for me. I began to giggle helplessly, and not a few of the people around me joined in. Impatiently, the minister hooked the boy's robe, pulled him back, and pushed him toward the stairs.

My mama, just visible on the staircase, hesitated briefly as the sodden boy climbed up past her. Then she set her lips tightly together and reached down and pressed her robe to her thighs. She came down the steps slowly, holding down the skirt as she did so, giving one stern glance to the two boys climbing past her up the steps, and then turning her face deliberately up to the painting of Jesus. Every move she made communicated resolution and faith, and the congregation stilled in respect. She was baptized looking up stubbornly, both hands holding down that cotton robe, while below, I fought so hard not to giggle, tears spilled down my face.

Over the pool, the face of Jesus watched solemnly with his pink, painted cheeks and thick, dark lashes. For all the absurdity of the event, his face seemed to me startlingly compassionate and wise. That face understood fidgety boys and stubborn women. It made me want the painting even more, and to this day I remember it with longing. It had the weight of art, that face. It had what I am sure art is supposed to have—the power to provoke, the authority of a heartfelt vision.

I imagine the artist who painted the baptismal font in that Baptist church so long ago was a man who did not think himself much of an artist. I have seen paintings like his many times since, so perhaps he worked from a model. Maybe he traced that face off another he had seen in some other church. For a while, I tried to imagine him a character out of a Flannery O'Connor short story, a man who traveled around the South in the fifties painting Jesus wherever he was needed, giving the Son of God the long lashes and pink cheeks of a young girl. He would be the kind of man who would see nothing blasphemous in painting eyes that followed the congregation as they moved up to the pulpit to receive a blessing and back to the pews to sit, chastened and still, for the benediction. Perhaps he had no sense of humor, or perhaps he had one too refined for intimidation. In my version of the story, he would have a case of whiskey in his van, right behind the gallon containers of shellac and buried notebooks of his own sketches. Sometimes, he would read thick journals of art criticism while sitting up late in cheap hotel rooms and then get roaring drunk and curse his fate.

"What I do is wallpaper," he would complain. "Just wallpaper." But the work he so despised would grow more and more famous as time passed. After his death, one of those journals would publish a careful consideration of his murals, calling him a gifted primitive. Dealers would offer little churches large sums to take down his walls and sell them as installations to collectors. Maybe some of the churches would refuse to sell, but grow uncomfortable with the secular popularity of the paintings. Still, somewhere there would be a little girl like the girl I had been, a girl who would dream of putting her hand on the cool, sweaty painting while the Son of God blinked down at her in genuine sympathy. Is it a sin, she would wonder, to put together the sacred and the absurd? I would not answer her question, of course. I would leave it, like the art, to make everyone a little nervous and unsure.

I love black-and-white photographs, and I always have. I have cut photographs out of magazines to paste in books of my own, bought albums at yard sales, and kept collections that had one or two images I wanted near me always. Those pictures tell me stories—my own and others, scary stories sometimes, but more often simply everyday stories, what happened in that place at that time to those people. The pictures I collect leave me to puzzle out what I think about it later. Sometimes I imagine my own life as a series of snapshots taken by some omniscient artist who is just keeping track—not interfering or saying anything, just capturing the moment for me to look back at it again later. The eye of God, as expressed in a Dorothea Lange or Wright Morris. This is the way it is, the photograph says, and I nod my head in appreciation. The power of art is in that nod of appreciation, though sometimes I puzzle nothing out, and the nod is more a shrug. No, I do not understand this one, but I see it. I take it in. I will think about it. If I sit with this image long enough, this story, I have the hope of understanding something I did not understand before. And that, too, is art, the best art.

My friend Jackie used to call my photographs sentimental. I had pinned them up all over the walls of my apartment, and Jackie liked a few of them but thought on the whole they were better suited to being tucked away in a book. On her walls, she had half a dozen bright prints in bottle-cap metal frames, most of them bought from Puerto Rican artists at street sales when she was working as a taxi driver and always had cash in her pockets. I thought her prints garish and told her so when she made fun of my photographs.

"They remind me of my mama," she told me. I had only seen one photograph of Jackie's mother, a wide-faced Italian matron from Queens with thick black eyebrows and a perpetual squint.

"She liked bright colors?" I asked.

Jackie nodded. "And stuff you could buy on the street. She was always buying stuff off tables on the street, saying that was the best stuff. Best prices. Cheap skirts that lost their dye after a couple of washes, shoes with cardboard insoles, those funky little icons, weeping saints and long-faced Madonnas. She liked stuff to be really colorful. She painted all the ceilings in our apartment red and white. Red-red and white-white. Like blood on bone."

I looked up at my ceiling. The high tin ceiling was uniformly bloody when I moved in, with paint put on so thick, I could chip it off in lumps. I had climbed on stacks of boxes to paint it all cream white and pale blue.

"The Virgin's colors," Jackie told me. "You should put gold roses on the door posts."

"I'm no artist," I told her.

"I am." Jackie laughed. She took out a pencil and sketched a leafy vine above two of my framed photographs. She was good. It looked as if the frames were pinned to the vine. "I'll do it all," she said, looking at me to see if I was upset.

"Do it," I told her.

Jackie drew lilies and potato vines up the hall while I made tea and admired the details. Around the front door she put the Virgin's roses and curious little circles with crosses entwined in the middle. "It's beautiful," I told her.

"A blessing," she told me. "Like a bit of magic. My mama magic." Her face was so serious, I brought back a dish of salt and water, and we blessed the entrance. "Now the devil will pass you by," she promised me.

I laughed, but almost believed.

For a few months last spring I kept seeing an ad in all the magazines that showed a small child high in the air dropping toward the upraised arms of a waiting figure below. The image was grainy and distant. I could not tell if the child was laughing or crying. The copy at the bottom of the page read: "Your father always caught you."

"Look at this," I insisted the first time I saw the ad. "Will you look at this?"

A friend of mine took the magazine, looked at the ad, and then up into my shocked and horrified face.

"They don't mean it that way," she said.

I looked at the ad again. They didn't mean it that way? They meant it innocently? I shuddered. It was supposed to make you feel safe, maybe make you buy insurance or something. It did not make me feel safe. I dreamed about the picture, and it was not a good dream.

I wonder how many other people see that ad the way I do. I wonder how many other people look at the constant images of happy families and make wry faces at most of them. It's as if all the illustrators have television sitcom imaginations. I do not believe in those families. I believe in the exhausted mothers, frightened children, numb and stubborn men. I believe in hard-pressed families, the child huddled in fear with his face hidden, the father and mother confronting each other with their emotions hidden, dispassionate passionate faces, and the unsettling sense of risk in the baby held close to that man's chest. These images make sense to me. They are about the world I know, the stories I tell. When they are accompanied by wry titles or copy that is slightly absurd or unexpected, I grin and know that I will puzzle it out later, sometimes a lot later.

I think that using art to provoke uncertainty is what great writing and inspired images do most brilliantly. Art should provoke more questions than answers and, most of all, should make us think about what we rarely want to think about at all. Sitting down to write a novel, I refuse to consider if my work is seen as difficult or inappropriate or provocative. I choose my subjects to force the congregation to look at what they try so stubbornly to pretend is not happening at all, deliberately combining the horribly serious with the absurd or funny, because I know that if I am to reach my audience, I must first seduce their attention and draw them into the world of my imagination. I know that I have to lay out my stories, my difficult people, each story layering on top of the one before it with care and craft, until my audience sees something they had not expected. Frailty—stubborn, human frailty—that is what I work to showcase. The wonder and astonishment of the despised and ignored, that is what I hope to find in art and in the books I write—my secret self, my vulnerable and embattled heart, the child I was and the woman I have become, not Jesus at the Jordan but a woman with only her stubborn memories and passionate convictions to redeem her.

"You write such mean stories," a friend once told me. "Raped girls, brutal fathers, faithless mothers, and untrustworthy lovers—meaner than the world really is, don't you think?"

I just looked at her. Meaner than the world really is? No. I thought about showing her the box under my desk where I keep my clippings. Newspaper stories and black-and-white images—the woman who drowned her children, the man who shot first the babies in her arms and then his wife, the teen-age boys who led the three-year-old away along the train track, the homeless family recovering from frostbite, their eyes glazed and indifferent, while the doctor scowled over their shoulders. The world is meaner than we admit, larger and more astonishing. Strength appears in the most desperate figures, tragedy when we have no reason to expect it. Yes, some of my stories are fearful, but not as cruel as what I see in the world. I believe in redemption, just as I believe in the nobility of the despised, the dignity of the outcast, the intrinsic honor among misfits, pariahs, and queers. Artists—those of us who stand outside the city gates and look back at a society that tries to ignore us—we have an angle of vision denied to whole sectors of the sheltered and indifferent population within. It is our curse and our prize, and for everyone who will tell us our work is mean or fearful or unreal, there is another who will embrace us and say with tears in their eyes how wonderful it is to finally feel as if someone else has seen their truth and shown it in some part as it should be known.

"My story," they say. "You told my story. That is me, mine, us." And it is.

We are not the same. We are a nation of nations. Regions, social classes, economic circumstances, ethical systems, and political convictions—all separate us even as we pretend they do not. Art makes that plain. Those of us who have read the same books, eaten the same kinds of food as children, watched the same television shows, and listened to the same music—we believe ourselves part of the same nation, and we are continually startled to discover that our versions of reality do not match. If we were more the same, would we not see the same thing when we look at a painting? But what is it we see when we look at a work of art? What is it we fear will be revealed? The artist waits for us to say. It does not matter that each of us sees something slightly different. Most of us, confronted with the artist's creation, hesitate, stammer, or politely deflect the question of what it means to us. Even those of us from the same background, same region, same general economic and social class, come to "art" uncertain, suspicious, not wanting to embarrass ourselves by revealing what the work provokes in us. In fact, sometimes we are not sure. If we were to reveal what we see in each painting, sculpture, installation, or little book, we would run the risk of exposing our secret selves, what we know and what we fear we do not know, and of course, incidentally, what it is we truly fear. Art is the Rorschach test for all of us, the projective hologram of our secret lives. Our emotional and intellectual lives are laid bare. Do you like hologram roses? Big, bold, brightly painted canvases? Representational art? Little boxes with tiny figures posed precisely? Do you dare say what it is you like?

For those of us born into poor and working-class families, these are not simple questions. For those of us who grew up hiding what our home life was like, the fear is omnipresent—particularly when that home life was scarred by physical and emotional violence. We know if we say anything about what we see in a work of art we will reveal more about ourselves than the artist. What do you see in this painting, in that one? I see a little girl, terrified, holding together the torn remnants of her clothing. I see a child, looking back at the mother for help and finding none. I see a mother, bruised and exhausted, unable to look up for help, unable to believe anyone in the world will help her. I see a man with his fists raised, hating himself but making those fists tighter all the time. I see a little girl, uncertain and angry, looking down at her own body with hatred and contempt. I see that all the time, even when no one else sees what I see. I know I am not supposed to mention what it is I see. Perhaps no one else is seeing what I see. If they are, I am pretty sure there is some cryptic covenant that requires that we will not say what we see. Even when looking at an image of a terrified child, we know that to mention why that child might be so frightened would be a breach of social etiquette. The world requires that such children not be mentioned, even when so many of us are looking directly at her.

There seems to be a tacit agreement about what it is not polite to mention, what it is not appropriate to portray. For some of us, that polite behavior is set so deeply, we truly do not see what seems outside that tacit agreement. We have lost the imagination for what our real lives have been or continue to be, what happens when we go home and close the door on the outside world. Since so many would like us to never mention anything unsettling anyway, the impulse to be quiet, the impulse to deny and pretend, becomes very strong. But the artist knows all about that impulse. The artist knows that it must be resisted. Art is not meant to be polite, secret, coded, or timid. Art is the sphere in which that impulse to hide and lie is the most dangerous. In art, transgression is holy, revelation a sacrament, and pursuing one's personal truth the only sure validation.

Does it matter if our art is canonized, if we become rich and successful, lauded and admired? Does it make any difference if our pictures become popular, our books made into movies, our creations win awards? What if we are the ones who wind up going from town to town with our notebooks, our dusty boxes of prints or Xeroxed sheets of music, never acknowledged, never paid for our work? As artists, we know how easily we could become a Flannery O'Connor character, reading those journals of criticism and burying our faces in our hands, staggering under the weight of what we see that the world does not. As artists, we also know that neither worldly praise nor critical disdain will ultimately prove the worth of our work.

Some nights I think of that sweating, girlish Jesus above my mother's determined features, those hands outspread to cast benediction on those giggling uncertain boys, me in the congregation struck full of wonder and love and helpless laughter. If no one else ever wept at that image, I did. I wish the artist who painted that image knew how powerfully it touched me, that after all these years his art still lives inside me. If I can wish for anything for my art, that is what I want—to live in some child forever—and if I can demand anything of other artists, it is that they attempt as much.

Louise Erdrich

Naked Woman Playing Chopin

The street that runs along the Red River follows the curves of a stream that is muddy and shallow, full of brush, silt, and oxbows that throw the whole town off the strict clean grid laid out by railroad plat. The river floods most springs and drags local back yards into its flow, even though its banks are strengthened with riprap and piled high with concrete torn from reconstructed streets and basements. It is a hopelessly complicated river, one that freezes deceptively, breaks rough, drowns one or two every year in its icy flow. It is a dead river in some places, one that harbors only carp and bullheads. Wild in others, it lures moose down from Canada into the city limits. At one time, when the land along its banks was newly broken, paddleboats and barges of grain moved grandly from its source to Winnipeg, for the river flows inscrutably north. And, over on the Minnesota side, across from what is now church land and the town park, a farm spread generously up and down the river and back into wide hot fields.

The bonanza farm belonged to Easterners who had sold a foundry in Vermont and with their money bought the flat vastness that lay along the river. They raised astounding crops when the land was young—rutabagas that weighed sixty pounds, wheat unbearably lush, corn on cobs like truncheons. Then there were six grasshopper years during which even the handles on the hoes and rakes were eaten and a cavalry soldier, too, was partially devoured while he lay drunk in the insects' path. The enterprise suffered losses on a grand scale. The farm was split among four brothers, eventually, who then sold off half each so that, by the time Berndt Vogel escaped the trench war of Europe, where he'd been chopped mightily but inconclusively in six places by a British cavalry sabre and then kicked by a horse so that his jaw never shut right again, there was just one beautiful and peaceful swatch of land about to go for grabs. In the time it took him to gather—by forswearing women, drinking low beers only, and working twenty-hour days—the money to retrieve the farm from the local bank, its price had dropped further and further, as the earth rose up in a great ship of destruction. Sails of dust carried half of Berndt's lush dirt over the horizon, but enough remained for him to plant and reap six fields.

So Berndt survived. On his land there stood an old hangar-like barn, with only one small part still in use—housing a cow, chickens, one depressed pig. Berndt kept the rest in decent repair, not only because as a good German he must waste nothing that came his way, but also because he saw in those grand, dust-filled shafts of light something that he could worship. It had once housed teams of great blue Percherons and Belgian draft horses. Only one horse was left, old and made of brutal velvet, but the others still moved in the powerful synchronicity of his dreams. He fussed over the remaining mammoth and imagined his farm one day entire, vast and teeming, crews of men under his command, a cookhouse, a bunkhouse, equipment, a woman and children sturdily determined to their toil, and a garden in which seeds bearing the scented pinks and sharp red geraniums of his childhood were planted and thrived.

How surprised he was to find, one afternoon, as though sown by the wind and summoned by his dreams, a woman standing barefoot, starved, and frowsy in the doorway of his barn. She was a pale flower, nearly bald, and dressed in a rough shift. He blinked stupidly at the vision. Light poured around her like smoke and swirled at her gesture of need. She spoke.

"*Ich habe Hunger.*"

By the way she said it, he knew she was a Swabian and therefore—he tried to thrust the thought from his mind—liable to have certain unruly habits in bed. He passed his hand across his eyes. Through the gown of nearly transparent muslin he could see that her breasts were, excitingly, bound tightly to her chest with strips of cloth. He blinked hard. Looking directly into her eyes, he experienced the vertigo of confronting a female who did not blush or look away but held him with an honest human calm. He thought at first that she must be a loose woman, fleeing a brothel—had Fargo got so big? Or escaping an evil marriage, perhaps. He didn't know she was from God.

In the center of the town on the other side of the river there stood a convent made of yellow bricks. Hauled halfway across Minnesota from Little Falls by pious drivers, they still held the peculiar sulfurous moth gold of the clay outside that town. The word "Fleisch" was etched in shallow letters on each one: Fleisch Company Brickworks. Donated to the nuns at cost. The word, of course, was covered by mortar each time a brick was laid. However, because she had organized a few discarded bricks behind the convent into the base for a small birdbath, one of the younger nuns knew, as she gazed at the mute order of the convent's wall, that she lived within the secret repetition of that one word.

She had once been Agnes DeWitt and now was Sister Cecellia, shorn, houseled, clothed in black wool, and bound in starched linen of heatless white. She not only taught but lived music, existed for those hours when she could be concentrated in her being—which was half music, half divine light, flesh only to the degree that she could not admit otherwise. At the piano keyboard, absorbed into the notes that rose beneath her hands, she existed in her essence, a manifestation of compelling sound. Her hands were long and thick-veined, very white, startling against her habit. She rubbed them with lard and beeswax nightly to keep them supple. During the day, when she graded papers or used the blackboard, her hands twitched and drummed, patterned and repatterned difficult fingerings. She was no trouble to live with and her obedience was absolute. Only, and with increasing concentration, she played Brahms, Beethoven, Debussy, Schubert, and Chopin.

It wasn't that she neglected her other duties; rather, it was the playing itself—distilled of longing—that disturbed her sisters. In her music Sister Cecellia explored profound emotions. She spoke of her faith and doubt, of her passion as the bride of Christ, of her loneliness, shame, ultimate redemption. The Brahms she played was thoughtful, the Schubert confounding. Debussy was all contrived nature and yet as gorgeous as a meadowlark. Beethoven contained all messages, but her crescendos lacked conviction. When it came to Chopin, however, she did not use the flowery ornamentation or the endless trills and insipid floribunda of so many of her day. Her playing was of the utmost sincerity. And Chopin, played simply, devastates the heart. Sometimes a pause between the piercing sorrows of minor notes made a sister scrubbing the floor weep into the bucket where she dipped her rag so that the convent's boards, washed in tears, seemed to creak in a human tongue. The air of the house thickened with sighs.

Sister Cecellia, however, was emptied. Thinned. It was as though her soul were neatly removed by a drinking straw and siphoned into the green pool of quiet that lay beneath the rippling cascade of notes. One day, exquisite agony built and released, built higher, released more forcefully until slow heat spread between her fingers, up her arms, stung at the points of her bound breasts; and then shot straight down.

Her hands flew off the keyboard—she crouched as though she had been shot, saw yellow spots, and experienced a peaceful wave of oneness in which she entered pure communion. She was locked into the music, held there safely, entirely understood. Such was her innocence that she didn't know she was experiencing a sexual climax, but believed, rather, that what she felt was the natural outcome of this particular nocturne played to the utmost of her skills—and so it came to be. Chopin's spirit became her lover. His flats caressed her. His whole notes sank through her body like clear pebbles. His atmospheric trills were the flicker of a tongue. His pauses before the downward sweep of notes nearly drove her insane.

The Mother Superior knew something had to be done when she herself woke, her face bathed with sweat and tears, to the insinuating soft largo of the Prelude in E Minor. In those notes she remembered the death of her mother and sank into an endless afternoon of her loss. The Mother Superior then grew, in her heart, a weed of rage against the God who had taken a mother from a seven-year-old child whose world she was, entirely, without question—heart, arms, guidance, soul—until by evening she felt fury steaming from the hot marrow of her bones and stopped herself.

"Oh, God, forgive me," the Superior prayed. She considered humunculation, but then rushed down to the piano room instead, and with all of the strength in her wide old arms gathered and hid from Cecellia every piece of music but the Bach.

After that, for some weeks, there was relief. Sister Cecellia turned to the Two-Part Inventions. Her fingers moved on the keys with the precision of an insect building its nest. She played each as though she were constructing an airtight box. Stealthily, once Cecellia had moved on to Bach's other works, the Mother Superior removed from the music cabinet and destroyed the Goldberg Variations—clearly capable of lifting subterranean complexities into the mind. Life in the convent returned to normal. The cook, to everyone's gratitude, stopped preparing the rancid, goose-fat-laced beet soup of her youth and stuck to overcooked string beans, cabbage, potatoes. The floors stopped groaning and absorbed fresh wax. The doors ceased to fly open for no reason and closed discreetly. The water stopped rushing through the pipes as the sisters no longer took continual advantage of the new plumbing to drown out the sounds of their emotions.

And then one day Sister Cecellia woke with a tightness in her chest. Pain shot through her, and the red lump in her rib cage beat like a wild thing caught in a snare of bones. Her throat shut. She wept. Her hands, drawn to the keyboard, floated into a long appoggiatura. Then, crash, she was inside a thrusting mazurka. The music came back to her. There was the scent of faint gardenias—his hothouse boutonnière. The silk of his heavy brown hair. His sensuous drawing-room sweat. His voice—she heard it—avid and light. It was as if the composer himself had entered the room. Who knows? Surely there was no more desperate, earthly, exacting heart than Cecellia's. Surely something, however paltry, lies beyond the grave.

At any rate, she played Chopin. Played him in utter naturalness until the Mother Superior was forced to shut the cover to the keyboard and gently pull the stool away. Cecellia lifted the lid and played upon her knees. The poor scandalized dame dragged her from the keys. Cecellia crawled back. The Mother, at her wit's end, sank down and urged the young woman to pray. She herself spoke first in fear and then in certainty, saying that it was the very Devil who had managed to find a way to Cecellia's soul through the flashing doors of sixteenth notes. Her fears were confirmed when, not moments later, the gentle sister raised her arms and fists and struck the keys as though the instrument were stone and from the rock her thirst would be quenched. But only discord emerged.

"My child, my dear child," the Mother comforted, "come away and rest yourself."

The younger nun, breathing deeply, refused. Her severe gray eyes were rimmed in a smoky red. Her lips bled purple. She was in torment. "There is no rest," she declared. She unpinned her veil and studiously dismantled her habit, folding each piece with reverence and setting it upon the piano bench. The Mother remonstrated with Cecellia in the most tender and compassionate tones. However, just as in the depth of her playing the virgin had become the woman, so now the woman in the habit became a woman to the bone. She stripped down to her shift, but no further.

"He wouldn't want me to go out unprotected," she told her Mother Superior.

"God?" the older woman asked, bewildered.

"Chopin," Cecellia answered.

Kissing her dear Mother's trembling fingers, Cecellia knelt. She made a true genuflection, murmured an act of contrition, and then walked away from the convent made of bricks with the secret word pressed between yellow mortar, and from the music, her music, which the Mother Superior would from then on keep under lock and key.

So it was Sister Cecellia, or Agnes DeWitt of rural Wisconsin, who appeared before Berndt Vogel in the cavern of the barn and said in her mother's dialect, for she knew a German when she met one, that she was hungry. She wanted to ask whether he had a piano, but it was clear to her that he wouldn't and at any rate she was exhausted.

"*Jetzt muss ich schlafen,*" she said after eating half a plate of scalded oatmeal with new milk.

So he took her to his bed, the only bed there was, in the corner of the otherwise empty room. He went out to the barn he loved, covered himself with hay, and lay awake all night listening to the rustling of mice and sensing the soundless predatory glide of the barn owls and the stiff erratic flutter of bats. By morning, he had determined to marry her if she would have him, just so that he could unpin and then unwind the long strip of cloth that bound her torso. She refused his offer, but she did speak to him of who she was and where from, and in that first summary she gave of her life she concluded that she must never marry again, for not only had she wed herself soul to soul to Christ, but she had already been unfaithful—with her phantom lover, the Polish composer. She had already lived out too grievous a destiny to become a bride again. By explaining this to Berndt, however, she had merely moved her first pawn in a long game of words and gestures that the two would play over the course of many months. What she didn't know was that she had opened to a dogged and ruthless opponent.

Berndt Vogel's passion engaged him, mind and heart. He prepared himself. Having dragged army caissons through hip-deep mud after the horses died in torment, having seen his best friend suddenly uncreated into a mass of shrieking pulp, having lived intimately with pouring tumults of eager lice and rats plump with a horrifying food, he was rudimentarily prepared for the suffering he would experience in love. She, however, had also learned her share of discipline. Moreover—for the heart of her gender is stretched, pounded, molded, and tempered for its hot task from birth—she was a woman.

The two struck a temporary bargain and set up housekeeping. She still slept in the indoor bed. He stayed in the barn. A month passed. Three. Six. Each morning she lit the stove and cooked, then heated water in a big tank for laundry and swept the cool linoleum floors. Monday she sewed. She baked all day Tuesday. On Wednesday she churned and scrubbed. She sold the butter and the eggs Thursdays. Killed a chicken every Friday.

Saturdays she walked into town and practiced the piano in the school basement. Sunday she played the organ for Mass and then at the close of the day started the next week's work. Berndt paid her. At first she spent her salary on clothing. When with her earnings she had acquired shoes, stockings, a full set of cotton underclothing and then a woollen one, too, and material for two housedresses—one patterned with twisted leaves and tiny blue berries, and the other of an ivy lattice print—and a sweater and, at last, a winter coat, after she had earned a blanket, quilted overalls, a pair of boots, she decided on a piano.

This is where Berndt thought he could maneuver her into marriage, but she proved too cunning for him. It was early in the evening and the yard was pleasant with the sound of grasshoppers. The two sat on the porch, drinking glasses of sugared lemon water. Every so often, in the ancient six-foot grasses that survived at the margin of the yard, a firefly signaled or a dove cried out its five hollow notes.

They drank slowly, she in her sprigged-berry dress that skimmed her waist. He noted with disappointment that she wore normal underclothing now, had stopped binding her breasts. Perhaps, he thought, he could persuade her to resume her old ways, at least occasionally, just for him. It was a wan hope. She looked so comfortable, so free. She'd taken on a little weight and lost her anemic pallor. Her arms were brown, muscular. In the sun, her straight fine hair glinted with green-gold sparks of light, and her eyes were deceptively clear.

"I can teach music," she told him. She had decided that her suggestion must sound merely practical, a moneymaking ploy. She did not express any pleasure or zeal, though at the very thought each separate tiny muscle in her hands ached. "It would be a way of bringing in some money."

He was left to absorb this. He might have believed her casual proposition, except that her restless fingers gave her away, and he noted their insistent motions. She was playing the Adagio of the "Pathétique" on the tablecloth, a childhood piece that nervously possessed her from time to time.

"You would need a piano," he told her. She nodded and held his gaze in that aloof and unbearably sexual way that had first skewered him.

"It's the sort of thing a husband gives his wife," he dared.

Her fingers stopped moving. She cast down her eyes in contempt.

"I can use the school instrument. I've spoken to the school principal already."

Berndt looked at the moon-shaped bone of her ankle, at her foot in the brown, thick-heeled shoe she'd bought. He ached to hold her foot in his lap, untie her oxford shoe with his teeth, cover her calf with kisses, and breathe against the delicate folds of berry cloth.

He offered marriage once again. His heart. His troth. His farm. She spurned the lot. She would simply walk into town. He let her know that he would like to buy the piano, it wasn't that, but there was not a store for many miles where it could be purchased. She knew better and with exasperated heat described the way that she would, if he would help financially, go about locating and then acquiring the best piano for the best price. She vowed that she would purchase the instrument not in Fargo but in Minneapolis. From there, she could have it hauled for less than the freight markup. She would make her arrangements in one day and return by night in order not to spend one extra dime either on food she couldn't carry or on a hotel room. When he resisted to the last, she told him that she was leaving. She would find a small room in town and there she would acquire students, give lessons.

She betrayed her desperation. Some clench of her fingers gave her away, and it was as much Berndt's unconfused love of her and wish that she might be happy as any worry she might leave him that finally caused him to agree. In the six months that he'd known Agnes DeWitt she had become someone to reckon with, and even he, who understood desperation and self-denial, was finding her proximity most difficult. He worked himself into exhaustion, and his farm prospered. Sleeping in the barn was difficult, but he had set into one wall a bunk room for himself and his hired man and installed a stove that burned red hot on cold nights; only, sometimes, as he looked sleepily into the glowering flanks of iron, he could not keep his own fingers from moving along the rough mattress in faint imitation of the way he would, if he ever could, touch her hips. He, too, was practicing.

*

The piano moved across the August desert of drought-sucked wheat like a shield, a dark upended black thing, an ebony locust. Agnes made friends with a hauler out of Morris, and he gave her a slow-wagon price. Both were to accompany into Fargo the last grand piano made by Caramacchione. It had been shipped to Minneapolis, unsold until Agnes entered with her bean sock of money. She accompanied the instrument back to the farm during the dog days. Hot weather was beloved by this particular piano. It tuned itself on muggy days. And so, as it moved across the flat expanse, Miss Agnes DeWitt mounted the back of the wagon and played to the clouds.

They had to remove one side of the house to get the piano into the front room, and it took six strong men a full day to do the job. By the time the instrument was settled into place by the window, Berndt was persuaded of its necessary presence, and proud. He sent the men away, although the side of the house was still open to the swirling light of stars. Dark breezes moved the curtains; he asked her to play for him. She did, the music gripped her, and she did not, could not, stop.

Late that night she turned from the last chord of the simple Nocturne in C Minor into the silence of Berndt's listening presence. Three slow claps from his large hands died in the waiting quiet. His eyes rested upon her and she returned his gaze with a long and mysterious stare of gentle regard. The side of the house admitted a great swatch of moonlight. Spiders built their webs of phosphorescence across black space. Berndt ticked through what he knew—she would not marry him because she had been married and unfaithful, in her mind at least. He was desperate not to throw her off, repel her, damage the mood set by the boom of nighthawks flying in, swooping out, by the rustle of black oak and willow, by the scent of the blasted petals of summer's last wild roses. His courage was at its lowest ebb. Fraught with sheer need and emotion, he stood before Agnes, finally, and asked in a low voice, "*Schlaf mit mir. Bitte. Schlaf mit mir.*"

Agnes looked into his face, openly at last, showing him the great weight of feeling she carried. As she had for her Mother Superior, she removed her clothing carefully and folded it, only she did not stop undressing at her shift but continued until she had slipped off her large tissuey bloomers and seated herself naked at the piano. Her body was a pale blush of silver, and her hands, when they began to move, rose and fell with the simplicity of water.

It became clear to Berndt Vogel, as the music slowly wrapped around him, that he was engaged in something that he would have had to pay a whore in Fargo—if there really were any whores in Fargo—a great sum to perform. A snake of hair wound down her spine. Her pale buttocks seemed to float off the invisible bench. Her legs moved like a swimmer's, and he thought he heard her moan. He watched her fingers spin like white shadows across the keys, and found that his body was responding as though he lay fully twined with her underneath a quilt of music and stars. His breath came short, shorter, rasping and ragged. Beyond control, he gasped painfully and gave himself into some furtive cleft of halftones and anger that opened beneath the ice of high keys.

Shocked, weak, and wet, Berndt rose and slipped through the open side wall. He trod aimless crop lines until he could allow himself to collapse in the low fervor of night wheat. It was true, wasn't it, that the heart was a lying cheat? And as the songs Chopin invented were as much him as his body, so it followed that Berndt had just watched the woman he loved make love to a dead man. Now, as he listened to the music, he thought of returning. Imagined the meal of her white shoulders. Shut his eyes and entered the confounding depth between her legs.

Then followed their best years. Together, they constructed a good life in which the erotic merged into the daily so that every task and even small kindness was charged with a sexual humor. Some mornings the two staggered from the bedroom disoriented, still half drunk on the unlikely eagerness of the other's body. These frenzied periods occurred every so often, like spells in the weather. They would be drawn, sink, disappear into their greed, until the cow groaned for milking or the hired man swore and banged on the outside gate. If nothing else intervened, they'd stop from sheer exhaustion. Then they would look at one another oddly, questingly, as if the other person were a complete stranger, and gradually resume their normal interaction, which was offhand and distracted, but upheld by the assurance of people who thought alike.

Agnes gave music lessons, and although the two weren't married, even the Catholics and the children came to her. This was because it was well known that Miss DeWitt's first commitment had been to Christ. It was understandable that she would have no other marriage. Although she did not take the Holy Eucharist on her tongue, she was there at church each Sunday morning, faithful and devout, to play the organ. There, she, of course, played Bach, with a purity of intent purged of any subterranean feeling, strictly, and for God.

So when the river began to rise one spring, Berndt had already gone where life was deepest many times, and he did not particularly fear the rain. But what began as a sheer mist became an even sprinkle and then developed into a slow, pounding shower that lasted three days, then four, then on the fifth day, when it should have tapered off, increased.

The river boiled along swiftly, a gray soup still contained, just barely, within its high banks. On day six the rain stopped, or seemed to. The storm had moved upstream. All day while the sun shone pleasantly the river heaved itself up, tore into its flow new trees and boulders, created tip-ups, washouts, areas of singing turbulence, and crawled, like an infant, toward the farm. Berndt rushed around uneasily, pitching hay into the high loft, throwing chickens up after the hay, wishing he could throw the horse up as well, and the house, and—because Agnes wrung her hands—the piano. But the piano was earth-anchored and well-tuned by the rainy air, so, instead of worrying, Agnes practiced.

Once the river started to move, it gained confidence. It had no problem with fences or gates, wispy windbreaks, ditches. It simply leveled or attained the level of whatever stood in its path. Water jumped up the lawn and collected behind the sacks of sand that Berndt had desperately filled and laid. The river tugged itself up the porch and into the house from one side. From the other side it undermined an already weak foundation that had temporarily shored up the same wall once removed to make way for the piano. The river tore against the house, and then, like a child tipping out a piece of candy from a box, it surged underneath and rocked the floor, and the piano crashed through the weakened wall.

It landed in the swift current of the yard, Agnes with it. Berndt saw only the white treble clef of her dress as she spun away, clutching the curved lid. It bobbed along the flower beds first, and then, as muscular new eddies caught it, touched down on the shifting lanes of Berndt's wheat fields, and farther, until the revolving instrument and the woman on it reached the original river and plunged in. They were carried not more than a hundred feet before the piano lost momentum and sank. As it went down, Agnes thought at first of crawling into its box, nestling for safety among the cold, dead strings. But as she struggled with the hinged cover, she lost her grip and was swept north. She should have drowned, but there was a snag of rope, a tree, two men in a fishing skiff risking themselves to save a valuable birding dog. They pulled Agnes out and dumped her in the bottom of the boat, impatient to get the dog. She gagged, coughed, and passed out in a roil of feet and fishing tackle.

When she came to, she was back in the convent, which was on high ground and open to care for victims of the flood. Berndt was not among the rescued. When the river went down and the heat rose, he was found snagged in a tip-up of roots, tethered to his great blue steaming horse. As Agnes recovered her strength, did she dream of him? Think of him entering her and her receiving him? Long for the curve of his hand on her breast? Yes and no. She thought again of music. Chopin. Berndt. Chopin.

He had written a will, in which he declared her his common-law wife and left to her the farm and all upon it. There, she raised Rosecomb Bantams, Dominikers, Reds. She bought another piano and played with an isolated intensity that absorbed her spirit.

A year or so after Berndt's death, her students noticed that she would stop in the middle of a lesson and smile out the window as though welcoming a long-expected visitor. One day the neighbor children went to pick up the usual order of eggs and were most struck to see the white-and-black-flecked Dominikers flapping up in alarm around Miss DeWitt as she stood magnificent upon the green grass.

Tall, slender, legs slightly bowed, breasts jutting a bit to either side, and the flare of hair flicking up the center of her—naked. She looked at the children with remote kindness. Asked, "How many dozen?" Walked off to gather the eggs.

That episode made the gossip-table rounds. People put it off to Berndt's death and a relapse of nerves. She lost only a Lutheran student or two. She continued playing the organ for Mass, and at home, in the black,

Reetika Vazirani

At the Society for the Promotion of Indian Classical Music & Culture among Youth

At the Society for the Promotion of Indian Classical
    Music & Culture among Youth,
Maestro plays a raga at dusk that means
God is powerful enough, and we have our misery.
It's true, though downtrodden, we talk to God.

Maestro plays a raga at dusk that means
Groceries are on stage. (Symbolism for starving people.)
It's true, though downtrodden, we talk to God.
(Thank you for the onions and cabbage.) But why

Are groceries on stage? Symbolism for starving people.
What will white people think of us? Corruption, poverty,
Thank you for the onions and cabbage. But why
Must the singer make sure the dreaded lament goes on?

What will white people think of us? Corruption, poverty,
Everyone feels devastated by the separation from God.
Must the singer make sure the dreaded lament goes on
For three hours? Happy New Year, it's the twenty-first century.

(Everyone feels devastated by the separation from God.)
On top of that my boyfriend slept with you out of state
For three hours. Happy New Year, it's the twenty-first century,
A moaning raga about restless humans and

On top of that my boyfriend slept with you. The out-of-state
Visitors (all white) walk out, they can't take it,
A roaring raga about jet-set humans and
The zany distribution of oil, gold, crack, cars, a world in which

Visitors (all white) walk out, they can't take it
At the Society for the Promotion of Indian Classical
    Music & Culture among Youth. . . .
The zany distribution of oil, gold, crack, cars, a world in which
God is powerful and we've had enough misery.

Patrick Sylvain

Volcanic Songs

We used to sit underneath palm trees,
or on porches where the sun could not reach
our skin. Sometimes, we would sit on a long
marble bench leaning against the wall
of our house that grandpa had built
before calluses and arthritis
had found refuge between his knuckles.

We sat around Manno to watch
his long black fingers
conversing with his guitar strings,
as his colossal voice exploded
songs as hot as burning oil.

He sang about our bent-back parents
threading needles on cows' skin
making baseball. Foreign signatures
carving deeper into the land and
into their skeletal like frames.

I will never bury the images
of his back arched like a bow,
holding his guitar like an arrow
with its six strings and echoing
the messages of his fingers
in a theater where waves of macoutes
could not touch his shore.

He sings with a tidal energy against
the military who have broken the radios
and try to prohibit his songs,
still we kept singing
"je nou byen kale, n'ap siveye."
Our eyes well lit, we are watching.

We're from a dark town
where monsters' teeth glow
in the dark, and our light
is a torch from our ancestors
that we carry in our hands
like his songs.

Marcie Hershman

Where the Markets Converge

I love going into Boston early on Saturday mornings, when the city is still quiet but already alert. When there are parking spaces and free meters, and roaming room for pedestrians. When strangers look up and grin like conspirators, each one knowing the same great secret: *This* is when our city is a joy, *these* moments when everything urban seems possible.

The outdoor markets are wide open then. Haymarket's pyramids of produce are precisely topped, the gleam still on the fruit. Vendors make small talk—no need to hurry, because the press of the crowds hasn't begun. My partner and I stroll, chatting. From the knockdown carts of apples, tomatoes, mangoes, jimica, eggplants, oranges, and herbs, we select all that we want. The variety of colors, textures, shapes, and scents is intoxicating. Only when the paper sacks are full to bursting, do we carry them back to the car parked in the shadows fallen between the massive modern structures of Government Center. Then we recross the public plazas and the narrowing draw of cobblestone streets. Beyond the peddlers' stalls of Haymarket lies Faneuil Hall and a series of century-old warehouses; the long brick buildings are burnished to an upscale luster they never possessed in their more functional youth. Quincy Market, the first of America's "festival marketplaces," has barely woken up. In its echoing food court we buy strong coffee, just-baked bagels, and the newspapers before we climb a curved staircase to the second story, where all is quiet as a library. Any table on the balcony—ours for the taking. We eat beneath the rotunda's balmy splendor, every so often gazing out the arched windows toward the financial district, where the sleek buildings are sharp-edged as new bills.

Not until I read a furious letter in the *Boston Globe* did I add another stop to these lazy, productive sojourns. The writer was angry about the New England Holocaust Memorial. Was it necessary, he demanded, to remind us of history's most vile atrocity in the middle of America's most historic city? The "atrocious contemporary" architecture of glass columns, metal, and gray stone marred the unity of Colonial brick.

I was jolted by his ferocity. More, I didn't hold with his idea that Boston is best labeled "City as Still-Life." The streetscapes I traveled weren't static. But what dismayed me most about his letter? I, too, had separated the Holocaust Memorial from the city surrounding it. Though the small plaza is set where the markets converge, I hadn't once visited it. The memorial honors the millions of citizens terrorized and murdered by the Nazis—among them, members of my own family. Still, I'd told myself it would be sacrilegious to see it on the way to filling bags with fruits and vegetables at Haymarket, or on the way back from having coffee and pastry in Quincy Market. Of course, as I stepped off the curbs I was making a choice. And each Saturday, without acknowledging it, I'd decided it would be better to glance at the six glassy towers from a distance. It would be better to view the memorial—sometime—on its own. Better to separate that visit from my other visits. So that I could concentrate on it.

Sometimes the truth is what we hide best from ourselves. The truth? The Holocaust occurred in the marketplace. It happened amid daily life, busy lives. You couldn't *not* see how other people—Jews, usually—were ordered through the center of town. Sometimes they were locked inside warehouses and large commercial buildings before being forced onto freight cars going "east" to the death camps near other towns.

History happens in the center of things. It happens when you are buying flowers.

One bright Saturday morning before Haymarket, I stepped across the memorial's first boundary. Carved into the paving stones was one word, *Re-*

member, in Hebrew. And then I read the next word, *Chelmo*—the name of a death camp. And then I walked across a metal grate in the pathway that made my footing insecure. I was aware of the airy vacancy beneath me, aware of a scattering of electric embers flickering below the grid. Massed, they smoldered with light. These are the ashes we stand upon. Or, not ashes—stars.

The eloquence of the architect Stanley Saitowitz's symbolic language is such that it can enrich and sustain the dualities of emotion and reality. Named for six of the death camps, the six towering, walk-through glass columns look like industrial chimneys. They might also be candles. They might carry ash to blacken the sky or tap light against a heaven too dark. They might defile or bless us. The numerals, from 1 to 6,000,000, etched on the glass walls are visible through the blur of visitors' fingerprints. The numbers can recall the anonymity of human arms tattooed, or they can account for individual beings: Take from the mass of the crowd *this* living soul. In the open stretches of land between the chimneys or candles, the weather is what it is and the boundaries wider, less clear. On either side of the path: simple, human testimony. Engraved on glass, on stones laid flat or set upright are the words of survivors, soldiers, philosophers. Words that make you wince or straighten your spine; words so real, they make you aware you've just caught your breath. And, at the last, theirs.

For all the horror of the Holocaust's historical scale, the New England Memorial is a profoundly contemplative work. What is most poignant and, at the same time, most unrelenting is that the site is surrounded by movement. Which marks the choice that citizens of great cities and modest villages have always had in relation to history. It's as quiet as this: Will you pass by—or, finally, stop?

Barbara Kingsolver

How Poems Happen

I have never yet been able to say out loud that I am a poet.

It took me some thirty years and several published novels to begin calling myself a novelist, but finally now I can do that, I own up to it, and will say so in capital letters on any document requiring me to identify myself with an honest living. "Novelist," I'll write gleefully, chortling to think that the business of making up stories can be called an honest living, but there you are. It's how I keep shoes on my kids and a roof above us. I sit down at my desk every day and make novels happen. I design them, construct them, revise them; I tinker and bang away with the confidence of an experienced mechanic, knowing that patience and effort will get this troubled engine overhauled, and this baby will hum.

Poetry is a different beast. I rarely think of poetry as something I make happen; it is more accurate to say that it happens to me. Like a summer storm, a house afire, or the coincidence of both on the same day. Like a car wreck, only with more illuminating results. I've overheard poems, virtually complete, in elevators and restaurants where I was minding my own business. When a poem does arrive, I gasp as if an apple had fallen into my hand, and give thanks for the luck involved. Poems are everywhere, but easy to miss. I know I might very well stand under that tree all day, whistling, looking off to the side, waiting for a red delicious poem to fall so that I could own it forever. But like as not, it wouldn't. Instead, it will fall right while I'm in the middle of changing the baby, or breaking up a rodeo event involving my children and the dog, or wiping my teary eyes while I'm chopping onions and listening to the news; then that apple will land with a thud and roll under the bed with the dust bunnies and lie there forgotten and lost for all time.

There are dusty, lost poems all over my house, I assure you. In yours too, I'd be willing to bet. Years ago I got some inkling of this when I attended a reading by one of my favorite poets, Lucille Clifton. A student asked her about the brevity of her poems (thinking, I suspect, that the answer would involve terms like *literary retrenchment* and *parsimony*). Ms. Clifton replied simply that she had six children, and could only hold about twenty lines in memory until the end of the day. I felt such relief, that this great poet was bound by ordinary life, like me.

I've learned since then that most great poets are more like me, and more like you, than not. They may be more confident about tinkering with the engine, but they'll always allow that there's magic involved, and that the main thing is to pay attention. I have several friends who are poets of great renown, to whom I've confessed that creating a poem is a process I can't really understand or control. Every one of them, on hearing this, looked off to the side and whispered, "Me either!"

We're reluctant to claim ownership of the mystery. In addition, we live in a culture that doesn't put much stock in mystery. Elsewhere in the world, say in Poland or Nicaragua, people elect their poets to public office, or at the very least pay them a stipend to produce poetry, regularly and well, for the public good. (Poles and Nicaraguans evidently have their own ideas about the nature of an honest living.) Here, a poet may be prolific and magnificently skilled, but even so it's not the poetry that's going to keep shoes on the kids and a roof overhead. I don't know of a single American poet who makes a living solely by writing poetry. Identifying your livelihood as "Poet" on an official form is the kind of thing that will make your bank's mortgage officer laugh very hard all the way into the manager's office and back. So we're a timid lot, of necessity. At the most, we might confess, "I write poetry sometimes."

And so we do. Whether anyone pays us or respects us or calls us a poet or not, most of us feel a tickle behind our left ear when we catch ourselves saying, "You know, it was a little big, and really pretty ugly." We stop in our tracks when a child pointing to the sunset cries that the day is bleeding and is going to die. Poetry approaches, pauses, then skirts around us like a cat. I sense its presence in my house when I am chopping onions and crying but not really crying while I listen to the lilting radio newsman declare, "Up next: the city's oldest homeless shelter shut down by neighborhood protest, and thousands offer to adopt baby Jasmine abandoned in Disneyland!"

There is some secret grief here I need to declare, and my fingers itch for a pencil. But then the advertisement blares that I should expect the unexpected, while my elder child announces that a shelter can't be homeless, but that onions make her eyes run away with her nose, and my youngest marches in a circle shouting "Apple-dapple! Come-thumb-drum!" and poems roll under the furniture, left and right. I've lost so many, I can't count them. I do understand, they fall when I'm least able to pay attention because poems fall not from a tree, really, but from the richly pollinated boughs of an ordinary life, buzzing, as lives are, with clamor and glory. Poetry just is, whether we revere it or try to put it in prison. It is elementary grace, communicated from one soul to another. It reassures us of what we know and socks us in the gut with what we don't, it sings us awake, it's irresistible, it's congenital.

One afternoon, while my one-year-old stood on a chair reciting the poems she seems to have brought with her onto this planet, I heard on the news that our state board of education was dropping the poetry requirement from our schools. The secretary of education explained that it takes too much time to teach children poetry, when they are harder pressed than ever to master the essentials of the curriculum. He said that we have to take a good, hard look at what is essential and what is superfluous.

"Superfluous," I said to the radio.

"Math path boo!" said my child, undaunted by her new outlaw status.

This one was not going to get away. I threw down my dish towel, swept the baby off her podium, and carried her under my arm as we stalked off to find a pencil. In my opinion, when you find yourself laughing and crying both at once, that is the time to write a poem. Probably, it's the only honest living there is.

Danielle Legros Georges

How to Kiss

The children know how to kiss,
to descend stairwells when called
into rooms of colored lips,

whispered *entendres*, demurring smiles,
and the patron uncle who *en Creole* calls us
"*kochon mawon,*" "wild pigs."

We walk into crooned *comment vas tu*
uus rolling too long from gold-filled mouths,
thistly jowls. We kiss

the cheek, the next cheek, and more
cheeks, the odors of Vitalis
(the smart man's hair tonic),

of Bain de Champagne, Chanel No. 5,
Eau de Floride, of various adult *eaus*.
We bristle in advance against the teen-ager

whose five o'clock shadow goes from sun yard
to sit in parlors, his knees eclipsed in cloth;
a foreshadow that we too would be the kissed.

But Pascal had the audacity, once,
to alter form, opening her mouth
to snake a tongue that swept

beige powder from the face of Madame
Altagrace LaVache; exposing a patch
of brown from chin to ear.

"Un veritable scandale."

"Tongue on cheek?!"

"Truth indeed, the wild pigs!"

Manfred Wolf

The Dance School

In 1948 when I was thirteen and living in Curaçao, a ballroom-dancing champion from the Netherlands came to the island and, in a flurry of publicity, opened a dance school. Articles in the newspaper proclaimed this yet another bounty for the colony from the mother country, which now, after the disastrous war years, was beginning to find itself again. First came the new DC4 from KLM, inaugurating a direct route between Amsterdam and Curaçao, then the new brewery—and now the Dance School de Beer for children. Within a few weeks, virtually every child I knew was enrolled in this school. There were many different classes for children, and they seemed to meet all the time.

Frank de Beer was a trim, florid-looking man in his thirties. Like many Dutchmen, he was flax blond and a bit pink from the new-found sunshine of the tropics. An animated small man, he walked, moved, and gestured like a dancer. Every step he took was either long and deliberate or short and deliberate. He insisted that in each dance all the boys should ask all the girls to dance. When we had approached within three feet of the girl of our choice, we were supposed to bow deeply, and ask, "May I have this dance with you?"

The rule was that the girl was not permitted to decline, which still did not mean that the boy could dance with only the girl he wanted. If someone else approached her first, just a second before you did, this then required a swift move to another girl who had not been approached yet, also with a bow. Mr. de Beer explained that such jockeying shouldn't cause embarrassment. "If the young lady of your choice is no longer available, you walk firmly, decisively, gracefully, up to another young lady." Despite his pleas for dignity, there was a certain amount of running to the girls several boys wanted to dance with. Some boys would have to bow three or four times before they were able to find a partner. The girls had to nod and smile but not bow back.

I looked forward to the afternoons in that reddish-colored house with its gingerbread trim, the two whitewashed rooms with their parquet floors giving on a breezy veranda. And it felt good to do something with girls without having to talk to them a lot. Mr. de Beer would play a record, and you had to decide quickly what dance was appropriate, make your deep bow, and start dancing. Despite the pressure of these decisions, I liked the school and its atmosphere. It was serious business, but we learned to dance.

Mr. de Beer's favorite dance was the *boté*, which he pronounced in his Dutch way, *boatay.* Sinuously you stood on one leg, leaned all your weight on that side, and then slowly, sensuously leaned on the other. The aim was to create a flawlessly fluid hip motion, Mr. de Beer explained. He said it was the basic Latin American step and that all the others, the rhumba, the guaracha, the mambo, the merengue, were all based on it.

"Mr. de Beer," said my friend Mundi, a tall Curaçaoan boy, a superb dancer, "I've never even heard of the *boté.*" Brash though he sounded, Mundi was actually being more deferential than usual.

"Well," said Mr. de Beer mildly, "we learned it in Amsterdam, and it took us right to the championship. Latin American dancing is very big in Holland right now."

He demonstrated the step all over again. "Gently, smoothly; this must be lithe and controlled," said Mr. de Beer to our class of twelve- and thirteen-year-olds, his ever-cheerful voice commanding attention. When the record stopped and we were done with our partner, he made us bow again from the waist and escort the girl all the way to the exact spot against the wall where she had been standing. Another bow, and "Thank you *very* much for this dance."

Mr. de Beer's brother Nico, tall and light on his feet, roamed the hall, smiling, encouraging, cajoling. Taller than his brother, he had the same flaxen hair but a heavier face. Nico was a stickler for posture. When the brothers introduced a new dance, they would often dance side by side, next to each other, one more supple than the other, and both extend their left arm to hold an imaginary woman with their right. Sometimes Mr. de Beer would whirl Nellie, his assistant, around, a redhead with an upturned nose, her colorful skirts twirling.

Curaçao was a dancing culture, but this was something new. The Curaçaoans did not need to be taught to dance, but of course many Curaçaoan children enrolled in the school. Mr. de Beer was lavish in his praise for their talents but never condescending to the others. He especially stressed the gravity of these occasions, their dignity. And he enjoyed having us all watched by dozens of leisurely staring Curaçaoans—men, women, children—all of them peering through the louvered porches around the veranda and occasionally whispering comments through the shutters. Mr. de Beer, fresh from Holland, could not understand some of these hissed remarks in Papiamento from staring boys as the girls swished by, such as "What delicious legs, what sweet thighs, what a luscious little ass," accompanied by a strange slurping sound made with indrawn breath.

Though there were not many Jewish children in Curaçao, they tended to be segregated from each other. The newcomers, to which I belonged, were the smallest group. More numerous were the Jewish kids born in Curaçao—children of Polish immigrants who had arrived in the thirties. Then there were Curaçaoan Jews, long-time residents, descendants of Spanish and Portuguese Jews. Most of them belonged to the Jewish Club, but I never felt at home there. They found my background odd and unsettling. Nor did I want to meet with their incomprehension. But here in Mr. de Beer's school, we all came together.

One of my dance partners, Annette, was in the category of the just-arrived. She had a rather resolutely Dutch manner, brisk and purposeful, and was a laconic dancer, her pigtails flipping briskly from side to side. Her father, Dr. Santkamp, picked us up in the afternoon. We envied him because, as a doctor, he was not bound by rationing, and received new tires for his car, whereas three years after the end of the war we still drove on tires that had been inserted one into the other. Dr. Santkamp was small and somehow never pushed his car seat forward, so he could hardly see where he was driving. If he drove by, you saw just a hat reaching for the steering wheel. On the island he was best known for his chicken phobia. There had been reports of Dr. Santkamp freezing in his tracks as he approached the house of one of his patients who had a chicken coop. When he walked through downtown, sly Curaçaoans made loud clucking noises to each other.

Annette was bold and took after her mother, a disdainful, aristocratic beauty, with a haughty manner. Unlike her father, she was not going to be led, not on the dance floor or anywhere else. I tried, but she insisted on moving her arms up and down and pulling me this way and that. Once in a while, the proximity of her body persuaded me that I liked her, and I started saying whispery things to her about the dance; but she gave me a hard, silent stare. She disliked all weakness.

"How can a doctor be afraid of chickens?" my father asked.

"Some people are afraid of snakes," said my mother. "Why not chickens?"

"Are there snakes in Curaçao?" wondered my father.

Every Saturday night I practiced all my steps. I had the radio on and danced the *boté* as if I had a partner, with my left hand out and my right arm encircling her waist. I sang with Radio Curaçao, "*Aunque ya tú no me quieres, yo se que algun día, tu me darás toda la felicidad*" ("Though you do not love me yet, I know that someday you will give me all happiness"). That is what the future would bring, and marriage, a life of total happiness. It would be just as good as the distant past in Holland, before the war spoiled everything and replaced pleasure with panic and happiness with dread. I could see the little house in Bilthoven, and in front of it my playmates, a round-headed boy and a girl who could not pronounce the name of the dog they had recently taken over from the Dutch people in whose house they lived. The family had come from France to Holland, because they thought Holland would remain neutral. I helped her say Hector, which she pronounced "Ector."

Both children were lost in the war, my parents said, using the word *lost*, which I found so odd, as if they had been endlessly misplaced, as if they could still return some day, when in fact they had been incinerated. In that little park across the street we rode our bicycles, the girl always looking over her shoulder at me, as if seeking approval or guidance. She always rode tentatively, questioningly. A music-induced wave of yearning for that idyllic time broke over me, and for a moment I reeled, the mist coming unstoppably to my eyes. My future bride would understand this in me, would appreciate it, love it. How could it be otherwise?

I continued dancing, almost grimly, concentrating now on how I would create that happiness, wondering which one of my classmates would be part of the future I fashioned. Slowly the hideous pictures of the little children and the barking dog suffocated by the burning cloud dimmed, and I saw instead myself and someone else, the two of us as adults, dancing, our arms around each other, the way it sometimes happened in American movies, especially when the evening breeze was said to "caress the trees, tenderly."

My brother was studying in our bedroom. My parents were out. I had the living room to myself, its overstuffed chairs lately acquired by my mother, who got no aesthetic appreciation from her male household. It was time for "Radio Curaçao Presents . . . By Special Request," and I listened for the song that invariably emerged, requested by "Wilfried for Mary," or "Chrisma for Enrico," or "Johannes for Carlita," a haunting French song that had first come out in 1938 and was popular again in the forties, "J'Attendrai" ("I Will Wait"), sung by Tino Rossi, the divine Corsican, the other Corsican, as he was known in France. My imaginary partner and I were still; we held hands and looked at each other with longing and joy. Such happiness wiped everything else out; that's what happiness was for. "Yes," I said to her, "I will wait for you, all the days of my life."

"J'Attendrai" was never part of the repertoire of the dance school. Mr. de Beer was not fond of the fox trot and perhaps wanted to discourage close dancing.

*

Soon Gloria started coming to our class. She was born in Curaçao a few years after her parents arrived from Poland in the early thirties. Auburn-haired, small, vivacious, Gloria knew all the dances but was frustrated that Mr. de Beer didn't teach the jitterbug. She wanted to be an American bobby-soxer and go to proms and sock-hops. At fourteen, Gloria had seen all the American movies that came to Curaçao and modeled herself on Esther Williams, though she was a bit round for the part. Her fondness for things American was matched by her patience: she had once read the English-Dutch dictionary from cover to cover. We traded movie magazines and she swooned over John Derek. In the Jewish Club, she sat at the piano and sang, again and again, "I Love You—For Sentimental Reasons . . . I hope you do believe me; I'm giving you my heart." Through the amazing immediacy of the years I can still hear her accent, "S*a*ntim*a*ntal reasons . . ."

Painfully aware of being a year younger than Gloria and not having seen many American movies, I copied out the words she sang. The only way I could think to approach her was to have her check the English. "Not santimantal *meeting*," she said irritably; "santimantal *reasons*."

After dance school, my friend Alex was always hungry. He was born in Curaçao of Turkish-Jewish immigrants, so both his Dutch and his manners were exotic to me. His brother was caught in the local brothel and his picture appeared in the newspaper. Alex's mother had packed an enormous sandwich, which he squashed between his two large hands, sometimes even leaning on it with all his weight. Then he scooped half of it into his mouth and chomped vigorously while talking.

"These girls drive me crazy," he said, his round face sweaty from the exertion. "They won't rub up against me."

"Why should they?"

"Because it's dancing, *pendejo*. Don't you know that's what dancing is for?"

"That's not what Mr. de Beer thinks," I said pedantically.

"Who are you, Wolf, some kind of fool? You're thirteen years old now. De Beer doesn't know what passion we South Americans have. Have you ever seen a bolero where the man and the woman stand so far apart from each other as we do in that school?"

Alex had a point, but I was reluctant to accept it. "The de Beers know a lot about dancing," I said.

"And you know nothing about girls. Girls are just as hot as we are." His round face was now glowing, and his short hair seemed to stand up on end, making him look younger than thirteen.

"Do you really think so?"

"I know so," said Alex expansively, his hand flattening his cheek bulging with food. "You know, I'm not going to marry a Jewish woman."

"You're not? Why not?" I asked.

"So people will know that a Jew can make a Gentile woman happy, that's why. But first I'm going to Germany, to Berlin, to study gynecology."

"Gynecology?"

"Yes, because I can never get enough of women."

"And why Germany?" I asked, this time genuinely shocked by Alex.

"I'm going to fuck all the women there. And they'll be grateful."

"Why does it have to be there?"

"It *has* to be there. There first. Then I'll fuck my way through the rest of the world. Wolf, you're growing up now. From now on, no more games, no more kid stuff. There are more important things. In the future it has to be all fucking." He used the Papiamento word for cleaning, one of the many that described sex. "*Limpia.*"

"Alex, why in Germany?" I repeated.

"We begin there," he said, not answering the question. "Promise me, don't ever say 'Oy' again; don't ever listen to anyone who says that. Never, never again, never, never."

I didn't even know that with his Sephardic background Alex knew the Yiddish word "Oy" and was about to ask him, but Alex never really answered a question. He was a born ranter.

"You know how to be Jewish?" he said, grabbing my collar violently. He still smelled of the sandwich he had just devoured.

"I know," I said, "*limpia, limpia.*"

"Yes, and go to Israel. Get Middle Eastern girls."

It was not to be. I didn't go to Germany or to Israel. Neither did Alex. He went to South America and somehow got into the furniture business in Colombia. Years later I heard he was in jail in Peru.

The latest arrivals were the Franshorsts. In their forties now, they had married right after the war. They had met in Bergen-Belsen, and even at thirteen I could instantly tell that their survival had something to do with an indestructible constitution. Mr. Franshorst had been a butcher, Mrs. Franshorst a sales lady in a department store. They were both red in the face from the tropical sun beating down on their pale skin.

For some reason, my mother adopted them. She spent every other evening with the Franshorsts and gave Mrs. Franshorst blouses and sundresses from our textile store, and they laughed when Mrs. Franshorst tried them on. My mother also doted on their child, a beautiful dark-haired boy of three. Often she would smile at them because the Franshorsts were not very genteel, saying things like "I eat like ten horses." They were not blunt exactly but blurted out what came into their minds, as if they had not been in polite company much.

The Franshorsts adored their child. The father would move his large horse face close to the child's belly and say, "Eddie, Eddie, the hippopotamus is nuzzling you," and the child pealed with laughter. Mrs. Franshorst gazed at Eddie with awe and wonder.

I saw Eddie several times, and, while I enjoyed the child, I felt a growing unease in his presence. A premonitory fist clenched my heart the more I saw him. What if this child were stolen, killed, or lost, the way so many children had been just a few years ago in Europe? He was too precious, too much in jeopardy. "People should always have more than just one child, but the Franshorsts were not able to have more," my mother explained, with that serious, melancholy look she could get. I changed the subject, pretending that I did not know what she meant, and that I wasn't interested anyway; but I knew exactly what she meant: this child was a fragile entity, a beautiful being easily removed, the Franshorsts' sole chance for happiness. I was all too aware of how dangerous and threatening the world was and could not enjoy the Franshorsts' pleasure in their child. I was too afraid.

Half conscious of turning away from such thoughts, I became fanatically curious about the future, eager for the present. In back of me was a dank, heavy mist; before me, an airy plain I wanted to cross. At the far edge of this plain stood a beckoning row of trees. What would lie beyond them? I wanted to hurry to those views, those fields and skies. Perhaps I would settle in a small town against a green hillside, with music, laughter, and the ever-palpable presence of love. Suddenly, on this plain stood Melda, a girl in one of my classes, whose presence distracted and excited me. I now lived in my crush on her.

Melda was thirteen, a clear-featured, brown-skinned beauty with lovely black hair and a small, thin nose. Her kind of coloring was most desirable on the island, not pale, not black, but glowing brown, honey-gold. She looked directly at me in dance school and one afternoon whispered, "Ask me to dance." The large white room seemed to shimmer, and I was dizzy with wanting to, dizzy with her glamorous presence. Her father represented the island of St. Martin in the local Parliament. We danced the *boté* under Mr. de Beer's watchful eyes, and she said over the music, "I like talking to you, because you have so much sense."

I wished she could see me in a more romantic light, but I didn't know how to bring that about. Maybe if I stayed her friend, she would someday give me "all happiness."

When she spread out her arms and sang, to no one in particular, "I want to go on a ship and be towed out to sea," I did not say anything. I felt that if I said I would tow her out to sea, I would somehow have to make good on that promise, would really have to try to do it. So I said nothing.

My classmate Carlo was not so cautious or so literal-minded. He picked it right up. "Let's build that ship together."

"Sure," said Melda, with her hand on her pretty hip. "Let's see you do that."

"I've got the wood all ready," said Carlo, making an unsubtle pun on *palo,* Papiamento for both wood and prick.

"You have the wood, but do you have the hammer?"

"My hammer is ready at a moment's notice."

"Let's see if you have the muscle power." And she kneaded the biceps on his upper arm and rolled his short sleeves up higher.

Carlo let her feel all she wanted. Soon they became a couple.

Disappointed, dejected, I could not conceive of how I could do without Melda. I continued to think about her, to picture her, to imagine her speaking to me. She saw I was wounded but was too happy to think about it. We still talked, and I hinted at my infatuation. The talk lessened. Soon I decided to pursue Annette instead.

The dance school lasted almost a year. Then something odd happened. The daily Dutch newspaper ran a series of articles on Mr. de Beer. The headline on the first article proclaimed, "Dancing 'Champion' Really in 37th Place." There had been thirty-eight contestants in the competition Mr. de Beer claimed to have won. This information was repeated in subsequent articles, and each time it sounded more ominous. At first Mr. de Beer denied it, but then there were more serious charges.

It seemed that right after the war, the de Beers had a dancing school in the little town of Amersfoort and then fled with all the cash to another town. How this could have remained undetected for any length of time in a tiny country like Holland was never clear, and the charges struck me—an avid newspaper reader even at thirteen—as strangely vague. Whose cash did they take? What is it they made off with? It then developed that the editor of the paper, the father of one of my classmates, had in the early days of the school withdrawn his child and demanded a full refund, against the rules. At least so Mr. de Beer charged. But the damage was done. Two months later the de Beers left Curaçao for the Netherlands. I don't remember many other examples of investigative reporting in Curaçao. And no other dance school was started while I lived on the island.

I kept missing the school for years. I regretted losing it as much as I now regret not knowing what Melda looks like or who Gloria is married to. Most of all, the school was not only a place to dance but a refuge from thoughts that jarred and feelings that could overwhelm a sunny day with darkness. And I continued to need such a refuge, because a few months after their arrival, the Franshorsts' little son Eddie died of amoebic dysentery.

After that, it was especially difficult not to think about the Franshorsts. But I succeeded better in those days than I do now, when I sometimes can't get them out of my mind at all.

Martín Espada

For the Jim Crow Mexican Restaurant in Cambridge, Massachusetts Where My Cousin Esteban Was Forbidden to Wait Tables Because He Wears Dreadlocks

I have noticed that the hostess in peasant dress,
the waitstaff and the boss
share the complexion of a flour tortilla.
I have spooked the servers at my table
by trilling the word *burrito.*
I am aware of your T-shirt solidarity
with the refugees of the Américas,
since they steam in your kitchen.
I know my cousin Esteban the sculptor
rolled tortillas in your kitchen
with the fingertips
of ancestral Puerto Rican cigar makers.
I understand he wanted to be a waiter,
but you proclaimed
his black dreadlocks unclean,
so he hissed in Spanish
and his apron collapsed on the floor.

May La Migra handcuff the waitstaff
as suspected illegal aliens from Canada;

may a hundred mice dive from the oven
like diminutive leaping dolphins
during your Board of Health inspection;
may the kitchen workers strike, sitting
with folded hands as enchiladas blacken
and twisters of smoke panic the customers;
may a Zapatista squadron
commandeer the refrigerator,
liberating a pillar of tortillas at gunpoint;
may you hallucinate dreadlocks
braided in thick vines around your ankles;
and may the Aztec gods pinned like butterflies
to the menu wait for you in the parking lot
at midnight, demanding
that you spell their names.

Touré

The Sad Sweet Story of Sugar Lips Shinehot and the Portable Promised Land

Trust me, if you'd asked any Negro in Harlem "Who's the coldest saxophone player around?" durin them two months in the summer ah 1942, they'da looked at you like you was crazy. "Sugar Lips Shinehot," they'da said. "You new in town?" Yeah, for a short while Sugar Lips Shinehot was the top saxophonist in Harlem and probably the best sax player livin. Now them history books won't whisper a thing bout Sugar Lips cuz them jazz historians is out there tellin the stories they want to tell. But I'll tell the story, cuz it ain't half-bad, and it's all true. If I'm lyin, I'm flyin.

Back durin them two months Sugar Lips was top dog, even Charlie Parker was scared ah him cuz anytime Sugar Lips wrapped them thick, pillow-soft lips round a mouthpiece, he swung hard nuf to make rain, thunder, and lightnin stop and pay attention. Womenfolk paid, too. They say one night ol Satchmo threw a party, and Lena Horne, Katherine Dunham, and Mahdaymoyzell Josephine Baker all went by Satchmo's hopin to have they lips caressed and massaged by Sugar Lips. Quiet as it's kept, not a few men was there for that, too. As the night lost its pigment word ah the widely shared thought got round and by time that night had turned high-yaller they had the biggest catfight you could imagine up in there. Per some accounts, Katherine slugged Josephine. Others said Lena soaked Katherine wit a glass ah vodka. All's certain is everyone in Harlem laid claim to bein there, and Sugar Lips had set three ah the finest Negro women alive to riotin.

Now, Sugar Lips had always been pretty good wit a horn, though he never struck fear in no Yardbird Parker. But for nine months he was locked hisself up in his apartment on 166th and St. Nicholas blowin til the paint cracked from the heat from his horn. That's when he knew he could smoke like West Hell. So, he looked out his window, saw the sun was in bed snorin hard, throwed on his jacket and porkpie hat, rolled on over to Minton's, where Bird and them was inventin Bebop, and walked in the way you walk in when you a Negro and you know you bad.

Minton's was a do or die sorta joint for jazz cats where players that blew the crowd away could become the king ah Harlem, but mos cats got blown away by dudes like Bird, Dizzy, and Monk, and if ya got blown away it was likely some patron would snatch ya off the stage, take ya out back, and whip ya head til it's red and flat like a dime. It was that sorta spot. But when Sugar Lips leapt up on the bandstand, he started to blowin some horn blowin like no one else belonged in the blowin bizness. Drinks stop bein served, reefers stop bein sold, and a couple that had been in the batroom mergin pull up they draws and stepped out to hear that horn.

Bird hisself happened to be under the bandstand sleepin at that time, so he woke up, grabbed his horn, and started a cuttin contest. He went at Sugar Lips hard as he could, notes spittin from his horn fast and furious as Negroes runnin in a riot, but from the gitgo Sugar Lips was scorchin through solo after solo, gettin that crowd whoopin and hollerin, shoutin and stompin, and when he blew into his last solo he was swingin so hard a few women fainted, a few men cried, and anyone anywhere near the joint thought the Holy Rollers was havin service wit the Holy Ghost hisself as guest preacher. Then Sugar Lips spat out a string ah notes no one had ever heard before and built them into a blazin cascade ah pitch and time and if you closed your eyes you'd have sworn from the sound that he and you was in the air flyin. By the time he finished, the sun had had a cup ah coffee and was ready for his day and Sugar Lips had even Bird admittin he'd outbirded Bird.

Now, Sugar Lips didn't go crowin round Harlem like he was the new mayor or nothin. He went bout bizness like always, but let him try to pay for a steak or taxi or anythin. No one in Harlem would take his money. Got to where he had to add a extra hour to gettin anywhere, wit folk wantin his autograph or askin him to play on they record or inquirin bout what time he might get back home so's maybe she could be there, too. Time slid on and men from them record-makin companies came callin wit contracts and promises bout makin him a big-time star. And Sugar Lips was bout to sign one ah them contracts when somethin butted in.

One night two months to the day since he cut Bird, Sugar Lips bounced outta Minton's wit his horn in his hand and, on his arm, a sealskin-brown broad with six months in front and nine months behind. She was hot as July jam. They was jus a block from his apartment when they made a shorecut thru ah alleyway and found two white Navy boys hidin out. For all youse too young to remember, in '42 servicemen was barred from jus settin foot in Harlem cuz they thought them boys was comin uptown and gettin all sorta vernearally classified diseases. So for them boys to sneak up to Harlem meant them riskin they whole Navy careers jus to knock the pad with a woman fine as the one Sugar Lips had.

"What's goin on here?" one ah them Navy boys said.

Sugar Lips jus looked at him and kept walkin, but they stepped in his way.

"Ain't gonna intradeuce me to the gal, darkie?" one said.

"Y'all should think ah somethin better than darkie if you hope to get under my skin," Sugar Lips said. "Try Sambo. Or coon."

He got up nose to nose wit Sugar Lips. "I was sailin all over the Pacific savin your *coon* hide when I thought that one up, *Sambo*, so I think you like it."

"Well, I don't. But you think on it and catch me right here tomorrow night, man," Sugar Lips said, and started to walk round the sailors.

"Did you call him *ma'am*?" one of them asked.

"No. Didn't."

"You callin me a *liar*, boy?"

Before Sugar Lips could open his mouth, both sailors leapt up, wrestled him down, and went to bangin on his head and shoulders and ribs like he was a steel drum. That woman hauled off, but long before the law showed up, Sugar Lips blacked out, right after seein a brick, wit white fingers wrapped round it, racin toward his soft lips.

When you a Negro, white folk is like doors. You got to go through them to get most anywhere. If you want to play at the Apollo, you got a door called Mo Leviathan. If youse to get a contract wit Savoy Records, there's a door named Herman Rubinsky. If you need space in a roomin house, or to see a movin picture, or to buy some fruit, or a beer, or sometimes jus to get cross town without gettin your head bust open, there you is, face to face wit a door. Even when you a Negro talkin to a Negro, lotta time you really dealin wit a door. Doors don't always open up, and sometimes them doors get heavy and Negroes get tired of openin door after door to get anywhere, and mostimes to walk through them doors you have to act a certain way you don't want to. But if you want to go through, there's lil choice. And when there ain't no door, either it's somethin you shouldn't be havin anyway, or the door is jus then bein built.

For Sugar Lips, it seemed like the Navy boys had chain-locked a whole lotta doors at once, cuz even months later, after mos ah the bones and bruises had healed on up, he still couldn't blow his horn, or kiss, or do anythin truly important. Where them sweet lips used to be he had jus a mangled ol fist. Bird was back top that sax hill, them record-sellin companies had put away they tracts of con, and he couldn't find no broad to boil his hambone. Times was hard for Sugar Lips then, and if not for throwin an occasional house-rent party, he'd never dirty no dishes.

So Sugar Lips was surprised one afnoon to hear somebody honkin outside his window like they honkin after him. It was a short, jet-black man wit a sharp fire-red Pontiac, wearin a checkered zoot suit and diamonds on every finger. Sugar Lips had never seen him before, but glad fer company, he threw on a coat and hobbled downstairs.

"Sugar Lips, I'm Gabriel," the man said.

"Afternoon," he replied.

"It's all in the street about your problems. I came to see if I could be of any service," Gabriel said.

"What do you do, sir?" he asked.

"I'm in the problem-solvin game, my friend," Gabriel said. "It was them crackers tore you up, right?"

"Yeah."

"You can't play your horn?"

"Nah."

"You can't kiss your women?"

"No, sir."

"Make you mad?"

"Sure."

"Make you mad at *all* crackers?"

"Uh, sometimes."

"So mad you *hate* them?"

"I don't know about all that."

"Wish you could wipe them honkeys from the Earth as you know it?"

"What Negro hasn't, once or twice?"

"Well, then," Gabriel said, "this here's *your* lucky day!"

Sugar Lips stared at him.

Gabriel whispered, "I've got a friend who can clear whitey right off your Earth forever."

Sugar Lips thought Gabriel was beatin up his gums and runnin his mouth, but he stayed curious.

"Hey, this is solid. I guarantee results. My friend will take care ah you. He's the world's best problem-solver. Take this card and meet me in three days," he said. "We need time to make sure everythin's set up."

Gabriel hopped into his Pontiac and raced off. Sugar Lips looked into his hand. There was a plain business card wit the name "Reverend Doctor Bernard Z. LeBub," and under it, smaller words sayin "Problems Solved," and under that, even smaller words sayin "For You Hoodoo." A Harlem address was printed in the bottom righthand corner, and three days after, his curiosity gettin better ah him, Sugar Lips went there.

Sugar Lips arrived at the office and tried the knob. Inside, there was Gabriel standin beside a man papa-tree-top-tall, blindinly handsome and so light you couldn't be sure he was Negro or not. He was draped down in the whitest white zoot suit your eyes could register, and wit one look you knew *this dude is righteous.* A man who could outchase the fastest skirt-chaser, outpick the best lock-picker, outroll the best dice-roller, outrhyme the best dozens player, and con the brilliantest of the brilliant. The sorta cat who could be a king ah kings if jus he wanted. He grinned widely at Sugar Lips.

"Sugar Lips," Gabriel said. "May I introduce my boss, Reverend Scratch."

"I thought his name was Doctor LeBub," Sugar Lips said.

"The Reverend has many names," Gabriel answered. "But enough idle talk. For a small price Reverend Scratch will do what you wish: remove the white man from the Earth as you know it. *Ad infinitum.*"

"What's the price?" Sugar Lips asked.

Gabriel began to speak, but Reverend Scratch raised up his hand. The Reverend stood slowly and said, "My son, I am a Reverend and a Doctor. You can trust me." He stood next to Sugar Lips, slid his arm around Sugar Lips's shoulder, and leaned into his face. "I am offering you relief from everythin that ails you. *Everythin.* When I am finished you will know boundless freedom. For this favor, do you ask the price?"

"Well, if you from Harlem you do," Sugar Lips said.

"You puny lamb amongst wolves in the valley of the damned!" Reverend Scratch roared. "When a shepherd comes bearin salvation on a platter, do you ask when can I eat the apple? Why can't I look back? How much will the nails burn? You have one chance and there is one cost. *When thou art offered salvation doth thou asketh the price?*"

Scratch threw up his desk to reveal a door in the floor. With ease he flung the door open, stepped in, and slammed the door back. Sugar Lips's heart got to punchin at its skin, and he was as close to leavin as ninety-nine is to a hundred when Gabriel rush up to his side. "Don't concern yourself with the price," he said. "We'll haggle about it later. You got a tremendous opportunity here. I wouldn't blow it if I were you."

Sugar Lips was justly afraid ah the Reverend, but as Gabriel spoke he calmed down. He thought there was opportunity, and somehow the Reverend had made his curiosities grow.

"Are you ready to rid yourself, my friend?" Gabriel asked.

"I think so," Sugar Lips said.

Gabriel led Sugar Lips through the door where Scratch had gone and down countless flights ah stairs to a room filled wit manila candles and a white bathtub brimmin wit milk. Gabriel helped him undress and get into that tub, then waited til Sugar Lips was relaxed. Soon, young boys in black robes, whose race Sugar Lips could not guess, began enterin one by one til they lined the walls and began chantin. Reverend Scratch came in and stood at the foot of that tub and stared straight at Sugar Lips, not sayin a word. Sugar Lips heard scufflin in another room, like three or four men was fightin. Over the chantin he heard screams, a boy's screams, then, suddenly, them screams stopped and a boy in a white robe came rushin in that room and shoved two whole eyeballs in Sugar Lips's mouth. His skin crawled wit the thought of eyeballs in his mouth, but slowly they taste took him over. He realized they was pleasantly salty, and not unlike a tender breast of chicken. Bitin them was easy as bitin a crunchy milk chocolate egg, though a liquid came out the middle that seeped down his chest, burnin like whiskey. While them crunched balls and they inner liquid eased down his throat, a man closed Sugar Lips's eyes, dripped hot wax on his lids, laid his head back, and put him to sleep.

When Sugar Lips woke that next afternoon, he found he could not remember what had happened after he'd swallowed them eyeballs—not walkin from Reverend Scratch's back to his apartment or takin his clothes off or even gettin to bed. Plus, he had a strong feelin to havin somethin new, somethin important. He couldn't recall what that was, neither. He felt a joy, but didn't remember what to feel joyous bout.

Then he heard a car honkin outside his window. It was the sound ah his girl from down in Grenitch Village. He was glad to hear that sound. She had been up in Paris for the summer and knew none ah his troubles. Sugar Lips had once had a taste for lotsa flavors, and his sweet lips had led him to every flavor from double chocolate to mocha to cinnamon to cherry to butter pecan to cookies n' cream and when he needed a lil vanilla, nothin tasted like Carolyn. Course, Carolyn was a door herself. A door to a certain sorta love and approval and sheet-burnin, and a door everyone tells Negroes not to open.

He leaned his head out the window to call to her and saw her blue Buick but no Carolyn anywhere. He flew down them stairs and opened the door but still, no Carolyn at all. Her car sat front ah him, the motor runnin, but no one in sight. He stood in that doorway for a long time lookin round, expectin her to jump out and surprise him, but nothin happened. Then, Carolyn's Buick suddenly shifted and zoomed off down that street.

Sugar Lips stepped out to look round. Some well-dressed Negroes was over here peacockin down the street like they was late to they coronation, and some Negro winos was lyin like crumpled-up pieces of paper over there, and some Negro children was slidin up, round, and through a double-dutch rope like magic, and it looked to be a normal day in Negro Heaven. Then he saw a Cadillac drive by wit no one inside it. Then another. He turned to run to the newsstand down the block to read bout this new driverless car, but got only a few steps before he hit what felt like a brick wall and was knocked on his backside. He looked up and saw nothin, then felt hisself jerked to his feet by his collar. A Negro man came runnin from nowhere, talkin frantically to the air, apologizin for Sugar Lips *to the air.* Sugar Lips fell back to his back, and that Negro bent to help him up.

"Ay, boss, what choo doin, juss all runnin inta white folk like dat?" the Negro said.

"What white folk?" he said.

"You crazy?" the Negro asked. "The one ya juss smacked inta. The one almoss beat ya into pulp."

"I ain't seen nothin," Sugar Lips said, but then everythin made sense. He leapt to his feet and looked round. The Man was nowhere in sight. The Woman, neither. But this was Harlem. He walked over to the bus stop, careful to walk in a straight line and not make sharp turns lest he run into someone he couldn't see, and hopped on that number six downtown. There were open seats all over, but jus to be safe he stood near the front and looked out the window. As the bus rumbled downtown he saw Negro shoeshine boys on one knee, snappin and crackin a rag as though polishin a shoe. But no one in the shoeshine seat. He saw Negro doormen in uniforms, mechanically movin through they ritual of noddin, smilin, and openin the door, but no one steppin through. He saw ice vendors handin blocks of ice over to the air, waiters placin food in front of tables wit nobody, and women pushin empty strollers. He saw a Negro havin a fistfight solo, a Negro in handcuffs trudgin along by hisself, and, once, a high-yaller with a right arm and leg and no left arm or leg—a man with jus half a body!

The bus got to 42nd Street and he got off. He looked round and saw less than half the normal number of peoples on that street, and they was all Negroes. No white cops directin traffic. No white waitresses takin orders. No white men in suits movin down the street. Jus Negroes percolatin everywhere, shoppin, drivin, sellin ice cream. And he felt the weight of tuggin on door after door drop away. Without bein able to get at them doors, it was like he couldn't go nowhere, but then again, without bein able to get at them doors, it was like he *could* go nowhere. Wit no place to go and no place bein exactly where he wanted to be, he felt somethin like a jus-freed slave.

"Is it a holiday?" he said out loud. "Tax day? Voting day? No!" he yelled, "It's Anti-Christmas!" A small crowd of Negroes was watchin, and he screamed louder, "It's Anti-Christmas!!! It's Anti-Christmas!!!"

He looked at his crowd and saw they wasn't lookin directly at him, but jus in front and in back ah him. Then came a loud crack from behind and a blindin pain at the back ah his neck. Sugar Lips fell to his knees. His wrists was handcuffed together and he was heaved into this empty paddy wagon. Punches and kicks and blows and stomps started comin from all over, but there was nothin to see, and they was comin again and again, openin up them breaks and bruises he'd jus gotten past and new ones, too. But Sugar Lips didn't feel no pain cuz he was laughin. Laughin so loud and hard he shook that paddy wagon, makin it rock from the force of his laughin and laughin and laughin.

Once he was well again Sugar Lips marched all over the Big Red Apple, and every street he set foot on was either barren or graced wit them colors and styles and smells and sounds ah Negroes and every place he went he felt deeply at home cuz every place seemed to be Harlem.

As the capital of Negro America, Harlem was supposed to be Negro Heaven and, much as one place can be that, it was. Negroes could live there wit a sense ah security and peace and community and freedom they lost soon's they stepped outside. Now, in some ways Harlem was keepin up a front to keep its prestige. Sugar Lips hisself had sometimes to live like mos folks, in a hot bed wherein a landlord rented a room to one and another fellow. One slept by day, another at night, wit only nuf time in between to turn the sheet. Still, Harlem livin was as good as Negro livin got. Them hot beds, folk said, was proof to Harlem's greatness, cuz it happened on count ah so many Negroes wantin to live there. And they felt like Harlem was a sort of promised land for them, and for Sugar Lips to feel like he was in the promised land wherever he went made him blessed as everyone in the Bible added up.

Sugar Lips found if he moved slow and in straight lines he got no trouble, like collidin wit folk, and he found his days mo peaceful than he could've ever imagined. He didn't miss playin his horn, cuz he was so filled wit a new sense of contentment, and sides, he was busy. Everyone in Harlem heard bout the Negro that couldn't see whiteys and though he couldn't hardly prove it, they believed it cuz they jus wanted such a thing to be. And Sugar Lips became even mo the celebrity than he'd been after he'd cut Bird. His picture made the cover ah *Negro Digest*, and in every bar, street, and room he was the center attention, cuz Negro men and women crowded round to watch and listen to the man wit the portable promised land. Folk gave him money jus to come to they parties and even jus for bein hisself. One Saturday night he had dinner wit Gordon Parks, Mister Bill Bojangles Robinson, and Joe Louis at Joe's Harlem restaurant. Then he woke up early so he could be special guest at the Sunday service of the legendary Father Divine. And don't you know, Father Divine invited Sugar Lips up to the pulpit in the middle of his sermon and declared him "the Modern Moses who parts the white waters with nothin but his eyes."

Finally, Sugar Lips knew it was time to do somethin big to share his gift and everythin it meant wit alla Harlem. Somethin to make everyone know exactly what bein a Negro could mean. He turned a corner and was on 133rd Street, in front of a bar called Sum Mo, crowded wit Negroes drinkin conk busters and throwin dice and chasin tail. When he walked in, that crowd hushed up.

"Harlem, I got somethin to say!" he screamed out. "I am Sugar Lips Shinehot . . ." he said.

"Well, awright!" folk yelled out.

". . . and I am the coldest thang Harlem ever did see!" he said.

"Ya might have a point there, son!" some jug head called from the back and set everyone to laughin.

"I can do things no man has ever done before!"

"Ya ain't lied yet!"

"For months I ain't seen one whitey or had none of them tell me about somethin I couldn't do or somethin I had to do. I haven't talked to one. I haven't heard from one. Not even had a postcard."

"Now ya cookin wit gas!"

"Can I get an amen!!" Sugar Lips roared.

Sum Mo cheered wildly.

"So tomorrow," Sugar Lips said when the uproar calmed down, "I'm gonna show y'all what freedoms Negroes can acquire if you can get the white man out of your life! I'll show you how light you'll feel without that weight!" Sugar Lips paused and then he said, "I am going," then he paused, "to fly."

And it was dead silent throughout Sum Mo.

Sugar Lips had never before thought ah flying, hadn't considered it until the words came outa his mouth, but as soon as he said it, he was sure he could do it. "I'm goin to show y'all what a Negro can do when he's freed of the burden of havin to deal with white people! I'm gonna fly! Tomorrow, at noon, y'all be out in front of the Apollo, and tell a friend! I'm gonna fly! This is somethin everyone is goin to wanta see. I'm goin to get up there on top of the world famous Ay-paul-o *Thee*-ay-ter, and sure as my name is Sugar Lips, I'm gonna fly!"

Wit that, he strutted outta Sum Mo. Once he'd walked down the street, someone in the bar sighed and said, "My people, my people. Not seein Mister Charlie done made that poor Zigaboo lose his mind."

"I bet he can do it."

"Don't you get fooled by that boogerbooin. Ain't no man that can fly."

"Ain't no man flown. Don't mean no man can fly. Sides, that boy there some kinda Negro superman or somethin, walkin round not havin to see these ofays. Wish I could do that."

"Yeah, then yo ass'd be out a job!"

*

That next day bout five hundred Negroes was standin in the street in front ah the Apollo Theater when Sugar Lips appeared on that roof. He'd played there a few times before his lips got bust up, and one them security guys that remembered him helped him find his way up. Now he was alone to get down. He looked out at the crowd and saw they was on his side, they wanted him to fly. For him to fly would be to do in front ah they eyes somethin he useta to do and somethin Bird Parker still did wit a horn: to throw off them white man shackles and fly. And jus as when Bird flew, if Sugar Lips flew somethin in all of them would fly.

For some folk, it didn't matter none if he flew. Jus for a Negro to believe he could fly was a feelin better than if a Negro turned into Joe Louis and knocked out Max Schmelin hisself. His actual flyin wasn't as important, cuz his *believin* he could fly was inspiration nuf. That a Negro could get that much good feelin bout hisself made em feel good. Others felt him flyin would put back some of the glory Harlem was losin and remind the world where was Negro Heaven. And then there was those Negroes who jus got to have the theater in they lives. If some Negro said he was gointa put on a show and fly, they was gonna have good seats.

"I'm about to go up!" Sugar Lips screamed out.

"Yeah!" everyone cheered.

"And I may not come down!"

"YEAH!!"

"I may just fly away from all of this, fly right on up to Heaven and see y'all when you get there. But even if I don't, I declare this to be a Negro holiday. Flyin Day!!"

The crowd started cheerin even louder a second later when Sugar Lips stuck his arms out in front of hisself, bent low, and leapt up into the air and screamed out, "I AM HARLEM!!!" Time slowed down for Sugar Lips then, and he felt hisself glidin, face first, hangin in the air, weightless, not quite flyin but perched and without a stitch ah fear. He shut his eyes then, knowin that through feelin hisself able to fly, he could die happy even if he didn't fly.

125th Street held its breath as Sugar Lips hung in the air, they dreams ah him, a Negro, flyin, seeminly realized. They wanted so much for him to fly that not one of them even moved when, after a few seconds of hangin, he began fallin, cuz of jealous Gravity snatchin him back, and once Gravity caught hold ah him she pulled harder and harder and he fell faster and faster and the ground raced up to them closed eyes and them mangled lips that was still screamin, "AAAAHHHH AAAAAMMM HAAAR-LLLEEEMMMMMM!!!!!" and Gravity was bout done pullin and all ready to hand him over to her cousin Death when the day manager of the Apollo, Fat Jimmy, waddled out onto the sidewalk to see why a few hundred Negroes was standin in the street lookin up into that sky above his joint and he looked up jus in time to see Sugar Lips crash right onto him.

Every so often after Sugar Lips got hauled off that day, folk set theyselves to tellin him bout the white man that broke his fall. Sugar Lips never bought they story. "Aw man, go head with that," he'd say. "I know I gotta work on my landin style." Now, wit half a chance, that white man woulda let Sugar Lips fall right into Death's hands, and if he could've laid eyes on Fat Jimmy, Sugar Lips would've known he hadn't really flown. Still, Sugar Lips needed Fat Jimmy to be able to think that he could fly jus like Harlem needs the rest ah the island called Manhattan to keep from fallin in the ocean. For quite some time after, Sugar Lips did believe he could fly, and that's a nice thing for a Negro to believe. Yeah, Sugar Lips believed he could fly even after his untimely demise on the second annual Flyin Day. He knows better now. Trust me. I told him. Right after he finished tellin this story to me, Uncle Scratch.

Major L. Jackson

Some Kind of Crazy

It doesn't matter if you can't see
Steve's 1985 Corvette: Turquoise-colored,
Plush purple seats, gold-trimmed
Rims that make little stars in your eyes

As if the sun is kneeling at
The edge of sanity. Like a Baptist
Preacher stroking the dark underside
Of God's wet tongue, he can make you

Believe. It's there; his scuffed wing-
Tips—ragged, frayed, shuffling
Concrete—could be ten-inch Firestone
Wheels, his vocal chords fake

An eight-cylinder engine that wags
Like a dog's tail as he shifts gears. Imagine
Steve, moonstruck, cool, turning right
Onto Ridge Avenue, arms forming

Arcs, his hands a set of stiff C's
Overthrowing each other's rule,
His lithe body and head snap back
Pushing a stick shift into fourth

Whizzing past Uncle Sam's Pawn
Shop, past Chung Phat's Stop & Go.
Only he knows his destination,
His limits. Can you see him? Imagine

Steve, moonstruck, cool, parallel
Parking between a Pacer and a Pinto—
Obviously the most hip—backing up,
Head over right shoulder, one hand

Spinning as if polishing a dream;
And there's Tina, wanting to know
What makes a man tick, wanting
A one-way trip to the stars.

We, the faithful, never call
Him crazy, crackbrained, just a little
Touched. It's all he ever wants:
A car, a girl, a community of believers.

Kevin Young

Jack Johnson

acrylic & oil paintstick on canvas (1982)

Jack decided that being a painter was less of a vocation than he had supposed. He would be a boxer instead. He had the punch; he had the speed; he was capable of moving half a second before trouble arrived in his neck of the woods.

—Denzil Batchelor,
Jack Johnson & His Times

BLACK JACK: *b. 31 March 1878*

Some call me spade,
stud, buck, black. That last
I take as compliment—

"I am black & they
won't let me forget it."
I'm Jack

to my friends, Lil'
Arthur—like that King
of England—to my mama.

Since I got crowned champ
most white folks would love
to see me whupped.

They call me dog, cad
or card, then bet
on me to win. I'm still

an ace & the whole
world knows it. Don't
mean most don't want

me done in. But I got words
for them too—when I'm through
most chumps wish

they were counting
cash instead
of sheep, stars. I deal

blows like cards—
one round, twenty
rounds, more. "I'm black all

right & I'll never let them
forget it." Stepping
to me, in or out

the ring, you gamble—
go head then dealer,
hit me again.

THE UPSET: *26 December 1908*

"Who told you
I was yellow?"
I wanted to know

taunted—"Come
& get it,
Lil' Tahmy"

in my best English
accent, inviting
Burns to dodge

my fists the way
he'd avoided me,
running

farther—Britain
France—than
that kangaroo

I once bet I could
outdistance & did.
Chased down

to Sydney
Stadium, now was nowhere
to go—no more

color line to hide
behind, no lies bout
my coward streak—

I will bet a few plunks
the colored man
will not make good!

That I wasn't game.
Baited him
like a race—first

round he fell
with his odds,
favored. By two

all bets were even
& I made him pay—drew
blood—pounded

his face into morse, worse
than what Old Teddy
Roosevelt could stand

to hear over the wire. Bully.
"You're white, dead
scared white

as the flag of surrender.
You like to eat
leather?" By twelve I bet

he wished
he was still
at sea, had stayed Noah

Brusso, not Burns
trapped in Rushcutters Bay
about to be smoked

like my finest
cigar. "Didn't
they tell us this

boy was an in-
fighter?"
By thirteen

rounds he bites
luck & dust—
the police

rush in like fools,
angels, afraid
for both of us

treading this ring
like water,
my wide wake.

The fight!—There was no fight! No American Massacre could compare to the hopeless slaughter that took place in the Sydney Stadium. The fight, if fight it must be called, was like that between a pigmy and a colossus. It had all the seeming of a playful Ethiopian at loggerheads with a small white man—of a grown man cuffing a naughty child—of a monologue by Johnson who made a noise with his fist like a lullaby, tucking Burns into a crib—of a funeral, with Burns for the late deceased, Johnson for the undertaker, gravedigger, and sexton, all in one.... It was hopeless, preposterous, heroic!... But one thing now remains. Jim Jeffries must emerge from his alfalfa farm and remove the golden smile from Jack Johnson's face. Jeff, it's up to you! The White Man must be rescued.

—Jack London,
Jack Johnson & His Times

THE CROWN: *4 July 1910*

In order to take
away my title
Jeffries—Great White

Hope—emerged
like a whale, lost
weight, spouted

steam. Said negroes
have a soft spot
in our bellies

that only needs
finding. Bull's
eye. He refused

our pre-fight shake—
my eyes clear
like the time, years

later, I saw Rasputin
at the Czar's Palace
weeks before the Reds

stormed in & knew that big
man—whom no one could
outdrink or talk—was grand

but finished. Heard
it took five tries
—poison, stabbing, etc.—

before he went at last
under. Jeffries was cash
by round one. Fresh

from his alfalfa
farm retirement,
only he was fool

or good enough
to challenge me, stage
a bit of revolution—

the Whites
couldn't have
me running

their show, much less
own the crown.
Called for my head.

"Devoutly hope
I didn't happen
to hurt you, Jeff"—

my fists harpoons,
hammers of John
Henry gainst

that gray engine
—*I think I can*—
steaming. Stood

whenever in my corner
facing the sun
after giving him

the shady one.
My trunks navy
blue as Reno

sky, Old Glory
lashed through
the loops—that Independence

Day, despite warning
shots & death threats
before the match,

I lit Jeffries like black
powder, a fire
cracker—

on a breakfast
of 4 lamb cutlets
3 eggs, some steak

beat him till he
hugged me
those last rounds

& I put him
out his misery.
You could hear the riots

already—from Fort
Worth & Norfolk
Roanoke to New

York, mobs
gather, turning
Main Street into a main

event, pummeling
any black cat
who crosses

their paths.
Neck tie
parties cutting

another grin
below any raised
Negro chins—

JOHNSON WINS
WHITES LYNCH
70 ARRESTED

BALTIMORE
OMAHA NEGRO
KILLED—

all because I kept
their hope
on the ropes. His face

like newsprint
bruised. On account
of my coal-fed heart—

caboose red
& bright
as his—what wouldn't give.

Amaze an' Grace, how sweet it sounds,
Jack Johnson knocked Jim Jeffries down.
Jim Jeffries jumped up an' hit Jack on the chin.
An' then Jack knocked him down agin.

The Yankees hold the play,
The white man pull the trigger;
But it makes no difference what the white man say,
The world champion's still a nigger.

—Traditional

THE RING: *13 May 1913*

The bed is just
another ring I'd beat
them white boys in—

double, four
poster, queen.
I'd go the rounds

with girls who begged
to rub my head
cause it was clean

shaven, polished.
Said it felt like billiards
to them, bald

black. Balling
was fine, but once
I began to knock out

their men & sweep
the women off their feet
—even bought one a ring—

well, that was too much.
When I exchanged vows
with my second wife

—before God & everyone—
they swore I'd pay. Few
could touch me anyway,

what did I care. Later
when she did herself in
in our bed, I knew

—sure as standing—
they'd pushed her
to the edge. After

I mourned & met
my next love
& wife—my mama,

Tiny, said
little but worry—
they trumped

up charges, 11 counts
of the Mann Act
so I couldn't fight. My dice

role came up thirteen—
a baker's dozen
of prostitution & white

slavery—a white jury
after one hour found me
guilty of crimes

versus nature. Put
me through the ringer.
Nigras, you see, ain't

supposed to have brains
or bodies, our heads just
a bag to punch. But I beat

the rap without fists—
disguised as a Black
Giant, I swapped

gloves—boxing
for baseball—traded
prison stripes for Rube

Foster's wool
uniform. Smuggled
north into Canada

like chattel, we sailed
the *Corinthian*
for England, staying below

deck. Fair France
greeted me with a force
of police—turns out to tame

the cheering crowds—
granted me amnesty,
let me keep my hide

whether world
champ, con, or stripped
like my crown.

Jack Johnson's case will be settled in due time in the courts. Until the court has spoken, I do not care to either defend or condemn him. I can only say at this time that this is another illustration of the most irreparable injury that a wrong action on the part of a single individual may do to a whole race. It shows the folly of those who think that they alone will be held responsible for the evil that they do. Especially is this true in the case of the Negro in the United States today. No one can do so much injury to the Negro race as the Negro himself. This will seem to many persons unjust, but no one can doubt that it is true.

What makes the situation seem a little worse in this case is the fact that it was the white man, not the black man who has given Jack Johnson the kind of prominence he has enjoyed up to now and put him, in other words, in a position where he has been able to bring humiliation upon the whole race of which he is a member.

—Booker T. Washington
for United Press Association,
23 October 1912

Some pretend to object to Mr. Johnson's character. But we have yet to hear, in the case of white America, that marital troubles have disqualified prizefighters or ball players or even statesmen. It comes down then, after all, to this unforgivable blackness. Wherefore we conclude that at present prizefighting is very, very immoral, and that we must rely on football and war for pastimes until Mr. Johnson retires or permits himself to be "knocked out."

—W. E. B. Du Bois,
Crisis, August 1914

THE FIX: *5 April 1915*

That fight with Willard was a fix
not a faceoff. Out of the ring
three years, jonesing

for the States, I struck a deal
to beat the Mann
Act—one taste of mat

& I'd get
let back home.
But I even told

my mama—
Tiny,
Bet on me.

Once in the bout—run out
of Mexico by Pancho
Villa himself—I fought that fix

the way, years back, Ketchel
knocked me down
even after we shook

& agreed I'd take the fall
if he carried me
the rounds without trying

to KO—crossed,
doubled
over, I stood up & broke

his teeth like
a promise. At the root.
On the canvas

they shined, white
as a lie. But with Willard
that spring, each punch

was a sucker, every round
a gun. Loaded. Still
I fixed him—strung

him along the ropes
for twenty-five
rounds. At twenty-six

the alphabet in my head
gave way—saw
my wife take the take,

count our fifty grand
& leave. Did the dive,
shielding my eyes—

not so much from Havana
heat—its reek my favorite
cigar—as from the ref's count.

Down, I counted too, blessings
instead of bets. Stretched
there on the canvas

—a masterpiece—stripped
of my title, primed
to return to the States.

Saved. Best
believe I stood up
smiling.

Rita Dove

Rosa

How she sat there,
the time right inside a place
so wrong it was ready.

That trim name with
its dream of a bench
to rest on. Her sensible coat.

Doing nothing was the doing:
the clean flame of her gaze
carved by a camera flash.

How she stood up
when they bent down to retrieve
her purse. That courtesy.

contributors

Kim Addonizio is the author of *Philosopher's Club* and *Jimmy and Rita.* She is co-author with Dorianne Laux of *The Poet's Companion: A Guide to the Pleasures of Writing Poetry.* Her book of stories, *In the Box Called Pleasure,* was published in 1999 by Fiction Collective 2. The title of her next book is *Tell Me.*

Dorothy Allison is a writer living in San Francisco. Her most recent novel is *Cavedweller.*

Greg Bottoms has been a Tennessee Williams Scholar at Sewanee and recently won an individual artist fellowship from the Virginia Commission for the Arts. His book, *Angelhead: A Memoir,* is forthcoming from Crown in fall 2000. "1967" is his first published work of literary nonfiction.

Jane Brox's most recent book is *Five Thousand Days Like This One: An American Family History.* Her first book, *Here and Nowhere Else,* won the L. L. Winship/PEN New England Award. Her essays frequently appear in *The Georgia Review* and other journals and magazines, and her commentaries can be heard on National Public Radio's *Living on Earth.* She lives in the Merrimack Valley of Massachusetts.

Marcus Cafagña's first book, *The Broken World,* was selected by Yusef Komunyakaa for the National Poetry Series. His poems have appeared in *Poetry, The Kenyon Review, The Southern Review,* and *The Threepenny Review,* among others. He teaches creative writing at Southwest Missouri State University.

Rafael Campo teaches and practices general internal medicine at Harvard Medical School and Beth Israel Deaconess Medical Center in Boston. He is the author of *The Other Man Was Me*, which won the 1993 National Poetry Series award; *What the Body Told*, which won a Lambda Literary Award for Poetry; and *The Poetry of Healing: A Doctor's Education in Empathy, Identity, and Desire*, a collection of essays now available in paperback, which also won a Lambda Literary Award for memoir. His poetry and prose have appeared in many anthologies, including *Best American Poetry 1995*, *Things Shaped in Passing: More "Poets for Life" Writing from the AIDS Pandemic*, *Currents in the Dancing River: Contemporary Latino Fiction, Nonfiction, and Poetry*, and *Gay Men at the Millennium*; and in numerous prominent periodicals, including *Double Take*, *The Lancet*, *The Nation*, *The New York Times Magazine*, *Out*, *The Paris Review*, *The Progressive*, *The Threepenny Review*, and *The Washington Post*. With the support of a John Simon Guggenheim Foundation fellowship for 1997–98, he has completed work on his next book, *Diva*, to be published by Duke University Press in the fall of 1999.

Neil Davidson, who was under consideration for a 1995 Pulitzer Prize for feature writing, has written widely on music and arts. His novel, *The Sweet Revenge of Melissa Chavez*, is the first in a trilogy which chronicles the life of a young woman growing up in the 1990s.

Brandel France de Bravo was born and raised in Washington, D.C. Her poetry has appeared most recently in *The Kenyon Review*, *Black Warrior Review*, *The American Voice*, and in several anthologies including *Fathers: A Collection of Poems* and *Outsiders: Poems about Rebels, Exiles and Renegades*. She divides her time between Los Angeles and Mexico City, where she is a member of the Tramontane Poetry Collective.

Junot Díaz is the author of the short story collection *Drowned*, published in 1996. His stories have appeared in *The New Yorker*, *Story*, and *African Voices*, as well as in *The Best American Short Stories* for 1996, 1997, and 1999. He teaches creative writing at Syracuse University. He is currently a Guggenheim Fellow and is completing his first novel.

Rita Dove is a professor of English at the University of Virginia. She has published a novel, *Through the Ivory Gate*, and several books of poetry, most recently *Mother Love*.

Louise Erdrich grew up in Wahpeton, North Dakota, and is a member of the Turtle Mountain Band of Ojibwa. Her books include *Love Medicine*, *The Beet Queen*, *Tracks*, and *The Antelope Wife*, as well as the soon to be published *The Last Report*. She lives in Minnesota with her children.

Martín Espada was born in Brooklyn, New York, in 1957. He has published five books of poetry, most recently *City of Coughing and Dead Radiators* and *Imagine the An-*

gels of Bread, which won an American Book Award and was a finalist for the National Book Critic's Circle Award. Espada has also won the PEN/Revson Fellowship and the Paterson Poetry Prize. His poems have appeared in *The Nation* and *The Best American Poetry*. A recipient of fellowships from the National Endowment for the Arts and the Massachusetts Cultural Council, Espada is currently a professor in the department of English at the University of Massachusetts–Amherst.

Steve Faulkner has worked as a truck driver, a grave vault maker, a carpet cleaner, a roofer, and a carpenter. He is presently a newspaper carrier, student, and part-time teacher. He lives in Topeka, Kansas, where he is at work on *Waterwalk*, a book about his thousand-mile canoe trip with his son.

Frank X. Gaspar teaches at Long Beach City College in California. He has published two volumes of poetry, *The Holyoke* and *Mass for the Grace of a Happy Death*.

Danielle Legros Georges is a writer and translator born in Gonaives, Haiti, and raised in the United States. She has poems forthcoming in *Beyond the Frontier*, an anthology of new works by African American writers, and has contributed translations to a forthcoming book on Haitian women's oral histories. She recently contributed a biographical entry on Haitian novelist Marie Chauvet to *Encarta Africana*. Her recent awards include the 1999 LEF Fellowship from the Boston Writers Room, a MacDowell Fellowship, and a grant from the Barbara Deming Memorial Fund. She is working on a second manuscript of poems. She lives and works as an editor in Boston.

Marcie Hershman is the author of two novels, *Tales of the Master Race* and *Safe in America*. A frequent book reviewer for *The Boston Globe*, her work has appeared in *The New York Times Magazine, Poets & Writers, American Fiction, Ploughshares, Ms.*, and numerous anthologies. She is a recipient of the May Sarton Award, and has received grants from The Bunting Institute of Radcliffe, *The Boston Globe*/Winship Foundation, The Massachusetts Artists Foundation, and the St. Botolph Foundation. She will be the 1999–2000 Fannie Hurst Writer-in-Residence at Brandeis University. She also teaches at Tufts University and at the Fine Arts Work Center in Provincetown, Massachusetts. She lives in Brookline, Massachusetts.

Brian Hocevar has published stories in several journals, including one in *The Louisville Review* that won its fiction contest, and another in *Potpourri* that was nominated for a Pushcart Prize. He is in the M.F.A. program at the University of Alabama.

Major L. Jackson, an accountant and arts administrator, is doing graduate work in creative writing at the University of Oregon. He was awarded a 1995 Pew Fellowship in the Arts and was named the 1994 MacDowell Poetry Fellow. A member of the Dark Room Collective, he has held residencies at Cave Canem, the MacDowell Colony, and the Third Avenue Performance Space.

Gish Jen has published two novels, *Typical American* and *Mona in the Promised Land.* Her most recent book is a collection of stories entitled *Who's Irish?*

Ruth Prawer Jhabvala was educated in England after fleeing from Nazi Germany in 1939. In 1951, she married the Indian architect C.J.H. Jhabvala and went to live in India. Since 1975 they have divided their time between New York and New Delhi. Ms. Jhabvala has published twelve novels and six volumes of short stories. During her long association with James Ivory and Ismail Merchant, she has written twenty of their films.

Ha Jin teaches English and creative writing at Emory University. His latest novel is *In the Pond.*

Suzanne Kamata is currently living in Japan. Her work has appeared in more than fifty publications including *Wingspan*, *Manoa*, *Calyx*, and *Palo Alto Review.* She edited *The Broken Bridge: Fiction from Expatriates in Literary Japan*, a recent anthology.

Nadine Kijner received her M.F.A. from the University of Southern California, where she was fiction editor of *The Southern California Anthology.* "Water" is her first published work.

Jamaica Kincaid's books include *At the Bottom of the River*, *Annie John*, *Lucy*, *A Small Place*, and *The Autobiography of My Mother.* She is editor of *My Favorite Plant*, a collection of writing on plants. She lives in Vermont.

Barbara Kingsolver is a writer living in Arizona. Her most recent novel is *The Poisonwood Bible.*

Yusef Komunyakaa's latest book of poems is *Thieves of Paradise*, and his latest recording is *Love Notes from the Madhouse* (with John Tchicai). He teaches in the creative writing program at Princeton University.

Hanif Kureishi is the author of several award-winning plays and novels. His most recent novel is *Intimacy.*

Denise Levertov's most recent book of new poems is *Sands of the Well.* In 1997 New Directions brought out two thematic selections of her previously published work, *The Stream and the Sapphire* (on religious themes) and *The Life around Us* (on nature). She died in 1997.

Brenda Miller is assistant professor of English at Western Washington University. She earned a Ph.D. in creative writing at the University of Utah, and an M.F.A. at the University of Montana. She received a Pushcart Prize for an essay that originally appeared in *The Georgia Review*, and her work has appeared in such periodicals as *Prairie Schooner, The Bellingham Review, Northern Lights*, and *Yoga Journal*. Her work is included in the books *Storming Heaven's Gate: An Anthology of Spiritual Writings by Women* and *In Brief: Short Takes on the Personal.*

Janice Mirikitani is a major poet in America who has published three volumes of poetry, *Awake in the River, Shedding Silence*, and *We, the Dangerous*. Her work has been published in numerous anthologies, journals, and scholarly publications. She has also edited several anthologies of poetry, prose, and essays, including an anthology of works by survivors of incest and abuse. Ms. Mirikitani is executive director of Glide Memorial Church, where she oversees more than forty programs serving the poor and the homeless in San Francisco.

Jewel Mogan is a writer living in Lubbock, Texas. Her book of short stories, *Beyond Telling*, was published in 1995. She has received the Pushcart Prize twice (1994–1995, 1996–1997), and her story "X and O" was included in Joyce Carol Oates's anthology *Telling Stories: An Anthology for Writers.*

Pat Mora writes poetry, nonfiction, and children's books. Among her adult books are *Agua Santa: Holy Water, Aunt Carmen's Book of Practical Saints*, and the memoir *House of Houses*. She has been a judge and recipient of the Poetry Fellowships from the National Endowment for the Arts and an advisor and recipient of the Kellogg National Leadership Fellowships. Among her other awards are the Premio Aztlán Literature Award and four Southwest Book Awards. A native of El Paso, Texas, she divides her time between the Southwest and the Cincinnati area.

Marilene Phipps is a poet and a painter who was born and grew up in Haiti. She studied anthropology at University of California, Berkeley and is an M.F.A. graduate of the University of Pennsylvania, Philadelphia. She has won fellowships at the Guggenheim Foundation, Harvard's Bunting Institute, the W. E. B. Du Bois Institute, and the Center for the Study of World Religions. She is a Grolier Prize winner, and her manuscript "Crossroads and Unholy Water" won the 1999 Crab Orchard Review.

Susan Rosalsky lives in Brooklyn, New York. "Closer" is her first published story.

Marjorie Sandor is the author of *Night of Music* (stories) and the winner of a 1998 Rona Jaffe Foundation Award for fiction. Her stories and essays have appeared in *The Georgia Review, The New York Times Magazine*, and *House Beautiful*, as well as in *The Best American Short Stories* of 1985 and 1988, *American and I: Stories by American Jewish*

Women Writers, and *The Pushcart Prize XIII*. Her first book of nonfiction, *The Night Gardener*, is forthcoming from the Lyons Press in October 1999. She teaches creative writing at Oregon State University in Corvallis.

Reginald Shepherd's books are *Some Are Drowning* (1993 AWP Award in poetry) and *Angel, Interrupted* (1997 Lambda Award finalist), both published by University of Pittsburgh Press. Pittsburgh will publish his third book, *Wrong*, this fall. After several years' residence in Chicago, he now lives in Ithaca, New York, and teaches at Cornell University.

Terese Svoboda's second novel, *A Drink Called Paradise*, was published in 1999. Her first novel, *Cannibal*, won the Bobst Prize and the Great Lakes New Writers Award.

Patrick Sylvain was born in Haiti, and now works as a bilingual public school teacher in Cambridge. He is also a video-photographer who works as a special researcher for *Frontline*. He has been published in numerous literary magazines, and published three volumes of poetry, a play, a short story collection, and a novel.

Larissa Szporluk is the author of *Dark Sky Question*, winner of the 1997 Barnard New Women Poets Prize. Her poetry has recently won the *Mississippi Review* Prize, the International Poetry Competition (sponsored by the W. B. Yeats Society), and will be featured in *The Kenyon Review 2000*. She has just completed a second manuscript, *Isolato*.

Touré has written for *The New Yorker*, *The New York Times Magazine*, *Rolling Stone*, *Playboy*, and *The Village-Voice*, and studied at Columbia University's graduate school of creative writing. His work will be featured in *The Best American Essays* of 1999. He lives in Fort Greene, Brooklyn, and plays guerrilla tennis.

Reetika Vazirani was educated at Wellesley College and the University of Virginia, where she was a Henry Hoyns Fellow. Her first book, *White Elephants*, won the 1995 Barnard New Women Poet's Prize. She received a 1994 "Discovery"/*The Nation* Award. She has taught at several schools including the University of Virginia. Her individual poems have been widely published in such places as *Agni*, *Antioch Review*, *Callaloo*, *Partisan Review*, *Ploughshares*, and others. She has received fellowships and awards from The Thomas J. Watson Foundation, *Prairie Schooner*, the Sewanee Writers' Conference, and others.

Laura Wexler has published in *DoubleTake*, *The Oxford American*, and *Utne Reader*, and is currently at work on a nonfiction book about a quadruple lynching that occurred in Georgia in 1946. She lives in Athens, Georgia.

John Edgar Wideman, a MacArthur Foundation Fellow, is author of numerous award-winning books of prose fiction and nonfiction prose, including *Fever*, *Philadel-*

phia Fire (1990 PEN/Faulkner Award), *Reuben, Damballah, Hiding Place, I Sent for You Yesterday* (1984 PEN/Faulkner Award), *Brothers and Keepers, The Cattle Killing,* and *Fatheralong.* He teaches at the University of Massachusetts–Amherst.

Manfred Wolf's works have appeared in numerous magazines and journals in the U.S. and in Europe. He teaches at San Francisco State University.

Kevin Young is an assistant professor of English and African-American studies at the University of Georgia. He is a graduate of Harvard College and a Wallace Stegner Fellow at Stanford University. He recently received an M.F.A. in creative writing from Brown University. His *Most Way Home,* which was selected by Lucille Clifton as part of the National Poetry Series, recently won the John C. Zacharis First Book Prize from *Ploughshares.* He is an advisory and contributing editor of *Callaloo.*

credits

"Like That" by **Kim Addonizio** originally appeared in *Alaska Quarterly Review,* vol. 17, nos. 1 and 2, Fall and Winter 1998.

"This Is Our World" by **Dorothy Allison** © 1998, *DoubleTake* magazine. Reprinted by permission of the author.

"1967" by **Greg Bottoms** originally appeared in *Alaska Quarterly Review,* vol. 17, nos. 1 and 2, Fall and Winter 1998. Reprinted by permission of the author.

"The Wilderness North of the Merrimack" from *Five Thousand Days Like This One* by **Jane Brox**. Copyright © 1998 by Jane Brox. First appeared in *The Georgia Review,* vol. 52, no. 4, Winter 1998. Reprinted by permission of Beacon Press.

"Gloomy Sunday" by **Marcus Cafagña** originally appeared in *Witness,* vol. 12, no. 2, 1998. Reprinted by permission of the author.

"Darkest Purple" by **Rafael Campo** from *Diva,* copyright © 1999 by Rafael Campo. Reprinted by permission of Duke University Press.

"Goodbye, Johnnie Walker" by **Neil Davidson** originally appeared in *The Sun.* Reprinted by permission of the author.

"Licking the Woman" by **Brandel France de Bravo** first appeared in *The American Voice,* no. 47, Fall 1998. Reprinted by permission of the author.

"The Sun, the Moon, the Stars" by **Junot Díaz**, copyright © 1998 by Junot Díaz, first appeared in *The New Yorker*, February 2, 1998. Reprinted by permission of the author.

"Rosa" by **Rita Dove**, from *The Georgia Review*, Winter 1998. Reprinted by permission of the author.

"Naked Woman Playing Chopin" by **Louise Erdrich** first appeared in *The New Yorker*, July 27, 1998. Reprinted by permission of the author.

"For the Jim Crow Mexican Restaurant in Cambridge, Massachusetts Where My Cousin Esteban Was Forbidden to Wait Tables Because He Wears Dreadlocks" by **Martín Espada**, copyright © 1998, first appeared in *Harper's Magazine*, September 1998. Reprinted by permission of the author.

"Common Water" by **Steve Faulkner** originally appeared in *DoubleTake*. Reprinted by permission of the author.

"The Lemons" by **Frank X. Gaspar** from *A Field Guide to the Heavens*, winner of the 1999 Brittingham Prize in Poetry. Reprinted by permission of the University of Wisconsin Press.

"How to Kiss" by **Danielle Legros Georges** originally appeared as an appendix for an article published in *MaComère*, vol. 1, 1998. Reprinted by permission of the author.

"Where the Markets Converge" by **Marcie Hershman** was originally published in *ArchitectureBoston*, no. 2, 1998. Reprinted by permission of the author.

"The Drowned Man's Notes" by **Brian Hocevar** originally appeared in *Alaska Quarterly Review*, vol. 17, nos. 1 and 2, Fall and Winter 1998.

"Some Kind of Crazy" by **Major L. Jackson** originally appeared in *Callaloo: Emerging Male Writers, Part 1*, vol. 21, no. 1, Winter 1998. Reprinted by permission of the author.

"Who's Irish?" by **Gish Jen**, copyright © 1999 by Gish Jen. First published in *The New Yorker*, Sept. 14, 1998. Reprinted by permission of the author.

"A New Delhi Romance" from *East into Upper East* by **Ruth Prawer Jhabvala**. Copyright © 1998 by Ruth Prawer Jhabvala. Appeared in *TriQuarterly*, vol. 103, Fall 1998. Reprinted by permission of Counterpoint Press.

"A Young Girl's Lament" by **Ha Jin**. Reprinted from *Prairie Schooner* by permission of the University of Nebraska Press. Copyright © 1998 by the University of Nebraska Press.

"Driving" by **Suzanne Kamata** first appeared in *Crab Orchard Review*, vol. 4, no. 1, Fall and Winter 1998. Reprinted by permission of the author.

"Water" by **Nadine Kijner** originally appeared in *Witness*, vol. 12, no. 2, 1998. Reprinted by permission of the author.

"Garden of Envy" by **Jamaica Kincaid**, copyright © 1998 by Jamaica Kincaid. First appeared in *DoubleTake*, reprinted with permission of The Wylie Agency, Incorporated.

"How Poems Happen" by **Barbara Kingsolver**, copyright © 1998, *Utne Reader*, July and August 1998. Reprinted by permission of the author.

"Venus of Willendorf" by **Yusef Komunyakaa** first appeared in *Atlantic Monthly*, September 1998. Reprinted by permission of the author.

"Intimacy" by **Hanif Kureishi**, copyright © 1998 by Hanif Kureishi, first appeared in *The New Yorker*, May 11, 1998. Reprinted by permission of the author.

"A New Flower" by **Denise Levertov** originally appreared in *Alaska Quarterly Review*, vol. 16, no. 3 and 4, Spring and Summer 1998. Reprinted by permission of the Levertov estate.

"The Date" by **Brenda Miller** originally appeared in *The Sun*. Reprinted by permission of the author.

"For a Daughter Who Leaves" by **Janice Mirikitani** originally appeared in *Chelsea* 64, August 1998. Reprinted by permission of the author.

"El Lobo Solo" by **Jewel Mogan** originally appeared in *River City: A Journal of Contemporary Culture*, vol. 18, no. 1, Winter 1998. Reprinted by permission of the author.

"Reluctant Death" by **Pat Mora** originally appeared in *Chelsea* 64, August 1998. Reprinted by permission of the author.

"pink" by **Marilene Phipps** first appeared in *River Styx*, vol. 52, 1998. Reprinted by permission of the author.

"Closer" by **Susan Rosalsky** originally appeared in *Alaska Quarterly Review*, vol. 15, nos. 3 and 4, Spring and Summer 1998.

"Orphan of Love" by **Marjorie Sandor** was first published in *The Georgia Review*, copyright © 1998 by Marjorie Sandor. Reprinted by permission of the author.

"A Boy Called Risk" by **Reginald Shepherd** was originally published in *Callaloo: Emerging Male Writers, Part II*, vol. 21, no. 2, Spring 1998. Reprinted by permission of Johns Hopkins University Press.

“Leadership” copyright © 1998 by **Terese Svoboda.** Published by arrangement with Georges Borchardt, Inc. All rights reserved. First appeared in *Bomb*, Summer 1998.

“Volcanic Songs” by **Patrick Sylvain**, copyright © 1998 by Patrick Sylvain, first appeared in *The Caribbean Writer*, vol. 12, 1998. Reprinted by permission of the author.

“Deer Crossing the Sea” by **Larissa Szporluk** was first published in *Green Mountain Review*, Fall 1998. Reprinted by permission of the author.

“The Sad Sweet Story of Sugar Lips Shinehot and the Portable Promised Land” by **Touré** originally appeared in *Callaloo: Emerging Black Male Writers, Part II*, vol. 21, no. 2, Spring 1998. Reprinted by permission of Johns Hopkins University Press.

“At the Society for the Promotion of Indian Classical Music & Culture among Youth” by **Reetika Vazirani** first appeared in *The Southern Review*, vol. 34, no. 1, Winter 1998. Reprinted by permission of the author.

“Waiting for Amelia” by **Laura Wexler** first appeared in *DoubleTake* magazine, Winter 1998. Reprinted by permission of the author.

“What Is a Brother?” by **John Edgar Wideman**. Copyright © 1998 by John Edgar Wideman. First appeared in *Esquire*. Reprinted by permission of the author.

“The Dance School” by **Manfred Wolf** originally appeared in *The Literary Review*, Summer 1998. Reprinted by permission of the author.

The excerpt from *Jack Johnson* by **Kevin Young** originally appeared in *Callaloo: Emerging Black Male Writers, Part I*, vol. 21, no. 1, Winter 1998. Reprinted by permission of the author.

publications

Alaska Quarterly Review is devoted to the publication of contemporary literary art with an emphasis on the works of new and emerging writers of fiction, poetry, literary nonfiction, and short plays. *The Washington Post Book World* deemed *Alaska Quarterly Review* "one of the nation's best literary magazines." Subscriptions for two double issues per year are $10 in the U.S. and $12 abroad.

The American Voice will cease publishing with No. 50, a fiction retrospective, in the fall of 1999. During its fifteen-year history, *The American Voice* has gained an international reputation as a high-quality literary journal, with work from its pages regularly reprinted in *The Pushcart Prize, The Best American Poetry, The Best American Essays*, and other prize annuals, in addition to earning Alternative Press Awards from *Utne Reader* and others. A poetry anthology from its pages has been published by the University Press of Kentucky, currently in a second printing; copies for classroom use can be ordered directly from the Press. With No. 50, a complementary fiction text will be available for classroom use; copies of this edition can be ordered directly from the Kentucky Foundation for Women, which has published *The American Voice* since its inception. With the publication of No. 50, the editors feel they have accomplished all they set out to do with a national journal, particularly in bringing new writers to the attention of the culture; they are now interested in focusing on emerging Kentucky writers.

ArchitectureBoston is a quarterly magazine published by the Boston Society of Architects. It is an issues-oriented publication for everyone who cares about the built environment. *ArchitectureBoston*'s writers, editors, and readers understand the importance of current and timely information on design, practice, technology, and cultural issues. For subscription information and a free copy call (617) 951-1433 extension 221, send fax to (617) 951-0845, or e-mail architectureboston@architects.org.

The Atlantic Monthly subscriptions are $17.94 per year. Contact *The Atlantic Monthly* Subscription Processing Center, P.O. Box 52661, Boulder, Colorado 80322, call (800) 234-2411, or e-mail web@theatlantic.com.

BOMB Magazine was founded in 1981 as a not-for-profit arts organization dedicated to publishing and promoting art and literature of the highest quality. Conceived as a forum for emerging as well as established artists and writers to discuss their work with colleagues and foster a committed dialogue. *BOMB*, now in its eighteenth year of publication, has continued to promote the understanding of literary, visual, and performing arts through interviews between peers as well as the presentation of fiction, poetry, and artwork. To subscribe, call (888) 475-5987. Subscriptions are $18 per year for four issues.

Callaloo is a quarterly magazine that gives special attention to Black South arts and literature. *Callaloo* also publishes black writers nationwide and black writers in the Caribbean, Africa, Europe, and South America. Subscriptions are $35.50 per year in the U.S. for an individual. To place an order for electronic or paper subscriptions, contact The Johns Hopkins University Press Journals Publishing Division, P.O. Box 19966, Baltimore, Maryland 21211-0966, call (800) 548-1784, or e-mail jlorder@jhupress.jhu.edu.

The Caribbean Writer is an international literary anthology with a Caribbean focus, sponsored by the University of the Virgin Islands and edited by Erika J. Waters, professor of English at the University of the Virgin Islands. Individual copies are $10 plus $1.50 postage. Two-year subscriptions are $18 (postage included). Back issues of volumes 3, 9, and 11 are still available at $5 plus postage. Visit their website at www.uvi.edu/Caribbean Writer/.

Chelsea is unaffiliated with any institution and has been publishing new, established, and soon-to-be-established voices in literature since 1958. Eclectic . . . lively . . . with an accent on translations, art, and cross-cultural exchange, *Chelsea* mixes general issues of unsolicited work with occasional features and guest-edited portfolios. Subscriptions are $13 for one year, $24 for two years. Outside the U.S., subscriptions are $16 for one year, $30 for two. Contact *Chelsea*, Box 773, Cooper Station, New York, New York 10276-0773.

Crab Orchard Review is published twice yearly under the auspices of the department of English at Southern Illinois University and features the best in contemporary fiction, poetry, creative nonfiction, interviews, and book reviews. Individual subscriptions are $10 for one year, $20 for two years, and $30 for three years. Please contact *Crab Orchard Review*, Department of English, Southern Illinois University, Carbondale, Illinois 62901-4503.

DoubleTake is a magazine of documentary writing (fiction, nonfiction, poetry, and book reviews) and photography that offers new and unexpected insights about the world around us and the various ways in which ordinary people struggle to get by and to get along. A one-year subscription (four issues) is $32 in the United States; $42 in Canada; $47 elsewhere. Foreign subscriptions payable by credit card or postal money order in U.S. dollars or a check drawn on a U.S. bank. To subscribe call (800) 964-8301, or write *DoubleTake*, P.O. Box 56070, Boulder, Colorado 80322-6070, or e-mail dtmag@aol.com.

Esquire is designed as a forum to deal with the changing role of the American male in today's society. This monthly magazine will appeal to men who are interested in maintaining awareness of current events and living trends. In each issue, readers will find new fashions, personality profiles, as well as articles about the arts, politics, and the media. A one-year subscription is $15.94 in the U.S. and its possessions, $27.94 in Canada and other countries. Call (800) 888-5400.

The Georgia Review was established in 1947 at the University of Georgia. It is a quarterly journal of arts and letters featuring interdisciplinary and general-interest essays along with short stories, poems, book reviews, and visual art. The cost is $18 per year (four issues of 200-plus pages each), $30 for two years. Outside the U.S. subscriptions are $23 for one year and $35 for two years. Single copies are $7, and sample back issues are $6.

Green Mountain Review is a bi-annual magazine publishing poetry, fiction, creative nonfiction, literary essays, interviews, book reviews, and photographs by both well-known artists and promising newcomers. Subscriptions are $14 per year or $21 for two years.

Harper's Magazine aims to provide its readers with a window on our world, in a format that features highly personal voices. Through original journalistic devices—Harper's Index, Readings, Forum, and Annotation—and its acclaimed essays, fiction, and reporting, *Harper's* informs a diverse body of readers of cultural, business, political, literary, and scientific affairs. Offering a distinctive mix of arresting facts and intelligent opinions, *Harper's Magazine* continues to encourage national discussion of topics not yet explored in mainstream media. A subscription in the U.S. for one year is $14. Call (800) 444-4653. In Canada, a one-year subscription is $25.68 Canadian. In other countries, one year is $41 U.S.

The Literary Review is a quarterly international journal focusing on contemporary works of fiction, poetry, essays, and review essays. Subscriptions are $18 for one year in the U.S., $21 outside the U.S.

MaComère is the refereed journal of the Association of Caribbean Women Writers and Scholars (ACWWS), devoted to the scholarly studies and creative works by and about Caribbean women in the Americas, Europe, and the Caribbean diaspora. The single issue current price is $20 for institutions, $15 for individuals. E-mail *macomere@jmu.edu* or contact Dr. Jacqueline Brice-Finch, Publications Editor, Department of English, James Madison University, Harrisonburg, Virginia 22807 for further information.

The New Yorker is a weekly magazine dedicated to ideas. It is timeless and immediate, energetic and thoughtful, serious and funny. *The New Yorker* is about good writing, a point of view, and a deeper understanding of the world. To subscribe, contact *The New Yorker*, Box 56447, Boulder, Colorado 80322-6447, or telephone (800) 825-2510 (United States) or (303) 678-0354 (outside the United States).

Prairie Schooner, a quarterly literary magazine, continues to emphasize the discovery of new imaginative talent as well as to present the work of established authors. Its list of contributors and subscribers is international. Each issue of *Prairie Schooner* contains an exceptional selection of poetry, fiction, translations, essays, and book reviews. Individual subscriptions are $22 for one year, $38 for two years, $50 for three years. A single issue is $7.95. Please contact *Prairie Schooner* at 201 Andrews Hall, University of Nebraska, Lincoln, Nebraska 68588-0334, or call (800) 715-2387.

River City is the nationally distributed magazine of the creative writing program at the University of Memphis. It comes out twice a year, often with thematic issues. The subscription price is $12 per year. Contact *River City*, Department of English, University of Memphis, Memphis, Tennessee 38152.

River Styx has published the best poetry, fiction, essays, interviews, and art they can find with no overriding agenda since 1975. To subscribe, please contact *River Styx*, 634 North Grand Boulevard, Twelfth Floor, St. Louis, Missouri 63103-1002. Subscriptions are $20 for one year, $35 for two years, and $48 for three years.

The Southern Review publishes poetry, fiction, criticism, essays, reviews, and excerpts from novels in progress, with emphasis on contemporary literature in the United States and abroad, and with special interest in Southern history and culture.

Subscriptions are $25 for one year, $40 for two years, and $55 for three years for individuals; $50 for one year, $75 for two years, and $100 for three years for institutions. The address for the subscription is *The Southern Review*, Louisiana State University, 43 Allen Hall, Baton Rouge, Louisiana 70803-5005.

The Sun is a monthly magazine now in its twenty-sixth year of publishing, featuring a wide range of essays, fiction, interviews, and poetry. A one-year subscription (twelve issues) is $34. Write to *The Sun* Subscription Department, P.O. Box 3000, Denville, New Jersey 07834-3000. Or call (888) 732-6736.

TriQuarterly is especially dedicated to short fiction, although substantial amounts of poetry, including long poems, are also published in every issue. Brief book reviews and occasional essays round out the contents. The subscription price for one year (three issues) is $20. Add $5 for delivery abroad. Use U.S. dollars only. Call (800) 832-3615.

Utne Reader is the magazine that helps you lead a more balanced, meaningful life by bringing you practical information, challenging viewpoints, and personal insights. A one-year subscription (6 issues) is $19.97 in the U.S. In Canada, one year is $30 Canadian. Other countries pay $30 U.S. for one year, prepaid. Contact *Utne Reader* Subscriber Services, P.O. Box 7460, Red Oak, Iowa 51591-0460, or call (800) 736-UTNE.

Witness blends the features of a literary and an issue-oriented magazine to highlight the role of the modern writer as witness. Every other issue is devoted to a subject of wide social concern. Individual subscriptions are $15 per year or $28 for two years. Institution subscriptions are $22 per year or $38 for two years. For postage outside the U.S. add $4 per year. Please contact *Witness* at Oakland Community College, 27055 Orchard Lake Road, Farmington Hills, Michigan 48334-4579.